A BRIDE UNTIL MIDNIGHT
BY
SANDRA STEFFEN

AND

SOMETHING UNEXPECTED
BY
WENDY WARREN

Dear Reader,

As I write this letter, a song about going home again is playing on the radio. The lyrics call to me, for a few years ago my childhood home was nearly destroyed in a fire. By some lovely miracle, my parents got out alive.

Recently I had the pleasure of watching them as they celebrated a milestone anniversary. When asked to share the secret for such a long and successful marriage, my soft-spoken mother said, "Divorce, never. Murder, maybe."

Ah, the stuff of good old fairytales. It's safe to say I came by my sense of humor and my determination naturally.

My parents couldn't go home again after the fire, but I invite you to step into that feeling of homecoming with me as you begin my new series, ROUND-THE-CLOCK BRIDES. Turn the page to read *A Bride Until Midnight…*

I hope you love every word.

Welcome home,

Sandra Steffen

A BRIDE UNTIL MIDNIGHT

BY

SANDRA STEFFEN

First published in Great Britain 2011
by Mills & Boon, an imprint of Harlequin (UK) Limited,
Eton House, 18-24 Paradise Road, Richmond, Surrey TW9 1SR

ISBN: 978 0 263 88906 2

23-0811

Harlequin (UK) policy is to use papers that are natural, renewable and recyclable products and made from wood grown in sustainable forests. The logging and manufacturing processes conform to the legal environmental regulations of the country of origin.

Printed and bound in Spain
by Blackprint CPI, Barcelona

Sandra Steffen has always been a storyteller. She began nurturing this hidden talent by concocting adventures for her brothers and sisters, even though the boys were more interested in her ability to hit a baseball over the barn—an automatic homerun. She didn't begin her pursuit of publication until she was a young wife and mother of four sons. Since her thrilling debut as a published author in 1992, more than thirty-five of her novels have graced bookshelves across the country.

This winner of a RITA® Award, a Wish Award, and a National Readers' Choice Award enjoys traveling with her husband. Usually their destinations are settings for her upcoming books. They are empty nesters these days. Who knew it could be so much fun? Please visit her at www.sandrasteffen.com.

For Denis & Mary Lou Rademacher,
two of the finest role models and
well-loved parents in the world.

Chapter One

Sheet lightning flirted with the treetops on the horizon as Innkeeper Summer Matthews started up the sidewalk of her inn. For a few seconds she could see the bridge over the river and the steeple of the tallest church in Orchard Hill. An instant later the starless sky was black again.

Directly ahead of her, The Orchard Inn beckoned. Nestled on a hill overlooking the river, the inn was just inside the Orchard Hill city limits. Built of sandstone and river rock, it was tall and angular and had a roof that looked like a top hat from here. The large windows, wide front walkway and ornate portico were welcoming. A single antique lamp glowed in the bay window on the first floor. Upstairs the flicker of laptops and televisions, modern technology in a 120-year-old inn, cast a blue haze on the wavy window panes.

Only one window remained dark.

Summer went in through the front door, the purling of the bell blending with the lively voices of her friends who were watching the front desk in her absence. She listened at the stairs for guests and checked the registration book on her way by. K. Miller, the last member of the restoration crew scheduled to begin work on the train depot first thing in the morning, still hadn't checked in. Wondering what was keeping him, she followed her friends' voices to her private quarters.

"You're home early." Madeline Sullivan, whose surprise engagement to Riley Merrick was the reason for tonight's emergency wedding-planning session, was the first to notice Summer. Madeline's blue eyes shone with newfound joy.

Chelsea Reynolds looked up from her laptop, and Abby Fitzpatrick turned in her chair.

Giving Summer a quick once over from head to toe, Abby said, "I saw the new veterinarian getting into his truck with roses and a bottle of wine. And you wore a dress, which means you shaved your legs. What are you doing home already?"

Summer went to the refrigerator for a Diet Coke before joining the others at her table. "Did you know that goats, when born, land on only three feet?"

There was a moment of silence while the others searched for the relevance in that little pearl of wisdom.

"Goats," Abby repeated as Chelsea deftly plucked a blade of straw from Summer's light brown hair.

"Do you have experience birthing goats?" Madeline asked.

"I do now." She popped the top of her soda can and poured the cold beverage into a glass. "Nathan's service called during dinner. One of the Jenkins's goats was struggling to deliver. I went along on the emergency house call. The twins are fine, and the mother is resting, but I definitely shaved my legs for nothing."

Madeline was a nurse whose blond hair and blue eyes gave her an angelic appearance. Blond, too, Abby wore her hair in a short, wispy style that suited her petite frame but camouflaged an IQ that rivaled Einstein's. Chelsea had dark brown hair, a curvy build and a no-nonsense attitude. All three of her friends burst out laughing, and Summer couldn't help joining in.

Looking at these women sitting around her table on this quiet Tuesday night, it occurred to her that when she'd arrived in Orchard Hill six years ago at the tender age of twenty-three, she'd been as fragile and wobbly as one of the Jenkins's newborn goats. Madeline, Chelsea and Abby had befriended her, and in doing so, they'd held her up until she'd gotten both feet firmly underneath her. A year and a half ago, they'd all done the same for Madeline when her fiancé was tragically killed in a motorcycle accident. Now Madeline was standing on her own again, about to be married to the man who'd received Aaron's heart.

"How are the wedding plans coming?" Summer asked.

"Amazing," Abby said. "In ten days the most miraculous wedding of the century will go down in history right here in Orchard Hill."

Summer wished Abby hadn't worded it exactly that way. She *wanted* Madeline's wedding to be a dream come true—nobody deserved this happiness more—but a wedding that went down in history would undoubtedly be high profile. The thought of *that* sent dread to the pit of her stomach.

She reminded herself that most people harbored a profound desire to be remembered for something, to leave their mark on the world. At the very least they wanted their elusive five minutes of fame.

Not Summer.

She'd already made her splash and a messy one at that. Not that anyone in Orchard Hill knew the melodramatic details of her former life. As much as she loved this town and the life she'd found here, she preferred her little secret to remain just that. Hers.

"I think we've done all we can do until morning," Chelsea said. The official wedding planner, she closed her laptop.

The others gathered up their things, too.

Leading the little entourage out the door, Chelsea said, "We have the church, the reception hall, the caterers, the gown and the guest list. We still have to talk about music, flowers, table favors and Madeline's vows, but we're in good shape. Don't you agree, Madeline?"

Summer wondered when Chelsea would notice that Madeline wasn't listening. She wasn't even following anymore. She'd stopped in the center of the courtyard and, as she often did, lifted her face to the dark sky.

"I want apple blossoms on the altar and no gifts," she said. "I want a simple wedding."

From across the courtyard, Chelsea said, "Apple blossoms on the altar will be lovely, and we can request no gifts. But a simple wedding with three hundred guests?"

"Two-hundred-ninety-eight," Madeline said, blinking up at the starless sky. "Riley spoke with his brothers. They don't see how they can possibly get out of their commitments on such short notice. They'll both be out of the country for the wedding."

"Two of the most eligible bachelors on the guest list aren't coming?" Abby asked.

"Shoot," Chelsea said at the same time.

It was all Summer could do to keep the relief from bubbling out of her. Kyle Merrick was Riley's older brother and had grown up in Bay City on Michigan's gold coast. He'd caused quite a stir when he'd gotten kicked out of his Ivy League college, but it was his exposé of a professor's wrongdoing that gained him real notoriety. He'd accepted the formal apology from the university but turned his nose up at their invitation to return. With an attitude like his, it wasn't surprising he'd become a nationally acclaimed journalist. As a newspaperman, he'd likely caught her exclusive the day she'd made the front page of the society section of every major newspaper on the eastern seaboard.

He wasn't coming to his brother's wedding. Summer couldn't contain her happiness about that. It was all she could do to keep from performing cartwheels across the courtyard.

"Before you go," Madeline called. "I want all three of you to close your eyes."

Abby was the first to do as Madeline asked. Although Chelsea complained, she closed her eyes, too. Summer was still smiling when she finally acquiesced.

"Take a deep breath," Madeline continued in her quiet, lilting voice that for a moment seemed almost otherworldly. "Now, slowly release it and draw in another. Relax. Breathe. With your eyes closed, picture the man of your dreams. Do you see him? Maybe he's rugged and moody, or shirtless and sexy, or brainy and pensive."

An image sauntered unbidden across Summer's mind. No matter how many dates she accepted, or how much she enjoyed the attention of the rugged, earthy men of Orchard Hill, her fantasy man wasn't clad in faded jeans or chinos. He was loosening the button on a fine European suit.

Champagne taste on a beer budget.

"Believe your paths will cross, and they will," Madeline said. "I'm living proof. Now open your eyes."

All four of them opened their eyes at the same time. They were still blinking when lightning flashed across the horizon. As if in answer, the lights in the inn flickered.

"The universe just sent us a sign," Madeline whispered in awe. "Your lover is on his way."

Summer didn't know if Chelsea and Abby believed in Madeline's prediction, but they got in Chelsea's car without disputing it. Madeline had always been intuitive and romantic. Since she'd discovered wealthy architect

Riley Merrick and had proceeded to fall in love with him, she'd become even more wise and serene. She believed in destiny and positive thoughts manifesting into positive results. And she believed the flickering lights were a sign.

Summer believed in the cantankerous electrical system in her inn. If that storm came any closer, a fuse would blow, and her lights would go out. There was nothing magical about it, she thought, after Madeline left, too. And the balmy breeze fluttering the loose gathers in her dress's bodice *wasn't* a prelude to a lover's touch.

It was just the wind.

Tall and muscular, the man crossing Summer's threshold watched her watching him. Although she couldn't see his eyes clearly, she saw his bold smile.

Bold with a capital B.

There were times when a woman didn't appreciate such over-confidence. This wasn't one of them.

His chest was bare. Why, she didn't know. He didn't seem to care that he was dripping on an impeccably tailored, white shirt lying on the floor. He kicked it aside with the toe of one worn boot. Summer knew there was something incongruous about his attire, but this was her dream, and she was enjoying it too much to rouse herself enough to analyze the inconsistencies.

Thunder rolled, ever closer, the sound moving through the darkness, approaching as rhythmically and steadily as the man. And what a man—a long, lean paradigm of natural elegance, honed muscle and masculine intent.

Apparently unaffected by the fury of the storm, he smiled as he leaned over her. She held her breath as she waited to be awakened with his kiss.

Thunder cracked right outside the window, and Summer jerked awake. She blinked. Floundered.

Where was she?

Rain pelted the windowpanes, and thunder rumbled again. As she ran her hand over the cushion beside her, her memory gradually returned. She'd curled her feet underneath her at one corner of the settee in the central foyer to wait for the last guest to arrive. She must have fallen asleep. Had she been dreaming? The details of the fantasy escaped her, but there was a yearning in her belly that reminded her how long it had been since she'd known a lover's touch.

Darn Madeline and her silly predictions.

Summer squinted into the darkness. Darkness?

The lights had been on when she'd curled up with her magazine. The power must have gone out. Luckily she'd anticipated the likelihood of that and had put her candle lighter and hurricane lamp on the registration counter soon after Madeline, Chelsea and Abby left.

Now that she had her bearings, she padded barefoot to the desk where she easily located the lighter and removed the glass chimney from the hurricane lamp. She was in the process of lighting the wick when a fist pounded the door behind her.

She spun around, the lighter still flaming. Lightning blazed across the sky just then, outlining the dark figure of a man on her portico.

She reeled backwards.

"I'm here for the room," he said, water sluicing off his rain slicker.

K. Miller, the missing carpenter, she thought. Of course.

With her heart still racing, she took her finger off the lighter's trigger then turned down the wick of the lamp. "The power's out," she called, after replacing the globe.

"It went out with that last streak of lightning as I was pulling in," he said loudly enough to be heard through her front door. "I don't need electricity. All I need is a dry corner to crash until morning."

She unlocked the door. Leaving him space to enter, she slipped behind the counter where she normally greeted guests.

There was something oddly familiar about the way he stepped over the threshold. Which was strange, because she was sure she didn't know him.

Wet, his hair was the color of her favorite coffee, dark and rich and thick. His eyebrows were straight and slightly lighter than his hair, his eyes too shadowed for her to discern their color from here. A drop of water trailed down his cheek before getting caught on the whisker stubble darkening his jaw. He hung his jacket on the coat tree next to the door then started toward the desk.

Green. His eyes were green and so deep they shot a bolt of electricity straight through her. The atmosphere in the room thickened—desire at first sight. He must have felt it, too, because he wasn't moving anymore, either.

"Are you the innkeeper?" he finally asked, dropping his duffel bag at his feet.

"Summer Matthews, yes. Welcome to The Orchard Inn."

Maybe it was the lamplight. Maybe it was the late hour and the rain, but her voice sounded throatier and somehow sultrier in her own ears. If one of them didn't put an end to this soon, clothes were going to start falling off.

"Everyone else arrived hours ago," she said, taking a stab at normalcy.

He delved into his back pocket. It took her a little longer than usual to realize that he was probably fishing for his credit card so he could register.

She pushed the leather-bound book toward him and said, "As long as the power is out, my computer is, too. If you'd just sign the registry, we can settle up in the morning."

He hurriedly wrote his name. Leaving the book open on the other side of the counter, he turned his attention back to her. That delicious warmth uncurled deep inside her again.

Well well well. Here she was having sexy thoughts about a rugged, earthy man who definitely was not wearing a two-hundred-dollar tie. There was hope for her yet.

"You're in Room Seven." She handed him a key, since the electronic key card wouldn't work during a power outage, the number seven dangling from a metal ring. "Upstairs, to your right, then all the way to the end of the hall."

He accepted the key and her venture back to decorum without saying a word. After picking up his duffel bag, he headed for the stairs.

"Wait," she called.

He turned around slowly, his gaze steady and bold. Bold with a capital B.

Outside, thunder rumbled. Inside, lamplight flickered like temptation.

"Yes?" he asked.

"You'll need this flashlight."

He wrapped his fingers around one end of the light. The logical corner of her brain that was still functioning knew she was supposed to release her end now, but she couldn't seem to do more than tip her head back and look at him.

He was handsome but not in a classical way. His features were too rugged for that, his jaw darkened with beard stubble and damp from the rain. His face was lean and angular, forehead, cheekbones, chin; his lips were just full enough to cause a woman to look twice. There was a small scar below his nose, but it was his eyes that caused a ripple to go through her. Something about him brought out a yearning to hold and be held, to touch and be touched.

He must have felt it, too, because his gaze delved hers before dropping to her mouth. From there, it was a natural progression to her shoulders, bared by her sleeveless dress, and finally to the V that skimmed the upper swells of her breasts.

He drew a slow breath, and it was as if they were both suspended, on the brink of taking the next step.

If either of them made the slightest movement, be it a gentle sway or the hint of a smile, there would be no turning back.

She finally garnered the wherewithal to release the flashlight and step away. Giving herself a mental shake, she said, "I hope you enjoy your stay at the inn. Good night, Mr. Miller."

She'd surprised him. No doubt a man with his masculine appeal was accustomed to a different outcome. But he didn't press her. Instead, he turned the flashlight on and followed the beam of light up the stairs.

"It's not Miller," he said, halfway to the top.

"Pardon me?" she asked.

"My name isn't Miller. It's Merrick. Kyle Merrick."

The thud of his footsteps had quieted, and his door had closed before Summer moved. Looking dazedly around the room, her gaze finally fell upon the open registration book. She ran to it and spun it around. By the light of the oil lamp she read the bold scrawl.

Kyle Merrick.

Oh no.

A few hours ago Madeline had said that neither of Riley's brothers was planning to attend the wedding. So what was Kyle doing here?

Regardless of his reasons, the wealthy, world-renowned journalist with a nose for scandal and a penchant for stirring up trouble was spending the night right upstairs, and it was too late for Summer to do anything about it.

The Merricks were self-made millionaires. The jacket hanging on the coat rack was likely made in Italy. Kyle probably owned a closet full of European suits. No matter how far she'd thought she'd come these past six years, her taste in men hadn't changed.

She'd been wildly attracted to him and had come very close to succumbing to the desire he brought out in her. There was no other way to describe the awareness that had arced between them. She couldn't explain it, and she couldn't deny that she'd felt it. A delicious current lingered even now. She had little doubt an attraction like that would have led to more passion than she'd experienced in a long time.

But he was Kyle Merrick.

And she was…well, Summer wasn't her given name.

Chapter Two

Kyle Merrick's Jeep Wrangler was equipped with the most advanced navigational system on the market, but he rarely turned it on. Relying on technology dulled a man's natural instincts. Besides, it was more fun to use the sense of direction he'd been born with. It came in handy when he needed to find a way out of dicey situations in some of the world's largest cities, poorest villages and, on occasion, women's hotel rooms.

Locating the house where his brother was staying didn't require navigational gadgetry, carefully honed skill or God-given talent. Once Kyle had narrowed it down to the general vicinity—east of the river and north of Village Street—Riley's silver Porsche in the driveway had been impossible to miss.

Kyle parked the Jeep and got out. As he sauntered to the door, he noted his surroundings, something else that came naturally. This neighborhood was in an old section of Orchard Hill, but, unlike the residences on the national historic registry, the houses here were small and nondescript. This bungalow wasn't Riley's type of house at all. Which meant it was Madeline Sullivan's.

Since there was no sense putting off the inevitable, he raised his fist and knocked on the door. A large, brown dog bounded outside the instant the door was opened.

While the dog took care of business on an unsuspecting hedge, the Merrick brothers faced one another, each carefully assessing the other.

Riley was the first to speak. "I wondered which one of you The Sources would send."

Kyle grimaced because this *did* feel a little like a mission. He'd wanted Braden to come but had lost the toss.

He and his brothers had a father in common and three separate mothers. It accounted for the similarities in their height and build and the differences in their eye colors and personalities. They hadn't always gotten along, but they'd always been a united front when it came to their mothers, otherwise known as The Sources. In this instance, Kyle didn't blame them for being concerned about Riley's recent, hasty engagement.

Apparently Riley understood that this confrontation was inevitable. He threw the door wide and said, "You might as well come in."

Kyle and the dog followed him through a comfortably furnished living room where blueprints were spread across a low table and a fax was coming in. They ended up in a yellow kitchen where a television droned and steam rose from a state-of-the-art coffeemaker.

Catching Kyle looking around, Riley said, "She's not here."

Instead of offering Kyle a seat at the table, Riley leaned against the counter and took a sip from one of the mugs he'd just filled. There was no delicate way to do this, and they both knew it. They also both knew that Kyle wouldn't leave until he'd had his say.

Carrying his coffee to a spot that was a safe distance from his brother, Kyle leaned a hip against the counter, too, and said, "You can't blame us for being concerned. Two years ago, you were dying. Two months ago, you still weren't yourself. Now you're getting married in a week and a half to a woman you proposed to after you'd known her a matter of days."

"Don't form an opinion until you've met Madeline."

"I'm sure she's a saint. I heard she was wearing your sheet the first time she met your mother." Kyle wouldn't have minded being a fly on that wall, but Riley didn't share the details of the encounter. Merrick men didn't kiss and tell.

"You have to admit it looks suspicious," Kyle said. "She's a nurse. You have money."

"Madeline doesn't care about money."

Everybody cared about money. But Kyle said, "She showed up uninvited at one of your construction sites, and she failed to mention that the heart beating in your chest came from her deceased fiancé."

"Water under the bridge," Riley insisted before taking another sip of coffee.

Following suit, Kyle said, "You fell for her. Hard. I get that. So live with her for a while. Make sure the penny doesn't lose its shine."

"I'm marrying her, Kyle, the sooner, the better."

The dog stood up and looked from one to the other.

"What's your hurry?" Kyle asked. "It's not as if you *have* to marry her." He stopped. The drone of the television covered an uncomfortable lag in conversation. "Is that what this is about? She's pregnant?"

Riley shot him a warning look.

And Kyle muttered the only word that came to mind.

"We're not telling anyone yet," Riley said. "So keep it to yourself. I don't know what I did to deserve Madeline, to deserve any of this, but whatever it was, I'm not wasting another minute of my life without her."

Kyle fought the urge to rake his fingers through his hair. "You slept with her, and now she claims she's going to have your baby. Don't hit me for what I'm thinking."

He could tell Riley wanted to hit him. It wouldn't be a sucker punch, either. Riley didn't fight dirty, but he fought to win, something else the Merrick men had in common.

"Have you ever *known* a virgin, Kyle?" he asked.

It took a few seconds for Riley's meaning to soak in. "You mean Madeline? For real? You're sure?"

"Positive."

Kyle put his coffee down. "I'll be damned. A virgin.

I didn't know there were any alive past the age of eighteen. Make that seventeen. Fine. The kid's yours. That's good. I guess. I'm just saying—"

"You're saying it's all happening fast and you, Braden and our mothers are worried about that. I trust you'll put their minds at ease. In your own good time, of course."

They shared their first smile. Riley knew him well.

"Anything else you'd like me to tell our mothers?" Kyle asked, suddenly not at all sorry he'd lost that toss to Braden.

"Tell them I can feel my heart beating."

This time Kyle didn't say anything. He simply stared in amazement at his younger brother.

He would never forget the panic and paralyzing fear that had ripped through the entire family twenty months ago when they'd learned that Riley had contracted a rare virus that was attacking his heart. In a matter of days, he'd gone from strong and athletic to wan and weak. He was only thirty years old. And he was dying.

Kyle, Braden and Riley's friend Kipp had stayed with him around the clock. They'd begged him, badgered him and bullied him to hold on. Two years younger than Kyle, Riley had been at death's door, literally, by the time he'd finally received a heart transplant. His recovery had been nothing short of a miracle, but, despite his robust health afterwards, there had been something different about him. It was as if his sense of adventure, his passion and even his laughter had been buried with his old heart. Strangely, he hadn't been able to feel the new one beating.

"How long has the feeling been back?" Kyle asked.

"Since Madeline." Riley placed a hand over his chest. "I used to climb mountains just for the view from the top. That view is nothing compared to what I see when I look into her eyes. I can see the future, and that's never happened to me before."

Kyle held up one hand. He didn't know how much more he could take on an empty stomach.

Riley laughed. And for a moment it took Kyle back to summer vacations and boyhood pranks they'd pulled together. He hadn't heard Riley laugh quite like this in a long time. It did Kyle's heart good.

"I'll tell The Sources you're happy and as healthy as the proverbial horse and I'll tell them you can feel your beating heart. I'm glad, man. It's good to see you. Real good. Now, I have a plane to catch to L.A."

He was already out the door when Riley said, "You look good, too, Kyle. More rested than I expected."

The brothers shared a long look, Kyle in the watery rays of late morning sunshine and Riley in the shadow of the doorway. If they were keeping score, this point would go to Riley, for, with his simple statement, he'd let Kyle know that Riley wasn't the only one their mothers were worried about. Kyle hadn't been himself lately, either. He was going through something. Running from something.

The Sources worked both ways.

"If I look rested," Kyle said, "it's because I slept like a baby last night."

"During that storm?"

Kyle couldn't explain it, but once he'd closed his eyes,

he hadn't heard a thing for nine solid hours. The inn had been empty and the power was back on by the time he'd wandered downstairs this morning. Now, standing in a patch of sunshine beneath his brother's watchful gaze, he found himself thinking about the woman with the large, hazel eyes and sultry, cultured voice that made hello sound like an intimate secret.

"Can your plane ride wait until after lunch?" Riley asked.

"That depends. Are you cooking?"

Again, the brothers shared a grin.

Riley, who often burned toast, said, "I thought I'd call Madeline at work and see if she can join us at the restaurant downtown. I'd like you to meet her."

"Let me know what time," Kyle said as he climbed into his Jeep.

Meanwhile, he had a woman to see about a room.

Robins splashed in the puddles in the inn's driveway as Summer pulled into her usual parking place. She lifted her cloth bags from her trunk and started toward the backdoor, the groceries in her arms growing heavier with every step she took. The sound of Kyle Merrick's deep voice coming through the kitchen window sent the headache she'd awakened with straight to the roots of her teeth.

She'd spent the first half of the night tossing and turning, her body yearning to finish what meeting Kyle Merrick had started. Between short bursts of fitful sleep, she'd lain awake staring at the dark ceiling, anticipating the hate mail she would receive from the people she'd duped should her secret ever be revealed.

Her father, for one. Her former fiancé, for another.

Sometimes she imagined her mother and sister sitting on a cloud, smiling down at her and singing a song about sweet revenge. To this day, she knew she'd done the right thing. That didn't mean she wanted to relive what was to have been her wedding day.

She heard Kyle's voice again. This time it was followed by a flirtatious, though aging, twitter Summer would recognize anywhere. Harriet Ferris lived next door and was always happy to watch the front desk when Summer needed to run errands during the day. Harriet told raucous stories and loved nothing better than having a captive audience, especially if it was someone of the opposite sex.

Summer almost felt sorry for Kyle.

Almost.

What was he doing in the inn, anyway?

He'd gone. She'd freshened the rooms after breakfast and made the beds. Room Seven had been empty. She'd checked.

Kyle Merrick's duffel bag was gone. And she'd been relieved. Okay, she'd felt a little unsettled, too, but that was beside the point.

For some reason he was back—she had no idea why—and was sitting at the table, no doubt sharing raucous tales with Summer's next-door neighbor. He looked up at her as she walked in and almost smiled.

"I thought you'd left," she said.

"Without paying for my stay last night? Your low opinion of me is humbling."

He didn't look humble. He looked like a man with sex on his mind, the kind of man who didn't ask for commitment and certainly didn't give it. Lord-a-mighty, the invitation in those green eyes was tempting.

"What makes you think I've formed an opinion about you?" she asked.

He smiled, and the connection between their gazes thrummed like a guitar string being strummed with one finger. Pulling her gaze from his wasn't easy, but she turned her attention to the woman watching the exchange.

"Would you like a cup of tea, Harriet?"

Seventy-eight-year-old Harriet Ferris had been dying her hair red for fifty years. Before every birthday there was a discussion about letting it go gray, but she never would, just as she would never stop wearing false eyelashes and flirting with men of all ages.

"No, thank you, dear, I really should be getting back home. I'm expecting an email from my sister in Atlanta. She refuses to text. So old-school, you know?"

Although she stood up, she made no move toward the door until Summer leaned down and whispered in her ear.

A smile spread across Harriet's ruby red lips. "What would I do without you? What would any of us do? This handsome man has brought you a gift." Harriet looked from Summer to Kyle and back again. "I won't spoil the surprise, but I dare say if you could bottle the electricity in this room right now, you could sell it to the power company for a tidy profit. If only I were twenty years younger."

"You're a cougar, Harriet," Kyle said, rising, too.

With a playful wink and a grin that never aged, Harriet tottered out the back door.

Now that he and Summer were alone, Kyle handed her the gift bag. "For the next time your power goes out," he said.

She opened the brown paper sack. Peering at the fuses inside, she shook her head and smiled.

He looked like he was about to smile, too, but his gaze caught on her mouth, and Summer knew Harriet was right about the electricity in this room.

"You wanted to settle up for last night's stay?" she asked.

"You aren't from Michigan are you?" he asked.

The question came from out of the blue and caught her by surprise. Years of practice kept her perfectly still, her expression carefully schooled to appear artful and serene.

"I can't place the inflection," he continued. "But it isn't Midwestern."

She pulled herself together. Carrying the milk, eggs and cheese to the refrigerator, she said, "I was born in Philadelphia and grew up in Baltimore. My grandparents had a summer house on Mackinaw Island. Until my grandfather died when I was fourteen, my sister and I spent every summer in northern Michigan. What about you? Where are you from?"

She was just making conversation, for she knew the pertinent facts about his past. She'd researched all three of the Merrick brothers after Madeline had announced her engagement to Kyle's brother Riley a few days ago.

"I was born and raised in Bay City," he said, his voice a lazy baritone that suggested he had all the time in the world. "I studied out east and have traveled just about everywhere else. What did you whisper to Harriet?"

She glanced at him as she closed the refrigerator. "I told her where she put her spare key this week. She keeps moving it and forgets where she hides it."

"Is that why they call you the keeper of secrets?" he asked.

Summer stopped putting away groceries and looked at him. She prided herself on her ability to identify a person's true nature at first sight. She wasn't the only one in this room doing that right now. Kyle was looking at her as if she were a puzzle he had every intention of solving. That felt far more dangerous than the heat in his gaze or the fact that she was wondering if he might kiss her.

She wasn't about to be the first to look away, as if she had something to hide. Which she did, but he didn't know that. And he wouldn't.

Okay. It was time to get both their minds on something else. "Are you flirting with me?" she asked, even though she knew he was.

She could tell her ploy had worked by the change in his stance, the slight tilt of his head, the even slighter narrowing of his gaze. Oh yes, his mind was on something far more fundamental than her past, for nothing was more fundamental than flirting with the opposite sex.

For months, Kyle had felt as if a spring had been coiled too tight inside him. This woman was slowly unwinding him. She'd taken a chance when she'd opened her door last night. Maybe she kept mace under the counter. If she had a stun gun, she hadn't needed it. He'd felt hypnotized at first sight.

Summer Matthews had hazel eyes and curves in all the right places. She was a pretty woman, and he knew his way around pretty women. He didn't understand them, God no, but he knew when a woman wanted what he wanted.

Summer was interested. She just wasn't acting on it. The question was, why? She wasn't wearing a ring, and she was no prude. Nobody with a voice that sultry and a mind that bright was shy and unsure of herself.

She was refreshing and intriguing. Deep inside him, that taut spring unwound a little more.

"If I were flirting with you," he said huskily, "you'd know it."

Her gaze went to his mouth, but instead of continuing the flirtation, she named the amount for last night's stay. His interest climbed another notch, and so did his regard for her.

He liked a woman who could keep her wits about her.

He wished he had enough time to turn those astute eyes starry, to run his hands along her graceful shoulders and feel her arms slowly wind around his neck as her lips parted for his kiss. Unfortunately he was out of time to do more than say, "I'm meeting my brother and future sister-in-law for lunch. After that I have a plane to catch, but I wanted to pay for my room before I leave town."

Pocketing the cash he gave her, she said, "It's not every day a girl meets an honest man."

And then she did something, and there was no turning back. She smiled as if she meant it.

Kyle couldn't help reaching for her any more than he could help drawing his next breath. He covered her mouth with his, before either of them thought to resist.

After that first brush of lips and air, the kiss deepened, breaths mingling, pulse rates climbing. It was a possessive joining, a mating of mouths and heat and hunger. It didn't matter that it was broad daylight, that he had to leave in a few minutes or that he barely knew her. He kissed her because he had to. It was primal, and it was powerful, and, when her mouth opened slightly, he wanted more. He wanted everything.

He'd imagined her body going pliant—he had a damned fine imagination—but it was nothing compared to the reality in his arms. Her hands came around his back, then glided up to his shoulders. She moved against him, and he held her tighter, melding them together from knees to chest.

Somewhere in the back of Summer's mind, warning bells were clanging. She was crazy to be doing this, to be starting something with a man in his field, this man in particular. Doing so was risking discovery. And yet she couldn't seem to help herself. She couldn't stop. She had to experience Kyle's kiss. She needed to know she could feel this way.

Last night when she should have been sleeping, her eyes had been wide open. Now, they closed dreamily, so that she had to rely on her other senses. Her other senses were floating on a serenade of sound, heat and passion.

His mouth was firm and wet, his breathing deep, his scent clean and brisk like mint and leather. The combination made her heart speed up and her thoughts slow like a lazy river on a sultry summer day. His arms and back were muscular, his legs solid and long. It had been a long time since she'd been kissed like this, since she'd reacted like this. Had she ever been kissed quite like this?

Her back arched, her body seeking closer contact even though they couldn't get any closer through their clothes. Until this moment, they'd been strangers. His kiss changed that, and it was spinning out of control. Control was the last thing she wanted, for passion this strong didn't come along every day.

She felt like a balloon held gently between a pair of firm lips, waiting to see if another puff of air would fill her, transforming her, or if those lips would withdraw, sending her careening backwards. The air was Kyle Merrick. Therein lay the risk.

She reminded herself that he was leaving town today, and if she ever saw him again, it would be on rare occasions and only because he was going to be Madeline's brother-in-law. Such meetings would be entirely controllable. It made this feel less dangerous, less likely to be something she would regret. And so, for a few moments, she let herself feel, let herself react, let herself go. And go and go.

For the first time in a long time, she felt like herself. And it felt good.

She felt free.

The kiss didn't end on a need for air. It ended with the sudden jarring and incessant ringing of both their phones.

Hers stopped before she could think clearly enough to answer. It went to voice mail, only to start up again. Whoever was calling was insistent. Kyle's caller was just as determined.

They drew apart, their eyes glazed, mouths wet, breathing ragged. She let her arms fall to her sides. Dazedly, he raked his fingers through his dark hair.

Moving more languidly than usual, as if her hands were having trouble picking up signals from her brain, she finally reached for her cell phone and answered. Normally Summer began speaking the moment she put the phone to her ear. Today, Madeline did that from the other end.

"What?" Summer asked. "Honey, slow down." Although vaguely aware of the low drone of Kyle's voice, too, Summer listened intently to what Madeline was saying. "Of course I'll come. I'll be right there," she said.

Summer was aware that Kyle had pocketed his phone and was watching her. "That was Riley," he said. "I was planning to meet him and Madeline for lunch. He had to cancel."

She glanced at him as she dropped her phone into her bag and fished inside for her keys. "I know. My call was from Madeline."

He watched her, waiting for her to say more. When she didn't, he said, "Riley said it's possible she's losing the baby."

Summer studied his eyes. Only a few people knew Madeline was pregnant. "Riley told you about the baby?"

This time Kyle nodded. "When I saw him this morning, he was happier than I've seen him in a long time."

"Madeline, too," she said quietly.

Summer wanted to shake her fist at fate and demand that this work out for Madeline. She'd already lost so much. Now she'd found Riley, and she was happy. Happy. Was it too much to ask that she could stay that way?

"Dammit all to hell," Kyle said.

Summer wasn't a crier, but tears welled because, for a few moments, she understood. They both felt frustrated and helpless over Madeline's possible medical emergency. Maybe what they said was true. Maybe there was strength in numbers, because she suddenly felt empowered. It went straight to her head. From there, it meandered to places she didn't normally think about in the light of day.

Dresses were her usual work attire. The sleeveless, gray dress she wore today had a fitted waistband and a softly gathered skirt. It wasn't formfitting, yet she was very aware of the places along her body where the lightweight fabric skimmed.

She felt Kyle's gaze move slowly over her, settling momentarily at the little indentation at the base of her neck. It was all she could do to keep from placing her hand where he was looking, for she could feel the soft fluttering of her pulse at her throat. She'd learned to school her expressions, but that little vein had a mind of its own.

Last night, she'd blamed this attraction on the storm. Everybody knew people did crazy things during atmospheric disturbances. Kyle's kiss a few minutes ago had created its own atmospheric disturbance.

But right now, Madeline needed her.

So Summer reeled in her thoughts, tamped down her passion and said, "I don't like to be rude, but I have to go." A handshake seemed a little formal after that kiss, so she settled on a smile. "It was nice meeting you. I mean that. Have a good flight."

Even though it was handled politely, Kyle knew when he was being asked to leave. Since he had no legitimate reason to hang around—he did have a plane to catch after all—he walked out with Summer.

She headed for a blue sedan, and he started toward the lilac hedge in full bloom near where he'd left his Jeep. Pea gravel crunched beneath his shoes. He wasn't sure what made him turn around and look at her. Perhaps it was the same thing that caused her to glance over her shoulder at him at the same time. Whatever the reason, it felt elemental and as fundamental as the pull of a man to a woman and a woman to a man.

Just then, a gust of wind caught in her hair and dress. And it struck him that he'd seen her before.

He knew he was staring, but he couldn't help it. He scanned his memory, trying to identify the reason she seemed familiar.

"Is something wrong?" she asked, obviously in a hurry to be on her way.

Deciding this wasn't the time or place to play twenty questions, he simply said, "No. You have to go. Good luck. Tell Riley I'll be in touch."

She drove away, and he finally got in his Jeep. Instead of starting the engine, he sat behind the steering wheel, thinking. The sensible thing to do would be to turn the key and head for the airport to catch his two o'clock flight to L.A.

Leaving the engine idling, he slipped his laptop from its case and turned it on. He typed Summer's name at the top of his favorite search engine. There were thousands of matches, among them a semi-famous opera singer, a retired drummer from a sixties rock band, and a teacher in Cleveland. There was even a racehorse by that name. Kyle tried another search engine and found an article archived from a local newspaper that listed Summer as the innkeeper of The Orchard Inn.

Minutes later he turned his computer off. Now what?

He wondered what was happening in the Emergency Room. He'd spent days on end at the hospital two years ago when Riley had been so close to death. Riley hadn't asked Kyle to come this time, which was fine with him. Female troubles made all men squeamish. Besides, this was intimate. It was something that was between Riley and Madeline and Madeline's closest friend. That brought Kyle back to Summer.

He was pretty sure he'd never met her. He would have remembered an actual encounter. As he sat strumming his fingers on the armrest, he couldn't shake the feeling that he was missing something.

What?

She hadn't looked familiar until a few moments ago. Did she remind him of someone else? Was that it?

His mind circled around a few possibilities then discarded them. No, she didn't look like anyone he knew. He would have noticed that earlier.

But she was familiar. Although he didn't know where or when, he'd seen her before.

Kyle Merrick never forgot a face.

Chapter Three

The founding fathers of Orchard Hill were an unlikely trio of entrepreneurs from upstate New York. One was said to have been a charming shyster who convinced his business associates back home that wealth awaited them "in the green hills of a promised land."

According to local historians, among the first arrivals were a prominent banker and his wife, who took one look at the crudely built clapboard houses in the village and the surrounding mosquito-infested ramshackle farms and fainted dead away. The second founding father was a botanist who, through much trial and error, developed three species of apples still widely grown in the local orchards today. The third was considered to be a simpleton by his aristocratic parents. This so-called dunce proved to be a man of great wisdom and ambition who eventually established The Orchard Hill Academy, now the University of Orchard Hill.

Historical tidbits were strange things for Summer to be thinking about as she waited at the traffic light at the corner of Jefferson and Elm, but it took her mind off worrying about Madeline or wondering if she'd really glimpsed a momentary recognition in Kyle Merrick's gaze as she was leaving the inn. She gripped the steering wheel and told herself not to jump to conclusions.

He couldn't have recognized her.

It *was* possible he'd seen her photograph in the newspapers six years ago. But she'd been younger then, and blond, and had been wearing a frothy veil and a wedding gown made of acres of silk.

He hadn't recognized her.

How could he? She barely recognized the girl she'd been then.

More than likely, what she'd thought was a fleeting recognition in Kyle's green eyes had simply been a conscious effort to coax the blood back into his brain after that kiss. She pried the fingers of her right hand from the steering wheel and gently touched her lips. He wasn't the only one still recovering.

Enough. They'd enjoyed a brief flirtation. Not mild, mind you, but brief. That was all it was. She had nothing to worry about. He was most likely on his way to the airport this very minute to pursue more pressing stories than a rehash of old news, even if that old news was Baltimore's most notorious runaway bride.

She and Kyle had said their good-byes. Or at least she had. She tried to remember how he'd replied.

"Good luck," he'd said as they'd parted ways. And everybody knew good luck was as good as goodbye.

She jumped when a horn blasted. People in Orchard Hill didn't generally honk their horn, which meant she'd probably been sitting at the green light longer than she should. Smiling apologetically in her rearview mirror at the poor driver behind her, she quickly took her foot off the brake and continued on toward the hospital across town.

Roughly seven square miles, Orchard Hill was a city of nearly twenty-five thousand residents. The streets curved and intersected in undulating juxtaposition to the bends in the river. A state highway bisected the city from east to west, but even that was riddled with stoplights. She'd learned to drive in congested city traffic. She'd learned patience here.

She had to wait a few minutes while a crew wearing hard hats moved a newly fallen tree limb out of the intersection. A few blocks farther down the street a delivery man threw his flashing lights on and left his truck idling in the middle of Division Street. Hosanna chimed from the bell tower as it did every day at half past eleven.

It really was just an ordinary May morning in Orchard Hill. The normalcy of it was like a cool drink of lemonade, refreshing and calming at the same time.

While she waited at another red light she found herself staring at the ten foot tall statue on her left. Nobody could agree where the bronzed figure came from, or how long it had stood on the courthouse lawn.

Summer remembered vividly the first time she'd seen

it more than six years ago. She'd been lost and nearly out of gas that day when she'd coasted to a stop at the curb. So exhausted that the lines and words on the road map in her hand swam before her eyes, she'd found herself gazing out the window at a whimsical figure at the head of a town square.

Most cities reserved a place of such importance for cannons and monuments and statues of decorated war heroes on mighty steeds, but that day she was drawn from her car by a larger-than-life replica of a fellow with holes in his shoes, bowed legs, patched trousers, and a dented kettle on his head. Johnny Appleseed was her first acquaintance in Orchard Hill.

She'd stood beside the statue and taken a deep breath of air scented with ripe apples and autumn leaves. Above the golden treetops in the distance she saw a smoke stack from a small factory, a water tower and several church spires. Somewhere, a marching band was practicing, and there were dog walkers on the sidewalks of what appeared to be a busy downtown.

It had been too early for streetlights, but lamps had glowed in the windows of some of the shops lining the street. Fixing her gaze straight ahead, she'd walked away from her unlocked car, leaving her ATM and credit cards in plain view on the seat inside. A thief wouldn't get far with any of them, for all her cards had been cancelled.

Nobody duped Winston Emerson Matthews the Third without consequences, not even his daughter. Especially not his daughter.

She'd entered the first restaurant she came to and sat

at a small table. A blond waitress a few years younger than Summer had appeared with a menu and a smile. Nearly overtaken with the enormity and finality of her recent actions, Summer stared into the girl's friendly blue eyes and blurted, "Ten days ago I left a rich and powerful man at the altar. My father has disinherited me and all I have left in my purse is ten dollars and some change."

After a moment of quiet deliberation, the waitress had replied, "I'd recommend Roxy's Superman Special." In a whisper, she added, "It's a savory chicken potpie. Roxy makes it from scratch. Her crusts alone could win awards."

Something had passed between their gazes. Summer's eyes filled up, and all she could do was nod.

"I'll be right back." The angelic waitress had soon returned, a plate in each hand. She sat down across from Summer and shook out her napkin. "I'm Madeline Sullivan," she said, handing Summer a fork and napkin and picking up another set for herself. "Welcome to Orchard Hill."

Before the meal was finished, Summer's second acquaintance in Orchard Hill had become the best friend she'd ever known. Madeline had taken Summer home with her, as if normal people took in disinherited young women with secret pasts every day.

She was the only person in Orchard Hill Summer had confided in, the only person who knew her given name.

Madeline had been working her way through college then. Today she was a nurse, and right now she lay in a hospital, possibly losing a baby she desperately wanted.

"I'm coming, Madeline," Summer whispered into the celestial sovereignty reserved for promises and prayers.

Buchanan Street curved one last time before the three-story brick hospital came into view. She followed the arrows and parked near the lighted E.R. sign around back. Grabbing her shoulder bag, she locked her car then ran through the automatic doors and down a short corridor. She rounded a corner.

And came face-to-face with *two* Merrick brothers, not one.

Years of practice with schooling her features very nearly deserted her as she looked from Riley to Kyle. She wanted to ask Kyle what he was doing here. Why wasn't he checking his bag at the airport?

And how had he beaten her here?

Instead she focused on a pair of brown eyes, not green, and said, "Riley, how is she?"

Riley Merrick was as tall as his brother and had a similar build. There was a depth in his eyes that put Summer at ease every time she saw him.

"You know Madeline," he said, his voice a deep baritone. "She keeps telling me not to worry about her, that everything's going to be okay."

That sounded like Madeline.

"What happened?" Summer asked.

"She passed out at work. Hit her head when she fell. The bleeding seems to have stopped."

"She was bleeding?" Summer asked.

"Too heavy to be considered spotting."

Oh. That kind of bleeding. "And the pregnancy?" Summer whispered.

"We're waiting for the results of blood work. A few minutes ago Madeline told me she doesn't *feel* she's lost the baby."

That sounded like Madeline, too.

Apparently Riley realized that Kyle was still standing beside him. He glanced at him, and said, "Summer, this is my brother Kyle."

"Hello, Kyle," she said.

"We meet again," he said at the same time, only slightly louder.

"You two know each other?" Riley asked, looking sideways at his brother.

"Remember when I told you I slept like a baby last night? It was at her place."

"At my *inn*. In Room Seven. Alone. At least I assume he was alone." Summer shot Kyle a stern look before turning back to Riley. "Where is Madeline now?"

Double doors clanked open and a man wearing scrubs pushed a gurney through the doorway. A television droned on the far wall in the waiting area. A little girl was crying, and a teenaged boy was holding his wrist. Other bored-looking people dozed or fidgeted, waiting for their turn to see a doctor.

"She's in Room Four," Riley answered quietly. "Talya's performing an examination."

Talya Ireland, pronounced like Tanya, only with an *l,* was a midwife and Madeline's new employer. She'd stayed at the inn when she first came to town several months ago. If Madeline was with her, she was in good hands.

Summer lowered herself into a nearby vinyl chair. Before she'd even finished smoothing her skirt, Riley said, "Madeline asked me to send you in the minute you arrived."

She was on her feet again and halfway to the door when she thought of something. "Riley?" she said.

Both Merrick brothers were watching her.

"If Madeline feels she's going to be okay," Summer said, "I believe her."

Relief eased the strain on Riley's face. Kyle's expression was more difficult to decipher. He stood looking at her, his shoulders straight, the collar of his shirt open, cuffs rolled to his forearms. He was one of those men who played hard and cleaned up well, and he sent her stomach into a wild swirl. He was ruggedly attractive from the waves in his coffee-colored hair to the toes of his Italian-made shoes.

She forced her eyes away but felt his gaze until she disappeared on the other side of the heavy metal doors. The vinyl flooring beneath her feet muffled the sound of her footsteps. From behind curtain one came the mechanical blip of a heart monitor. Behind curtain two, a child cried forlornly. Hushed voices and a few groans that didn't sound like pain were coming from behind curtain three.

Summer stuck her head inside room four. The hospital bed took up the majority of the narrow cubby; monitors and IV racks competed for space with an efficient-looking midwife.

"Hey," Summer said, drawing Madeline's gaze.

From her pillow, Madeline gave Summer a weak smile. "Hey yourself."

Summer looked at the third woman in the room. In her late thirties, Talya Ireland had exotic gray eyes and five shades of brown hair beauty salons would love to replicate. If there was an ounce of Irish blood in her as her name suggested, it wasn't readily apparent.

While Talya studied the blood pressure printout and fussed with a switch on the IV, Summer sidled closer to the bed and studied Madeline. The two of them were identical in size, yet today Madeline seemed slight and pale and smaller somehow.

"How are you feeling?" Summer asked.

On a shuddering breath, Madeline said, "Oh, Summer. All these sounds and smells and people scurrying around. I used to work here, but this morning all I could think about was the day Aaron died."

Summer took Madeline's hand. Madeline and Aaron Andrews had been childhood sweethearts and inseparable until nearly two years ago when a motorcycle accident cut his life tragically short. Madeline had been with him when he'd taken his last breath in a hospital room similar to this one. It was only natural that the horrors would come back at a time like this.

With a sniffle, Madeline pointed to the thin wall between her room and the room next door, from which came another creak and a muffled moan. "Are they doing what I think they're doing?" she asked.

Nobody could make Summer smile like Madeline.

"Are you blushing?" Madeline asked.

Smoothing the sheet at her patient's waist, Talya said, "Summer is such a lady."

"Take that back." But Summer knew she was smiling again. Friends made life so rich.

"We're talking about you," she said to Madeline. "And you haven't answered my question."

"I'm scared and shaken but better, I think."

Sinking to the edge of the bed, Summer sighed. "You're really okay?"

Madeline nodded. "Talya wants me to stay off my feet for a few days."

"At *least* a few days," came a stern voice from the other side of the bed.

"And the baby?" Summer asked quietly.

"I'm not far enough along to have an ultrasound, but Talya is guardedly optimistic that my pregnancy is still viable and will continue to be so for a good long time."

Talya said, "Sometimes spontaneous bleeding occurs early in a pregnancy. It isn't normal, but it isn't altogether uncommon, either. It's possible her placenta has attached a little low in her uterus. If that's the case, I've seen it spontaneously move up a little to a safer holding place. Right now all we can do is wait and see."

A nurse who used to work with Madeline bustled into the room. "Here's your lab results," she said, handing the report to the midwife. "Hi, Madeline."

Talya read the report. "Your beta levels are elevated. That's a good sign."

The moment she grinned, Summer jumped to her feet. "I'll get Riley."

"I'll go," Talya said. "I like to deliver good news."

With a swish of the curtain, she was gone, only to pop her head through the folds again. "Those sounds coming from your neighbors? Two twelve-year-old girls texting their grandma in Spokane." She made a tsk, tsk, tsk sound with her tongue. "I know what's on your minds." She pointed her finger at Madeline. "None of that for you until I see you again in my office." She winked at Summer. "You are under no restrictions."

An instant later the curtain fluttered back into place. In the ensuing silence, Madeline burst out laughing. It was music to Summer's ears.

"I'll call Chelsea and Abby," Summer said. "We'll contact the caterers, Reverend Brown and everyone on the guest list." Since there hadn't been time to follow normal wedding protocol, most of the invitations went out via email, so it wouldn't be difficult to send another. "We'll tell them the wedding is being postponed for a few weeks."

Madeline was shaking her head. "I want to talk to you about that."

Summer had known Madeline for more than six years. This stubborn streak had begun to emerge *after* she'd discovered newfound happiness with Riley Merrick.

"What is it?" Summer asked.

"I have a favor to ask."

"The answer is yes."

"You haven't heard the request," Madeline insisted.

For years Summer had wanted to repay Madeline in some small or profound way for taking her under her wing when she'd first arrived in Orchard Hill. "No matter what it is, I'll do it." She studied the mischievous glint in Madeline's eyes, another quality that had only recently come out of hiding, and posed her next question more haltingly. "What is the favor?"

Madeline crossed her ankles beneath the sheet, fluffed her pillow and tucked one hand under her head. When she was comfortable, she told Summer what she had in mind.

By the time Talya returned with Riley and Kyle in tow, Summer and Madeline had everything worked out and their plan in place. Summer gave her best friend a warm hug, told Riley goodbye and skirted around Kyle, who still had time, if he hurried, to catch his plane.

She smiled to herself as she walked out into the gorgeous May sunshine. Madeline was right. Everything was going to work out just fine.

Harriet Ferris never did anything halfway.

When Summer returned to the inn, the sassy redhead was talking to a man Summer didn't know. She wore violet today, her slacks, her blouse, her earrings, even the broach on her collar, were a shade of her favorite color. Five feet two in her two-inch purple heels, she rested her elbows on the top of the registration desk and cast Summer a friendly smile. "This is Knox Miller checking in."

The missing K. Miller was here at last.

"Isn't Knox the most masculine name you've ever heard?"

Harriet didn't flirt halfway, either.

It didn't matter that he wore a wedding ring and had

a receding hairline and expanding waist. Harriet didn't discriminate when it came to men.

For his part, Knox was flattered and kind. He explained that he was a day late due to a family emergency, chatted for a few more minutes and accepted Summer's welcome to The Orchard Inn.

After he left to join the crew hired to begin restoration of the old train depot, Summer filled Harriet in on Madeline's condition. In return, Harriet relayed the messages that had come in during Summer's hour-long absence. Mentally she calculated the time it would take to launder the guest towels, dust the hardwood floors, pick a bouquet of lilacs for the dining room table and plan tomorrow's breakfast. In the back of her mind, she thought about Madeline's request.

She also wondered if Kyle had managed to catch his flight.

As if thoughts really did manifest into reality, the front door opened and Kyle walked in. Once again she had the distinct impression that nothing escaped his notice. It reminded her that she needed to stay on her toes with him.

"I left the inn ahead of you," she said. "And yet you arrived at the hospital before I did. How?"

He took his time removing his sunglasses, took his time replying. "I have a genetic predisposition to catch lights green and to bypass construction zones. I guess you could say I always get where I want to go."

Summer knew there was no logical reason to believe Kyle was referring in any way to sex, but *she* had a genetic predisposition to pay attention to innuendo. "I thought you had a plane to catch."

"Are you trying to get rid of me?" he asked.

"You evade a lot of questions," Summer said.

"We're alike that way," he countered.

Harriet looked up from the computer where she'd been checking out her new profile online and watched the exchange. Still sharp as a tack, she raised pencil-thin eyebrows at Summer as if concurring. Summer definitely needed to stay on her toes with this one.

"I didn't go to the airport because I decided that meeting my future sister-in-law was more important than catching a plane," Kyle said. "My brother's a lucky man. I don't think Madeline's midwife likes me, though. What's her secret?"

He was looking at Summer in waiting expectation, but it was Harriet who said, "Tayla doesn't like men. That's not a secret, though. I mean, she dates men on occasion, but she doesn't wholly trust the lot of you. And for your information, Summer doesn't reveal our secrets. She's a saint that way."

He met Summer's gaze. "You have a lot of fans."

"I have a lot of friends."

"Talya," he said thoughtfully. "It's the name of the Greek muse of comedy."

"You know the Muses?" Summer asked, thinking of the nine sister goddesses in Greek mythology presiding over song, poetry and the arts.

"As a writer, I'm well-acquainted with the muses." He leaned his elbows on the registration desk, the action bringing his face closer to Summer's. "How do *you* know them?"

"I studied mythology in college."

"What college?" he asked.

Summer didn't like answering questions about her past. Luckily Harriet liked to be the center of attention and saved Summer the trouble of trying to reply without revealing anything pertinent.

Harriet batted her fake eyelashes at Kyle and said, "Give me a second and I'll tell you what the name Kyle means."

Summer could have kissed her.

While Harriet clicked buttons on the computer, Kyle took out his credit card and slid it across the registration desk toward Summer. "I'm going to need that room for another night or two."

"You're not leaving for L.A.?" she asked.

He shook his head.

You have to be kidding me, she thought. But she feigned an apologetic smile and said, "I'm afraid all my rooms are taken." She could tell he didn't believe her.

"Here it is," Harriet said. "Kyle. It means handsome. They've got that right. I handed over the key to Room Seven ten minutes ago."

Kyle's green-eyed gaze was causing an atmospheric disturbance again. In the six-plus years Summer had lived here, she'd adjusted to an entirely new life, different in every way from the one she'd left behind. No more shopping trips to London or yachting on Sunday afternoons or going wherever she pleased whenever she pleased without having to worry about expenses. Now she worked for a living, and she worked hard.

When it came to friends, she'd taken a giant step up. She liked her new life. She loved her inn, and her friends and neighbors, and she enjoyed her niche in Orchard Hill.

Men were the only category she had trouble with. It wasn't that she didn't have opportunities to date. She went out often and truly enjoyed dinner and conversation. But she hadn't been wowed by any of them.

Until Kyle.

He was doing it again right now with just a look. "Have dinner with me," he said.

Peering up at Kyle through her trifocals, Harriet said, "I'd want to be home before seven. I hate to miss The Wheel."

Kyle seemed at a loss. Summer didn't try to hide her grin.

"Why don't you put Kyle in the attic apartment, dear?"

Just like that, Summer was the one at a loss, and Kyle's smile grew. He rounded the desk and planted a kiss on Harriet's lined, rouged cheek. "I'll take it. What time would you like me to pick you up for dinner? I promise to have you home in time for The Wheel."

Harriet fairly swooned as she named a time. "Would you like me to show him the attic?" she asked Summer.

"If you don't mind all those stairs," she said to her neighbor.

"It'll save me from having to get on the StairMaster."

With a wink at Kyle, Harriet added, "I like a tight butt."

There was a slight lifting of Kyle's right eyebrow as he looked down at the audacious, bodacious woman. He glanced at Summer and said, "So do I."

"How long will you be staying with us?" Summer asked, making a failed attempt to refrain from looking at Kyle's rear end as he sauntered toward the stairs.

"I'm not sure." He turned and caught her looking. "Oh. You need to know because of the room. I'll pay for an entire week. I'm doing Riley a favor, and I'm not sure how long it will take."

Summer was getting a bad feeling about this. "What kind of favor?" she asked.

"Madeline has doctor's orders to stay in bed, and Riley is going to wait on her hand and foot. They won't hear of postponing the wedding, so until Madeline's out of danger, I'm filling in for the groom. I'm not at all sure what that entails, exactly, since I've never been married. Do you?"

While Summer was shaking her head, Harriet put one hand on the newel post. In a stage whisper to Summer, she said, "If I'm not back in ten minutes, don't come looking for me."

Summer couldn't help smiling. "Don't do anything I wouldn't do."

Harriet's twitter preceded her up the stairs.

Kyle didn't immediately follow her. Sunlight spilled through the bay window, turning the air golden yellow. He stood in the middle of all that sunshine, feet slightly apart, hips narrow, the slight cleft in his chin more pronounced with the light behind him. He was tall and lean and wouldn't be very comfortable in the full-size bed in the attic apartment Madeline had recently vacated. He'd rented it sight unseen. That alone was cause for concern, for it suggested an agenda of some sort.

If that wasn't bad enough, he was looking at her again as if she were a puzzle he had every intention of solving. His name may have meant handsome, but he spelled trouble with a capital *T*.

"Are you coming?" Harriet called from the top of the first landing.

He glanced up the staircase and heaved a sigh. With his face turned slightly, his eyes hidden, Summer glimpsed a pallor not evident before. With his guard down, his fatigue was almost palpable.

She wondered if he'd been ill, or if there was something else at the root of his exhaustion. There was a weight in his step as he followed the purple-clad woman up the open staircase, the quiet thud of their footsteps overhead the only sounds Summer heard over the wild beating of her heart.

She faced the fact that Kyle Merrick wasn't going to be someone who'd once spent a night in her inn. He wasn't even going to be someone she'd once kissed. He would be staying in Orchard Hill for several days, and he would be sleeping right upstairs.

He'd agreed to fill in for the groom.

That was not what she'd wanted to hear. She could

feel the vein pulsing at her throat. That favor she'd wholeheartedly granted Madeline?

Summer had agreed to fill in for the bride.

Chapter Four

"You missed your *bleeping* flight? Are you *bleep-bleep-bleeeeeeeeeep?*"

Kyle held the phone slightly away from his ear to prevent permanent damage to his hearing. Grant Oberlin had a corner office on the top floor of a New York City high-rise with one of the most prestigious newspapers in the country. It had been one hell of a steep climb from the streets of south Boston where he'd grown up. Pushing sixty now, he hadn't lost his drive, the accent or the language.

"Where the *bleep* are you right now?"

Kyle had learned to mentally block out Grant's profanity. It was one of a handful of useful skills he'd gleaned from his father.

"On second thought," Grant said loudly. "I really

don't give a *bleep* where the *bleep* you are. Here's what you're going to do."

People in the business called Oberlin The Cowboy. He rolled his own cigarettes—he probably had one clamped between his lips right now—wore snakeskin cowboy boots and had a chip on his shoulder the size of Wyoming.

"Do you know how many *bleepity-bleep-bleep* strings I had to pull, how many favors I had to call in to get you this *bleeping* gig?"

The tirade continued. Kyle's mind wandered.

Harriet had opened the windows on either end of the attic before she'd gone. Kyle stood in the gentle cross breeze, his shirt unbuttoned, his feet bare.

The attic apartment was long and narrow. With its sloped ceilings and painted wood floors, it was the kind of space his interior decorator mother would have a name for. There was a bed and dresser on one end, a kitchenette and living room on the other, and a crooked chimney dividing the two halves. Harriet had said Madeline Sullivan had lived here after college. She must have taken all her personal touches with her, because the apartment was shades of gray and splashed with yellow. Like Summer.

"Get your bony *bleep* on the next plane, and I'll call Anderson and tell him you'll be in touch."

Oh. Grant was still talking.

The cagey newspaperman had given Kyle his first break fourteen years ago. Kyle had high regard for the man. There was a part of him screaming that Grant was right, that he was making a mistake or, as Grant put it, a mother-*bleeping* gargantuan *bleep*.

Kyle was too tired to care.

He took the verbal beating—he owed Grant that much—but he felt far removed from it. How long had it been, he wondered, since he'd felt anything? How long since his experiences had found their way through the top layers of his skin and moved him, touched him or just plain fazed him?

He was thirty-four years old and had become like one of those kids born without the sensor in their nerve endings that allowed them to feel pain. Without it, they didn't understand the concept of fire or sharp objects or broken bones. It was a dangerous way to live because, without pain, joy had a lot in common with a shot of Novocain.

"You haven't heard a *bleeping* word I've said, have you?"

Grant Oberlin was one of the few newsmen left willing to cut Kyle any slack. Maybe the only one. Kyle was numb to that, too.

He'd felt Summer's kiss, though. He conjured up the sensation from memory, her soft lips, her warm breath, her pliant body. He wasn't dead to everything.

"I heard you, Grant." His voice could have been coming from anybody, anywhere. "I'm on the scent of something here."

"Blonde, brunette or redhead?"

A year ago Kyle might have been able to rustle up a smile. "I have a hunch."

"Yeah, well, your *bleeping* hunches hold as much

water these days as a leaky bucket." How nice that Grant was moving from gutter slang to cliché.

"I'm not sure I care if I fix the bucket, Grant."

The blasé remark sparked a long litany of bleeps. "That's the trouble with you *bleeeep* kids who come into this profession already rich. You're not hungry enough."

Kyle had heard it before. That no longer fazed him, either. "I'll be in touch, Grant." He disconnected in the middle of the lecture.

Squeezing the phone in his fist, he almost hurled it against the wall. He yanked his shirt off, balled it up, and flung that instead. With that, the adrenaline leaked out of him like a stuck balloon.

Oberlin was wrong. Kyle *was* hungry. Hungry for something out of his reach, hungry for oblivion.

Flying day and night, night and day, living in airports and hotel rooms while hunting down people who didn't want to be found and sniffing out stories they didn't want to tell, sifting through lies and searching for a grain of truth, then writing an accurate account of the events only to have it slashed in half to make it fit in a column between a political cartoon and a story about a heroic cat that found its way home over the Rockies had grown wearisome.

Who wouldn't be tired?

Other than an occasional fluke, he'd lost the ability to sleep more than a few hours at a time. A friend of his who liked to play at psychiatry claimed his internal clock needed an adjustment. She said he needed to wake up and go to bed in the same time zone.

He needed to restore his reputation, too. And Kyle didn't see that happening.

He went to the window Harriet had opened. From here he had a bird's-eye view of the grounds and the river. In its day, rivers like this one had been an integral part of life in the Midwest. During the timber barons' heyday, logs were floated on the river to thriving sawmills downstream. Harriet said a riverboat used to travel from Lansing to Grand Haven and back every day, carrying commuters and travelers before the railroads were built and highways cut through the forests, around lakes, swamps and dunes.

He wondered if the river minded that it was no longer of use to anybody. Kyle knew the feeling.

Rumor was he'd sold out an informant. The proper terminology was that he was being investigated for revealing a source. He hadn't revealed anything, and he sure as hell hadn't taken money for it. But he couldn't prove it, and it had broken down the line of trust he'd worked so hard to build. And an investigative reporter without leads wasn't an investigative reporter for long.

He probably should care about that.

He had it from a good source that he was burned out. He wasn't burned out. And he wasn't experiencing writer's block, whatever the hell that was. He was just tired of fighting for meaningless front-page stories while the real news was given a two-inch spot after the obituaries.

Last night he'd slept more than he'd slept in weeks. It hadn't lasted. Already fatigue was engulfing him.

He turned his back on the view and glanced around

the room. Sloping ceilings, painted wood floors, a slip-covered sofa, mismatched lamps, and a bathroom too small to turn around in. He sank to the bed, because the accommodations didn't matter, either.

He laid back. And was asleep before he'd closed his eyes.

Summer's footsteps were quiet as she climbed the stairs to the third floor. At the top, she adjusted the stack of linens in her arms and finger combed her hair. She didn't really expect to see Kyle. After all, it had been three hours since Harriet had returned after showing him to his room. Although Summer hadn't heard the purling of the front door chimes or seen him leave through the kitchen where she'd been working this afternoon, it didn't mean he hadn't slipped out.

Just in case he was inside, she tapped lightly on the door. Placing her ear close, she listened. She didn't hear music, voices or the TV. There was only silence.

She hadn't spent much time in the third-floor apartment since Madeline had moved out two weeks ago. She'd given the place a thorough cleaning, but that was all she'd done. Since Kyle would need these towels before he could shower, and she wanted to make the bed up with fresh sheets, she knocked again. Her apartment off the kitchen and this one on the third floor were the only doors that required actual keys anymore. She had a spare key with her, but first she tried the knob. Surprisingly, it turned.

She'd have thought that somebody who'd lived in L.A.

and New York and half a dozen other bustling cities would have locked up behind him. Obviously not.

She would just run in, put the towels in the bathroom, freshen up the bed, then leave. She pushed the door open and instantly felt the gentle breeze.

The natural light slanting through the small windows on either end of the space left the center portion in shadow. Her hand was on the light switch when she saw Kyle lying on the bed across the room.

Shirtless and barefoot, he was clad in low-slung jeans. His face was turned toward her, his lashes casting deeper shadows on his cheeks. She saw no movement whatsoever, no fluttering of his eyes, not even a rise and fall of his chest. She thought about the pallor she'd glimpsed before he came upstairs and wondered—

She didn't like what she was thinking.

There were times in her life when she'd felt as if she were being steered toward a blind curve by an invisible hand pressed firmly against her back. Today she was being *pulled* toward it as if by an invisible cord.

As she crept steadily closer, she automatically categorized the space. She didn't see Kyle's duffel bag anywhere. His shirt lay half on, half off the chair beside the bed, his shoes lined up neatly beneath the window. The man was a study in contrasts. Somehow she'd expected that.

She hadn't expected him to be dead to the world. Cringing at her terminology, she saw no liquor bottles or sleeping pills on the nightstand, or anything else that might have explained his comatose appearance.

She leaned slightly over him. Now that she was only

a few feet away she could see his chest rise and fall shallowly. He was breathing. Thank heavens.

Okay, he was simply sound asleep. The voice of reason told her to stop looking at him, but my oh my oh my, she wasn't listening.

A man's chest really was his most attractive physical attribute. No man wanted to hear that, but it was true. Kyle's chest was muscled, the skin taut and tan and darkened with a sparse mat of fine, brown hair. His ribs showed, suggesting a lanky, wiry build. His waist was lean, his abs tidily halved by a narrow line of hair that disappeared beneath the closure of his CK's.

She had no idea how he kept in shape, but he was every woman's fantasy and had a broad appeal that could have been an advertisement for anything from blue jeans to sports cars to European vacations. His legs were long and lean, too. Shame on her for allowing her eyes to linger at his fly.

Summer took a step away and let her gaze glide back along a safer path—waist, abs, ribs, chest, shoulders. His jaw was darkened with whisker stubble. His mouth was closed.

And his eyes were slightly open.

She froze like a deer trapped in the glare of headlights. He was looking at her.

Or was he?

She looked closer and realized she was wrong. His eyes were open a slit but his pupils weren't focused. He was still sound asleep.

And she was getting out of here before he woke up and caught her watching him or worse. But what could be worse? He could accuse her of liking what she saw. She couldn't have refuted it, for she evaded the truth when necessary, but she didn't lie.

She scurried to the door on tiptoe, leaving the towels and sheets on the table where Kyle had left his keys. She backed out the door, her gaze on his prone form, an image that was going to be nearly impossible to get out of her mind.

Kyle was aware of two things when he wandered downstairs. His brain was fuzzy despite his quick shower, and he was starving.

He wasn't wearing a watch, and he'd left his cell phone charging next to the stack of towels he'd discovered by his door, so he couldn't be certain of the time. He'd missed lunch. From the look of the activity of other guests at the inn, their work was over for the day.

Two men in blue jeans and work boots stood on the portico, their voices carrying through the screen door. Three others sat around what appeared to be an old game table in the front room off the foyer. A kid who didn't look old enough to shave was eating fast food in the dining room. The aroma of greasy fries had Kyle's stomach growling all the way to the kitchen.

He hadn't known what he was looking for until he saw her. *Summer.*

She stood at the counter, her back to him. She was whipping up something with a wire whisk, her actions slowing each time she glanced at the recipe book open in front of her. Her light brown hair swished between her shoulder blades and her hips swayed to and fro with every repetition of that metal whisk.

She must have had ultra-sensitive hearing, for she glanced over her shoulder. Stilling momentarily, she said, "You're awake."

He sauntered the rest of the way into the room, letting the door swing closed behind him. "Jet lag's a b— a bear."

"I see you found the bath towels," she said, resuming whatever it was she was doing.

So, she'd noticed his damp hair. Obviously he wasn't the only observant type in the room. He stopped at the kitchen table and said, "Until I spotted the towels, I thought I'd imagined seeing you in my room."

She stopped stirring. "You saw me?"

"I've got to tell you, it was a relief finding evidence that you'd been there. Chronic insomnia and an insatiable hunger are bad enough. Hallucinations would have been a lot tougher to ignore."

She smiled at his dry wit. He found he liked that, too.

"I thought you were dead," she said, as she faced him. "Seriously, I've never seen anybody sleep so soundly. If you saw me deliver your towels, why didn't you say something?"

"Like I said, I thought I was dreaming. I'd be happy to tell you about the rest of the dream."

She rested her back against the counter, folded her arms and tilted her head slightly. He half expected a mild admonishment. He felt a sexual stirring again. Oh, he definitely wasn't numb to everything.

"Harriet is the one who enjoys dirty stories," she said quietly.

Did she say Harriet?

There was a nagging buzzing in the back of his mind. He looked from Summer's hazel eyes to the clock on the stove. It was after seven.

Harriet.

He'd stood her up. Muttering Grant Oberlin's favorite word under his breath, Kyle headed for the door.

"Take these," Summer told him. She handed him a vase filled with fragrant lilacs. "Purple is Harriet's favorite color."

It was dark outside when Kyle parked at the curb in front of Madeline's house on Floral Avenue later that night. He recognized Riley's silver car in the driveway and also Summer's blue sedan. Two other vehicles were there, too. It might have explained why every light in the house was on.

He climbed out of his Jeep, only to hesitate. Madeline's doctor had prescribed bed rest, so it was unlikely there was a wild party going on, and yet for a few seconds he wondered if he should go in. Riley would have called Kyle a choice brotherly name if he knew Kyle was so much as considering the possibility that he was intruding.

Riley, Braden and Kyle had been raised by three very different mothers in three separate households. The boys had all wanted the same thing from their father: his attention, some fatherly advice and a good example. Brock Merrick hadn't had it in him. He'd shared his immense wealth, and he'd loved his sons; he'd loved their mothers, too. The problem was, he'd loved a lot of women. By the time the boys were adults, they'd learned to accept his flaw. Ultimately, since they couldn't get what they'd needed from him, they'd gotten it from each other. They'd also gotten black eyes and bruised egos, but that was part of growing up with brothers.

They'd vowed to be there for one another no matter what, no questions asked, and while they'd all been adults for a while now and didn't see each other as often as they wanted to, being there for one another would never change. Feeling back in his game, Kyle walked to his brother's door.

Riley answered Kyle's knock and threw the door wide. He motioned him in as if Kyle were a lifeboat and Riley was swimming in shark-infested water. "I'm glad you're here."

"Is something wrong?" Kyle asked.

This morning only Riley and his dog, Gulliver, had been home. Tonight, Kyle heard voices, several of them. All female.

"No," Riley said. "On the other hand." He paused again. "No, come on back."

Kyle wondered, was there something wrong or not?

Just then a chorus of laughter carried through the house. One was throaty, one breathy, one a giggle. Again, all were feminine. Maybe there was a party going on after all.

Gulliver looked expectantly at Riley then waited for his master to nod before leading the way. The brown dog and Riley took the same route through Madeline's house they'd taken this morning. They led Kyle past a narrow staircase in the living room then through a brightly lighted dining room and into the kitchen. From there they entered an arched hallway where Kyle saw a door that had been closed earlier.

They stopped outside a small bedroom with old-fashioned floral wallpaper and period furnishings. There was a mahogany desk and dresser on the far wall. On an adjacent wall was an antique four-poster bed. And on that four-poster were four women.

Kyle recognized Summer. She sat on the side closest to the door, her back to him, her body blocking the faces of two others. Kyle assumed the slight woman lying down was Madeline. He had no idea who the other two lined up against the headboard were. One had a notebook open on her lap, the other was gesturing wildly with her hands. Whatever she said caused laughter to erupt again.

Kyle and Riley shared a look, and Kyle quietly said, "This kind of thing would never happen between men."

Riley's sudden chuckle drew four sets of eyes. It occurred to Kyle that laughter looked good on Summer. Her cheeks were flushed, the curve of her lips enticing a second look. Rimmed by dark lashes, her eyes crinkled slightly at the corners. She was smiling, genuinely happy.

There was an innate elegance in the way she placed her teacup on its gilded saucer and set it on the nightstand before introducing him to her friends. Chelsea

Reynolds was the curvy brunette, Abby Fitzpatrick the wispy-haired blonde.

"It's nice to meet you," he said to each in turn.

"How did it go?" Summer asked him.

"Better than I expected."

"Did she forgive you?"

"Who?" the petite blonde asked.

The brunette shushed her with a nudge.

"She made me work for it," he said, his gaze steady on Summer. He and Summer were the only ones who knew they were referring to Harriet Ferris, and neither of them chose to explain to the others. "But eventually she warmed up," Kyle said. "The flowers were a big help."

"I'm glad." She was looking at him as if she meant it.

Kyle wondered if anybody else in the room noticed that he couldn't seem to take his eyes off her. He was interested. He was intrigued. And he hadn't been either of those things in a while.

"Am I interrupting something?" he asked her.

Summer shook her head. "Chelsea is Madeline's wedding planner. She's been prioritizing the most pressing details for the coming week."

The blonde, Abby, said, "Summer's going to be filling in for Madeline."

"Is that right?" He smiled at Abby, but his gaze ultimately went to Summer again, for this was the first he'd heard that.

The weather had been unseasonably warm and humid today. It brought out the beast in a lot of people. As far as Kyle was concerned, the conditions were perfect for peeling off layers of clothing, for gliding a zipper down a slender back, for lowering the straps of a certain someone's bra and for taking his time removing it.

That was a good place to halt his wayward thoughts. "If you have plans to make," he said, looking directly at Summer, "I won't keep you from them." Even he could hear the huskiness in his voice. "I just stopped over to talk to Riley." Kyle nodded at all four women. He smiled last at Summer.

He'd been accused of being vain a time or two. When he happened to look over his shoulder as he was leaving and caught four women looking at him, he knew why he'd never apologized for it.

From the doorway, he directed a question to the official wedding planner of the group. "I'm curious about something. What does a fill-in bride do?"

Chelsea held up the fingers of her right hand and began listing off responsibilities. "She hosts a bridal shower, samples wedding cake, chooses the menu, wears pink, the bride's favorite color." That was spoken with a shudder. "She helps the bride select the music, meets with the photographer and basically does whatever needs to be done, even if it means keeping the appointment with the seamstress for the final dress fitting, since, luckily, Summer and Madeline are the same size."

Summer was shaking her head. "Trying on someone else's wedding gown is bad luck."

Obviously, this was an ongoing debate.

"Now you sound like Madeline," the petite blonde

said. "Usually she's the one with all the uncanny intuitions and crazy premonitions."

"I'm right here," Madeline said. "And I can hear everything you're saying, Abs."

Kyle couldn't help smiling. He would have enjoyed continuing along that vein, but he said, "And what does the fill-in groom do?" He'd already spoken to Riley about this, but his brother's answer had been sketchy at best.

He doubted there were many women who could pull off appearing businesslike while sharing a bed with three other women, but Chelsea made an admirable attempt as she held up the fingers of her right hand again and prepared to count the ways Kyle could help this week. In the end, all her fingers remained straight.

"I suppose the groom's responsibility during the week prior to the wedding is to support the bride."

His gaze returned to Summer's. In this instance he would be supporting the *fill-in* bride. "I can do that," he said.

Her hair had fallen across her cheek. He would have liked to brush it away. As long as he was touching her, he would glide his finger to her chin, his thumb smoothing over her lower lip. He'd let his hand trail down her neck, stopping at the little vein pulsing in the delicate hollow.

Kyle felt the way he had earlier. Alive and aware. Especially aware. If he and Summer had been alone, there was no telling what he might have done. Instead, he reined in his hormones and smiled all around.

"It was nice meeting both of you," he said to Abby

and Chelsea. "Take care of yourself, Madeline." At last he spoke to the woman he couldn't seem to stop looking at. "Summer. I guess I'll see you at the inn."

Summer swore the temperature lowered ten degrees the minute the men left the room. She heard three collective sighs from the other women on the bed. Pleased to discover that her hand was still steady, she took a sip of tea.

"Holy moly," Madeline declared.

"What was that?" Abby whispered.

"That," Chelsea declared, "was one amazing example of pure masculine appeal."

"That," Summer qualified, "was Kyle Merrick being supportive."

Madeline was looking at Summer, one eyebrow raised. With a point of her finger, Summer said, "Don't start."

Madeline grinned knowingly. And Summer thought it was going to be a long week.

"He wants you," Chelsea said matter-of-factly.

"Film at eleven," Abby piped in.

Arguing that they were wrong would have been futile, and Summer had a feeling she needed to save her strength. For a few moments, she'd almost forgotten that Kyle was in a profession she mistrusted. For those few blessed minutes, he'd simply been someone who slept too soundly and lost track of time and made her lose track of it, too. He was someone who took a bouquet of lilacs to a kind old lady, someone who brought out yearnings Summer hadn't expected to feel. It was too late to chide herself, for Chelsea was right.

He wanted her.

He hadn't tried to hide it. She hadn't expected that any more than she'd expected him to show up here tonight or arrive last night during that thunderstorm. But he had, and he wasn't leaving anytime soon.

Being wanted by a man like him was heady. It was tempting, and normally Summer didn't tempt easily. What she didn't know was what she was going to do about it.

Chapter Five

Kyle tossed the crime novel he'd been reading onto the bed. It landed facedown on the rumpled pillow beside him. Picking up the remote again, he aimed it at the small television on the nearby wall, adjusted his pillows and tried to get comfortable. He'd already caught the beginning of a comedian's act, a portion of the race Braden had qualified for in Europe, and the end of a black and white war movie. He'd watched an infomercial selling kitchen knives, a lot of garbage, and a piece about the disappearing rain forests in South America.

He stayed away from the news.

Powering off the television, he sat up on the edge of the bed. By the light of a small lamp in the alcove that distinguished the bedroom from the living room, he padded quietly to the window. He stood in the shadows looking up at the sky. There, in the west, was Pleiades.

According to an ancient Greek legend, the bright cluster of stars represented seven sisters who'd been openly pursued by a relentless hunter named Orion. Zeus, the ruler of the gods, took pity on the beautiful maidens and changed them into doves before setting them free into the heavens.

Those ancient stargazers sure knew how to tell a story. They must have spent a lot of time studying the night sky. Kyle wondered if they'd been insomniacs, too.

The inn settled around him. Somewhere a car downshifted. The air outside his window was still, the night so quiet he could hear the river flowing over the rocks in the distance. The dark windows of the neighboring houses reflected the crescent moon. Old post lamps lined the driveway and lit the inn's front lawn. The only illumination in the backyard was a square patch of yellow stretching onto the grass close to the inn. He couldn't see the origin of that light but he could tell from the angle that it was coming from the first floor.

He wasn't the only one awake at this hour.

Summer swirled the pale wine in her glass. After enjoying a generous sip, she returned to the stove where she stirred hot cream into a bowl containing beaten egg yolks and sugar. Humming with the radio, she then poured the mixture into the saucepan, adjusted the flame and began to slowly stir.

She loved cooking at night, loved the rhythm, the aroma and the steam. The process of measuring and mixing, folding and stirring was soothing. It cleared her mind, which helped her contemplate solutions to problems.

Take Kyle Merrick for instance. He was an investigative reporter. Of all the legitimate professions in the world, his had the potential to be the most damaging to the new life she'd built. That made this attraction anything but safe.

No wonder she'd been genuinely *relieved* when she'd learned he wouldn't be attending Madeline's wedding. Now he was staying in The Orchard Inn. What were the chances of that happening? she wondered.

She'd fairly melted in his arms when he'd kissed her in this very kitchen. She couldn't very well pretend indifference now without raising his suspicions. Besides, she wasn't that good an actress.

As she stirred the mixture in the saucepan, it occurred to her that having Kyle under her roof might not be so terrible after all. She needed to set some boundaries, for sure, but having him in close proximity meant she could keep an eye on him.

She took another sip from her fluted glass and turned down the flame under the front burner. The stove was forty-five years old and was often cantankerous, but tonight it was cooperating beautifully. Her crème brulee would be a masterpiece. She stirred and hummed, and hummed and stirred, her mind on the sweet concoction and the little oasis of light she'd created in the otherwise dark inn.

She liked nearly everything about her life as an innkeeper. Keeping this place running smoothly and in the black brought her a sense of accomplishment she hadn't known until she'd taken on the responsibility shortly after coming to Orchard Hill. She enjoyed serving breakfast and especially liked meeting new people and hearing all about their lives and dreams. She'd come to appreciate the steady progression and the one hundred and one tasks from check-in to checkout. She didn't mind the daily punctiliousness of freshening rooms and shopping and seeing to her guests' needs. The daylight hours belonged to them.

The night was hers.

Tonight the air was unseasonably warm. Thanks to the apple trees in the nearby orchards resplendent with blossoms, it was also wonderfully fragrant.

Turning off the flame beneath the thickened concoction, she sniffed the rising steam. With a moan, she closed her eyes.

When she opened them, she was no longer alone.

Kyle stood in the doorway where the light was faint, one hand on his hip and an easy smile playing at the corners of his mouth. "Am I interrupting?"

Always with that lilting sensuality. Deciding there was no time like the present to implement the boundaries she needed to set, she gave him a friendly smile and said, "You're welcome to come in, on one condition." She scooped up a spoonful of the hot mixture and gently blew on it. "Try this."

He sauntered to the stove wearing loafers, faded jeans and a T-shirt with wording in French. Bringing his nose close to her spoon, he took a trial whiff.

There was a certain level of trust involved as he

touched his lips to the still warm dessert. It was his turn to moan.

She reached for another spoon and sampled some, too. "That's not half-bad, is it?"

"Half-bad? Are you kidding? It's magnificent." Kyle moved slightly to make room for Summer as she went to the sink and washed her hands. She was wearing a white tank top and those knit pants that looked so damn good on women. Hers rode low on her hips and were held up by a string tied in a loose bow.

"Do you always cook when everyone else is sleeping?" he asked.

"It's when I enjoy it the most, and when I have the most time for it. The first strawberries of the season are ripe," she said as she dried her hands on a yellow towel. "I thought I'd spoon the crème brulee over them and offer a bowlful to my guests with breakfast which, by the way, is served every weekday between seven and nine."

Her movements were fluid, her voice quiet, as if in reverence to the night. She must have seen him looking hungrily at the crème brulee, for she took a bowl from the cupboard, filled it, added a clean spoon and handed it to him.

The bottom of the dish was warm in his palm, the aroma wafting upwards so sweet smelling his mouth watered. He didn't dig right in, though.

"Is something wrong?" she asked.

"Aren't you going to have any?"

It didn't take her long to make up her mind. Soon

they were leaning against opposite cupboards, ankles crossed, bowls in one hand, spoons in the other.

"So," she said between bites, "are you going to see Harriet again?"

Kyle didn't know whether to laugh or scoff. Everything about Summer Matthews was a contrast. The way she'd ladled her concoction into bowls and daintily ate it was refined. Her reference to his date bordered on brazen. Earlier she'd been sipping tea. Now her wine glass was empty. She was as regal as royalty, and yet she seemed to run this inn single-handedly. It couldn't be easy to keep up with the repairs of a building this old—floors pitched, doors didn't close, pipes rattled. And yet every item in the house had so obviously been *chosen*. The retro range and state-of-the-art refrigerator and the scratched oak table and cane-bottom chairs sitting tidily on an aubusson rug didn't scream good taste. They whispered it.

"I think I met Harriet's secret tonight," he said, scraping the bottom of his bowl.

Summer's eyebrows rose slightly. "Her secret?"

"Walter."

"You met Walter?"

"He joined us for dinner." Kyle emptied his bowl only to have it miraculously refilled. It happened again before he'd finished telling Summer about the evening.

Walter Ferris was a large man with beefy hands, thick gray hair and bushy eyebrows. He'd probably been a handsome devil once. In his late seventies, he was straightforward and astute. He hadn't been able to take his eyes off Harriet all night. Harriet had given Kyle plenty of attention, but he'd caught her eyes going soft on Walter a time or two when she'd thought Kyle wasn't looking.

They had history, no doubt about it. And since they had the same last name, and they didn't act like kissing cousins, Kyle wondered what their connection really was.

He didn't normally give relationships more than a passing thought. It had been a long time since he'd been in one that lasted more than a month or two. He'd *never* stood in a woman's kitchen eating warm crème brulee at three in the morning. Maybe there was something to the adage that the way to a man's heart was through his stomach, although Kyle preferred other more evocative ways.

"Do I have crème brulee on my chin?" she asked.

He shook his head but didn't apologize for staring. "What were we talking about?"

She seemed to have forgotten, too. It made them both smile.

"Walter," they said in unison.

Walter Ferris had a story for every occasion but, other than a vague recollection of Summer mentioning a mother and sister who'd died before she'd moved to Orchard Hill, neither he nor Harriet seemed to know a lot about her past.

"I'm a little surprised Walter joined you tonight," Summer said. "They usually have dinner together on Tuesdays and Fridays."

Kyle stared at her, his spoon poised between his

mouth and bowl. "Are you saying Harriet and Walter have regular dinner date nights?"

She'd spooned another bite into her mouth and therefore couldn't answer. He wondered if evading questions was intentional or automatic.

"Are they married then? Ah," he said, finally understanding the dynamics. "They're divorced. If I were to harbor a guess, I'd say Walter wants her back. Men are easy to read that way."

"I don't like to talk about people behind their backs," she said.

"If you'd rather we can talk about us."

Summer used the ruse of carrying Kyle's empty bowl to the sink to buy her a little time. It also gave her a little much-needed space.

By the time she'd rinsed the bowls, he was leaning against the countertop in the inn's main kitchen again, his ankles crossed, arms folded. If she'd stopped there, she would have believed he was completely at ease. But it only required one look at his lean face, his lips firmly together, his green eyes hooded, and she knew the ease was secondary. He was a man who took nothing for granted, a man who didn't rush or gloss over details. He was the kind of man who would take his time pleasuring a woman.

"There is no *us,*" she said. What was wrong with her voice?

"Not yet, you mean."

It was the perfect opening for her to say, "You and I don't know each other, Kyle. You're just passing through

Orchard Hill, but I live in this town. My livelihood is hinged on my reputation."

He uncrossed his ankles and straightened, leading her to assume he was going to take the rejection with a grain of salt and go back upstairs. Instead he joined her in front of the sink.

"Sunrise or sunset?" he asked.

"What?"

"Sunrise or sunset?" he repeated.

She'd turned the radio down when he'd first joined her in the kitchen. Now the low hum barely covered the quiet. "What are you talking about?" she asked.

"I'm getting to know you. I think the modern terminology refers to this stage as the date interview. You're right, that's an easy one. You are sunset all the way. It's your turn. Go ahead, ask me anything."

She started the faucet and squirted dish soap into the stream. "This isn't a date," she reminded him sternly, but she couldn't help thinking he was right about her and sunsets.

What could it hurt, she thought, to participate in a little harmless middle of the night conversation? After considering possible safe topics, she said, "Bourbon or Merlot?"

"Bourbon, hands down."

She was surprised. She'd have pegged him as the kind of man who had an extensive wine collection.

"Hard rock or Rap?" he asked when it was his turn. "First, what are you doing?" He pointed at the sink she was filling with sudsy water.

"The dishwasher's broken, and there won't be money

in the budget to have it repaired until July," she explained. "Hard rock and Rap are both okay on occasion, but my favorite musician of all time is Leonard Cohen."

As two iridescent bubbles floated on the rising steam, he said, "So you're a romantic at heart."

Had he moved closer? Or had she? Putting a little space between them again, she scoured a saucepan.

Kyle said, "I'd offer to fix your dishwasher, but I'm afraid my brother Braden is the mechanical genius in the family. I'm good with my hands in other ways."

"I'm sure you'll be very happy with yourself."

His laugh was a deep rumble, the kind that invited everyone to smile along. They were standing close again, her shoulder nearly touching his arm. This time he was the one who moved slightly. Picking up a towel, he began to dry. "I believe it's your turn."

Hmm, she thought as she washed measuring cups and spoons. "Baseball or football?"

"Football, but I like races the best. European Auto Racing is my favorite, probably because my youngest brother is trying to break records and hopefully not his neck. Chicken or fish?"

"I'm more of a pasta girl. Dogs or cats?"

"Dogs," he said. "Friends or family?"

Rinsing her wine glass and carefully handing it to him by the stem, she said, "I don't have much family."

"Then it wasn't a family connection that brought you to Orchard Hill?"

Keeping her wits about her, she said, "Madeline likes to say Orchard Hill found me. The elderly couple that used to own The Orchard Inn had been looking for someone to take it over. I applied, and the rest is history."

"So you work for this old couple?" he asked.

"I bought the inn from them with the money my grandmother left me. She'd been very ill and died right after I moved here." Summer's grandmother had been the only one who knew where she went, and the estate attorney had promised to keep her location confidential.

"The grandmother you and your sister spent summers with on Mackinaw Island?" he asked.

She supposed she shouldn't have been surprised he'd been listening when she'd mentioned that. Keeping her eyes on the dish she was washing, she said, "I wasn't kidding when I told you I don't have much family."

"If you'd like, you can borrow some of mine. Other than Riley and Braden, most of our relatives are female. One mother, two stepmothers and too many grandmothers, aunts and family pets to count. Action-adventure or horror?"

She laughed at the awkward segue. "I live alone in a hundred-and-twenty-year-old inn. Definitely not horror." It was her turn to ask a question. She took her time deciding which one. "Crime dramas or reality TV?"

"Could I get another choice here?"

"You don't watch much television?" she asked.

He made a sound universal to men through his pursed lips. "Three hundred channels and there's still nothing on half the time."

She looked up at him and smiled, for she'd often thought the same thing.

"See what I mean?" he said, his voice a low croon befitting the dark night. "We have a lot in common. We're practically soul mates."

She wished she could blame the warm swirl in the pit of her stomach on the lateness of the hour or the wine. "Out of all these questions," she said, "we've found only one thing we have in common. I don't believe in soul mates."

His gaze went from her eyes, to her lips, to the base of her neck where a little vein was pulsing. He folded the towel over the edge of the sink and got caught looking at her lips again. He didn't pretend he didn't want to kiss her. And yet he waited. A man who had enough self-confidence to want a woman to be sure wasn't an easy man to resist.

A gentle breeze stirred the air. Somewhere a night bird warbled. Moments later an answering call sounded from across the river. Summer didn't recognize the birdsong, but she understood the language of courtship. It seemed to her that birds had a straightforward approach to life. They built a nest in the spring, raised a brood and, as if guided by some magical internal alarm clock, they gathered in flocks and flew south to a tropical paradise for the winter, only to return and start all over again in the spring.

Summer had started over once. She never wanted to do that again, which brought her right back to where she and Kyle had started. Whatever this was, be it a date interview or simply a pleasant interlude, it was ending. It had to.

Taking a deliberate step back, she said, "Good night, Kyle."

He handled the mild rejection with a degree of watchfulness and his usual charm. She wasn't expecting the light kiss. Little more than a brush of air, it was over by the time she'd closed her eyes. The dreamy intimacy lingered as he walked to the door.

"Thank you for the midnight snack," he said quietly, "and for having a sunset personality."

She smiled. And he was gone.

It was a few minutes before Summer's heart settled into its normal rhythm. Occasionally Madeline used to join her in the kitchen late at night. Kyle was the only *man* who ever had. Strangely, his presence hadn't been an intrusion. Without even trying, he'd made her feel understood. Kyle Merrick would make a good friend.

He would have been a good lover, too. Of that, she had no doubt. All things considered, his middle of the night visit had gone well. He seemed to have accepted the limits she'd set. It was a relief, and yet, with every swish of the drawstring at her waist and every rustle of the fabric at her midriff, she was reminded of what she was missing.

She stuck her hands on her hips and huffed. She supposed there was always the next best thing.

On the counter sat the uncorked bottle of wine and the bowl containing the remaining crème brulee. She pushed the wine out of the way and reached for a spoon.

Friday morning dawned cloudy and gray. The temperature had dropped overnight and the barometric pressure had been on the rise ever since. Spring had returned to Orchard Hill.

Seven of Summer's eight guests had shuffled to the breakfast table groggy or grumpy or both, adversely affected by the atmospheric change. Kyle was the last to amble downstairs. Looking surprisingly rested and amiable, he took a seat at the long dining room table as she was clearing away the place settings of five men who'd already left for their day's work restoring the train depot.

"Good morning," she said, as she did to each guest every day.

"Morning," he answered. "Beautiful day, isn't it?"

The last two remaining carpenters looked askance at him. When thunder rumbled an exclamation point disguised as weather, Kyle had the grace to counter his sunny outlook with, "Easy for me to say. I'm not being forced to work in it today."

With a few grumbles, he was forgiven.

"Coffee and juice are on the sideboard," she said. "I'll be right back with your breakfast."

Kyle was alone at the table with his coffee when she returned with his plate of crisp bacon, whole wheat toast and a stack of piping hot pancakes. In a separate bowl was a generous serving of fresh strawberries sans crème brulee.

"Have you already had breakfast?" he asked.

She thought about the slice of toast she'd eaten two hours ago while the bacon was frying and answered simply, "Yes."

"A cup of coffee, then?" he asked.

Summer had hit the snooze button once, and then she'd hit the floor running. She hadn't slept well the previous night, and, after only three hours last night, sleep deprivation was catching up with her. Caffeine sounded wonderful. In fact, she could have used a direct IV line of the stuff. She went to the sideboard and poured herself a piping hot cup.

It wasn't unusual for her to have a cup of coffee with a guest. Her boarders all happened to be men this month, but that wasn't always the case. Sometimes families stayed here. Throughout the year, groups of women came for girlfriends' weekends of wine tasting and shopping and marathon chick flick rentals. Summer's mainstay came from sales reps and other men and women employed by companies with projects too far away for a reasonable commute.

She sipped her coffee while Kyle dug into his breakfast. They talked about everyday things. He told her about a book he was reading, and she relayed a funny story from a former guest. Out of the blue, he asked her if she'd ever been married.

She looked him in the eye and with complete honesty said, "No, have you?"

He offered her a pancake before he drizzled the stack with syrup. She took it and daintily ate it with her fingers while he explained why he'd never married.

She was laughing by the time he summed it up. "Women are complicated."

"And men aren't?" she asked.

Cutting into his stack of pancakes, he said, "I'd be

happy to explain the differences to you, but I have to warn you, it's not a topic for sissies."

Somehow she believed he was only half joking. In a like manner, she said, "I'm fairly certain I can handle it."

He seemed to be enjoying the opportunity to share his expertise. The man obviously had a playful side to go with his voracious appetite. The pallor she'd glimpsed yesterday was less noticeable this morning. His eyes crinkled at the corners, as green and changeable as the weather. He hadn't bothered to shave. The stubble on his jaw was a shade darker than his hair. The collar of his shirt was open at his throat, the green broadcloth a color and style that would fit in anywhere.

"Basically there are five classifications of men," he began as he spread jelly on his toast. "The butt heads are by and large the worst. Normally I would refer to them as something more crass, but I'm going to try to do this delicately, so we'll stick with butt heads. These are the guys who make promises they have no intention of keeping. They're hard and heartless. These are the liars, stealers, cheaters, politicians, CEOs, anybody with no conscience. They give all men a bad name."

She was listening, for she'd once known a few of those. Intimately.

"Next are the sorry-asses. Forgive me but there's no delicate way to describe this category. They're the drunks, the guys who mean well but are too lazy to bring home a paycheck, get their own beer or mow the lawn. You know, your basic losers."

She couldn't help smiling again.

"Third is the—let's call the third category the dumbbells. If sorry-asses are your basic losers, dumbbells are your basic users. This is the guy who doesn't have any money with him on Pizza Friday, who has to be shown repeatedly how to use the business system at work but can navigate every search engine for his personal use on company time. He's more obnoxious than harmful."

She made an agreeable sound, which earned her an appreciative masculine grin that went straight to her head.

"The last two categories are the smart alecks and the wise guys. At first glance you might think they're one and the same. They're both on the mouthy side, but smart alecks are irritating and wise guys are charming and entertaining." He took a big bite of his pancakes and smiled smugly, as if his work here was done.

"You've certainly cleared that up," she said over the rim of her coffee cup. "Tell me this. Why do women put up with any of you?"

Those green eyes of his spoke a full five seconds before he said, "Because some of us are irresistible."

"You don't say."

They fell into a companionable silence. She finished the plain pancake and sipped her coffee, and he made a good-sized dent in his breakfast.

Thunder rumbled overhead. Kyle felt an answering vibration that was more like the pulsing beat of a distant drum than weather. It started deep inside, radiating outward. This was desire, the kind that burned slow and got hotter. There was only one way to appease it, and she was sitting across the table from him.

Summer's dress was the color of pecans today. When was the last time he'd met a woman who wore a dress every day? He wasn't referring to buttoned-up suits with pencil-thin skirts and stiletto heels with toes so pointy they could draw blood. Summer wasn't out for blood. Was that why she drew him?

No. There was something far more elemental at work here.

Her dress was sleeveless, and the neckline covered all but the inside edges of her collarbones. It wasn't formfitting or tight and had no business looking sexy. He wanted to push his plate away and reach for her, but burning off this hunger with her wasn't going to be that simple.

Luckily Kyle was a patient man.

When his plate was empty, she came around to his side of the table and took it. Pausing at the kitchen door, she glanced back at him and said, "Which type are you?"

He wiped his mouth on his napkin and stood. "If you have to ask, I'm doing something wrong." With that he sauntered out the front door.

In the kitchen, Summer turned on the hot water and squirted in dish soap. As suds expanded over the dishes in the bottom, she placed one finger over that little indentation at the base of her neck. Feeling the pulse fluttering there, she thought, a wise guy, definitely.

Since there were no parking spaces in front of Rose's Flower Shoppe, Summer parked in front of Knight's Bakery and Confectionary Shoppe a block away. The steady pitter-patter of raindrops on her umbrella muffled the click of her heels as she started toward Rose's, but it didn't dampen her mood. Betty Ryan smiled from the window of her daughter and son-in-law's bakery when she saw Summer walking by. Looking up from the newspaper he was reading in his barber chair, Bud Barkley wiggled his fingers at Summer. She couldn't help returning his classic wave.

She hurried past two clothing stores that had survived the ongoing feud between their owners *and* the recession. The big chains had drained the life out of the old drugstore on the corner. Now the building was home to Izzy's Ice Cream Parlor. Summer loved that she knew the stories and the struggles of the courageous, tenacious people who called Orchard Hill home. Being accepted by them was an honor and a gift.

As if on cue, her phone jangled in her purse. Sliding it open, she began talking the moment she put it to her ear. "I'm on my way, Chelsea. How's Madeline this morning?"

"She's going stir-crazy and Riley's hovering." Chelsea's voice in her ear was clear and concise. "I don't know who I feel sorrier for. Let me know what Josie says about Madeline's bouquet, okay? I know you can't be away from the inn more than absolutely necessary, so somebody from Knight's Bakery is bringing four samples of wedding cake to the inn later."

Flowers. Check.

Wedding cake. Check.

There was something Summer was forgetting, but Chelsea was on a mission, and, when that happened, there was no stopping her. "Reverend Brown has agreed to go to Madeline's house after services on Sunday to talk to her and Riley about the ceremony and vows. That'll take us to the final five-day countdown. Can you believe it?"

Summer thought it *was* amazing how fast the wedding was approaching, but she didn't have an opportunity to make more than an agreeable murmur before Chelsea had to take another call. Outwardly Chelsea Reynolds was the most organized young woman on the planet. But underneath her buttoned-up shirts and practical manner smoldered a dreamer. Only those closest to her knew the reason she kept it hidden.

The world was feeling like a good place as Summer dropped her phone back into her shoulder bag and walked into Rose's Flower Shoppe. As always, the scents of carnations and roses met her at the door.

"I'll be right with you." Josie Rose's muffled voice sounded as if she was speaking into the cooler. Eight months pregnant with her third child, she entered the room with one hand at the small of her back and the other on her basketball-size belly. "There you are, Summer. Someone was here a little while ago asking about you. A man," she said in a stage whisper.

For the span of one heartbeat, Summer's only thought was, *they've found me*. She waited, unmoving.

"Can you say tall, dark and handsome?" Josie asked, oblivious to Summer's inner turmoil.

Oh. Okay. Summer could breathe again, because that description ruled out Drake and her father.

When she'd first moved to Orchard Hill and shortened

her name and bought her inn, she'd often caught herself looking over her shoulder. There had been times when she'd been certain someone was following her. She wasn't afraid, physically, of her former fiancé or her father. It was the havoc they could wreak and the media circus they were capable of creating that she so dreaded. Her father had connections to people in high places. She'd seen him in action with her own two eyes and knew he had the ability and the capability to ruin people for pleasure or personal gain.

Nothing had ever materialized out of those certainties that she was being followed. Eventually her paranoia subsided. She relaxed and began to enjoy the life she was painstakingly building, but old habits died hard, and this morning dread had reared.

"He had the greenest eyes I've ever seen on a man," Josie continued.

Summer knew only one man who fit that description. "I think you're referring to Riley's brother Kyle. He's staying at the inn this week." Offhandedly she asked, "What did he want to know about me?"

"Oh, your favorite color, what kind of flowers you like, that sort of thing. Now, I can't say more without spoiling the surprise, but it's like I told him, a man never goes wrong with red roses. Come on back. I'll show you what I had in mind for Madeline's bridal bouquet."

Summer had been on edge these last few days because Kyle was a reporter. Other than choosing his profession, he'd done nothing to warrant her distrust. In fact, except for asking her a few questions about her background, which was a very normal thing to do when people were getting to know one another, he'd done nothing except come to his brother's aid, sample a bowl of crème brulee at three in the morning and beguile her with his wit and charm over breakfast.

He'd hinted about making love, but she'd been thinking about that, too, so she could hardly chide him for it. She was beginning to like him. Summer took pride in the fact that she showed everyone common courtesy. She granted people who earned it her respect, but her affection wasn't given lightly. And she liked Kyle Merrick, truly liked him.

After consulting with Madeline over the phone, Summer finalized the order for the flowers for the wedding. Josie Rose was right. The bridal wreath spiraea, lilacs and baby's breath were going to be perfect compliments to the sprigs of apple blossoms from Madeline's family orchard. She spoke with Chelsea first and then Abby, as she started back toward her car. Since the rain had dwindled to a mild sprinkle by then, she didn't even bother with an umbrella.

She smiled a greeting to Brad Douglas, one of the accountants with the CPA firm located across the street, waved to Greg and Celia Michaels, owners of the antique store around the corner, and held out a steadying hand to Mac Bower who'd been the proprietor of Bower's Bar & Grill for sixty-five years.

A pair of strappy, high-heeled sandals in the window of the shoe store on the corner caught her eye. Lo and behold, they were even on sale.

The world felt like a very good place, indeed.

Chapter Six

The door between the kitchen and dining room was open when Summer returned to the inn late that Friday morning. As she hung her shoulder bag on the hook next to the refrigerator, she could see all the way to the parlor where Kyle was reading a magazine. He looked pretty comfortable hunkered down in an old leather chair favored by many of her guests. His elbows rested on the padded arms; one ankle balanced on his opposite knee.

She left her new shoes in her room then went to the registration desk in the foyer to check for messages. Catching a movement in her peripheral vision, she glanced up and found Kyle looking at her over his magazine.

She closed the inn's website and gave him her full attention. "Did you need something?"

"I wanted to give you these." He reached beside the chair. When he stood, he had a bouquet of flowers in his right hand.

The gesture stalled her heartbeat and invoked a sigh, for the flowers weren't red roses at all, as Josie Rose had hinted. They were daffodils, at least two dozen of them, all yellow—bright, sunny yellow, Summer's favorite color. She didn't remember walking into the parlor, but she must have because she found herself standing before Kyle, her mouth shaped in a genuine O.

He looked pleased with her response, and it occurred to her that looking pleased looked good on him.

"I have something else for you." He turned and bent at the waist, a marvelous shifting of denim over man. Just as quickly, he was upright again, and in his other hand was an ornately decorated box of Godiva chocolates.

She almost moaned. "You're very fattening to have around. Did you know that?"

"Women worry too much about their weight."

With a tilt of her head, she said, "You're saying you would date a woman who weighs three hundred pounds?"

"As long as she put it in the right places, sure."

Summer laughed out loud, and it sounded far sexier than she'd intended. After thanking him for the bouquet and the chocolates, she said, "You're a wise guy, definitely."

His grin was approving and mischievous, his posture relaxed. "I can't take sole credit for the system of analysis. It was a Merrick brother joint effort a few years back. You don't want to know what prompted it. Which reminds me. Riley said I'm to meet with you here at five to eat cake."

Well, she thought.

So.

Okay.

Something was seriously wrong with her ability to think in complete sentences, but she finally managed to say, "Someone from the bakery is bringing an assortment of sample wedding cakes here about then."

There was a nagging in the back of her mind again. What was she forgetting?

"I'll see you at five," Kyle said as he settled back into the chair and picked up his magazine.

Summer took the gifts to the kitchen where she put the flowers in water and the chocolates in the cupboard behind her baking supplies. All the while, something continued to bother the back of her mind.

What on earth could she be forgetting?

Freshening guest rooms took approximately two hours each day. Summer began on the first floor and worked her way upstairs. Being careful not to disturb personal belongings such as clothes, cameras and laptops, she straightened desks and dresser tops, smoothed wrinkles from beds and fluffed pillows. She made sure faucets weren't dripping and rugs were straightened. She also put out clean towels.

Often she listened to music and let her mind go blessedly blank while she performed these daily tasks. This afternoon, she found herself thinking about Kyle's five classifications of men. Her father and former fiancé fell into the first category. By Kyle's exposition this type was the worst, but that came as no surprise to Summer.

Since coming to Orchard Hill, she'd met a few men she considered users, several losers, a smattering of smart alecks and even a dumbbell or two. Kyle was right. The wise guys were the most entertaining. Madeline's three older brothers, Marsh, Reed and Noah Sullivan, belonged in that category, and so did Madeline's fiancé, Riley.

When Summer finished freshening the guest rooms on the first two floors, she carried her basket of cleaning supplies and another armload of fresh towels up the staircase leading to the attic apartment. She knocked to be sure Kyle wasn't inside. As she'd suspected, the apartment was empty.

Unlike the other rooms where the sheets and blankets hung on the floor, Kyle had thrown his spread loosely over the pillows. She opened the windows, freshened the bathroom and hung clean towels. Returning to the main part of the room, she rinsed out the coffee pot, pushed in a chair, then went to the bed to finish the job Kyle had started. As she fished an open novel from under one of the pillows, a sheet of paper fluttered out, landing face-up on the bed.

She picked it up automatically and couldn't help noticing her name scribbled at the top. Beneath it he'd compiled a list.

1. Baltimore
2. Merlot
3. Mackinaw Island

4. Ancient Mythology
5. Six years
6. The Orchard Inn, free-and-clear
7. Refined and educated
8. Evasive—hiding something

Suspicion reared, and the pit of her stomach pitched. Her average guests didn't make a list of perceptions and things she'd told them. In fact, this discovery was a first.

Her hand shook at the implications, the words on the paper blurring before her eyes. Making a list of things she'd told him didn't make him a thief, but Kyle Merrick was an investigative reporter. That wasn't the same as a private investigator, but it didn't mean she should trust him, either, chocolates and flowers notwithstanding.

She slid the paper into the book where she'd found it and placed the book on the nightstand as she normally would, as if she'd discovered nothing out of the ordinary. She smoothed wrinkles from the sheet, tucked in the blanket and made up the bed with her signature hospital corners. All the while, the word *ordinary* resonated inside her, for what she wanted, *all* she wanted, was an ordinary life.

From the door, her gaze strayed to the top edge of the paper peeking from the book on the nightstand. She didn't know what Kyle was up to, but finding that list was a reminder to her to remain cognizant of everything she stood to lose.

At a few minutes before five o'clock, Summer showed Betty Ryan from Knight's Bakery and Confectionary

Shoppe to the back door. Behind her, four neatly labeled miniature wedding cakes were lined up on the inn's kitchen table beside a large bouquet of bright yellow daffodils.

Several of her guests had already headed home for the weekend. In the ensuing lull, Summer called Madeline. "The cakes are here, right on schedule," she said while getting plates from the cupboard.

"I don't like asking this of you," Madeline said.

"You know I don't mind," Summer murmured. "In fact, I'm happy to do it."

"I know you say you don't mind, but I'm lying here doing nothing and you're—" Madeline burst into tears.

"And I'm about to eat cake. Madeline, what is it? What did Talya say at your appointment today? Better yet, you can tell me when I get there. I'm on my way."

"No! It was a good appointment. I don't need you to come over. I just sent Riley out. I love all of you so much, but all this hovering is making me crazy. Riley and I just had our first fight over it."

Summer paused, her hand suspended over the drawer where she kept the cake knife. While Madeline gave Summer an update on her condition and progress, Summer put forks and napkins on the table next to the dessert plates. Madeline had received good news from her nurse practitioner/midwife this afternoon. Talya confirmed that Madeline's beta levels were still elevated, a wonderful indication that she was still pregnant.

"Yesterday there was minimal spotting," Madeline said over the phone. "Today there's been none. Talya said that as long as this continues, today is my last day of prescribed bed rest. As of midnight tonight I'm relieving you of fill-in bride duties. Poor Riley doesn't know what to do with me, crying one minute, pointing my finger toward the door the next. What if he doesn't come back?"

Madeline sniffled again, and Summer's heart swelled. "Are you kidding me? He's a smart guy. He'll be back, probably sooner than you think. In fact, he's probably pacing outside in the driveway right now. You're marrying the man, Madeline. It's called for better and for worse."

"I'm afraid Riley's getting the worse first."

"Riley is getting the best, and he knows it," Summer declared.

"I hope you're right," Madeline said, sounding more like herself. "Just this morning we were talking about names…."

Laughing at Madeline's anecdotes, Summer looked around the room. Everything was ready in the kitchen. She was prepared in other ways, too. Madeline had said that as of midnight tonight, Summer would no longer be a fill-in bride. She wasn't going to wait until midnight to demonstrate a new-and-improved, friendly-but-businesslike manner with Kyle. No more shared middle-of-the-night crème brulee, no more laughing over morning coffee, no more heartrending emotion over something as sweet and simple as a bouquet of daffodils.

Her guard had slipped but she'd resurrected it. She felt a twinge of disappointment over that, for Kyle was a hot-blooded man, and he'd brought out her passionate side, too. But it was something she—

"Summer are you there?" Madeline asked.

"Hmm," Summer said.

"Summer?"

"Hmm?"

"You seem distracted."

Kyle had just entered the room. He stood in the doorway, feet apart, one hand on his hip. She could see him taking everything in, the cakes, the flowers, her.

"I'm still here, Madeline," Summer said quietly.

"Good. Kyle left a little while ago and should be arriving at the inn any minute."

"Here he is now," Summer said.

He'd showered and changed into brown chinos and a white, knit shirt. He was cleaned up, buttoned-up, tucked in. He'd even shaved. Without the whisker stubble, the lines of his jaw and chin were more pronounced, the skin above his white collar tan.

He smiled at her and let his gaze trail over her once from head to toe. The pit of her stomach did a dainty little pirouette, and she faced the fact that the return to decorum was liable to be a steep, slippery slope.

"Ready?" he asked.

She nodded.

Ten minutes later, all four cakes had been cut and Summer and Kyle had tasted each one. Twice.

"Okay," she said, doing everything in her power to ignore the expression of rapture on his lean face as he took a third bite of the first sample. "Madeline wants a simple wedding. Among other things, that means only one cake. We need to eliminate three. First, let's narrow it down. I think the one with the coconut can go."

"You're kidding." He reached around her and scooped up another forkful of that one. When his elbow accidentally brushed her breast, her heart jolted.

She drew away as if unaffected, but her body betrayed her. Rather than glance at him to see if he noticed, she said, "Coconut is one of those foods people either love or hate, which is why it's a logical choice to eliminate first."

"If you say so." He pushed the white cake sprinkled with coconut to the center of the table away from the other three. Scooping up a forkful of a light-as-a-feather white cake on the plate closest to him, he said, "I like this one."

"It's too sweet," she insisted.

"Who are you?"

Her gaze swung to him. And time suspended.

Did he know that Summer was only a nickname? Is that what he meant?

"You can't be the same woman who stood in this very kitchen eating crème brulee at three o'clock this morning."

He hadn't meant *who was she* literally.

She'd jumped to conclusions. He was joking. What a relief.

"You're sure this one's too sweet?" he said. He took another bite and held a forkful out for her to try again.

She sampled it off the end of his fork, contemplated, and nodded again.

With an exaggerated sigh, he pushed the middle cake out of the lineup. "Now we need to concentrate."

She couldn't help smiling because he made eating cake very serious work. They both tried the wedge with strawberry cream filling again, and then the chocolate-vanilla marble with the fudge filling again. And again.

"This," he said, "could take all night."

Laughing, she noticed a dab of frosting on his lower lip. Her thumb, of its own volition and without so much as a thought to decorum, glided across his mouth to wipe it away.

He caught her wrist in his hand and took the tip of her thumb into his mouth. Her heart hammered, but Summer held perfectly still. Playfulness became something else, something weightier, something living, breathing and instinctive. Her breath caught and her eyes closed, as traitorous as the rest of her.

The next thing she knew, she was in Kyle's arms. And his mouth was on hers. And everything merged, every thought converged, every heartbeat stammered, and the entire length of her body was melded to the entire length of his.

Kyle heard Summer's breath whoosh out of her, he felt her hands glide up around his neck, and he tasted the frosting they'd both sampled. None of it was enough.

He kissed her. At least that was how it began, with a kiss that exploded into something uncontrollable and invincible. It was possessive and hungry, a mating of heat and heart, discovery and instinct. Need filled him, too intense to question, and so tumultuous it became a tumbling free fall without a parachute, an adrenaline rush with only one end in sight.

He backed her to the nearest wall, his mouth open against hers, his hands all over her back. And still it wasn't enough. He molded her to him, her body soft where his wasn't, yielding and pliant where his was seeking and insistent.

Her mouth opened, and his tongue found hers. She moaned deep in her throat, the sound setting off an answering pounding in his ears, like the echoing beat of pagan drums. Slightly making room between them, he took her breast in his hand. It was full and soft and puckered and fit his hand so perfectly it was his turn to moan.

Two doors led off the back of the kitchen. He was fairly certain the first opened into a storage room. That meant the second must lead to her private quarters. He wanted to swing her into his arms and carry her there, for he needed a bed to pleasure her the way he wanted to pleasure her. And he needed it now.

He let his lips trail down her neck and loved that she tipped her head back, giving him better access. Her hands got caught in the fabric of his shirt, her touch insistent, at once strong and gentle as only a woman could be. He wanted to feel those hands on his bare skin. He wanted a lot more than that, and he would start by getting her out of her clothes.

"Summer. Are you home? Summer? Where are you?"

Kyle heard a voice in the distance. "Yoo-hoo. Summer. Jake's here." It came from far away, outside this haze of passion.

He felt the change in Summer before the words registered in his brain. She stiffened, then went perfectly still.

"I know she's here somewhere." Whoever was talking was getting closer. "I'll just be a moment. Make yourself comfortable."

Summer drew her neck away from Kyle's lips and awkwardly pressed her hand to his chest where his heart was beating hard. Through the roaring din inside her skull, she recognized Abby's voice.

She slipped out from between Kyle and the wall. She didn't have time to straighten her clothes or run a hand through her hair. She barely had time to take a shallow breath before Abby swished through the swinging kitchen door.

She stopped in her tracks the moment she saw Summer and Kyle. "Oh." Her blue eyes were round with surprise as she said, "There you are."

The feeling was returning to Summer's limbs, but the roaring in her ears hadn't lessened. "What is it, Abby?"

Upon meeting Abby Fitzpatrick for the first time, and seeing her wispy light blond hair and petite build, her bow lips and ready smile, people often assumed she was flighty. First impressions weren't always accurate, for she had an IQ that put most people to shame. It didn't require great brilliance to recognize the reason for Summer's disheveled appearance and glazed eyes, however, or the reason Kyle kept his back to the door.

"I'm sorry to interrupt," Abby said apologetically. "But Jake's here."

Summer's hands went to either side of her face. Jake. Of course. That was what she'd forgotten.

To Summer, Kyle said, "Who the hell is Jake?"

It was Abby who answered. "He's Summer's date." Her voice rose on the last word, turning the statement into a question.

Summer and Jake Nichols had been in the middle of dinner two nights ago when he'd had to make an emergency house call to help a mother goat deliver twins. He'd promised to make it up to Summer. Tonight. Summer wasn't sure what Abby was doing here, but it probably had to do with helping them choose the wedding cake.

"Shall I tell him something came—er, that you stepped out?"

"Yes," Kyle said.

"No," Summer said at the same time. She pulled a face at her friend and took a deep breath. Walking to the counter on rubbery legs, she said, "I won't lie. Tell him— What should we tell him? Tell him I'm running a little late. Can you keep him entertained for a few minutes?"

"Are you sure?" Abby asked.

The friends shared a look.

Trying on a shaky smile, Summer said, "I'm sure, Abby. Just give me a few minutes, okay?"

Abby spun on her heel and swished out the way she'd entered.

"What are you doing, Summer?" Kyle asked.

She went to the hook beside the refrigerator and opened her purse. After fishing out a brush and small mirror, she fixed her hair and applied lipstick and blush. Steadier now, she finally looked at Kyle again.

He'd turned around and now faced her. His shirt was untucked—she'd untucked it. His collar was askew, again her doing. His green eyes were stormy and narrowed, but there was little she could do about that.

She ran a hand down her dress, adjusted the waist and straightened the neckline. Taking a deep breath, she said, "I'm going to dinner."

"The hell you are."

The edge in Kyle's voice held Summer momentarily still. He walked toward her like a stealth bomber, determination and displeasure in every step. He didn't stop until he was close enough for her to see that he meant business.

"I have to go, Kyle."

"You don't have to do anything you don't want to do."

She could tell he was trying to hold on to his temper—trying but not entirely succeeding. He was a force to be reckoned with, and she understood why he was upset. She was wildly attracted to him. There was no sense trying to deny it. Her heart rate still hadn't settled back into its normal rhythm, her breathing was shallow and her legs were shaky. He'd touched her body and she'd felt his need. If Abby hadn't interrupted, they would probably be in her bedroom right now. But Abby had interrupted, and Summer did have to go tonight.

"Jake knows I'm here. I'm not going to stand him up."

He took her hand, then promptly released it. "So what we started he'll—"

Summer's chin came up a notch. A few responses came to mind, none of them nice. In the end, she met his gaze and quietly said, "Nobody else could finish what you started."

She glanced at the table beside him, and, after another calming breath, she said, "I'll ask Abby to tell Madeline we're recommending the chocolate-vanilla swirl."

Leaving the cake to dry out, and Kyle to cool off, she lifted her chin and went to greet her date.

Every bar Kyle had ever set foot in had basic similarities and a peculiarity or two that made each one unique in its own right. The three he visited in Orchard Hill were no exception. He'd knocked back a shot with his beer in the first, played a few games of pool in the second, and ordered a bar burger to go with a cold draft in the third. It wasn't the way he wanted to spend his Friday night, not by a long shot.

He'd gone up to his room after Summer left for her *date*. He had three voice mails from Grant Oberlin, each one more heated than the last, a text message from Riley, two missed calls from his mother and nothing from the source he needed to talk to. He'd tried to read, but Summer's touches in the room were everywhere, and he'd wound up pacing.

Summer insisted she wouldn't lie. That was a good

trait. But he was still mad. The answer was simple. He didn't like the thought of Summer having dinner with Jake whoever-the-hell-he-was. He liked what that dinner might lead to even less, because no matter what she insinuated she wouldn't do with anyone else, Jake whoever-the-hell-he-was was a man. Summer was a beautiful, vibrant woman, and this guy would have to be a fool not to try. Kyle had no claim on her. He had no right to feel like putting his fist in the middle of some stranger's face, either, but that didn't mean he hadn't cracked his knuckles in anticipation.

He'd dropped in on Riley and Madeline. Even in Kyle's foul mood, he could see that he'd interrupted them in the middle of making up. After that he'd driven around Orchard Hill, getting a feel for the lay of the land. There were several more bars on the strip across the river near the college. Those catered to students, and the last thing Kyle wanted to deal with tonight was a college girl.

A barroom brawl would have been a good diversion. The second bar he'd visited was a seedy dive where fights broke out with little provocation, but Kyle hadn't stayed. Sometime before he'd turned thirty, he'd learned that the pain of a split lip, a black eye and a broken hand lasted longer than the satisfaction of feeling invincible that preceded it. Though he might make an exception if he encountered Jake Whoever-the-hell-he-was.

Giving up his bar stool to some poor sap in a worse mood than Kyle, he dropped a twenty-dollar bill on the counter and left Bower's Bar and Grill. It was only nine-thirty. It was going to be a long night.

Since he'd parked his Jeep in a lot behind the second bar he'd visited, he started in that direction, in no particular hurry to get there. Most of the businesses on Division Street were closed, the storefronts emitting the blue haze of security system lighting. One window glowed bright yellow, and when Kyle went to investigate, he found himself peering into an antiquated newspaper office.

Walter Ferris was leaning on one elbow at a counter that divided the front door from the rest of the office space. Glancing up from whatever he was studying, he spotted Kyle and motioned him inside.

With nothing but time to kill, Kyle sauntered in and was given a tour of *The Orchard Hill News.* With steel desks and black telephones and an old printing press that had been retired and all but enshrined, Walter told him, when he took over the business after his father retired, it looked like something out of an old Clark Gable movie.

"You didn't tell me you were a news man," Kyle said after Walter had bent his ear for a good hour telling him about the good old days when newspapers reported real news.

Gesturing to the high ceilings and brick walls lining the interior of the building, Walter said, "She's my second-best girl. You walkin' or driving?"

"Walking, for now."

The old leather desk chair creaked as Walter lowered his tall frame into it. Motioning for Kyle to have a seat in a chair across from him, he opened a low drawer and brought out two stout glasses and a brown bottle with a crown on the label.

"Do you always work on Friday nights?" Kyle asked.

In answer, Walter opened the bottle and poured. "What I do doesn't feel like work. Used to annoy the bejesus out of Harriet." He stared into his whiskey. After swirling the amber liquid a few times, he said, "Never hurt a woman you love. Believe me, son, it isn't worth it. It'll change her forever. And that's a hard thing to live with, harder than living with the original sin."

Kyle swirled his drink, too. "You seem like a man who knows what he's talking about. How long have you and Harriet been divorced?"

"Thirty-two years." Walter picked up his glass and downed the whiskey in one gulp. Wiping his mouth on the back of his hand, he said, "I was old enough to know better, but, hell, a man isn't thinking with his brain at a time like that. Harriet and I were having problems, and my secretary was willing. Classic, isn't it?"

Kyle emptied his glass, too. "Harriet found out?"

"She knew from the start. Maybe if I'd been a little discreet she would have gone on pretending."

When Walter grew pensive and lost in his reveries, Kyle leaned across the desk, snagged the bottle and poured them both another round. "She caught you with the secretary?"

Walter brought his glass a few inches from his mouth. "In the act. In our marriage bed." He looked at the whiskey then set the drink down as if he'd lost the taste for it. "Are you surprised?"

Kyle sipped his whiskey, letting it burn his lips and tongue and throat on the way down before replying. "I have two younger half brothers and two stepmothers. After the third wife, my father stopped marrying his mistresses. Nothing surprises me."

"Where is he now, your father?"

"Sleeping peacefully beneath a maple tree in a cemetery in St. Claire. At least I hope he's at peace. The man never did like sleeping alone." Kyle capped the bottle.

"Do you hate him?" Walter asked.

"He told me I could be anything I wanted to be, and he believed it. Every summer he took all three of us boys someplace we would never forget. Sometimes it was in the middle of the wild somewhere, other times in the middle of a city. I guess you could say he had a fatal flaw, but I loved him. Luckily I didn't have to be married to him."

"And his ex-wives? Did they hate him?"

"There were a lot of catfights when I was a kid. Now that he's gone, they've formed a united front. It's Riley and Braden and me against The Sources."

Walter laughed, then his gaze followed the course Kyle's had taken.

Summer was strolling by. Kyle stared at her as if he had a radar lock on her.

She was walking next to but not touching a guy with a tattoo of an American Flag on his bicep and a Detroit ball cap on his head. She didn't look in the window, and Kyle wondered if she'd had a good time. God, he hoped not. The streetlight picked up at least five shades of brown in her hair and bleached her dress to a hue barely darker than her skin.

"It isn't much fun to watch a woman you want out with another man," Walter said.

Kyle's head turned with the speed of light. He hadn't even realized he'd made a fist of his right hand.

"Is that why Harriet flirts the way she does? Is she getting even?" he asked.

Walter put the bottle away and shut the desk drawer with a loud clank. "Harriet was a flirt before I married her and she'll likely be one until she takes her last breath. Don't get me wrong. She might dye her hair red now, but she had a redhead's fire from the get-go. She threw me out of the house the day she walked in on me. That little bitty gal dragged our mattress to the backyard and set it afire in the middle of a raging snowstorm. She filed for divorce a week later. I was belligerent back then. I showed her. I married somebody else. It was the second biggest mistake I've ever made."

"How did you two get from that burning bed to this arrangement?" Kyle asked, curious. "Any fool can see you're deeply committed to each other."

Walter's expression changed. His eyes softened, his mouth relaxed and his fingers eased on the grip he had on the arms of his chair. "She's some woman, isn't she? She forgave me."

"But I thought—"

"You thought what? That we keep separate houses? We do. I hurt her, son, the worst way a man can hurt a woman. Some women stick it out, but it changes them, and that's reality. Harriet and I made a new reality, one we can both live with. If you want Summer, find a way to make it a reality."

Kyle stood up too fast and felt a whoosh in his head.

With a chuckle, Walter said, "Come on. I'll give you a ride to the inn."

Over the legal limit, Kyle let the old newspaperman drive. From the passenger window, he watched the inn come into view. It was a handsome stone building in a historic district where the lawns were large and the houses had once been owned by the crème de la crème of Orchard Hill society. Tall and sturdy, it had a roof that looked like a top hat from here.

He wondered if Summer was back yet. He hoped she hadn't brought the vet home with her.

As Kyle opened the aging Cadillac's big door, Walter said, "Remember, son. Never hurt a woman you love."

He stood on the walkway in front of the inn until Walter had backed out of the driveway. Kyle had one foot on the first step of the front portico when it occurred to him.

Who said anything about love?

Once again the Orchard Inn beckoned Summer home.

She waited to go in until after Jake's taillights had disappeared on the other side of the bridge across the river. Above the soft silver glow of the lights on the antique posts lining her driveway, the stars were faint pinholes in the midnight blue sky. With most of her guests gone for the weekend, the windows on the second and third floor of the inn were pitch black. Only the lamp in the bay window could be seen from here.

She punched in the code on the electronic keypad, and went in through the front door. There was a knot between her shoulder blades and the start of a tension headache in her temples.

There were no medical emergencies tonight, no mares in trouble, no dogs or cats hit by cars, no iguanas falling down stairs, no parakeets suffering from apparent amnesia, or hamsters hyperventilating. As she'd listened to his marvelous stories about all those incidents—her mind wandered. Jake had known before dinner was over that she wouldn't be seeing him again. He was good about it, although not terribly happy. It would have been so much safer to care about Jake. Instead, she couldn't stop thinking about Kyle.

Abby had called Summer around eight to tell her she agreed with their choice of wedding cakes and had turned on all the usual night-lights before she'd gone home. Only one guest remained this weekend, and Abby said there had been no sign of him.

Stifling a yawn, Summer listened at the stairs. All was quiet in the old inn. Kyle's Jeep wasn't parked in the lot. Obviously he was still out. If he returned he would have to use his electronic key. Installing those locks was the first change she'd made upon purchasing the inn. It had been worth the expense for the peace of mind it gave her.

With the lamp in the window guiding her, she slowly made her way toward the back of the inn and the little apartment she kept there. The lack of sleep two nights in a row had caught up with her, and she yawned again.

Her heels clicked over the hardwood floors in the dining room. As she swung the kitchen door open, she found the room dark. She flipped the switch. And nothing. The room remained pitch black. The light must have burned out. She was forever changing lightbulbs in this old place.

She easily followed the countertop to the sink. Her fingertips were on another switch when a voice sounded behind her.

"Are you going to see him again?"

She jumped straight up as the light came on.

Heart in her throat, she spun around. Kyle sat at the kitchen table, his feet propped on a chair, eyes squinting against the sudden bright light.

Removing her hand from her throat, she said, "You nearly scared the life out of me, Kyle Merrick."

"Sorry."

He didn't look sorry. He looked lethal, like a man begging for trouble.

"So are you?" he asked. "Going to see the vet again, I mean."

Lowering his feet to the floor, he stood.

It wasn't fear that made her heart speed up. It was the expression in Kyle's green eyes, the slow, deliberate step he took toward her, and the way he reached his hand to her shoulder and gently drew her closer.

She could have stopped him at any point. He gave her time to turn away, to hold up a hand, to tell him no and mean it, but she made no sound, no movement. Her gaze remained fixed on his, her heart beating a staccato rhythm in her chest. The vein at the base of her neck fluttered up before settling down to a steady thrum.

Before either of them moved again, she knew. He was going to kiss her.

And this time, there would be no interruptions.

Chapter Seven

The light over the sink cast Summer's shadow across Kyle's chest and left shoulder. The small wedding cakes were no longer sitting on the table, and the dishes they'd used to sample them had been stacked beneath the cabinet where they belonged. Summer noticed those things the way she noticed everything, but her attention was focused on Kyle.

His face was lean and chiseled, his cheekbones hollowed slightly, his mouth open just enough to reveal the even edges of his front teeth. Beneath his gaze her fatigue and the knot between her shoulder blades was dissolving into thin air.

Awareness, brought to life out of shadows and moonlight as if just for the two of them, thrummed all around them. She'd thought the path to decorum might be a slippery slope. There was no slope; there was only this deep blue sea of possibility.

She went up on tiptoe, and sound became a strum of heartbeats, his touch stirring her longing, his arms around her a haven. His lips found hers, and suddenly they were in the center of a whirlwind, grounded in a kiss while the rest of the world spun all around them.

She had no idea where he'd been tonight, but he tasted like whiskey and burned like moonshine. There was no question in her mind about whether she was making a mistake. Some things transcended logic. She'd known, not intellectually, but instinctively, this moment was coming since the night she'd met him. She just hadn't known she'd known.

She'd become a new woman in so many ways six-and-a-half years ago. In the process, she'd begun a new life, and painstakingly learned how to be an innkeeper. At first she'd had to do a lot of pretending. She pretended nothing in Kyle's arms tonight. This was human nature in its purest form, and what she felt, felt right.

His hands went to either side of her face, levering her there as his mouth covered hers again and again. His kiss was hard and a little reckless, seeking and insistent. It filled her with so much longing she lost all sensation of time and place and reality. When his hand went to her breast, she gasped once then promptly forgot to breathe. It didn't matter. All that mattered was that he didn't stop. All that mattered was that she didn't either, that she returned his touch, pleasure for pleasure.

"Help me out here," he whispered hoarsely.

"With what?" she asked, her head tipped back, her

eyes closed, engrossed in the feel of his lips working their way down her neck.

"Where's the zipper?"

Her laugh sounded provocative and breathless. "Allow me," she whispered.

But first, she took his hand and drew him with her toward her room. Once they were both inside, he kicked the door shut, and she turned the lock.

Kyle had a hazy impression of a small suite of rooms with sloped ceilings and dark wood floors. She must have turned on the metal lamp on a table next to the bed across the room before she left. Beneath it was a black-and-white picture of three women, arm-in-arm. He was more interested in the picture Summer made, her mouth wet from his kiss, her lips full and lush, her color heightened by desire.

She was a woman, with a woman's wiles and a seductress's smile. She demonstrated both as she lowered the sneaky zipper down the *side* of her dress.

He whisked the lightweight fabric over her head, unbuttoned his shirt and peeled that off, too. He kicked off his shoes, but she was a step ahead of him. She was already barefoot, her body now covered only by the semi-transparent fabric of her bra and panties.

She held his gaze as she reached behind her and unfastened the back closure of her bra. As the garment fell away, his gaze raked down her body. Her legs were long, her panties scant. Her naval was a dip he would get to later. The delicate lower ridges of her ribs were slightly visible through her skin. Her breasts were round and creamy white and perfect.

He started there. He pressed his lips to the plump upper swells as he took them into his hands. They spilled over his palms, her nipples puckering instantly.

Her arms came around his neck, her body arching so perfectly into his. He kissed her mouth, again and again, pressing her backwards, one step and then another.

She didn't simply fall onto the bed when the backs of her knees touched the mattress. Oh no, not Summer. She turned around, threw the spread back and climbed on. The sight of her momentarily bent over in those scanty panties sent his heart rate to stroke level. His chinos landed on the floor before he'd drawn another breath.

Naked, he stretched out beside her and glided his hand along the entire length of her, his lips heating a path from her mouth to her breast and back again. Her moan of pleasure was the only music in the room, the wind against the window their only witness.

Her eyes were half-closed, as if she were learning him by heart through touch. He loved her hands on him, loved touching her in return, loved exploring and discovering what she liked, what drove her crazy and what drove her wild. Pliant and eager, she drove him wild in return.

He finally whisked her panties off. Both fully naked, they rolled across the bed, tangling the sheets and tearing out the covers as they went. He'd intended to take his time, but the blood pounding in his ears grew too insistent to be ignored, and he knew there was only so much he could do to slow this down.

She made a sound in the back of her throat. It was part demand, part plea, a request for a favor he couldn't help granting. Luckily she had the presence of mind to open a drawer in the beside table and remove a box of protection. Kyle took over from there.

Summer had been told she was beautiful in the past. Kyle said nothing with words, and yet, beneath his gaze, she felt revered. She heard foil tear, a wrapper being discarded. Then he was with her again, and it was as if the bed rose up to meet her back, and he was easing on top of her, one knee straddling her legs, his chest pressed tight to hers, his mouth on her lips.

She lost track of time then, of who moaned and who sighed. Nature had taken over, and instinct arose. He moved faster and faster, until she cried out lustily. He shuddered, and she whimpered again. It was a beautiful, noisy, raw act of possession, and it took both their breaths away.

Gradually her thoughts cleared, and her breathing ceased to be ragged. When her eyes finally fluttered open, she found that Kyle was on his side next to her, his gaze on her face. He really had the most amazing green eyes. He had a nice nose, too, for a man, and a mouth that could inspire poetry. She would have liked to continue, but she was having trouble keeping her eyes open.

She felt the mattress shift beside her, felt the sheet being drawn to her shoulders. Two nights with too little sleep had caught up with her at last.

"You never answered my question," he said after he stretched up on one elbow and reached for the chain on the lamp.

"What question?" she asked.

"Are you going to see the vet again?"

Her answer seemed to come from a great distance. "Not unless I get a dog."

Kyle chuckled in the dark. By the time he laid his head back down on the pillow, Summer was fast asleep.

He rolled over, listening to the wind and the river and the soft sound of Summer's breathing. She wasn't clingy or needy or demanding. She didn't ask to be held, and she didn't want to talk. Just the opposite, in fact. She lay on the other side of the bed, her head on her pillow, her bare thigh the same temperature as his.

With a sigh of contentment, he did something he hadn't done in more than a year. He closed his eyes and *drifted* slowly to sleep, too, a smile on his face.

Once, a few years ago, Summer had caught a miserable strain of flu that had confined her to bed for two days. It wasn't the flu that kept her here this morning. This was a fever of another sort.

She and Kyle had awakened the first time as the sun was coming up. They'd made love, slept more, and made love again. Now rays of late morning sunlight were slanting through the slats in the blinds on her windows.

Although she hadn't been completely celibate these past six years, she'd never invited a man to spend the night. She liked sleeping alone. So why did the soft rumble of Kyle's steady breathing as he slept next to her make her feel so full?

He may have been the only guest staying in the inn this weekend, but she still had eight rooms to clean, eight beds to change, and that was just the beginning. There were breakfast menus to plan for the upcoming week, and she had accounting to work on and reservations to verify and emails to answer. She needed to get up and begin her tasks, or she would never be ready when the other guests returned tomorrow evening.

Careful not to jostle him, she held in her sigh of contentment and eased to the edge of the mattress. The sheet fell away from her as her toes touched the floor.

Before she got any further, a strong arm encircled her waist. "Where do you think you're going?"

She let out a little yelp as Kyle drew her with him to the center of the bed where he fit her back to his front.

"I have an inn to run," she said, but her argument was losing steam to what he was doing to her.

He nuzzled the back of her neck with his lips, the stubble of a day-old beard making an already-sensitive area tingle. She couldn't believe he was aroused again, for they'd already made love several times.

When he'd run out of protection, she'd fumbled through a drawer until she found an unopened box. For some reason, he seemed pleased when she had to blow the dust off the top. Of course, everything she did seemed to please him.

"Chelsea, Abby and I are meeting with Madeline and the caterer this afternoon," she said. It might have made a stronger impact if her head hadn't lolled back when his hand covered her breast.

"What time?" he asked, nipping her shoulder with

his teeth while his hand continued to work magic where he touched her.

"Two o'clock."

"That's four hours from now." The deep rasp of his voice held a note of humor as he said, "We'll be cutting it close."

With a speed and agility that surprised them both, she turned onto her right side so she was facing him. Going up on one elbow, she tilted her head and arched her eyebrows. "You sound very sure of yourself."

He began to show her just how sure he was. It was a long time before either of them said another word.

This was one of those rare weekends when Summer didn't have to be careful not to use all the inn's hot water. And yet she didn't linger in the shower.

She had no reason to hurry. She had the entire place to herself, no one to answer to, two days to prepare for the coming week.

Why did she feel compelled to rush?

Kyle and Riley were meeting with Riley's tailor, and then the two of them were taking Riley's dog, Gulliver, for a run. Summer was officially off fill-in bride duty. Kyle was officially finished filling in for the groom, not that there had been a lot for Kyle to do. It was wonderful to know that Madeline was back on her feet and happy and ready to manage her remaining wedding plans. Riley Merrick had a strong woman on his hands, and, while Summer had a sneaking suspicion that it wasn't always going to make his life easy, it was exactly the kind of life he wanted.

As she dried her hair, smoothed on lotion and applied a single coat of mascara and lip gloss, a similar question played through her mind. What did she want?

She'd invited Kyle to her bed. It had seemed so natural while she'd been in his arms. Today reality was setting in.

She'd only been twenty-three when she'd arrived in Orchard Hill, and although people here saw her as worldly, she'd never been one to settle for casual sex. Though there had been nothing casual about making love with Kyle. Wild, yes, consuming and uncontrollable, definitely, but not casual.

Summer was accustomed to steering her life; she'd had no one to rely on for so long. This sensual experience was uncharted territory for her.

She doubted that was true for Kyle.

The realization gave her pause, and, in some bizarre way, it calmed her anxiety. Kyle was one of those men who exuded sex appeal. He traveled the world, and probably had exotic women slipping their room keys into his pocket on a regular basis. Surely he knew his way in and out of encounters of all kinds. Since she was out of date regarding the protocol for this kind of thing, she decided to take her cue from him.

If all they'd had was one night, so be it.

In fact, that would be best. He was a reporter who traveled the world, and she was an innkeeper who had no intention of leaving Orchard Hill. She knew better than to romanticize this. She'd stopped believing in fairy-tale endings a long time ago.

As she left the bathroom, she automatically catalogued

her surroundings. The shoes she'd been wearing last night were still where she'd toed out of them. The bed was rumpled, the sheet pulled out, one pillow on the floor.

Her gaze went to the framed photograph on the dresser. She saw that it was turned slightly, as if it had been picked up and put back down. Kyle must have looked at it.

Summer went to her dresser. Lifting the frame closer, she stared into the faces of her beloved mother and sister. She recalled her surprise upon discovering the list in Kyle's room. If he was looking for something about her past, he wouldn't find it here, for her mom and sister had died before Summer moved to Orchard Hill. Looking at their images brought a smile and left an ache. Both girls resembled their kind-natured and trusting mother, but Claire, the oldest, had been most like her. The photo had been snapped just before their mom's diagnosis. She was gone three months later. A year later Claire died, too.

Summer was glad her sister hadn't known that their father considered them pawns to be used in his business deals. At least she hoped Claire hadn't known before she'd died so suddenly of a brain aneurysm a year after their mom died from cancer. That day in a two-hundred-year-old cathedral in front of God and some of the most influential and wealthy people on the east coast, Summer had shown her father just how like him she could be. He wouldn't underestimate her again.

The media had turned her runaway bride act into a circus sideshow. It was only after she'd started over in

Orchard Hill that she'd been able to mourn her mom and sister and the life they'd shared.

Feeling melancholy, she set the photo back on the dresser and wandered from her room. She started a load of laundry then decided to work on upcoming reservations. She hadn't gotten far when her gaze homed in on a small piece of yellow paper lying on the registration desk.

How about dinner tonight?
Just so there's no confusion, now I'm officially interested.

A warm glow went through her, and a smile played across her mouth. Despite the warning bells clanging in her head, she couldn't tamp down her exhilaration. With a shake of her head and quiet chuckle, she thought, *now* he was officially interested?

If the residents of Orchard Hill wanted fine dining, they drove across the river to Dusty's English Cellar, by far the nicest restaurant in town. If it was gossip, good food, laughter and lunch they were looking for, The Hill was the perfect choice.

Summer had been meeting her three closest friends for lunch at The Hill every Saturday for six years. The décor was Americana Diner, the tables were square, the service was good, and, as usual, the place was packed.

Madeline looked radiant. Everyone who stopped by the table she was sharing with Summer, Chelsea and

Abby said so. Orchard Hill's darling beamed at each and every well-wisher.

After the last one shuffled away, Madeline whispered, "Do you think people know?"

Chelsea shook her head. Abby shrugged.

And Summer said, "I think they'll be counting backwards when the baby's born, but even then they won't know for sure. Do you care?"

Madeline beamed again. "I have morning sickness every day until eleven and the rest of the time I can't get enough to eat. I'm spilling out of my bra. Seriously, I don't even recognize my own body. I cry when it's inappropriate and I can't remember my own phone number. And yet just this morning I pinched myself because I didn't dream I could ever be this happy. I'd like to broadcast it to the world. Now, who wants dessert?"

The other three couldn't believe their ears.

"Dessert," Abby quipped. She looked good in red, her short, wispy blond hair in adorable disarray. "Are you the same person who, not twenty-five minutes ago, polished off the beef Wellington, the stroganoff *and* the stuffed chicken breast at the caterer's? Does anybody else remember hearing her say she couldn't eat another bite?"

Madeline giggled. Summer did, too. She'd been laughing a lot today. She couldn't believe the other three hadn't mentioned that. Chelsea, however, was having trouble forcing even a semblance of a smile. The reason was sitting across the room wearing a torn black T-shirt and faded jeans. Summer wondered what Sam Ralston was doing back in Orchard Hill.

Chelsea adjusted her necklace and smoothed her wrinkle-free collar, her equivalent of fidgeting. Pasting on a happy face, she signaled to the waitress to bring them all a slice of pie.

"So, Summer," Madeline said, resting her elbows on the table directly opposite Summer. "What did you and Riley talk about?"

Madeline either had cameras hidden all over town, or she really did have a sixth sense about matters of the heart. How else could she have known that her fiancé had taken Summer aside two hours ago and spoken of his concern for Madeline?

Looking into Madeline's blue eyes, Summer said, "I told him the truth. I said you're resilient and stubborn, caring and hormonal. I advised him to keep his appointment with his tailor. After all, he needs to look good for his wedding, too. I told him to enjoy a few hours away and not to worry because I've got you. Chelsea, Abby and I all do."

Emotion brimmed in Madeline's eyes all over again. Before the tears spilled over, the waitress arrived with dessert. Summer moved slightly to make room. The action must have bared the side of her neck formerly covered by her hair, because Chelsea placed a gentle fingertip over the abrasion there and quietly said, "Your date with Jake must have gone well."

Four slices of pie were forgotten as three sets of eyes narrowed speculatively.

"Dinner with Jake was okay." Summer looked at Abby, for she knew whom Summer had been kissing first.

It was Madeline who said, "Okay didn't leave whisker burn on your neck."

"That happened later, after Jake dropped me back at the inn and left."

Since they all knew there was only one guest spending the weekend at the inn, it didn't take any of them long to react. Abby covered her mouth with one hand. Chelsea's eyes widened, and Madeline put down her fork.

"Do you mean you and Kyle?" she asked.

Summer lifted one shoulder and nodded at the same time.

"Riley's *brother,* Kyle?" Madeline persisted.

"I didn't plan it, but, yes, that Kyle. Do you mind?"

The imp in Madeline had come out of hiding since she'd returned to Orchard Hill after her quest to find Riley Merrick. Summer had been surprised when her angelic friend had cut her long blond hair a few weeks ago. Yes, she was eating for two, but inside she was still the same caring girl who'd taken one look into Summer's eyes six years ago. She'd often told Summer that she'd found the sister she'd never had that day.

"Mind? I've been trying to match you up with my brothers for years. I'd love you to be my sister-in-law."

Summer held up one hand. "Nobody said anything about marriage. But you should know this is your fault."

"My fault?" Madeline quipped.

Abby and Chelsea were all ears, too.

"Remember Tuesday night when you told all of us

to close our eyes and envision the man of our dreams?" Summer asked.

"You pictured Kyle?" Abby said.

"I dreamed of a man who was shirtless and sexy, water glistening on his chest. Kyle arrived at the inn that same night soaking wet."

Pushing her dessert plate back, Abby said, "I drew a blank."

Summer noticed Chelsea looking into the distance. Sam Ralston was staring back at her, his jaw set, his shoulders back, arms folded across his chest as if begging for trouble.

The waitress returned to top off their coffees. "There's a man in town asking about you, Summer," Rosy Sirrine said.

Looking up at the iconic waitress, Summer said, "Does he have dark hair and green eyes?"

Rosy fanned herself. "Oooeee. That's him. When I refilled his coffee cup and gave him extra cream he called me Aphrodite, the goddess of love. When I told him charm doesn't work on me, he muttered something about furies."

Summer smiled to herself, because in Greek Mythology The Furies were avenging female spirits mere mortals feared. Rosy was tall and had broad hips and steady hands. Nobody could remember a time when she hadn't been the head waitress here, and yet there was no gray in her black braid, no lines in her face. She finished pouring the coffee and turned to leave as quietly as she'd arrived.

"Wait," Summer called to her back. "What did Adonis ask?"

Rosy glanced at Summer over her shoulder, and for a moment her eyes looked as old as time itself. Summer knew something about nearly everybody she'd met in Orchard Hill. She knew that most men were intimidated by Abby's IQ, and she knew why Chelsea refused to give Sam Ralston the satisfaction of looking directly at him, and she knew that the couple that owned The Hill were thinking about retiring. But she knew almost nothing about Rosy Sirrine.

The older woman finally spoke. "When a body's looking for the truth, it's best to go directly to the source."

Summer got lost in her reveries as she pondered that. Kyle Merrick was an investigative reporter, and yet he'd asked her very few personal questions. She'd seen that list in his room, so she knew he was gathering information about her. The details of her past weren't buried very deep. With his investigative skills, he could have easily discovered her secrets. Why hadn't he said something or done something?

Did she have this all wrong? Was he the one hiding something? What was *his* secret?

By the time Summer turned her attention back to her friends, Abby and Chelsea had dropped their napkins on the table next to their uneaten dessert. Summer did the same.

Looking at each of her friends, Madeline said, "Aren't any of you going to eat your pie?"

At the same time, Summer, Abby and Chelsea pushed

their plates toward Madeline. Not even Chelsea could help laughing when Madeline dug in.

Summer was on the second floor of the inn when she caught her first whiff of something wonderful wafting on the air. By the time she finished her work in Room Seven, she'd identified the tangy aroma of Chinese take-out.

She went to the window. Sure enough Kyle's shiny silver Jeep was parked down below. She stood listening for footsteps overhead. Hearing nothing, she was about to walk away from the window when she noticed a movement near the river.

The lone figure of a man paced back and forth on the bank. Dark pants, dark shirt, dark hair. Even from this distance she knew it was Kyle.

Fairly gliding down the stairs, she put away her dust cloth and window cleaner and hurried past the registration desk where half a dozen small, white cartons sat waiting. She had no clear plan in mind as she pulled on a light, heathery sweater and was on the winding path leading down to the river when he stopped pacing. The leaves on the birch trees lining the banks were just beginning to uncurl from their buds, the river itself an orange and yellow reflection of the setting sun.

There was tenseness in Kyle's shoulders, a coiled restraint in the muscles down his back and legs. She wondered if whomever he was talking to on the phone was aware of how close Kyle's coiled control was to springing.

He said something. Listened. Repeated it, louder

the second time. Although she couldn't hear the words themselves, his tone was angry.

He muttered something crass and final, told whoever was on the other end what he could do with his opinion, and hurled the phone into the river with so much force it skipped three times before sinking out of sight.

The river babbled, the wind crooned and, from twenty feet behind him, Summer said, "That's one way to deal with poor reception."

Kyle turned slowly, first his head and then the rest of him.

As he stood looking at her in the gathering twilight, she witnessed a gradual change in him, as if something was dissipating like vapor into thin air.

Beneath his watchful gaze, she held perfectly still. She didn't know whom he'd talked to or why they'd argued, but she knew something momentous had just occurred.

The sun was below his shoulders now, his shadow stretching all the way to the tips of her shoes. They called her the keeper of secrets. She hadn't set out to uncover people's most intimate riddles. She'd simply listened.

That was the secret ingredient, quietude. More often than not, if she said nothing, people said something.

As she waited, she couldn't help noticing Kyle's rangy physique covered by his black pants and shirt. His eyes delved hers, and whatever she'd been thinking about seemed to have dissolved into thin air, too.

She wasn't the only one saying nothing. And it occurred to her that there was more than one option. He could tell her what had just transpired over the phone. Or he could take her inside and take her to bed.

Talk about a win-win proposition.

Chapter Eight

Kyle wondered how long it was going to take to come to terms with the fact that the black mark behind his name was permanent. He'd known this day was coming. Secretly, he'd been in denial, but the frustration and inevitability had been keeping him up nights for months. He hated having his hands tied. And he hated—

He turned his back on the river, on the setting sun and on the futility of his thoughts. And there was Summer.

The lighted kitchen window glowed a soft yellow in the distance behind her. A pontoon loaded down with a boisterous group of adults enjoying the spring evening and whatever was in their heavy-duty cooler chugged past, the rumble of the oversized outboard motor at odds with the heavy bass blasting from their radio.

When the boat was slightly downriver, he said, "I promised you dinner. I left it in the inn."

"I noticed." She shivered in her lightweight sweater.

"I hope you like Chinese," he said.

"I do."

He didn't know why he was talking about food. Probably because it was easier than talking about what had just transpired. He'd made an irrevocable decision. It had been coming for almost a year, the end of his career. He'd been fighting it, searching for a resolution or a solution. But there wasn't one, at least not one he could live with. He and his lawyer had participated in a long-distance conference with three men from the paper's legal department and Kyle's immediate boss. His former immediate boss.

He still had to call Grant Oberlin. He didn't know what he was going to say to the man. He didn't know what had possessed him to pitch his phone into the river, either, for he wasn't often given to fits of rage. If Summer had witnessed it, she didn't appear affected by it. Not questioning or judging, a quiet presence in a complicated world, she looked back at him.

She wore jeans and a sweater today. And flat shoes. And a gray shirt that was feminine but not frilly. Like her. A silver charm hung from a delicate chain around her neck; a pearl drop earring gleamed on each ear. He wondered if he dared ask her to come closer, for he wanted to cover her mouth with his, to wrap his arms around her and to lay her down right here. He wanted to bury his face in her neck and make love to her until the stars came out and the fire of his damnation was forgotten, doused as surely as his phone.

Looking at Summer, he realized that making love to her that way wasn't out of the realm of possibility. Looking at Summer, he was struck by the realization that anything was possible.

"Kyle?"

He started.

"Did you hear me?"

He hadn't, and he didn't apologize for it. He was too busy processing everything he was feeling. The bolt of sexual attraction was the easiest to identify, although that wasn't what had rendered him speechless.

He didn't question the discovery. He was in love with the woman staring back at him in waiting silence. He, Kyle Merrick, was in love. With Summer Matthews. A woman who apparently hadn't existed until six-and-a-half years ago.

"We don't have to do any of the things I mentioned," she said. "Even though it's getting cold out, and it'll be dark soon." She gave him a small smile that went straight to his heart. "We don't have to go inside. We don't have to eat or talk, and you don't have to come back to my room with me. We can stand out here all night if you want to."

In a hundred years Kyle hadn't expected to smile. It was hard to believe he'd zoned out enough to miss the fourth option.

"I'd like to," he said.

He had to give her credit for patience.

He'd never been so completely overwhelmed by circumstances out of his control *and* so certain he knew exactly what he was doing. He started toward her. "I'd like to eat, talk and take you to bed. Why don't you choose the order?"

Smiling that sexy-as-hell all-knowing woman's smile of hers, she let him take her hand. Together, they went inside. And although she didn't tell him where she planned to start, he was pretty sure she'd made up her mind.

"Oh, Kyle. Yes, yes and yes." Summer's eyes slipped closed, and she let her head loll back in ecstasy.

Eat. Talk. And then make love.

Hadn't that been her plan?

Luckily there were no other guests in the inn tonight; therefore nobody had heard all the noise she and Kyle were making. They hadn't quite gotten to her bedroom yet. When they'd first come in from the river, she thought she would light the closed sign in the window and gather up all the cartons of food and take them to the kitchen.

Eat. Talk. Then make love.

The closed sign was on, but the boxes of takeout were still sitting on the registration counter. All were opened, and several of them were half gone. What was there about this man that made her so ravenous? She'd always had a high metabolism, but this voracious appetite was for more than food.

Eat, talk and make love.

She hadn't really thought it was possible to do all three simultaneously. They talked a little while Kyle opened the cartons. They ate a little between kisses.

There had been a lot of kissing.

"Try this," she said, squeezing a bite-sized morsel of Guai Hua Shrimp with scallops between the ends of her chopsticks.

He smiled when her first attempt didn't make it to his mouth. It landed next to the registration book with a quiet plop. She thought his smile looked tired.

"I guess I should let Riley and Madeline know I'll be attending the wedding after all," he said.

Between bites of fried rice and egg rolls, he'd calmly told her that there was no longer a story waiting for him in L.A. He was officially no longer gainfully employed.

"I don't imagine being able to attend the wedding is much consolation," she said, spearing a piece of Chengdu Chicken with the tip of her chopstick.

"There's consolation, and then there's consolation," he said, unbuttoning her top button.

She put down her chopstick and held his hand in place. The kissing was good, and so was the takeout, but there was something lurking behind his eyes and beyond his touch. He had something on his mind, something he needed to say but hadn't yet managed to broach. So she waited. She wouldn't push him. She never pushed.

As she held his hand to her breastbone, she was glad he'd thought to plug his iPod into her computer. Although not so sure this was the time or place for

The Barber of Seville, at least the comic opera's lively overture covered the silence as Kyle decided where to begin.

She could tell by the way he withdrew his hand from hers that he was almost ready.

In a deep, slightly removed tone of voice, he finally said, "A year ago I received a tip that had to do with the trafficking and extortion of illegal immigrants. The source checked out. I saw the photographs of young kids and women, shoddily dressed and filthy, fear in their eyes as they were herded into a warehouse on the Lower East Side of Manhattan. The EIEO was behind me one hundred percent, and everybody knows how much power they wield in human rights' cases. The piece I wrote made the front page of *The Herald.*" He paused for emphasis. "Three hours *before* the authorities busted into an *empty* warehouse on the lower east side."

"There were no illegal immigrants being held against their will in living quarters unfit for rats?" she asked quietly.

He shook his head, and, although he leaned his hip against the desk, too, she knew he was far from relaxed.

"Someone leaked your story early?" she asked.

He nodded. "The EIEO wasn't pleased. When money I couldn't explain showed up in my bank account, things got even more interesting."

Summer moved the carton of fried rice out the way. Resting her elbow where the food had been, she faced Kyle.

When he was ready, he continued. "The paper

printed a retraction and launched the required investigation. They didn't prove anything. I couldn't prove anything, either, such as where that money came from or how that story could have been submitted without my knowledge. It came from my computer, contained my access code and my protected password. I couldn't be reached to verify. The paper had no reason to doubt me and every reason to trust me, so they ran it. It's like I told every lawyer I've talked to, I don't know who hacked in to my computer, and I don't stinking need money."

From the registration desk, the opera music swelled and Figaro boasted how clever he was. Kyle didn't say any more. He didn't have to. Summer believed there was a great deal he wasn't telling her, but the condensed version was that somebody had successfully and methodically ruined his career. Kyle couldn't prove his innocence, and the paper didn't need to prove his guilt. Democracy had been founded on the ideal that a person was innocent until proven guilty. Too often it was the other way around.

Summer looked into Kyle's eyes, and her heart turned over. He'd grown quiet again. Whoever had said it was the quiet ones you had to watch was wrong. The quiet ones were often the good ones. Kyle was one of the good ones, perhaps one of the few good men left in this complicated world.

She took a deep breath of air scented with meandering river and springtime. He breathed deeply, too, and looked at her in waiting silence. Everything inside her strained toward him.

She wanted to kiss him. She was going to kiss him, but first she pressed herself closer, her hands on his upper arms. Turning her face into his shoulder, she pressed her lips to his neck. The shuddering breath he took was more erotic than a moan.

She looked up at him, then lifted her hands to either side of his face. Raking her fingers through his coffee-colored hair, she went up on tiptoe and, pressing her mouth to his, let him know he didn't have to prove anything to her.

Her senses whirred and blood rushed through her veins. Kyle's kiss was familiar, yet it contained a new urgency, one she understood, for she felt it, too—this need to feel, to live and breathe and touch and be touched. Pagan perhaps, lusty definitely, but it was human and it was beautiful.

Their passion went from zero to sixty in an instant. Summer tugged his shirt from the waistband of his pants, giving her hands access to the bare skin of his back. She kneaded the taut muscles between his shoulders, slowly working her way lower. As the tips of her fingers delved the edge of his waistband, she felt his hands come around her back.

The next thing she knew she was bodily lifted to right where he wanted her. She wrapped her arms around his neck and hooked her ankles around his waist. Already the world was spinning.

Kyle needed more—more of Summer's sighs, her throaty moans, more of her hands on him, more of her skin uncovered.

He couldn't keep his mouth off hers, couldn't keep from seeking closer contact with every inch of her body pressed so close to his. But it wasn't close enough. It would never be enough through their clothes.

He set her on the registration counter and swept the cartons out of his way. And all the while he kissed her, their mouths open, tongues meeting, groans blending with the undulating final strains of the age-old opera.

"Now I know why I prefer dresses," he said, hindered by the barrier of her jeans.

How she managed to laugh when he was kissing her, he didn't know. But laughter trilled out of her, spilling over into the jagged hollows inside him.

"Kyle," she whispered, her mouth close to his ear.

He stopped fumbling with her jeans long enough to listen.

"I think I'll self-combust if you don't take me to bed."

She slid down his body. And darted for her room.

Kyle caught up with her just before she got there. He swung her into his arms, and they fell together onto the bed. He didn't think about what he was doing. There would be time for thinking later. Right now he had passion to burn off and the woman he loved to please.

Unlike last night, Summer didn't fall asleep immediately after she and Kyle made love. Once again they'd been wild, their movements so heated and frenzied her mind felt a little singed, even now.

She wasn't complaining. Kyle was an amazing lover.

The lamp was on, but he wasn't asleep, either. He lay on his back, she on her side, her head resting lightly on his chest, listening to the even rhythm of his heartbeat and the uneven sound of his breathing.

He was quiet, probably lost in thought.

They hadn't gotten around to finishing dinner. She would take care of the cartons on the registration desk later when she double-checked that the doors were locked.

She recalled the fit of frustration she'd witnessed by the river and everything that had come after. She understood his anger and the futility he was surely feeling. She'd once experienced very similar emotions.

She didn't believe he was guilty of indiscretions as the people in his profession claimed he was. Although he'd undoubtedly left a great deal unsaid, she distinctly recalled that he'd mentioned seeing photographs of the people being used as slave labor and worse. If there had been photographs, there must have been victims.

"Are you awake, Summer?"

She hummed an answer.

"Do you have a mentor?" he asked.

"I've never put it in exactly that context," she said, slipping her hand between his chest and her cheek where his chest hair was tickling her nose. "But I suppose I'd have to say my mentor is Rosy Sirrine."

The sound he made had a lot in common with a growl. She didn't think he'd asked because he wanted her to justify her choice, although she easily could have. The head waitress at the restaurant Summer frequented was at once ageless and as old as time. Rosy had worked and lived in Orchard Hill for years, and yet Summer had never heard anybody mention a single untoward detail of her life. She was wise and serene and seemed happy with her solitary life. She rarely offered advice, but when she did, people listened. Summer listened.

"What about you?" Summer asked. "Do you have a mentor?"

"There's a man who took me under his wing when I first started in the news business. He rode me harder and expected more from me than anybody I'd ever known. He survived a childhood on the streets of Boston and has a mouth on him that makes seasoned sailors blush. He taught me about life and sour mash whisky and women. And somehow, in the process, he taught me about integrity."

Summer tipped her head back in order to see Kyle's face. "Was he the one who showed you those photographs?"

The deep breath he took moved the entire bed. "His son did."

Her hair swished across his chest as she went up on one elbow, and emotion brimmed in her eyes and chest. "Are you and the son close?"

"I considered him my best friend."

"Did he have access to your computer and password?"

"I can't prove it." His gaze was on hers as she drew closer. She saw so much raw emotion in his green eyes. She wondered if he had any idea what an incredible man he was.

"You aren't going to tell this man, your mentor, about his son are you?"

He shook his head. "It would kill him."

She wanted to wrap her arms around him, to offer him comfort or solace, a haven in the storm. But he was reaching for her again, and, although the raw emotion hadn't waned, it shared the space with another kind of need.

Placing her hands on the sides of his face, Summer covered his mouth with hers. She made love to him, and it was more gentle than anything they'd shared before, slower and less frenzied, but no less fulfilling.

She was pretty sure he fell asleep later. They both did. When she awoke in the morning, the other side of the bed was empty.

Summer was stepping out of the shower when she heard the inn's back door open and close early Sunday morning. Kyle was back at the inn, at least. She wasn't sure he was coming back to bed.

She had slipped her arms into the sleeves of a long robe and was combing out her wet hair when he shouldered through her door. Wearing the same dark clothes he'd been wearing last night, he was windblown, his hair a mess, his face unshaven. He looked disreputable and not quite tame. There were shadows beneath his eyes, as if he hadn't slept well.

Although he didn't smile when he saw her, there was a subtle easing in the tension in his shoulders. She was glad about that.

Waving a white paper sack in his right hand and

lifting a cardboard drink tote in the other, he said, "I hope you like donuts."

"Have I struck you as a fussy eater?" She led the way through a low archway that separated her bedroom from a tiny kitchenette and living room she rarely used.

They settled into chairs around a small table. After divvying up the orange juice and coffees, he handed her the bag of donuts. Although the fact that they both chose an apple fritter wasn't lost on either of them, neither of them mentioned that they'd just discovered something else they had in common.

Seeing him looking at the small apartment where she'd lived these past six years, she said, "A man named Ebenezer Stone had the house built nearly one hundred and forty years ago. He died before it was finished and left the project and property to his half brother Josiah. Josiah knew that location was everything, and after the house was finished, he turned it into an inn on the newly established stage line between Lansing and Grand Rapids. Many inns fell into disrepair after the railroads were built. Josiah's grandson Mead Johnson had the business sense to sell a parcel of the property he'd inherited to the railroad for the sole purpose of building a train depot. The last of Ebenezer's ancestors was a man named Jacob. He and his wife, Marguerite—"

She stopped talking when she realized that Kyle had finished eating and was looking at her, an indecipherable expression on his face.

"I'm boring you to death," she said. "I'm afraid I get carried away when I talk about this place."

His eyes probed hers. "I like it when you get carried

away." He stood, but instead of reaching for her, he reached for his coffee and took a final sip. "I have to go," he said. "I need to grab a shower upstairs."

She studied his eyes but couldn't determine the reason for the change that had come over him. She stood, too, and cinched the sash of her yellow robe tighter.

"I ran into Walter Ferris at the donut shop," he said on his way through her bedroom. "He invited me to ride along while he delivers papers to businesses in nearby towns. Never promise a man anything when he offers to let you cut in front of him in the donut line."

She followed the course of his gaze around her room. The bed was unmade, their pillows rumpled, her pearl earring lying precariously close to the edge of the dresser. He glanced at the lamp that was no longer on and stood looking at the black-and-white photo underneath it.

Not one to press, she let him look. In his own good time, he turned his attention back to her and said, "Maybe later you can finish telling me about Jacob and his wife, Marguerite."

She smiled. The kiss he gave her then was a culmination of all their previous kisses. Although she felt reluctance in the big hands cupping her shoulders, he still released her.

Church bells were ringing in the distance when he went upstairs while she finished dressing. The pipes rattled slightly, an indication that somebody was indeed taking a shower someplace else in the inn.

Although she didn't hear his footsteps, when she looked a little while later, his Jeep was gone. For the rest of the day, she couldn't shake the feeling that something beautiful was coming to an end. And she couldn't quite put her finger on the reason.

Chapter Nine

At midnight on Sunday, Summer crossed her ankles and adjusted her pillows behind her shoulders. Noticing her foot jiggling again, she brought both knees up beneath the covers and opened her book to the page she'd just read.

Now. Where was she?

Painstakingly, she started over at the top.

The blinds were closed, the inn was quiet, and the coming week promised to be a busy one. Madeline and Riley were getting married in five days. Tomorrow was Madeline's gown-fitting and, on Wednesday, a bridal shower at Abby's. The wedding rehearsal was scheduled for Thursday and, on Friday, Riley and Madeline would become husband and wife. Madeline had become nearly ethereal, gliding through the remaining preparations with a serene smile and sense of calm and purpose that was a joy to witness.

Comparatively, Summer was a bundle of nerves.

She tried to refocus on the book in her hands. It had been written by her favorite author, was on all the best-seller lists and was currently being made into a movie for the big screen. The fact that she was having trouble remembering the premise wasn't the author's fault.

All but two of the inn's guests had returned hours before she'd checked all the exterior doors and retired for the night. The two remaining carpenters, who were not yet settled comfortably into their rooms upstairs, had called to tell her they would be arriving first thing in the morning.

She didn't know where Kyle was. She didn't even know if his Jeep was parked out in the lot with the other guests' vehicles, and she refused to allow herself to check.

He'd been in and out of the inn all day. Although she'd caught him looking at her a few times, he hadn't made any attempt to seek her out. She knew better than to be upset, and she wouldn't allow herself to be disappointed. Two days ago, she'd decided she would take her cue from him regarding the protocol for an affair. It was good advice, although admittedly easier said than done.

She'd made a valiant effort, though. All day long she'd been reminding herself that, for all intents and purposes, Kyle Merrick was a passing fancy. She wasn't sorry she'd met him, and she wasn't sorry she'd discovered the passion he'd brought to life for these few short days. And nights. She was glad she'd been there when he'd been coming to grips with the irrevocable circumstances that had brought about the end of his career.

Surely he had loose ends to tie up. She wasn't one of them.

What they'd had was a week of sex. Okay, it hadn't lasted an entire week, and it had been more than sex. For her, at least. They'd shared laughter and food, sunsets and moonlight, but she'd known from the start that whatever was between them had a beginning, a middle and an end.

The end was near.

With a sigh, she punched the pillow at her back and closed the novel she'd started an hour ago. There was no sense marking her page, for she couldn't remember a word she'd read.

She was reaching for the switch on the lamp when a soft knock sounded on her door. "Yes?" she said quietly.

"It's me, Summer," Kyle said.

She felt a lurch of excitement as she swung her feet to the floor. Every word of caution and every ounce of self-restraint she'd applied to this situation flew away as she turned the lock and opened the door.

Kyle stood on the other side, his shirt unbuttoned, the top closure on his chinos undone, as if he'd left his room in a hurry. He still hadn't shaved, and although he wasn't dripping wet, he looked very much as he had in her dream.

"I didn't think you were coming," she said.

Kyle didn't know how to respond to that so he said

nothing. The truth was, he hadn't intended to leave his room after he'd climbed the stairs two hours ago. He sure hadn't intended to knock on Summer's door.

It was Sunday night. She had an inn to run and secrets to keep. It thoroughly ticked him off that one of them was his.

Oh, he wasn't worried she would tell anybody. He didn't care who knew. What made him so damned angry was how little she shared with him in return. What made him even angrier was that he was mad about that.

What was wrong with him? This was the perfect arrangement. She was beautiful and smart, and warm and willing.

He wasn't accustomed to being the one wanting more.

It was bound to have happened sooner or later, but hey, the sex had been great. All day he'd been putting that in the past tense, as if it was over, done, long gone. All day he'd told himself it was time to move on. He should have barricaded the damn door.

"I'm glad you did," she said. "Come downstairs, that is."

Just like that, nothing else mattered. She was glad he was here, and Kyle faced the fact that, even if he'd barricaded the door, he would have found a way to Summer's room, into her arms, into her bed.

He stepped over the threshold and his mouth came down hard on hers, harder than he'd intended. He'd kissed her often these past several days, and every time was an indulgence. This was different. From the onset it was a rocket launch at three G's.

She was wearing some sort of pajamas, slightly bedraggled, and not intentionally sexy. Her nipples showed through the thin fabric of the top. The bottoms were a mere technicality.

He kicked the door shut and back-walked her to the bed. Their bodies melded, thighs, bellies, chests and mouths. She shuddered in his arms, warm and responsive and giving.

See? He didn't have a problem. What he had was a passion to burn off and a need to satisfy. It was the same for her. They were on even ground.

He stopped kissing her long enough to peel off her top. While she shimmied out of the bottoms, he shed the rest of his own clothes.

They fell to her bed together, her legs already going around him. She wanted him. And he wanted her. Even-steven. They didn't speak of the future. She'd always made sure of that, hadn't she?

What they did had nothing to do with the future, anyway. It had everything to do with this moment. So what he did was his damnedest to tangle the sheets and burn off this passion that somehow refused to be appeased for long.

Eventually, Kyle and Summer both stilled. She lay underneath him, catching her breath. Recovering enough to put two thoughts together took a little longer. She'd never known passion could be like this, could make her feel like this.

He eased to his side.

And she took a deeper breath.

The first word out of his mouth was "Damn."

She'd wondered when he would realize they'd forgotten about protection. It had only just occurred to her, too. "If it's any consolation," she said, still slightly breathless. "I'm on the pill."

"I don't forget that," he said. "I never forget."

She gave him a reassuring smile. "You're the first man I've slept with in a long, long time, and as long as you've always made sure to…you know…we're both okay, aren't we?"

He settled on his side, and she drew the sheet up over them.

"My father is probably turning over in his grave," he said. "God knows he had no self-control when it came to women, but he never forgot protection."

She wondered about the stern line of Kyle's lips. "Do fathers and sons really talk about that?" she whispered.

Releasing a deep sigh, he said, "My dad had a lot of faults. You could say his life lessons were a little on the tawdry side, but he had a good side, too. He was the reason Braden, Riley and I are close. The three of us grew up with different mothers, in different homes and in different circles. We started life at odds. Our father couldn't abide by that, so as soon as we were all old enough, he brought us together for a month each July. Every year, he traveled from one side of the state to the other, gathering us together. At first he rented a house on Lake Michigan. When we were older, we stretched it to six weeks and ventured farther—to Spain, to Italy and, once, to Timbuktu, but only because Riley didn't believe there was such a place. Beneath those sunny skies every summer we were simply and profoundly three brothers with the same dad. I haven't thought about that in a long time."

"Which of you is more like him?" she asked.

"Like it or not, we all ended up with a piece of him. Riley has his aptitude for architecture. My father's work is truly noteworthy. To this day, his buildings and designs are cited. Braden got his need for the thrill of the chase. Dad chased women. Braden for the most part limits his chase to boats, motorcycles and race cars. I wound up with our father's appetite. The two of us could eat our weight in just about anything."

She smiled. "I noticed. What about your mother? Do you take after her, too?"

"My mom is the most stubborn, determined and organized woman on the planet. Did I mention interfering? She never remarried, never tried to make me hate my father."

"You love her," Summer said.

"Yeah."

"What about your stepmothers?"

"My father's wives got progressively younger and smarter. If you repeat that, I'll deny it."

She laughed, and everything felt the way it had yesterday and the day before, relaxed and carefree and good. "What do the women in your family do?" she asked, curious now.

"They strategize, scheme and interfere. Oh, you mean when they're not trying to *help* one of us? My mom is an interior decorator. Her clients are some of the wealthiest and most spoiled and indignant people on the planet.

They're putty in her hands. Riley's mother is a biochemical engineer. She has her own line of makeup and skin care products. Braden's mom is an orthopedic surgeon. God knew what He was doing because my youngest brother has had more broken bones than Riley and I combined. One time Regina literally had to set Braden's broken arm with two sticks and some twine string at the bottom of the Grand Canyon."

When Summer chuckled, Kyle noticed that his heart rate was almost back to normal and his irascible mood was all but forgotten. He supposed he could attribute his improved outlook to endorphins, and those were the result of great sex. It was possible that the figure-eight pattern Summer was tracing on his chest had something to do with the reason he was thinking about doing it again.

"Now your mother and stepmothers are friends," she said, after he'd told her that he, Braden and Riley referred to their three mothers as The Sources.

"I'm in bed with a beautiful woman," he said, nuzzling her neck with his lips. "A beautiful, *naked* woman. Talking about my mother feels wrong on so many levels."

She laughed, and it sounded sexy and happy. He was contemplating covering her bare breast with his hand when something drew his gaze to the bedside table. A younger, black-and-white version of Summer smiled back at him from beneath the glass in the picture frame. In the photograph she stood arm-in-arm with two women. One was obviously her sister and the other, their mother.

"What about you?" he said, leaving his hand where it was beneath the covers, in safe territory between them. "Do you take after your mother in temperament, too?"

She followed the course of his gaze to the photograph. "In looks, I do, but my sister was most like her."

"Was?" he asked.

"That picture was taken just before my mother's diagnosis. Stage four leukemia, not even a particularly rare form. She lived three months. It wasn't nearly long enough, but she was wise and beautiful, and she used the time she had left to reminisce and tell us goodbye. My sister died without warning of a brain aneurysm a year later."

When she fell silent, he said, "And your father? Where is he?"

She answered without looking at him, her gaze still on the black-and-white photo. "He's not in the picture."

By the time Summer turned around again, Kyle was getting out of bed. They didn't talk any more. Oh, they exchanged a few polite pleasantries and a quick kiss after he dressed, but the atmosphere had changed.

Alone in her room, she couldn't shake the feeling that tonight had been a prelude to goodbye.

"Do you want to talk about it, dear?"

Summer hadn't realized her disquietude was so obvious.

Stirring a cube of sugar into her cup of tea at Summer's kitchen table on Tuesday morning, Harriet Ferris said, "God knows you've listened to me *kvetch* about

Walter often enough. What good does it do anyway? He's never going to pry himself away from that newspaper long enough to accompany me on my dream vacation to Ireland. It's like I told him. Taking me out for a green beer at the Irish pub in Hubbardston on St. Patrick's Day doesn't qualify as a trip to Ireland."

Summer couldn't help smiling at the inside joke about the nearby town whose inhabitants were mostly of Irish decent. The older woman's hand quivered slightly as she poured more steaming tea into their china cups. Although Summer didn't mention it, she knew that that little quiver annoyed Harriet to no end. With her dyed hair and painted fingernails and shoes with heels she loved so much, she'd kept herself up admirably all these years. Summer could picture her kissing the Blarney Stone in Ireland one day.

"There's a smile," Harriet said, looking at Summer over the rim of her teacup. "The first I've seen on your face since I arrived. You're ruminating on something. Believe me, I recognize the signs. If I were to harbor a guess, I'd say it has to do with that green-eyed Adonis who wandered through this kitchen on his way out a few minutes ago. He couldn't keep his eyes off you."

"He couldn't?" Summer set her teacup in its saucer and covered her reddening cheeks with her hands. She hadn't blushed since she was in the eighth grade.

"Walter's eyes are getting rheumy, but I still see fine," Harriet said. "What's wrong? Why are you so quiet today? Did you and that hottie have a lover's spat? Don't worry about singeing my ears. I could use a little sex, even if it's only vicarious."

Summer couldn't keep her eyebrows from lifting slightly.

"Come on, lay it on me," Harriett prodded.

Slowly, Summer began to talk. She told her dear old friend about the first time she and Kyle had kissed in this very kitchen and about other kisses, too, and how those kisses had led to a passion that neither of them seemed to be able to curb.

"So you've seen him naked. I knew it."

Summer stopped in the middle of her confessions and simply stared at Harriet.

"I know you're too classy to divulge the really good details, but you can't blame a girl for trying. Tell me this. How was it?"

Summer crossed her hands over her heart and sighed.

"So what's the problem?" Harriet asked.

"Well." Summer ran the tip of her finger around the rim of the delicate bone china cup in front of her. Time was spinning so fast. It was Tuesday already. Yesterday she'd accompanied Madeline to her final dress fitting. Afterward, Chelsea and Madeline had come back to the inn with Summer, where the three of them had put the finishing touches on the layout and wording for the wedding programs that would be handed to each guest at the candlelight ceremony Friday night. Kyle had taken the original program to the newspaper office for final printing. Between the time he spent with Riley and helping Walter at the office, and the time Summer spent seeing to her guests and helping Madeline with wedding plans, Summer and Kyle had seen little of one another. Except at night. Which brought her back to Harriett's question. So what was the problem?

"The first night he woke me up all night long, and the second night was pretty amazing, too. But then last night and the night before…"

Harriet set her teacup down, too. "Did he peter out on ya? Is that it?"

Summer sat up and then she sat back. "No. It's not that."

"Then what is it?"

"It's just…it was…he was different."

"No offense, dear, but has it ever occurred to you that he might have been *tired?* If you know what I mean."

Summer eyed the wise old woman.

"Men have their limits," Harriet said, twisting the purple beads at her neck. "In their defense, they have to do more of the heavy lifting in the bedroom than we do."

When she winked, Summer smiled in spite of herself.

"Sure," Harriet continued after she tottered to the counter and brought back a plate of cookies. "They like to boast that all they need is sex and supper, but, in the bedroom, we're Wonder Woman, and sometimes they're Batman, and sometimes they're Robin." She bit into a cookie. "Mmm. Macadamia-nut-chocolate-chip. My favorite. Could I get the recipe?"

Evidently the advice-giving session was over.

Summer took a cookie, too, and thought about Harriet's superhero analogy. For the rest of the morning and throughout the afternoon, she spent far too much time thinking about it and even more time wondering what had happened to change the passionate cyclone between her and Kyle into a freefall without a parachute.

Was it her imagination, or was the ground getting closer all the time?

As he had the previous two nights, Kyle knocked on her door just before midnight on Tuesday. Summer hadn't been pretending to read, and he didn't pretend he hadn't known he would end up in her room.

Whatever was happening between them, she let him in. And he definitely wasn't the Boy Wonder. Kyle Merrick was all man, all the way.

They talked, about the station she was listening to on the radio and about what he'd done that day and about the final wedding preparations and how Summer was of the opinion that she, Abby and Chelsea looked liked triplets in their matching pink bridesmaids' dresses. Every now and then, their breathing hitched, for they both had something else on their mind. It was desire, and it was there in the way his eyes closed halfway when she twirled her hair just so, and it was there in her sigh when he smiled.

What followed was another record-breaking, mind-boggling, body-tingling experience, further heightened because now each knew the other's pleasure points. He touched her all over, first through her gown and then without it. She was just as bold. They wound up on the bed, her bedspread beneath her back, his body pressed on top of hers. Coherent thought was replaced with feelings and textures.

He remembered protection this time, and she remembered the pleasure, the pure rush of joy that being with him this way brought her. When their bodies became one, it was powerful. Her heart throbbed against his and his mouth covered hers again and again. Small tremors gave way to the greatest bursting of sensations. She cried out his name and closed her eyes to the pounding certainty that every time was better than the last.

While she was in Kyle's arms, Summer believed she'd been imagining that anything was wrong. Afterwards, things fell apart a little, and conversation seemed slightly stilted, and she couldn't put her finger on the reason.

They fell asleep together sometime in the wee hours Wednesday morning, his arm around her and her leg over his. Before dawn she woke up alone.

She lay in her big bed in the dark, listening to the wind and the river and the creaking of her century-old inn. Riley and Madeline's wedding was only two days away. Kyle was staying in Orchard Hill until then. And she wondered when she'd started wishing that time didn't have to run out.

Chapter Ten

Strains of Big Band Music reached Kyle's ears as he was leaving his room on Wednesday morning. With no clear destination in mind, he slid his new phone into his pocket and followed a Benny Goodman medley down two flights of stairs.

He found Summer in the kitchen with her back to him. She glanced casually at him over her shoulder before the door had stopped swishing. He didn't know how she'd known he was there, for the music blaring from the portable stereo on the counter covered any sound he might have made.

After turning down the volume, she finished rinsing a plate before turning her attention to him. She was wearing a dress again. This one was powder blue and would have looked as fitting in the Big Band Era as it did today. The woman had class; there was no doubt about that.

"I hope the music didn't wake you," she said over "Serenade In Blue."

"It didn't."

His new phone rang, startling him. His nerves were shot to hell. He took the phone out, looked at the number, then turned the stupid thing off.

"You've spoken with your mentor?" she asked.

He considered not answering. On principal alone, he would have been justified. She was good at asking questions but not answering them and sharing bits and pieces of her past. "The one and only," he said.

He supposed the fact that she knew him well enough to surmise that he'd spoken with Grant could have been construed as encouraging. Kyle was in no mood for encouragement. He walked around the table, looked out the window, and shoved his hands into his pockets.

He'd shaved.

It was Summer's first impression when Kyle had walked into the room. Drying her hands on a kitchen towel, she studied him further. He'd showered, too, but that observation came moments later, after she'd wisely chosen to keep her distance. The bottoms of his designer jeans were frayed, as if he'd had them for a long time and wore them often. His shirt was unwrinkled, the cuffs rolled up to reveal the veins in his forearms.

"Are you hungry?" she asked.

"I could eat." There was something about him this morning, something barely leashed.

She quickly gathered up a place mat and cutlery.

Using the towel in her other hand as a pot holder, she reached into the oven and brought out the plate she'd filled for him an hour ago. "Do I dare come close enough to set this in front of you?"

There was reluctance in the easing of his scowl, but at least it lessened. "I won't bite the hand that feeds me, if that's what you're worried about."

She laid the place setting, set down the plate and arranged the cutlery around it. By the time she filled a glass with orange juice and carried it to him, he'd taken his first bite of spinach-and-sausage quiche.

She poured them both a cup of coffee but took a sip of hers from her position back near the sink. After taking another bite of the quiche, he tried the baked apples. She watched his gaze stray to her mouth. From there it was a natural progression down her body.

Something in his eyes held her still. It was a raw emotion that produced an almost tangible current. Feeling emboldened by the male appreciation she saw, she decided to broach a topic she'd never considered until she'd met him.

"What would you call…this?" she said, motioning between them.

He swallowed audibly, and said, "What would you call it?"

She swallowed, too, and she wasn't even eating. "I'd call it complicated."

He cut into the baked French toast with enough force to cut through the plate.

"Kyle, what's wrong? I mean, I know this is a horrible time for you, career-wise. I in no way wish to minimize the upheaval you're experiencing and the disappointment you surely feel."

"I'm dealing with that."

"Good. Then this isn't the worst time to bring up our—" She brought her hand up to cover the little vein pulsing at the base of her throat. "Relationship?"

He put his fork down and shoved his chair back. He was on his feet, but he didn't come closer. "I'd hardly call this a relationship."

She'd angered him. She wasn't expecting that. She'd been thinking about this for hours, and while she hadn't been able to predict his reaction to her question, she'd assumed it would prompt something closer to denial or goodbye. She'd tried to prepare herself for either of those. This felt a little like driving in fog, and she had no idea what she would find around the next curve.

"What's wrong?" she repeated.

"What could possibly be wrong? We have the perfect arrangement. Great sex, and I mean great. Great food. You're a hell of a cook. Communication leaves a little to be desired, but that's a small price to pay, right?"

She looked at him looking at her. She was bewildered.

"What's the matter, Summer? Cat got your tongue? There's a surprise, isn't it?"

"What do you mean? What are you getting at?" Okay, now she was getting angry, too. "I've been thinking about this, Kyle. About…us. I know you're going through a rough time. And you probably have no idea what you'll be doing next week, let alone in the distant future, but I was wondering if you saw this, maybe, lasting a little while."

"How long is a while?"

"Honestly?" she asked. "I care about you."

Kyle turned his back on Summer, on the evidence of what her simple declaration was doing to him. He wanted her again. And it was starting to tick him off. Keeping his back to her, he said, "Honestly, Summer?"

Something in his tone must have caused her to pause. "What is that supposed to mean?"

"Have you been honest with me? Really?" he asked.

"I haven't told you anything that isn't true."

"You haven't told me much of anything, period, have you?" He spun around, and the anger seeped out of him. In its place was a renewed sense of enlightenment. He felt calm, suddenly, because he knew exactly what he needed to do.

"You've shared the most intimate secrets of your body," he said. "We've practically burned up the sheets sharing those. I know you like pasta and wine and music. I know your friends call you the keeper of secrets. Isn't that what everybody says? Who do you confide in? Not Harriet. Not Chelsea or Abby. I bet even Madeline doesn't know your biggest secret."

"My secret?" she asked, obviously uncomfortable with the direction this conversation had taken.

Glenn Miller's "Roll 'Em" whirred from the speakers across the kitchen. How fitting.

"Yes," he said, taking first one and then another step toward her. "You know, those intricate, little, inconsequential details of your life, like your mother's name and your sister's, and where you went to college and what you did before you came to Orchard Hill. Don't you find it interesting that you told me the entire history of this inn? Ebenezer Stone was the original owner, wasn't he? After him there was Josiah and Mead Johnson and Jacob and his wife, Marguerite. You've imparted their names, but you haven't told me yours."

He let that sink in.

"I've entrusted you with my secrets, Summer." He laughed, but there was no humor in it. "And I want you. You might as well know I'm in love with you. There, another secret revealed. I've been easy, but I'm not free. Come see me when you're ready to share more than that luscious body with me. Tell me a secret, Summer."

She stared back at him in utter silence. Her hazel eyes were round, her features frozen. Even that adorable, little vein in her neck was perfectly still. He wasn't surprised she didn't say anything. A sledgehammer wouldn't have stunned her any more.

He couldn't remember the last time he'd told a woman he loved her. And he'd never told one quite like this. He'd never felt like this, had never been in love like this. That was because he'd never known a woman as infuriating and intriguing as Summer, or as illusory, either.

He couldn't have known this was going to happen when he'd left his room a little while ago. Now that it had, he was relieved to have gotten it out in the open. He'd given her an ultimatum, and, by doing so, he'd effectively drawn a line in the sand. Her response remained as big an enigma as she was.

He'd thrown a lot at her. Now the proverbial ball was in her court. It was her move.

There was nothing else for him to do but wait.

He walked jauntily out of the kitchen, leaving his uneaten breakfast on the table and leaving Summer standing in the middle of the room, her mouth gaping.

Kyle moved his beer an inch to the right of the ring it left on the table at Bower's Bar and Grill. Riley sat across from him, Walter Ferris to his left. All three were pensive.

Evidently Riley's beer was just a prop, because he hadn't even taken a sip of it. Pushing his glass out of his way, the middle Merrick brother said, "Why is it that we're damned if we do and damned if we don't?"

"Because we're m-e-n," Walter said, wiping the suds from his upper lip. "And proud of it," he stated with added vehemence.

Even Riley, who drank only rarely since his heart transplant nearly two years earlier, lifted his beer to that. He and Kyle had been quietly killing time when Walter had wandered into the bar and grill on the third block of Division Street. Evidently he and Harriet had had a spat. Kyle wasn't sure why Riley was so morose. He didn't need to know. The fact that they were willing to watch water stains form on the table in a hole-in-the-wall bar in a town of mostly strangers made a strong statement by itself.

"So what are you in for?" Walter asked.

Riley looked confusedly at the older man. "In?"

"In the doghouse."

Riley practically growled, and, in that moment, he reminded Kyle of their father. "I'll have you know I don't hover!" Riley insisted.

"Good for you," Walter said.

Rather than call Riley out on the falsehood, Kyle took another drink. Hell, Riley had been hovering all week. Madeline couldn't make a move without him asking how she was feeling or, worse, if she should be lying down. In Riley's defense, he was in love with the woman. And love made men do stupid things.

Look at him, Kyle thought. He'd had it made. He'd found a woman who practically came apart in his arms every night, a woman who had good taste in music and was a magician in the kitchen. And what had he done? He'd told her he loved her in the same breath he'd issued an ultimatum.

Tell me a secret, he'd said.

In the heat of the moment he'd felt vindicated, invincible, ten feet tall. Now, ten hours later, he wondered what he'd been thinking.

What was wrong with him?

"What's wrong with women?" Walter said, his face reddening from his jowls up. "Why do they have to be so difficult?"

"How do they do it?" Kyle asked, getting into the spirit. "How do they make us so mad our blood boils and still make us want them?"

Before the other two came up with an answer, three guys who looked almost as morose as Kyle and his tablemates came in.

Riley jumped to his feet. "What are you doing here? Is Madeline alright?"

"Relax," a muscular man sporting a day-old beard and a baseball cap said.

Another man who looked a lot like the first, only younger and rougher, shouldered his way between the other two. "If we were going to tear you limb from limb, we would have done it a few weeks ago."

It looked to Kyle as if any one of them could have gone a few rounds with Riley, if they'd been so inclined. Kyle wondered who they were.

"Madeline asked us to come on down," the third man and only blond in the group said. "Demanded is more like it." This one had the same taste in clothes as Kyle. "That baby sister of ours gets more difficult every damn day."

Baby sister? *Ah,* Kyle thought. These were Madeline's older brothers, the Sullivan men.

The billiards game in the back of the room was getting loud, and the air in the room was getting dank, just like the air in a hole-in-the-wall bar should.

"Pull up a seat," Walter said, moving his chair slightly to the left. "I just proposed a toast."

The waitress brought out three more beers and Riley performed the introductions. In almost no time, Marsh, Reed and Noah Sullivan were practically family.

"To difficult women," Walter said, lifting his beer.

Each man around the table pictured someone. Walter was thinking of a spirited redhead, Riley his newly pregnant soon-to-be bride. The Sullivan brothers had somebody in mind, too. One was blond. One was a brunette.

And one was a mistake. The woman who sauntered unbidden across Kyle's mind had hazel eyes, impeccable taste and a stubborn streak a mile wide.

Lifting his beer in a salute of sorts, Kyle said, "To lines drawn in the sand. And why it's better to be a man."

Six glasses clanked. And six men drank to that.

Glasses clanked and silverware clattered as Abby and Chelsea gathered up dessert plates and silverware. Laughter trilled and the word *thank-you* was issued a dozen different ways.

Summer was oblivious.

Dazed. Fazed. And amazed.

That summed up her frame of mind.

She'd surfaced enough throughout the bridal shower to look around Abby's living room and participate enough to keep the others from calling 9-1-1. Now, lamps were on, and golden light pooled on tabletops and spilled onto the floor where ribbons and torn tissue paper lay, forgotten. Gift bags containing everything imaginable a new bride could need were waiting near the door. Chairs were still scattered throughout the room. Every one was empty except Summer's.

Madeline's bridal shower was over, but Summer had barely noticed.

Voices carried from Abby's open bedroom door. Summer sat in the adjoining room, her head in the clouds where Kyle's voice seemed to be echoing.

I'm in love with you.

Tell me a secret.

I may be easy, but I'm not free.

The breakfast dishes were still soaking in the kitchen sink in the inn. Summer's guests had returned after a long day's work. They had exchanged pleasantries, but she couldn't recall a single word they'd said. It seemed she hadn't been able to remain focused long enough to complete anything she'd started.

She'd put on ten miles in her new shoes. And that was before she'd left the inn.

I'm in love with you, Kyle had said. *I've entrusted you with my secrets. Tell me yours.*

Guys had told her they loved her before. They might have even meant it at the time or thought they did. Nobody had made the declaration the way Kyle had, and nobody had stunned her more.

"Well?"

Summer recognized Madeline's voice.

"Just a minute. Let me get the last button fastened."

That was Chelsea's.

"What do you think we should do about Summer?"

The lilting third voice belonged to Abby.

A movement in the doorway caught Summer's attention. Madeline stood on the other side, Abby on her left, Chelsea not far behind.

Summer's breath caught. As dazed as she was, she couldn't help reacting to the vision Madeline made in her wedding gown.

The dress had belonged to her mother, who had died when Madeline was a young girl. Just this afternoon, the last of the alterations had been made. This would be the last time Madeline put the gown on before she dressed for her wedding day.

As Summer found her feet, Madeline floated closer. Since Riley was staying with Madeline, Abby was storing the gown for safe keeping until Friday. It had something to do with it being bad luck if the groom saw the dress before the wedding began. Madeline didn't believe in luck. She believed in destiny, and, looking at her—her cheeks rosy, her blue eyes shining, the dress rustling as she came closer—Summer wished she believed in it, too.

The silk had aged like fine wine, mellowing from the bright white it had been on Madeline's mom's special day to the soft, shimmering ivory of today. The gown was sleeveless, the skirt loosely gathered.

"The seed pearls were a good idea, weren't they?" Madeline asked.

Just today Jolene Monroe had finished sewing the delicate row of pearls to the gown's neckline and hem. There was no other adornment, and the effect was ethereal. Or maybe that was just Madeline.

"I think I'll pull one side of my hair up and leave the rest down." Madeline demonstrated with her right hand. "What do you think?"

Tears sprang to Summer's eyes. Abby blew her nose. Even tough-as-nails-on-the-outside Chelsea sniffled softly.

"You are going to take Riley's breath away," Summer said.

It was the perfect answer. For the perfect bride-to-be. For what would undoubtedly be a perfect wedding day.

Madeline linked her arm with Summer's and gently drew her into the circle of her friends. Summer felt surrounded and as wobbly as the newborn goat whose birth she'd witnessed last week, unable to stand on both feet. Her dear, dear friends were here, holding her up.

They'd been doing it for six-and-a-half years. A lot of people believed she was strong. Sometimes Summer thought it, too. The veil was thinning before her eyes, and she was seeing her life more clearly than ever before.

What was strong and brave about pretending to be someone else?

"Help me get out of this dress." Madeline presented the three of them with her back. "Who wants ice cream?"

Ice cream, Summer thought. She was sifting through layers of self-discovery, and Madeline wanted ice cream. It was profound and fitting, and it made Summer smile.

"Tell me you don't want pickles, too," Chelsea said.

"No, just ice cream."

Chelsea and Abby unfastened the buttons down Madeline's back and gently lifted the gown off her. Unmoving, Summer stood in the midst of them.

When she was dressed again and her wedding gown was safely and meticulously hung in Abby's closet, Madeline linked her arm with Summer's. "Are you going to talk to him?"

There was no sense wondering how she could have known.

"Kyle gave me an ultimatum," Summer said.

"Who does he think he is?" Abby declared.

"What sort of ultimatum?" Chelsea asked.

Madeline said nothing. She and her soul sister shared a long, meaningful look. Chelsea and Abby fell silent, watching the hallowed exchange.

When Summer finally spoke, she began with her response to Abby's question. "I know who Kyle is. He's a man who needs to be trusted."

Her eyes strayed to Madeline's again, for Summer realized that the real question was, *Who am I?*

Wasn't that what Kyle was asking?

There was a short answer and a long answer. Summer knew where to begin.

Kyle was a man who needed to be trusted. And she was a woman who needed to trust.

It all seemed so natural suddenly. Summer ran to Madeline and hugged her. She gave Chelsea and Abby a hug, too.

Next, she spun around and let herself out of Abby's apartment. In her mind, she was already back at the inn, gently, tentatively perhaps, finally putting her other foot on the ground.

Chapter Eleven

The stars were out when Kyle finally got back to the inn, but he didn't give them more than a cursory glance. The wind sighed and two dogs howled from opposite corners of distant neighborhoods. He dismissed those, too.

It was one o'clock in the morning, and the lamp was on in the bay window, just as he'd expected. After letting himself in with his keycard, he listened for a moment. The stately old inn was perfectly quiet. With his right foot on the first step and his right hand on the newel post, he hesitated once more.

Fixing his gaze straight ahead, he climbed the stairs. Somebody was snoring in a room he passed on the second floor. All was quiet at the top of the third. By the light of the nearby wall sconce, he took his key from his pocket and opened his door.

"My name is Serena Nicole Imogene Matthews."

Kyle jolted in the dark. He banged his elbow so hard God only knew whom he woke up, yet he still felt a smile coming on. Cradling his buzzing hand, he peered in the direction of Summer's voice.

"You smell like a brewery," she said. "I hope you're not drunk. I really don't want to have to say this twice."

She talked tough, but he heard the little tremor in her voice. His eyes had adjusted enough to make out the hazy shape of her head and shoulders at the table ten feet away.

"I smell chocolate," he said. "What are you eating?"

He heard rustling, footsteps and paper crinkling. A lamp he'd never used came on, and at last his eyes met hers. She was standing now, one hand on the back of a chair.

The ends of her hair brushed the delicate edges of the neckline of a dove gray tank, and her long skirt nearly brushed her ankles. The box of chocolates he'd given her lay open in the center of the table. He didn't see any pieces missing.

He couldn't decide what to react to first. How damn good she looked in his room. How damn good she looked, period. Or how profoundly relieved he was that she'd come. "Serena Nicole Imogene Matthews is a lot of—"

One second Summer was standing ten feet away. The next she was in front of Kyle, her fingertips over his lips, afraid that if he spoke, she wouldn't be able to.

He smelled of beer and late night breezes and peppermint. There was a dark smudge on his chin—she thought it might be ink. His eyebrows were drawn together, an indication that patience came at a price. Something about that small imperfection gave her the courage to begin.

"In every life there comes one pivotal moment so monumental and profound it becomes a reference point to everything that came before and comes after. My moment occurred six years, seven months and three days ago.

"I was born into an affluent family from Philadelphia. My father's name is Winston Emerson Matthews the *Thurd*." She exaggerated the pronunciation, and added, "His ancestry can be traced to the Mayflower. I suppose that means mine can, too.

"My sister, Claire, and I had every imaginable luxury and opportunity growing up. In the deepest vagaries of our minds, we knew that not every girl shopped for school clothes in Paris and went to London to see plays and had maids at her beck and call.

"In those circles, it's still the man of the house who makes the money and the woman who runs the household. It was our mother who took us to dance recitals and music lessons, who made certain we belonged to the right clubs and learned the proper etiquette. She was wise and kind. Everyone loved her. On nights our father wasn't home, and there were a lot of those, she often spun stories about mythological places and divinities with names we'd never heard. I wish she'd written them down because her words painted pictures of chariots blazing across the sky.

"Our father touched our lives peripherally. He doled out praise sparingly and bestowed his smiles the same way. On occasion he engaged us in conversation. I was twenty-three when I realized it was a test."

"A test of what?" Kyle asked.

Summer looked at him. Instead of answering directly, she wandered to the far side of the room where the window looked out over the backyard and the river. Staring unseeingly into the dark, she said, "When Claire was twenty-four she became engaged to a man from a family nearly as wealthy as ours.

"From the beginning, there was something about Drake Proctor that bothered me, but Claire was head-over-heels in love with him, and our mother was dying. Maybe Claire needed to love someone then.

"After Mom died, Claire threw herself into planning the wedding. Two months before her wedding day, my phone rang in the middle of the night. Claire was crying and talking out of her head. She said she had migraine, and it felt like her skull would explode. I wondered where Drake was, but I told her I was coming, hung up and dialed 9-1-1."

Kyle listened from the other side of the room. Summer opened the window, and her words seemed to flow like the river, haltingly at times, stumbling over rocks, gaining momentum as if nearing a powerful waterfall. And he knew that pivotal moment she'd spoken of would soon be revealed.

"My sister died on the way to the hospital. I held her

hand until it grew cold and my father and Drake arrived. For the next several weeks I felt my father watching me. At the time I thought he was looking for hysteria. I couldn't have been more wrong.

"One afternoon I'd curled up on a cushion in the window seat in a little alcove in a room next door to my father's office. It was a seldom-used odd little nook and contained a dainty desk and heavy velvet drapes and floor-to-ceiling bookshelves. It had been my mother's favorite room and was the only place in that monstrous house that didn't feel as empty as a crypt."

Summer could almost feel herself being transported back to that nook. Once again, it was as if she could hear the voices that had carried through the wall. The first belonged to her father; the second was Drake's. She didn't recognize the third. The tone of the conversation was serious, the words too low to be heard clearly. Summer assumed they were discussing business. After all, Drake's marriage to Claire would have merged two of the largest, privately owned companies on the east coast.

She'd known that with the merger, the company would have gone public, opening to shareholders and stocks. A great deal of money would have been made by both families, who were already decadently wealthy and didn't need any more money. She'd learned there was a fine line between need and greed. Through the wall that day she could hear her father outlining the timeline his lawyers were working under, now that the merger was a moot point. Her father was as controlling as a nobleman or a king, and he wouldn't have considered the idea of merging without the marriage between the two families.

"My son would like to talk to you about that, Simon." For the first time Summer recognized Drake Proctor's father's voice.

"With all due respect, sir," Drake Junior said, "You have another daughter."

Summer hadn't heard her father laugh often. She would never forget the sound of it then.

"I do, don't I? I couldn't have said it better myself. You have my blessing. But I'm warning you, Serena isn't as malleable as her mother and sister were. She won't look the other way if she catches wind that you frequent the red-light district and worse."

Summer didn't move. She couldn't. Her stomach pitched. Her thoughts reeled. Was that where Drake had been the night Claire died? She prayed her sister hadn't known.

She understood her father better in that moment than she had in her entire life. To him, his wife and daughters were collateral to be used in business deals, more binding than cold hard cash and far easier to manipulate and placate with trips abroad and the finest luxuries money could buy. Summer wanted to wretch, but she didn't dare for fear the men in the next room would hear.

Her father had given Drake his blessing. His *blessing.*

As the fog in Summer's brain had cleared, her spiraling thoughts had formed a united front. Suddenly she'd known what she was going to do.

When Drake sought her out a week later on the

pretense of spending time with the only other person in the world who missed his beloved as much as he did—gag—she was ready, or as ready as she could be. She sniffled and nodded and reminisced. He began stopping over, and they began spending time together.

From that day forward, she cried only crocodile tears. In a matter of weeks Drake had taken their shared grief to the next level. It required super-human acting on Summer's part to pretend that the touch of his hand on hers didn't repulse her. The first time he kissed her, she almost threw up.

Sometimes she caught her father watching her. She met his gaze unflinchingly, saying nothing.

The imminent merging of two multi-billion-dollar empires was back on schedule. In the meantime, the pre-wedding parties were lavish, the guest list the Who's Who of Philadelphia society.

Telling him it wouldn't feel right, under the circumstances, until their wedding night, she wouldn't sleep with Drake. Somehow word got out. Drake took a lot of ribbing for it. Sometimes he almost seemed to respect her for it.

Claire's wedding morning dawned crystal clear. Even though the wedding had been postponed a few months, that was how Summer thought of that day—as Claire's.

Summer's vision cleared, and she found herself staring at Kyle. Had he been this close all the while she'd been talking? Close enough to touch if she needed to touch him. Close enough to feel the heat emanating from him. Close enough to look into his eyes and continue.

"Claire's wedding day dawned crystal clear. I underwent the transformation. I was made-up, manicured, spritzed, moisturized and scented like a virgin sacrifice about to be dropped into the mouth of a volcano. I stepped into Claire's gown, let my father fasten the clasp of my grandmother's pearls at my nape, sat for the photographer, and smiled for all the bridesmaids. And then it was time."

Once again Summer felt transported back to that day. It was as if she was standing on the steps of that cathedral, the polished marble cool beneath her shoes, the light shining through the magnificent stained glass windows feeling more like stage props than evidence of a divine presence.

The music started, and her father held out his arm. She didn't recognize the woman who took it. She didn't know the woman who smiled demurely as she fairly glided to the front of the cathedral, her elaborate elbow-length veil fluttering behind her. She went through every motion with grace, poise and dignity.

She placed her hand in Drake's. She answered the bishop's questions with the appropriate responses.

And then the bishop said, "Do you Serena Nicole Imogene Matthews take Drake Elliot Proctor the Second to be your lawfully wedded husband?"

Serena Nicole Imogene Matthews stood mute.

A hush fell over the guests, all five hundred of them. The bishop cleared his throat. Drake smiled encouragingly, but his Adam's apple wobbled slightly. Every one of the bridesmaids gestured in some way, as if they believed she had stage fright. Drake's groomsmen shifted uncomfortably from foot to foot. Her father's eyes narrowed.

Summer turned to the bishop and quietly said, "Would you repeat the question, please?"

He nodded as if relieved. Finding his page in his book again, he said, "Would you Serena Nicole Imogene Matthews take Drake Elliot Proctor the Second to be your lawfully wedded husband?"

Using the stage voice she'd perfected in drama class, she looked at Drake and said, "I wouldn't marry you if you were the last man on earth."

She wrenched herself away. Leaving Drake's side in a gown that felt as if it weighed a hundred pounds, she went down the steps while half the guests were gasping and the others were asking each other what was going on.

Her father had risen to his feet in his place of prominence in the front pew. She stopped before him.

"That was for Claire." She handed him her bouquet. "These are for Mom. It looks as if you should have had another daughter."

Gathering her skirt in both hands, she started down the aisle. Cameras flashed. The photo of her dashing from the church would appear on the front page of the society section in newspapers up and down the East Coast. Her father disinherited her immediately. And then Summer was really and truly alone in the world. She would take the nickname her mother had given her when she was small, and she would stumble into a new life.

But that day, she'd walked, faster and faster and faster

down the aisle, until she was running, until all she saw in the sea of faces were eyes and all she heard was the thundering of her own heartbeat.

"I didn't stop running for a long, long time."

Kyle watched as the haze slowly cleared from Summer's eyes. She was coming back from a distant place. He wanted to say something profound, but it wasn't his to say. Halfway through the telling, he'd noticed the sliver of the moon out the window behind her. It hung as if suspended from a thread over her right shoulder. He wanted to pluck it now and place the moon in her hand, wrapping his hands around it until its glow spread all the way through her.

There had been several instances throughout her story when he thought he'd identified her pivotal moment. The first came when her mother died and, then, when Claire had. Those were life-altering circumstances, but the pivotal moment had occurred later. It hadn't happened that day when she'd walked out of that church and walked away from a life of luxury.

Her pivotal moment was that instant when she'd heard her father laugh after Proctor had said, "You have more than one daughter."

Everything prior to that was Summer's before, and everything since, her after. Kyle was experiencing a similar moment now, a moment on which the axis of his existence rested.

The way she was looking at him now made him suspect that some time had passed.

"Are you ever going to say anything?" she asked.

He wanted to swing her off her feet, to wipe the pain

from her memory. He couldn't do that. Nobody could, so he did the next best thing. He wrapped his arms around her and held her, just held her. She came stiffly into his arms. Gradually, she relaxed. That was when he felt her tremble.

When the trembling stopped, he said, "That's a good secret."

She looked up at him and rolled her eyes. "You are going to be the death of me, do you know that?"

"Yeah? I guess we're even because you're the life of me."

She sniffled, and a smile spread across her lips. "Kyle, do you think you could kiss me now?"

Summer watched Kyle react to her request. He had a way of setting his jaw just so, of not quite closing his mouth, of taking a deep breath and holding it, only to release it slowly before drawing another. His dark hair was mussed, his cheeks less hollowed than they'd been a week ago. But it was his eyes, those green, green eyes that let her know what he had in mind a moment before he took a step closer.

He made a sound deep in his throat, part growl, all male. "I think I can do better than that."

He placed a hand on either side of her face. Slowly, he brought his face down, until his features blurred before her eyes and his breath mingled with her breath.

He'd kissed her often since he'd rumbled in on a thunderclap all those days ago. But he'd never kissed her quite like this.

There was a reverence in the way he held her face in his big hands. Absorbing the rhythm of his heartbeats and the heat that was uniquely him, she brought her body closer. Gliding her hands around his neck, she sighed.

Summer didn't rush.

She didn't push for more. She didn't hurry. For the first time in her life, she felt as if she had all the time in the world.

He swung her into his arms, eventually. He lay her down, and he lay down, too. They made love in his bed, under the eaves in her century-old inn, as the sliver of the crescent moon outside the window slowly floated across the sky, silently calling in another day.

Chapter Twelve

Summer double-checked the information on the confirmation form regarding a room reservation for October. Hosanna chimed from the bell tower on the Congregational Church as it did every weekday at half past eleven. The breakfast dishes were done, two days' worth, actually, and all the beds were made except one.

She was back in Innkeeper Mode.

She'd fallen asleep in Kyle's arms last night. Luckily, her internal clock had awakened her before her other guests had stirred. Although she would have loved to linger in bed long enough to kiss Kyle awake, too, she'd eased out of bed and pulled on her clothes. Leaving him snoring softly and carrying her shoes, she'd crept down the stairs.

A quick shower, a single coat of mascara and lip gloss, clean clothes, and she was back in the kitchen. She may not have beaten the sun up, but she was ready when her guests shuffled to the table for breakfast. Rugged carpenters that they were, they acted as if they'd died and gone to heaven when she set down their plates of scrambled eggs, American fries and ham. It made her rethink the asparagus quiche she'd been planning for tomorrow.

She'd spent yesterday in a fog. Finding the courage to step up to the invisible line Kyle had drawn in the sand hadn't been easy, and yet telling him her story had released something inside her, something that had been weighing her down for a very long time.

Today she was more like a glowing comet spinning through her chores. Baring one's soul was good medicine. Baring one's body was a close contender. She smiled to herself, feeling lighter, freer and truly understood. All because she'd shared her secrets with the only man she'd ever trusted.

She needed to call Madeline and ask if there was anything she could do before the wedding rehearsal, which was scheduled to begin at six. Tomorrow Riley and Madeline's wedding would go down in history in Orchard Hill. Just a week ago, she'd dreaded the thought of history being made here. Now she was looking forward to it.

The door chimes purled. She glanced up from her computer screen as a man with silver hair and cowboy boots entered, a cigarette clamped tight between his lips. Evidently remembering his manners, he wet his fingers and put the cigarette out.

"May I help you?" she asked.

"This is The Orchard Inn, isn't it?" His accent was Boston, but not quite the one the Kennedys had made famous. This man had climbed out of his humble beginnings, though, for his shirt had cost a pretty penny and his cowboy boots several more.

"This is The Orchard Inn, yes," she said.

He studied her with brown eyes that had probably seen more than anybody knew. She wasn't afraid. For one thing, she had pepper spray behind the counter, and, for another, she knew self-defense. Besides, she considered herself a good judge of character, and first impressions counted. This man had lines beside his mouth and unwavering rectitude in his eyes.

"May I help you?" she asked again.

"I'm looking for Kyle Merrick. Is he here?"

She couldn't give out personal information. This silver-haired man undoubtedly knew that because he smiled. "I already tried his phone. He's not answering."

He was resorting to charm. She liked it. It didn't work on her, but she liked it.

Kyle saved her the trouble of explaining that to him.

"You would try to charm the spots off a leopard as he was spitting you out."

Summer and the man both glanced at the stairs. His shirt tucked neatly into a pair of unwrinkled pants and his Italian shoes planted a comfortable distance apart, Kyle stood halfway to the top.

"What are you doing here, Grant?"

Summer started. Kyle's mentor Grant?

While Kyle descended the remaining stairs, she tried to recall everything he'd told her about his mentor. It seemed as though his last name began with an O. Not O'Connor or Oliver or Orson. Oberlin. Grant Oberlin, that was it.

"Grant Oberlin," Kyle said, descending the remaining stairs and coming to a stop on the other side of the registration counter. "Innkeeper, Summer Matthews."

"I was just making her acquaintance when you so rudely interrupted. Look at you. Just getting up and it's almost noon. The life of leisure will ruin you. Turn you into a sloth. I got here in the nick of time."

Summer studied the man who'd been harder on Kyle than anybody in the business, the man who'd taken him under his wing and who'd taught him about life and women and integrity. This was the father of the man who Kyle suspected had ruined his career.

"Maybe you have nothing better to do than sleep half the damn day," Oberlin said. "But I've been up since four. I'm *bleeping* starving. 'Scuse my French," he said to Summer. Back to Kyle, he said, "There must be some place in this one-horse town where we can eat. You can say no, but I'll dog your steps until you hear me out."

There was grudging affection in Grant Oberlin's tired eyes and grudging respect in Kyle's rested ones. With the sole intention of giving them privacy, Summer excused herself and went to the kitchen.

Kyle spun her around while the door was still swishing. Before she knew what was happening, he kissed her.

One long kiss, then he turned and left, his gait jauntier than when he'd descended the stairs.

They were both smiling now. And neither had spoken a word to the other.

Kyle was almost late for his brother's wedding rehearsal.

He practically jogged to the front of the small stone church on the outskirts of Orchard Hill where Riley was standing with a group of men that included Madeline's three older brothers, Riley's future brothers-in-law. Kyle didn't see Summer, but Madeline was busy with the reverend and an older man Kyle didn't recognize who'd apparently been assigned to walk her down the aisle. Kyle remembered now. That was Aaron's father. Aaron Andrews had been Madeline's childhood sweetheart. He'd died tragically, and, by some miraculous and mysterious stroke of destiny, Riley had received his heart.

"You'll never believe who just called me," Kyle said as quietly as he could to Riley's back.

Riley turned around and stepped aside, and Kyle came face-to-face with his youngest brother. "You called me from here?"

Braden Merrick gave Kyle a bear hug.

"It's good to see you," Kyle said emphatically.

"Yeah?" Braden groused. "Riley just told me I look like something the cat dragged in."

The Merrick brothers were almost identical in height. Riley had a way of standing, his hands on his hips, feet apart, shoulders back, eyes assessing. Kyle had been told *he* looked good coming and going. The baby of the family, Braden still wore his hair too long and played too hard. If he'd ever known fear, it didn't show when he was trying to win a race.

"I thought you weren't going to make it," Kyle said.

"I thought you weren't, either."

Kyle grinned. "I came to Orchard Hill to try to talk Riley out of this."

Braden made a show of looking around the bustling church. "Looks like you made quite an impact."

That attitude was the reason the older two had ganged up on him when they were kids. Riley said, "I'm glad you're both here."

What followed was one of those awkward moments between men, when a cuff in the arm felt like too little and a handshake too stuffy and a hug too girlie.

"I'm glad I didn't miss this," Braden said, shoving his hair behind his ears. "There's a lot of potential here."

Witnessing the silent exchange between his older brothers, Braden took a step back and said, "You can't flush my head down the toilet. You've tried. Now cut me some slack. I flew all night, moved heaven and earth and drove all day to be here. How about giving me a point for that? You can introduce me to that cute little blonde with the short hair and big—" he grinned "—eyes later."

The Merrick brothers laughed in unison for the first time in months. It was beginning to look as if the wedding really would go down in history.

In every corner of the small church there was activity. Nobody was listening to anybody else, and nobody seemed sure what he or she was supposed to be doing.

Chelsea Reynolds, the official wedding planner for tomorrow's big event, was running from group to group, her notes fluttering, her normally calm demeanor in a tattered shambles.

She consulted with a middle-aged woman holding a flute and had a discussion with a teenager tuning a violin. There was a florist somewhere and a reverend who appeared even more frazzled than Chelsea.

Kyle followed directions and stood where he was told to stand. The flutist started fluting. The first bridesmaid, Abby Fitzgerald, started up the aisle, only to be told to start over, slower next time. The flute music began again.

Marsh, Reed and Noah Sullivan, who'd shared a beer with Riley and Kyle last night, took seats in the front pew. Abby finished her trek up the aisle, and then it was Chelsea Reynolds's turn. Somebody must have said what Kyle had been thinking, because the curvy brunette took a deep breath and made a conscious effort to relax her shoulders.

Then came Summer. She wore another one of her pretty dresses. It consisted of two layers of silver fabric, the hem and sleeves fluttering in a breeze Kyle couldn't feel. Nobody had to tell her to relax. Nobody had to tell her to slow down. She glided up the aisle with the poise of Cinderella at her ball.

Kyle hadn't seen her since he'd kissed her before noon, hadn't spoken a word to her all day. When her gaze met his, something passed between them, and no words were necessary.

She took her place at the front of the church opposite

him. As Madeline started up the aisle, the flute music changed to the undulating strains of a single violin. Kyle heard sniffling and rustling and murmurs and sighs. Madeline was a beautiful bride.

Kyle had another bride on his mind.

He couldn't help imagining what it had been like that day when Serena Nicole Imogene Matthews had walked down the aisle of a different church, one filled with politicians and executives and brokers and playwrights and a prima donna or two. She'd been undeniably brave that day.

Summer was just as brave today. It couldn't be easy to put a smile on her face and walk up this aisle when surely memories of that other wedding march were close at hand.

The reverend ran through the vows, the blah-blah-blahs and the do-you's. And then the flutist and the violinist played together, and Riley and Madeline rehearsed their big exit.

Kyle met Summer at the center of the aisle. As she placed her hand in the crook of his arm, she said, "Did you and Grant get everything worked out?"

"Pretty much."

They followed Madeline and Riley. Behind them the violinist broke a string, and the flutist squeaked on the wrong note.

"Where is Grant now?" Summer asked.

"He went back to New York hours ago," Kyle said, secretly hoping the music sounded better tomorrow.

Someday he would tell Summer that Grant had come to see him today because he'd figured out who had leaked Kyle's story and why. He'd offered Kyle a prestigious job with the newspaper, his newspaper. And he'd told Kyle he wouldn't blame him if he exposed his son. Kyle had said no to both.

One day he would tell her how it had felt when Grant had clasped him by the shoulder and told him he was proud of him. Right now Kyle had something else on his mind.

"What have you been doing with yourself since Grant left?" Summer asked.

He thought she sounded like a wife already.

He looked down into her eyes and said, "I've been planning my strategy. Do you have a date for the wedding?"

"For Madeline and Riley's wedding?" she asked.

"Do you know of any other wedding that's slated to go down in Orchard Hill history tomorrow?"

He caught that little roll of her eyes. "I don't have a date."

"Would you be mine?" he asked.

She looked at him as if he'd lost his mind.

"We haven't been on a proper date yet," he said. "And I think every couple should go on at least one before they get married."

Kyle had never noticed that little dimple in her right cheek. He wondered what else he would uncover during the next fifty or sixty years. "I think we should go to the justice of the peace." He gestured to all the people running around like gerbils in a science experiment. "Why would anybody choose to go through all this?"

"I don't recall saying I would marry you."

He thought he saw a ghost of a smile on her pouty pink lips. "That's why," he said, as if it was obvious, "I think this date thing is a good idea."

They were at the back of church now, and everyone was talking at once. Chelsea had cornered the poor reverend, who was now frantically taking notes. The musicians were discussing changes, and the Sullivan men were silently relieved that they weren't going to have to employ the shotgun element to this wedding after all, as if they could have forced their sister to do anything she didn't want to do.

"Are you coming back to the inn tonight?" Summer asked.

A man Summer hadn't been formally introduced to jostled one shoulder in front of Kyle's. "Riley is getting married tomorrow. It's our brotherly duty to take him out for one last hoorah."

With a flick of a gaze, Summer looked the slightly younger man over. She couldn't help smiling as she held out her hand. "I'm Summer. You must be Braden."

Ignoring his brother, Kyle leaned closer, his breath tickling her ear. "Your room or mine?"

The breeze toyed with her hair, and a smile toyed with the corners of her lips. "Both," she said.

There was a dinner following this rehearsal and toasts to be made and more plans to finalize and laughter to be savored and schedules to coordinate and wedding speeches yet to be written. The mothers were arriving in the morning. There were always surprises when The Sources rode into town. Tomorrow Riley and Madeline's wedding would go down in history in Orchard Hill as the largest and most hastily planned event anyone could remember.

Kyle and Summer were going to be a part of that history-making moment. He'd been strategizing all afternoon.

He could hardly wait for tomorrow. Tonight he was looking forward to discovering what Summer had in store for him back at the inn.

Chapter Thirteen

Anybody who happened to be walking past the old stone church on Briar Street in Orchard Hill on Friday evening would have felt the underlying excitement in the air. Not that anybody was walking by. It seemed everybody was inside waiting for Madeline and Riley's wedding to begin.

Bouquets of apple blossoms adorned the altar; more delicate sprigs were tucked into bows made of airy netting on every pew. The windows were open, letting in a current of air that seemed to carry a giggle that couldn't quite be restrained. Guests were being seated. In the vestibule, ushers were preparing to light the tapers for the candlelight ceremony. The musicians were in their designated places where the choir normally sat.

In a small room down a narrow hallway that led to

the back of the church, Madeline and her bridesmaids were nearly ready.

Chelsea put away her brushes and powders and wands. "Okay, everybody, what do you think?" she said, turning Abby toward the floor-to-ceiling mirror.

Abby looked at her reflection. They all looked. And what they saw were four lovely young women, three dressed in the palest pink and one dressed in white. Abby and Chelsea stood in front, Summer and Madeline off to the side slightly behind them.

"Not bad," Abby said, smiling at the way her light, wispy hair framed her face.

"What I want to know," Chelsea said, tucking an errant strand of her own thick, auburn hair back into her loose chignon, "is why Madeline and Summer look so rested, while Abby and I needed a gallon of concealer to hide the dark circles under our eyes."

Abby's breath caught as she said, "Because they're both in love."

Madeline beamed, and for a moment, Summer thought the ruby necklace Riley had given his bride glowed a little brighter, too. Although she said nothing, Summer didn't deny Abby's observation. She didn't want to deny it. She was in love with Kyle.

Chelsea was right, too, she thought, turning this way and that in front of the mirror. She really did look rested. She never required a lot of sleep, but last night she'd gotten more than she'd expected. She'd left a note on the registration counter for Kyle, telling him where he could find her.

She'd fallen asleep waiting for him and awoke this

morning to her clock radio playing. Kyle was fast asleep beside her. There was something poignant about the knowledge that he cared enough about her well-being not to wake her. She'd done the same for him this morning.

Other than catching a glimpse of him in his dark suit and tie a half hour ago, she hadn't seen him all day. His mother and stepmothers, brother Braden and Riley's friend Kipp were in town for the wedding. Summer wasn't the only one who'd been busy. She would see him soon, and, when they had a moment alone, she would tell him what it had meant to her to share her innermost secrets with him.

A knock sounded on the door. "Yes?" Madeline said.

A stocky man who looked a little uncomfortable in his tight collar and tie poked his head inside. "They're ready for us, Madeline."

Madeline kissed the kind man's ruddy cheek. She was ready. They all were.

They formed a procession and followed Esther Reynolds's flute music through a labyrinth of hallways and lined up as they'd rehearsed. Abby opened the double doors, and the music changed to the heavenly strains of a single violin.

Abby went first, a butterfly of a woman and Madeline's first friend. Chelsea was next, so strong on the outside, so tender underneath.

It was Summer's turn. She squeezed Madeline's hand then stepped to the doorway, her right foot poised an inch off the floor.

All eyes were on her.

Her heart fluttered, but she didn't panic, for her gaze went beyond the sea of faces, all the way to the front of church where Kyle was looking back at her. His back straight, his shoulders broad beneath his suit jacket, he stood with his brothers and another groomsman. Above his white shirt, he had the classic bone structure of the fabled gods in Greek mythology, chiseled nose and cheekbones, deep-set eyes and a poet's mouth. But he was very much a human, very much a man. Her man.

As she started toward him, her right foot must have touched the floor. Her left foot, too. She couldn't be floating. It only felt that way.

Candlelight flickered from the window ledges. Above it the weak rays of the evening sun infused the air with the hazy purple, red and gold hues of the stained glass. Summer smelled apple blossoms. And she felt—

"Serena. Over here."

She jolted and looked at the man who'd called her name. Her former name.

She blinked as a camera flashed. Only a few of the guests noticed she missed a step. Their attention had turned to the back of the church where Madeline was starting up the aisle on Aaron's father's arm.

Summer took her place at the front of the church. Chelsea and Abby both crinkled their eyebrows in silent question. She looked at Kyle, who had taken a step toward her. With one stern shake of her head, she turned her attention back to the wedding taking place.

From that moment on, Kyle didn't hear a thing. Not music. Not the shuffling of feet, not a damn word the reverend said. Riley was the one who'd had a heart transplant. Before the ceremony was over, Kyle was going to need one, too, because he was pretty sure a hole had blown through his left ventricle.

He tried to see who had snapped Summer's picture, but the weasel was hiding behind a woman wearing a big hat. Or were there others? He looked out at the sea of faces, and suddenly everyone was suspect.

He heard a throat being cleared.

Everyone was looking at him.

"Kyle?"

He glanced at Braden.

"They're waiting for the rings, man."

Oh.

Yeah.

The rings.

He fished into his pants pocket. He almost took out the wrong ring. By some stroke of luck, he managed to withdraw Madeline's and Riley's wedding bands without dropping them. As if they'd rehearsed it this way, Braden plucked the rings from Kyle's palm and handed them to Reverend Brown.

The ceremony went on around Kyle. He supposed Reverend Brown addressed the wedding guests in some sort of a sermon. Riley and Madeline undoubtedly said, "I do."

If there was more music, he didn't hear it. Summer didn't look at him again. He knew because he barely took his eyes off her.

He heard clapping. And then Riley and Madeline were walking from the church, hand in hand.

By rote, Kyle met Summer at the center of the aisle. He couldn't read her expression as she placed her hand in the crook of his arm. At the back of the church, he recovered enough to clasp his brother in a bear hug and kiss his new sister-in-law's smooth cheek.

All three of The Sources asked him what was wrong. He kissed each of them on the cheek, too. Summer stayed close to Madeline, greeting each of the guests who went through the receiving line. He kept watch for whoever had snapped her picture but saw no one now.

He lost Summer in the throngs of well-wishers moving between the church and the banquet hall next door. He caught sight of her slipping away from the crowd and finally caught up with her in a quiet little courtyard beside the church.

"I know how this looks," he said.

Summer turned around and squinted into the setting sun. Shading her eyes with one hand, she said, "Oh, Kyle, there you are."

Wait just a cotton-picking minute, Kyle thought. What was going on? Summer sounded tired but basically fine.

"I didn't call the press. I haven't told a soul."

She looked up at him, her eyes pools of gray surrounded by coal-black lashes. "I never doubted you, Kyle."

Summer watched the transformation that came over Kyle. His eyebrows came down. His chin went up a fraction. He was as handsome as she'd ever seen him in his hand-tailored suit. He smelled like the clean, brisk breeze. Once, she'd thought he was a risk. She'd been wrong.

"I didn't doubt you when that camera flashed," she said. "Why? Because the reporter in you would have dug into my background the first time your curiosity wasn't satisfied. You've known who I am since that first morning you were here, haven't you?" She hadn't realized it at the time, but it made perfect sense now. He'd known, but instead of using it against her or to further his career or redeem it in some way, he'd guarded the information. He'd wanted her to trust him with it, with her love.

The sun was sinking and the shadows were lengthening. The dread that had held his shoulders and arms rigid turned to vapor, popping like the cork on a fine bottle of champagne. What remained after the bubbles cleared was the best part. What remained was the heart of the man Summer loved.

He moved closer, his body making contact, key contact with hers, arms, chest, hips, thighs. "I knew," he said, "but if I didn't contact the press, and I *didn't,* who did?"

She started to shrug. Remembering those times throughout the years when she'd thought she was being followed, the answer became clear.

"Drake," she said.

"Proctor," Kyle said at the same time. "Your ex-fiancé knows where you are."

Summer nodded. Drake probably did know. He'd probably always known. Her father would have known, too. Any investigator could have located her. She'd changed her name, but there were records. She didn't think her father was responsible for the photographer at Madeline's wedding, though. He'd had his revenge when he'd disowned her. The last she knew, he'd married again, a much younger woman this time. He now had a new daughter to use as collateral in future business deals.

Just then a shadow flickered at the edge of the courtyard. Kyle and Summer saw a stranger in a cheap suit and with his hair slicked back start to snap a picture.

They both looked at him, bored.

He lowered his camera as if even slime balls knew when there wasn't a story to capture.

He slunk away, and Summer said, "I smell food."

The reception was beginning in the banquet hall next door. She started toward it, but Kyle caught her hand in his and simply held it.

The breeze ruffled the fabric of her pink skirt and fluttered her five shades of brown hair. This wasn't how he'd planned to do this. Some things didn't need to be planned.

Smoothing his thumb in a circle on her wrist, he gently turned her so she was facing him. Reaching a hand into his pocket to make sure the ring was still there, he said, "I've been thinking. About making a career change."

He had her undivided attention.

"It was Walter's idea, so I can't take the credit for the initial notion, but how would you feel about marrying a guy who's about to become a partner in operating a newspaper in a small college town in mid-Michigan?"

"Did you slip a marriage proposal in there somewhere?" He looked into her eyes and nodded.

He took the smile spreading across her lips as a good sign. Although it might have been risky to bring up the second phase, he braved the risk and said, "I don't know how you feel about children. But if you're willing to give me a chance, I think I'd like to start filling those bedrooms in that inn of yours."

There was a hitch in Summer's breathing. What followed was the most amazing burst of possibilities. She hadn't thought about children, at least not in the context of her own. She'd always been afraid, in the back of her mind, that she was like her father: flawed. Looking into Kyle's green eyes, she saw herself the way he saw her, strong but cautious—and maybe a little wicked—but in a good way.

"You think we should turn the inn back into a house?" she whispered.

"Wasn't that what it was always intended to be?" he asked.

He reached for her other hand. Bringing both her hands together gently in both of his, he stared into her eyes. "I never thought I would find someone like you, never dreamed I could feel this way. I love you. I love the way you daydream in the middle of the afternoon and stargaze in the middle of the night. I love your courage and I love your loyalty to your friends. Let me be as loyal to you. Would you marry me, Summer?"

The next thing Summer knew, she was staring at a diamond that caught the final rays of the setting sun. Her throat felt thick and her eyes dewy as she said, "I love you, too, and I'll marry you, Kyle Merrick." He slipped the ring on her finger and she whispered, "On one condition."

He looked ready for any condition she could name.

She pushed the dark hair off his forehead. Letting her fingers trail down his face, she skimmed his lips. "Tell me a secret."

Kyle rose to the challenge and whispered in her ear.

Her breath caught and her color heightened. Nobody in the world could make her blush but him. "I wonder if anybody would miss us if we slipped away from the reception for a little while."

Taking her hand, Kyle led her toward the banquet hall, for what he had in mind was going to take longer than a little while. They joined Madeline and Riley and Chelsea and Abby and Walter and Harriet and the Sullivan brothers and Braden and Kyle's mother and his stepmothers, too. They celebrated the marriage of two special people.

They danced, and they toasted to ever after. And they ate. Everybody loved the cake, but nobody loved it more than Summer and Kyle. As the sweet frosting melted in their mouths, their gazes met. Both were thinking about how they would celebrate when they got back to the inn.

They had the same vision in the back of their minds. What they had in store was going to last for the rest of their lives.

* * * * *

SOMETHING UNEXPECTED

BY

WENDY WARREN

First published in Great Britain 2011
by Mills & Boon, an imprint of Harlequin (UK) Limited,
Eton House, 18-24 Paradise Road, Richmond, Surrey TW9 1SR

ISBN: 978 0 263 88906 2

23-0811

Harlequin (UK) policy is to use papers that are natural, renewable and recyclable products and made from wood grown in sustainable forests. The logging and manufacturing processes conform to the legal environmental regulations of the country of origin.

Printed and bound in Spain
by Blackprint CPI, Barcelona

Dear Reader,

For a very sweet while, I lived in a kind of latter-day Mayberry, a small town in Oregon still so innocent that the mayor's giant squash provided the lead story on the local news.

Twice a day in the summer, horses clopped down our block pulling a carriage, and in December the locals, dressed in elaborate Victorian costumes, handed out hot cider and chestnuts on the street corner.

Marrying my true love dictated a move; today I make my Mayberry in the middle of a busy city. But I go to work every day in Honeyford, a replica of the wonderful town I lived in.

In *Something Unexpected*, Rosemary is running from her life in the city. Smarting from the pain of lost dreams and broken trust, all she wants is peace. Then she meets Dean Kingsley, Honeyford's favorite son, a man who has played by the rules all his life, but who realizes he may have to bend them a bit to show Rosemary that her home is in his arms.

Welcome to book two of Home Sweet Honeyford!

Wendy Warren

For Tim, my "something unexpected" of
—oh, lord, is this possible?—twenty-five years.

Despite the fact that I was only five (okay, ten) when we met, I was fortunate enough to find a man with sterling qualities I never even thought to look for. Your integrity, tolerance, compassion and broad, broad shoulders have never let me down.

My "Mayberry" is in your arms.

I love you.

Wendy Warren lives in the Pacific Northwest with her actor husband, their wonderful daughter and the assorted four-legged and finned creatures they bring home.

A two-time recipient of Romance Writers of America's RITA Award, Wendy loves to read and write the kind of books that remind her of the old movies she grew up watching with her mom and now shares with her own daughter—stories about decent people looking for the love that can make an ordinary life extraordinary. When not writing, she likes to take long walks under leafy trees, lift weights that make her sweat and her husband laugh, settle in for cozy chats with great friends, and pretend she will someday win a million dollars in a bake-off. Check out her website for more information on Honeyford, some great recipes from the townsfolk and other fun stuff. www.authorwendywarren.com.

Chapter One

The Tavern on the Highway
Ten miles west of Honeyford, Oregon
December

"He's a firefighter."

"No way. Ballroom-dance instructor. Specializes in Argentine tango."

"Please. His pants aren't tight enough. And he lacks that chronic self-involved air. He has nice hands. I bet he's a surgeon."

Rosemary Jeffers smiled over the rim of her lemon-drop martini as her three best friends dished about a man at the bar to her right. She didn't turn to look.

The bar scene was not her thing. Neither were lemon-drop martinis, come to think of it, but Ginger Kane, Vi Harris and Daphne Nordli had driven three hours from Portland, Oregon, to Honeyford, intent on rescuing her from a thirty-second birthday that had looked as if it might require the use of antidepressants.

Single, recently relocated and waiting for her new job to begin the following week, she had planned to spend her birthday alone at home, dying the three gray hairs she'd found earlier in the day back to brown.

"Where are we going to eat?" she ventured, attempting for the second time that night to steer the conversation around to her growling stomach.

Vi's red brows swooped in frank disgust. "We're not here to feed our stomachs. We're here to indulge our senses. And yours have been sadly neglected, my friend."

Rosemary shrugged. She did not want to have this conversation. Again. "Taste is a sense. I hear there's a great Italian place—"

"Stop!" Vi slapped her hand on the myrtle-wood table. "We did not doll you up and take you out so you could dribble marinara down your dress. You haven't gone on a date in *two years*. Now turn and look at the dude by the bar. He's been ogling you since we got here."

Daphne nodded eagerly. "He really is a cutie." Two reassuring dimples appeared in her ivory cheeks.

"It *is* time to get back in the dating pool," Ginger added, though she had the grace to look a smidge apologetic.

Rosemary's empty stomach threatened to dry heave. The thought of diving into the dating pool was roughly as appealing as dunking herself in chum and plunging into shark-infested waters.

"I've given dating some thought," she ventured, taking a pretzel from a bowl in the center of the table and sucking salt as she tried to sound offhand. "I've decided not to do it until I find a completely honest man."

She was met with three pairs of wide eyes and a pregnant

pause until Ginger said quietly, "That's going to severely limit your prospects, sweetie."

Rosemary lowered the pretzel to her cocktail napkin while the others reached morosely for their drinks. Of the four of them, only she had married, proving that she'd never *intended* to spend her thirties like a nun. But neither had she planned to return home from work early one evening to find her husband *in flagrante delicto* with his paralegal. That miserable night had occurred two years ago on this very date, which unfortunately had also been her tenth wedding anniversary.

Faith Hill came on the jukebox, singing about the perfect kiss while the aroma of mini tacos wafted from the happy-hour buffet.

"You know what the trouble is?" she pondered aloud, plucking the lemon twist from her martini and winding it until it broke. "The trouble with romance and infatuation and falling in love?" Vi arched a brow. Ginger and Daphne shook their heads. "It isn't that people break your heart because they lie or they leave. What makes you absolutely miserable is the hope that next time will be different. That the next guy is going to be *the* guy, or that 'tonight' is going to turn into 'forever.' Hope," she said earnestly. "That's our problem."

"Wow. That's cynical." Vi tapped a toothpick-speared pearl onion on the edge of her Gibson glass. "I like it. Keep talking."

Rosemary's caramel eyes narrowed. In her chest there was a deep well where her heart used to be, and for too long that well had been filled with confusion and grief. She wanted her heart back.

"I know I don't want to get married again." She tested the words aloud for the first time. "Or even to live with anyone."

"Never?" Daphne looked appalled.

"No." Rosemary shook her head. "Not ever." She felt stronger merely from saying it. "But you're all right about one thing—I shouldn't live like a nun."

"Damn straight," Vi toasted.

"I just have to find a way to date without pain. Like men do."

Disappointed, Ginger reached for her margarita. "I thought you were going to say something profound." She sucked frosty liquid from two skinny red straws, swallowed and proclaimed, "It's not possible to date like men do. Men are born without a conscience. That's why they need women. We're like software—we download guilt onto their brain computers."

Vi stared. "That is seriously twisted." She smiled hugely. "I like that, too." She waved a hand at Rosemary. "You're talking about dating without strings. Been there. In fact, I live there."

"No." Rosemary shook her head. "More than that. I'm talking about dating without hope. No texting girlfriends from the restaurant to see if they'll be your bridesmaids. No doodling potential wedding dates on every scrap paper in sight."

Daphne's hand snaked out guiltily to crumple her cocktail napkin.

"Carpe diem dating," Rosemary improvised like the pitchman of an ad campaign. "When the date itself becomes not simply the means to an end—" she stabbed her finger on the table, punctuating her words "—but the only goal you'll ever have!"

Dead silence followed her big finish. Then Vi stood up and applauded. Ginger followed, albeit more slowly, and Daphne had to be lifted up by the arm. Once they were all standing, Rosemary took a humble bow, and Vi praised, "Brilliant. Show us how it's done."

Resuming her seat, Rosemary laughed. "Maybe I will."

"Not 'maybe.' Right now. The cute dude at the bar hasn't been able to take his eyes off you. He stared the whole time you were talking. I think he just sent over a drink."

The cocktail waitress arrived at that moment with not one, but four peachy-gold drinks she called Honey Slides. The girls approved.

"Very generous," Daphne whispered.

"Good manners." Ginger nodded in approval.

"Wow, that is one sickeningly sweet drink," Vi said after taking the first sip, but she raised the golden concoction and aimed a beautiful smile toward the bar. Before the others knew what she was going to do, Vi crooked one talon-tipped finger and beckoned the man over.

"Vi, no!" Rosemary warned. "We don't even know him."

"Which makes him perfect for your experiment." Abandoning the Honey Slide, she returned to her Gibson. "I dare you to dance with that gorgeous hunk and not allow yourself to think beyond this one night. If you can do that, I promise not to bug you ever again about dating, because clearly you will have proved yourself a more evolved woman than I."

Rosemary looked at her friends' enthusiastic expressions. "You won't bug me *ever* again? Any of you?" They shook their heads. "And then we can go to the Italian place?" Nods all around.

Rosemary knew she wasn't like other women her age, the ones who could flirt, get up and salsa, even touch and kiss men they'd just met. She'd never developed the ability to be casual with males. Spending time, even a little time, with a strange guy in a bar not only would not fill her with hope, it was unlikely to do more than give her a few hives. This was a bet she could win in a walk.

One dance, and they can never pressure me to date again.

She gave it another few seconds of consideration then said quickly, before she could change her mind, "All right. I'll do it."

She was the most stunning creature he had ever seen.

With his back to the bar, Dean Kingsley observed the four vivacious females who shared a table in the sawdust-strewn lounge of Tavern on the Highway. The lady who had caught his interest was not the sexiest of the quartet (that honor belonged indisputably to the redhead), nor did she have the most perfect features (the petite blonde looked like a china doll come to life). But the girl with the dark chocolate curls and the light-as-milk skin was the one he couldn't stop watching.

He'd been studying her for the past half hour, and it had been the most satisfying thirty minutes he'd spent in months.

So far, he'd seen her only in profile, but already he was familiar with several of her mannerisms. She ducked her chin and smiled with her lips closed shortly before she said something that made the other women laugh….

She bit her thumbnail when she was thinking hard then scowled and shook her hand once she realized what she was doing, as if nail biting was a long-standing habit she wanted to break….

She listened carefully when her friends spoke, and she cared about what they were saying….

And, she liked only the salt on pretzels, as the growing stack of soggy sticks on her cocktail napkin attested. That particular habit would wreak havoc on his stash of Rold Gold, but no relationship should be *too* perfect.

Dean grinned. For the first time in weeks, he felt something other than dull resignation. Interest and desire kindled in his body, making him feel alive again. He liked it.

"Forget about her." Len Perris tapped him on the forearm. "She hasn't looked at you once." Tilting his tan Stetson back on his head, Len narrowed his eyes in a thoughtful assessment and nodded. "Go for the blonde. She's an angel. So to speak."

"Which is exactly why he shouldn't go for the blonde." Fred Werblow, Dean's pal from the time he, Len and Fred were all more interested in their rock collections than in women, slapped him on the back. "The last thing our boy needs is an angel. Right, Deano? If you're going to make it through the next two years without wanting to do yourself in then you need a woman who can whip up some excitement." Leaning close, he advised, "Go for the redhead. She looks like a wildcat. Grrrrrr."

"Did you just growl?" Shaking his head, Dean set his draft beer on the bar behind them. The tension he'd momentarily been able to dispel slammed into him again, full force.

"Listen, I don't want to talk about my 'plans' tonight," he said. "I particularly don't want to discuss how or whether I'm going to make it through the next two years." Talking about his predicament, even casually, made his blood pressure spike.

Len put an arm around Dean's shoulders. "That's why we're here, buddy. We're riding shotgun for you."

Fred slapped him on the back again. "That's right. You're being forced to take a wife, and we're going to help you find one you can stomach."

Swearing beneath his breath, Dean hung his head.

His father, Dr. Victor Kingsley, may he rest in peace, had died this past April, leaving a will that bequeathed his sons exactly what they wanted—as long as they married within twelve months of their father's death and remained wed for at least two years.

Afraid his sons might permanently shun marriage, the doctor had prescribed a couple of daughters-in-law.

It was now December. Dean had four months left to marry.

Anyone who knew Dean and his younger half brother would have expected Fletcher to flip the birdie to the will, and Dean to be thoughtful, rational and ultimately compliant. And in fact, that was exactly how the men had reacted—at first. Fletcher had flatly refused to consider marriage, but then, shockingly, he had met someone who'd managed to transform him from gruff loner to tender lover. Two weeks ago, he'd gotten married.

Dean, on the other hand…

Feeling the muscles in his neck contract, Dean considered swapping his beer for bourbon, but he'd never had a taste for hard liquor. Or for escaping life's problems.

After the reading of his father's will, he had forced himself to be practical. A marriage of convenience was not, after all, such a far cry from what he had planned for himself all along.

At thirty-five, he had been engaged once, to a woman as logical and reasonable as he. When Amanda's career had required her to move out of state, they'd ended their relationship, wished each other well—meant it—and had been no worse for the wear. Afterward, Dean had wondered why he'd felt only mildly disappointed when she gave him back his ring.

Eventually, he'd come to accept that deep emotions and powerful yearnings tended to escape him where relationships were concerned. There was only one dream for which he was willing to go to the mat. His father had understood that and was capitalizing on Dean's single passion to coerce him into marriage.

"Maybe Dean's looking for something less permanent tonight. A last hoo-rah." Fred's booming voice was jovial and wholly approving. "Is that why we're here? Do you need to party a little before you settle down? Because no one is going to blame you for that."

Dean sighed. "I'm here because you two wouldn't shut up until I came," he muttered.

What did he want? He wished to God he knew.

Some unnameable impulse tugged his focus once more to the brunette. He'd sent over drinks and each woman had already tasted her Honey Slide. Each woman except for the girl with the curly hair.

I want you.

The answer came so swiftly and clearly that he couldn't refute it.

He wanted to know what she was thinking in this very moment. Why her skin glowed as if she was lit from within. Whether she came here often, why she'd ordered a martini when she didn't seem to like them and what she was doing for the next twenty-four hours, because he wanted to spend them with her.

He saw the redhead toast him, offering a dazzling, if artificial, smile. The brunette didn't even turn around. Dean pushed a responding curve to his lips. *You're welcome,* he nodded to the redhead. It was done. Time to go.

He was about to suggest to Len and Fred that they try the new Italian place in Honeyford, when the brunette stirred. Leaning forward, she put a thumb and delicate forefinger on the fine straws in the frosty drink.

Len said something about barbecue, but Dean only half heard. He waited, gazing like a landlocked sailor staring out to sea, engrossed and longing, hoping for some action to release him from the spell.

And then she moved, turning her head before she lifted her gaze to his. Their eyes caught and held. Eyes the color of butterscotch taffy, big and curious, acquired a spark of surprise when she saw him. Her smile, tentative at first, grew progressively wider and more relaxed, turning the elegant portrait of her face into a masterpiece.

Thank you.

She mouthed the words. Or perhaps he simply couldn't hear her from where he stood.

Thank you was not an invitation to join her, but he wanted to ask her, at least, to dance one dance, to talk, to spend just a few moments getting to know each other before they returned to their real lives. The moments of gazing into her eyes enclosed him in a bubble that floated him lightly above the practical, the mundane. Above his ambivalence about his life and the path that awaited him.

He wanted to remain where he was, sharing a long mutual stare, even if it went no further than that.

But she surprised him.

Raising a loose fist, she briefly rested her knuckles against her mouth, then unfurled her index finger, crooked it, and beckoned him over.

Instantly, Dean knew: though Tavern on the Highway was not a place he frequented, and although he believed much more in free will than manifest destiny, he—pragmatic, level-headed Dean Kingsley—knew that for perhaps the first time in his life he was in exactly the right place at exactly the right time.

Chapter Two

Honeyford, Oregon
March

"Here you are, Mrs. Bowman. One copy of *What to Expect in the First Year*." Rosemary twinkled at her heavily pregnant customer. "Just in the nick of time, by the looks of it."

Elliana Bowman placed her canvas book bag atop the checkout desk of The Honeyford Public Library and slid the parenting tome carefully inside. "Two more weeks," she told Rosemary, her handsome, bespectacled face as giddy and enchanted as a child's. "I meant to order the book online months ago. Ordinarily I'm highly organized, but ever since I met my husband, I'm very…distractible."

Her high cheeks turned furiously red, and Rosemary smiled. She hadn't known Elliana at all prior to the other woman's marriage to Dan Bowman, Honeyford's resident mechanic, but she'd been told that although Dan and Elliana had lived in Honeyford all their lives, they hadn't hooked up until they were solidly in their thirties. Now they were expecting their first child.

Rosemary waited for the pangs of envy she used to feel when confronted with another woman's pregnancy. Through her teens and her twenties, she'd been certain that motherhood was her mission.

Not anymore. Her mission now was her work, and the residents of this darling town she'd been fortunate enough to find were becoming her makeshift family.

"I'm going to make myself a note," she told Elliana, "to renew that book for you automatically if you don't return it on time. You just enjoy your pregnancy and don't worry about a thing."

Elliana beamed, waving goodbye as she left, and Rosemary told herself once again how lucky she was.

"Plug your nose! Incoming!"

Rosemary turned to see her assistant, Abby, a twentysomething library clerk who wore shoulder pads and had a predilection for World War II novels, approach the circulation desk. In one hand, Abby held a book as far from her body as possible. With the thumb and forefinger of her other hand, she pinched her nostrils shut.

"Brady Silva just upchucked on *Captain Underpants,*" Abby announced nasally. "His mother's in the bathroom, cleaning him up."

"Oh, dear."

Glancing at the grandfather clock that, Rosemary was told, had graced the entrance of the Honeyford Public Library for more than fifty years, she felt a rush of relief when she saw there were only seventeen minutes left to closing time. Since beginning her job as head librarian here, she'd stayed late more nights than not, finding any number of delightful tasks to perform. In two months, she had implemented a new literacy program benefiting local youth and had several more programs planned. She didn't mind staying late.

Her sole motivation for wanting to leave on time tonight was the flu that had been snaking through Honeyford like one of the evil Dementors in Harry Potter. Because she'd felt funky on and off since morning, Rosemary feared she, too, might be coming down with the bug. Brady Silva's accident with the book made her more than a little queasy.

"Not to worry." Rosemary reached for one of the used plastic shopping bags she kept beneath the desk, shook it open and had Abby drop the book inside.

"We'll all be puking by tonight." Abby shook her head, depositing the book and plucking a moistened wipe from the box Rosemary kept on the counter. "My fiancé has it, too. The first twenty-four hours are sheer misery."

Rosemary swallowed. She detested throwing up. "Wash your hands with soap and hot water every hour for as long as it takes you to sing 'Happy Birthday,' and whatever you do, don't touch your eyes, nose or mouth."

Abby gaped at her. "Are you phobic or something?"

"Germs can live eleven hours on nonporous surfaces like door handles, steering wheels and shopping carts. I'm not phobic—I'm cautious."

Abby's full lips twitched at the corners. "Cautious about everything or just germs?"

"Every—" Rosemary stopped abruptly.

Almost three months ago, she would have completed that sentence without a second thought. *I'm cautious about everything.* Now she avoided her clerk's curious gaze and muttered, "It's still cold-and-flu season. It can't hurt to take extra precautions."

Nodding, Abby moved off to return a stack of books to the large-print section. Rosemary pressed a computer key so she could check in DVDs, but her mind was a mile away.

Make that ten miles and two and a half months away.

As if she'd pressed a play button in her brain, her head filled with images.

Tavern on the Highway...Faith Hill on the jukebox...a drink called a Honey Slide that she'd barely touched...and a man named Dean, whom she had touched a lot, in ways she would never, not in a million years, have imagined she could touch a stranger.

Not that he had remained a stranger for long.

By the time the library closed and Rosemary was able to head to her car, she had replayed that night with Dean a dozen times...and felt herself blush almost as many.

That evening in the bar, she had intended to thank the tall, handsome man for the drinks, perhaps to chat just a bit so the girls wouldn't rag on her later and then to say goodbye. That was all. Harmless.

Seated in her car, alone in the library parking lot, Rosemary clapped her hands over her face and groaned.

After dancing, Dean had escorted her back to her table and chatted amiably with her friends, but his demeanor with them had been nothing more than courteous. Brotherly. So different from the way he'd looked at her. They had returned to the dance floor again and again. At some point in the evening, leaving the bar with him had seemed perfectly sane. In her entire adult life, she could not recall feeling the sexual urgency she'd felt that night.

Flushing anew at the memory, Rosemary flipped her visor down to check her face in the mirror. Mascara was smudged beneath her eyes. Licking a finger, she carefully wiped it away and thought that if she lived a hundred more years, she would not understand how she had morphed in one evening from the woman who never went anywhere without her AAA card, cell phone, a calling card in case the cell phone went dead and at least half a dozen quarters in the event the calling card didn't work, to the woman who jumped into the arms and the bed of a total stranger.

Despite her brave talk of carpe diem dating, in her heart the words *casual* and *sex* were antonyms.

Now somewhere in the world there was a man with whom she had gotten naked and made love with the lights on, yet whose last name, age, address and occupation she still did not know.

What kind of woman did that?

"The kind who's finally joined the twenty-first century," Vi had assured her approvingly the day after.

Right. The kind who believed in carpe diem dating. No strings. No hope. And no recriminations.

That last part was gonna take a while.

Lifting her head, Rosemary turned the key in the ignition, gripped the steering wheel with fingers stiff from the March chill and threw the car into Reverse.

Chicken soup.

The sudden craving for something warm, uncomplicated and comforting gave her a direction, and she headed for Sherm's Queen Bee, the grocery store on the east end of town. With a population of nearly nineteen hundred people, Honeyford was large enough to support two markets. Sherm's was the larger, and it stayed open later.

On her way into the store, Rosemary grabbed a handled basket. The act of shopping distracted her from troubling thoughts. By the time she'd picked up aspirin, tea and orange juice, she felt a bit better. Grabbing a box of saltines from the cracker aisle in case her nausea returned, she started toward canned soups, one aisle over, when she overheard a conversation that managed to make her smile.

"You do not need to use canned soup to make macaroni and cheese." The woman's voice was vehement and vaguely disgusted. "Get a good English Cheddar."

"Cheddar-cheese *soup* makes it feel more like comfort food, Amanda," came the man's much gentler reply. "Trust me. This is the best mac and cheese you'll ever taste. You'll feel like you're ten again."

"I don't want to feel ten again…."

Rosemary laughed to herself. Right there was one of the perks of being single. She used to use cheddar soup to make macaroni and cheese, but Neil had loathed that particular meal, saying it tasted "cheap." During the first year of their marriage, she'd found a recipe for fettuccini Alfredo and had abandoned her beloved mac and cheese altogether.

With no need to please anyone but herself tonight, and hungry for the first time all day, she skirted a display of Goldfish crackers and rounded the soup aisle, intent on making a big casserole of creamy pasta tonight. She wanted to thank the gentleman with the macaroni craving for reminding her about this treat and then tell him to grab his own can of soup and run, before he spent the better part of his life acquiescing to someone else's desires, but, of course, it was none of her beeswax.

As she entered the aisle, Rosemary couldn't help but glance at the woman with the firm opinions on cheese and the strongly judgmental tone. Tall enough to partially block Rosemary's view of the man, the blonde wore black-rimmed glasses, a belted coat, stiletto-heeled leather boots and a perturbed expression. "I'm going to call Beezoli's and have them make a fettuccini Alfredo to go," she said as she fished her cell phone from her pocket. "Do you want one?"

Hiding her grin, Rosemary stepped in front of the couple to reach for the soup. "Excuse me."

As she straightened, she angled her body, hoping to take a quick, nosey-bones peek at the man. Good English Cheddar was clearly a gal who got her own way. The poor guy might never enjoy a decent mac and cheese again.

Sorry, buddy, she told him mentally as she turned, deciding to give him a smile. *Believe me, I relate—*

Dear God!

The can of soup dropped from Rosemary's hand, clunking onto the hard floor.

She stared stupidly, frozen as a statue, while Dean Whose-Last-Name-She-Did-Not-Know stared back at her.

"You dropped something," the blonde intoned drily, which should have snapped Rosemary out of her stupor, but didn't.

Dean, however—as neatly groomed and handsome as he'd been two and a half months ago—dived for the can of soup, rose and handed it back to her, his blue gaze glued to her face.

"Hello," he said.

She should have recognized his voice right away. Smooth and rich rather than deep, like the best milk chocolate, it had wrapped her in delicious sensation that magical night.

Rosemary couldn't answer him. Her mind buzzed with a dozen questions.

Do you live in Honeyford?

Does Good English Cheddar live in Honeyford?

Were you and she together when you and I…?

Mortified, by the possibility that she had slept with another woman's man, Rosemary could feel her face flush and perspiration build beneath her heavy clothing.

"Do you two know each other?" The blonde sounded bored as she flipped her hair back and brought her cell phone to her ear.

Rosemary glared at Dean. He seemed not to have heard his companion's question. His brows lowered in deep thought.

She turned toward the woman, wondering whether she should answer, then saw something that strangled any words that might have emerged.

From the hand holding the phone, a simple ring glittered. A simple, emerald-cut diamond engagement ring.

Fury sped through Rosemary's veins like fire along a line of gasoline.

"We should do this again…for the next forty years." The words he'd murmured while they'd danced came back to taunt her.

She knew better than to trust in forever. That was one reason she'd left before dawn—so she wouldn't be tempted to buy into a fairy tale. But she'd assumed, at least, that her prince-for-a-night was as charming and decent as he'd seemed.

Snake! Rat! Philanderer! She was tempted to pick up the can of cheddar-cheese soup and aim it at his head, but then another thought struck. Because of Dean's dishonesty, she had done to another woman what had been done to her. She had become a mistress by mistake!

The blonde—Amanda, was it?—lowered her chin, peering at Rosemary above her rectangular glasses. "Are you all right? You look like you're going to pass out. Dean, take out your phone in case you have to call 9-1-1. Beezoli's has me on hold."

The last thing Rosemary saw before she turned and ran through the store was Dean's hand reaching toward her. As she chucked her basket of goods and raced for the door, she heard him call, "Rosemary, wait!"

And then Amanda's voice, more faintly: "You *do* know her."

For the third morning in a row, Rosemary huddled on her side beneath a fluffy white comforter ninety minutes past the time her alarm went off. She'd missed two days of work, and now, on her regularly scheduled day off, she could no longer deny the facts: from the moment she opened her eyes in the morning, nausea hit so hard she could barely raise her head.

She'd thought she had the flu that was going around, but by midday she typically got better, and around dinnertime she was ravenous…only to begin the cycle again the next day.

And, she'd missed two periods.

At first, she'd chalked the interruption to her monthly cycle up to the stress of her recent move and a new job. Now it seemed far more ominous than that.

Grunting, Rosemary pushed the covers aside and slowly sat up. Her feet had barely touched the hardwood floor when her stomach rebelled, and she raced to the bathroom.

"I hate throwing up," she told her sad reflection as she brushed her teeth after the fact. More than anything, she wanted to crawl back into bed, pull the pillows over her head and stay there.

She'd worked so hard to create a new life for herself after her divorce. Now, if her suspicion proved correct, that sweet new life was going to turn into a very bad soap opera.

"Stupid, stupid, stupid!" Sniffing back tears, she returned to the bedroom to get dressed. She hadn't been on birth control since her divorce. There hadn't been any need since she hadn't intended to be sexually active.

On that now deeply regretted night in December, she and Dean had used a condom….

The first time. And the second.

But the third? She honestly couldn't remember.

A glance in the mirror above her dresser told Rosemary that she looked like death warmed over. She shrugged as she dressed in jeans and a heavy wool sweater then twisted her curly hair into a knot atop her head. From her hall closet, she withdrew a shin-length camel-hair coat with a collar she could turn up to partially hide her face, and a pink cloche that she tugged down around her ears.

Honeyford wasn't small enough to run into people one knew every day, but she hoped to minimize the odds that someone in this quaint, conservative town might stop her to strike up a conversation as she ran her errand: the purchase of an at-home pregnancy test to determine whether she was knocked up from a one-night stand with an engaged stranger.

Grabbing her purse and heading into the brisk March day, Rosemary fought back tears once again. She'd thought her divorce was the low point in her life. Now she was deeply afraid she was about to hit a new bottom.

It took ten minutes to walk from her home on Oak and 4th Street to downtown Honeyford. As a string of bells jingled merrily against the glass door of King's Pharmacy, Rosemary began to wish she'd driven to another town to make her purchase.

It certainly didn't escape her that if Dean and his fiancée lived in Honeyford then she was likely to bump into them again sooner or later. She comforted herself with the knowledge that this was a workday for most people, and given that it had taken her over two months to run into Dean the first time, she could reasonably expect luck to be on her side today.

In fact, if she was *really* fortunate, her nausea would turn out to be some exotic disease or possibly intermittent salmonella or merely garden-variety stress. Anything other than pregnancy. And then she could simply ignore her one-night stand and his bride-to-be the next time she saw them.

Quickly, Rosemary entered the store, which was larger than she'd expected, with an old-fashioned soda fountain to her left and gift shop up front. A cash register was located at the entrance, but also, she saw as she made her way back, in the rear of the store by the pharmacy.

Locating the aisle with the EPTs, Rosemary grabbed two boxes to be on the safe side then gathered a few additional items before she approached the cash register near the pharmacy.

The cashier had teased, bright red hair and pince-nez glasses perched low on the end of her nose. Her forehead creased deeply as she perused an issue of *OK! Magazine.* Rosemary never forgot a face and took a relieved breath when she realized the woman was a stranger to her.

Unloading her items onto the counter, she slid a large box of candy ahead of the EPT. In addition she'd selected a white teddy bear holding a sign that read Friends Forever, and a greeting card, reasoning that if she did see someone she knew, she could say she was on her way to give moral support to a friend whose husband was overseas, and who thought she might be pregnant and didn't want to be alone when she found out.

Hopefully, it would sound better coming out of her mouth than it did in her head.

A forced smile strained her lips as she mumbled her "Hello."

The cashier greeted her without fanfare and efficiently rang up the purchase. "Thirty-two ninety-five."

She hadn't reacted in the slightest to the EPTs. Rosemary relaxed, realizing she'd been paranoid. This was a pharmacy, after all. They probably sold EPTs all the time.

"Thirty-two ninety-five," she repeated with more spring in her voice, opening her purse.

"I don't think I have a bag large enough for the candy box," the older woman muttered, peering beneath the counter. "Do we have any of those gift bags left from Valentine's Day?" she called out.

Opening her deep handbag, Rosemary fished for her wallet.

From the pharmacy behind the cash register, someone responded, "Why don't you head on up to the front now, Millie. I'll look for the bags."

As Rosemary registered the warm male voice, the strangest

feeling she had ever experienced overcame her. Fire ignited in her belly and rushed through her veins so quickly that for a moment she felt as if she might pass out.

No. Please, no.

Impulse almost compelled her to look up, but she resisted, keeping her head as low as possible.

"I don't need the bag," she protested to the cashier even as the woman walked around the counter. "I'll just pay, and—"

"Dean will take care of you, honey."

Dean.

Ohmygod, ohmygod, ohmygod.

As the older woman walked away, Rosemary's gaze zeroed in on the EPT, which seemed to be glowing like a flare. She couldn't breathe.

Frantic, she looked around for a way to hide the evidence. Eye-level to her right were rolls of vitamin C and throat lozenges. *Too small.* Below them hung bags of cough drops.

Diving, she seized several bags, dumping them on the counter. By the time a white lab coat appeared in her field of vision, there was barely an inch of counter surface visible. Tugging her hat as low as it would go, Rosemary dug through her purse. *Where was her damned wallet?*

"All right, how large a gift bag do we need?" Dean inquired pleasantly as he halted in front of her. With only the counter to separate them, Rosemary felt her entire body tense. Her *engaged* lover was the friendly neighborhood pharmacist.

Surveying her goods, he whistled. "Looks as if you're medicating quite a cough." He picked up one of the packages. "These are fine for a cough related to the common cold, but if you're treating the bug that's going around, you'll need something stronger. May I recommend a couple of products I think will be more effective for you?"

Oozing compassion and care, his voice could make a

woman believe she was safe in his hands. An excellent trait in a pharmacist; a treacherous quality in a lover.

"No need," Rosemary croaked, morphing her normal tones into something that resembled a bullfrog on Marlboros. "I'm stocking up."

What were the chances she could pay her bill, collect her items and leave without having to look up?

"Rosie?"

Her trembling fingers closed around the wallet, and she felt a mustard seed's worth of relief. Pulling out several bills, she tossed them onto the counter, opened her wide-mouthed purse and began sweeping her purchases inside. She had no hope that everything would fit, but prayed she could get the EPT in there without Dean noticing.

"I've been looking for you," he said. "Where have you been all these months?"

Her hand froze. "You've been looking for me for *months?*"

"Since December."

Anger raced through her, and she stared at him, hard. As always, Dean's face was incredibly handsome, but this time the attractiveness was blunted by the fact that he was a low-down, lying boy-slut.

All through her divorce, Rosemary had preferred to skirt issues rather than to confront them, afraid her feelings would overpower her. Now she experienced no such compunction.

"I wonder how you had the time to look for me?" she said. "Didn't your *fiancée* have plenty for you do?"

She gave him points—but only a couple—for not trying to deny the existence of a fiancée. Neil had lied even after she'd caught him red-handed.

He frowned. "I want to explain—"

"Good," she interrupted. "You can start by explaining *me* to *her.*" She reached again for the items on the counter, righteous indignation—no, rage—trumping all other emotion.

Cheating didn't ruin only the immediate relationship: it robbed the cheated-on person of her dreams. If you'd loved and been lied to once, it was damned difficult to trust in love a second time. Rosemary actually felt a kinship with Good English Cheddar.

"Hey, stop." Dean reached for her forearm. "Don't run away again. Talk to me."

She sent him a withering glance. "You have got to be kidding. Let go of my arm."

"Rosemary, is that you?"

Oh, good lord.

Dean let her go, and Rosemary unclenched her gritted teeth to smile limply at the new arrival. Irene Gould, a regular participant at the library's book club approached the pharmacy counter. "Hello, Irene."

"Darling girl! The book club has been so worried about you. We heard you have that awful flu that's going around. Are you better?" she asked.

"Yes," Rosemary lied. "Doing fine."

"Oh, good. Listen, darling, I won't be at the library this Thursday. I'm going on a seniors' bus trip to Portland. We're touring the Chinese Garden and eating dim sum in China Town."

Rosemary nodded politely, acutely aware that Dean was listening to every word. To him, Irene said, "You make sure she goes home with vitamin C and zinc. We want our librarian back."

"I'll make sure," Dean murmured pleasantly enough.

The moment Irene left, Rosemary reached again for the items on the counter. This time Dean grabbed her wrist and held on tight.

"You work at the library? That's where you've been all this time?"

"Let go of my wrist," Rosemary ordered, looking up, but if

Dean heard her, he gave no indication. His attention lowered, riveted now on the goods rather than on her. With his free hand, he extracted from the pile of cough drops and candies one of the two EPT test boxes.

Panic turned Rosemary's body cold. Thoughts ran through her mind so quickly, she couldn't pin one down.

"It's for a friend," she blurted. "A friend who thinks she might be pregnant and doesn't want to be alone when she finds out." The fib she'd prepped in case she ran into anyone she knew rolled off her tongue before she could think twice. "Her husband's out of the country, so I said I'd bring along a pregnancy test…."

"And cough drops?"

"Those are mine. I've been sick."

"Maybe you should see a doctor." He studied her. "But make it an ob-gyn." His expression was somber. "Your nose turns red when you're lying."

Chapter Three

Her ears turned red, too.

A blush infused her cheeks, and her eyes began to glisten.

Dean sensed her genuine panic and confusion; he'd have liked to comfort her, but he had his own teeming emotions to deal with. How many weeks ago had they met? *Ten.* Anything could have happened since that night. Anything could have happened before. He knew so damn little about Rosie or her lifestyle, yet when he looked from the EPT box to her eyes, he was certain she was purchasing the test because of their night together.

Frustration tightened his gut. For weeks he had tried to find her, never realizing she worked less than a mile from the building on Main where he worked and lived.

She'd run out on him after a night filled with passion, had bolted as soon as she'd recognized him in the market and obviously wanted nothing to do with him now. And still when he looked at her he felt something he almost never felt: need. An interest and desire and hope that weren't matched anywhere else in his life.

"Where did you go?" he asked.

"Back to my real life."

When he'd woken to find her side of the bed empty, he'd considered a number of possible scenarios: she was married; she had an appointment she couldn't break; he had been a disappointing lover. Remembering her reactions to him, he felt safe discarding the latter scenario, but if it was true, he wanted another chance.

Frustration made his chest muscles ache when he realized how eager she was to escape the pharmacy. Red splotched her cheeks under her crazy pink hat, and her eyes—which still reminded him of candy—refused to meet his.

Talk to me. I've been looking for you for weeks.

Letting her go, he yanked a bag from beneath the counter and packed most of Rosie's items inside. He slid the EPT into his pocket.

He needed to tell her about Amanda, but they had other business to attend to first.

"Come on."

"What?" She shook her head. "I'm not going anywhere with you."

"Polly!" he called to a young woman stocking a shelf nearby. The girl, a teenager who'd worked for him the past two summers, loped over. "Ask Millie to come back and man the pharmacy for a while while you stay up front. I'm taking a break."

"Sure thing." Polly smiled at him then looked at Rosie. "Oh, hi, Ms. Jeffers! I didn't recognize you in that hat. It's awesome."

Rosie nodded, obviously dismayed at being seen by yet another person. Dean used her discomfort to his advantage.

"Ms. Jeffers and I have some business to take care of. We'll be upstairs if anyone needs us." He stared at her. "Right?" he demanded softly.

Rosie's jaw clenched, but she accurately read his expression: he wasn't going to let this go. If she left, he'd follow, sooner or later. Probably sooner.

"Right." The word barely emerged through her gritted teeth.

Good enough.

"If you'll follow me, Ms. Jeffers." Dean walked around the counter and toward the stairwell leading to his apartment above the pharmacy. At least now he knew her last name and place of employment. And strangely, although he was about to take a pregnancy test with a woman he barely knew, he suddenly felt more optimistic than he had in weeks.

As he walked away, Rosemary sweltered beneath her winter clothing and an even more cumbersome layer of embarrassment. She felt hot, apprehensive and foolish.

"I'm bringing my friend an EPT...and some cough drops..." What a dork! She was an awful liar, which was why she hadn't fibbed since she'd failed to complete a book report in fourth grade and told her teacher it got ruined when her mother washed her backpack.

Dean appeared about as convinced as Mrs. Karp had been. Seeing him again while she was trying to ascertain whether she was pregnant with his child had quite simply sent her into a flight-or-fight panic.

Hesitating before she followed him, Rosemary dug all the cough-drop bags from her purse and returned each one to its peg. The cashier had not rung them up, and while Rosemary might be a woman of questionable judgment, she was no shoplifter. She had allowed her ex-husband's treachery to turn her into someone she was not: a woman who spent the night with a total stranger. Whatever happened now—whatever the pregnancy test revealed—she was going to reclaim her former integrity.

Dean reappeared at her side. "What are you doing?"

"Returning these things. The cashier didn't ring them up, and I don't need them."

"Okay." He watched her a moment then said, "I'll be right back." When Rosemary was placing the last bag of cough drops on its hook, Dean returned, holding a small rectangular box. Another EPT test, but a different brand. "This one is more accurate," he informed her stoically. "So I'm told."

Rosemary eyed the box. "You have experience with this," she concluded darkly.

"Not personally, no. I'm a pharmacist. My customers talk to me."

Rosemary knew she had no right to judge. She was as responsible as he for the fact that she was about to pee on a stick. But at least she wouldn't be *engaged to somebody else* when she got the results.

"I don't have any experience with this, either," she blurted. "This isn't something I've done before."

Dean's brows rose. "No kidding?" He tilted his head toward the cough drops she'd hastily replaced. "You were so smooth purchasing the EPT I never would have guessed."

Rosemary flushed. "I mean, I don't have experience with *needing* to buy one. I don't do…what we did. I don't go to bars, and I don't go home with men. Just for the record."

"I see." His blue eyes, as placid as a summer sky, glowed with gentle humor. "Well, just for the record, I didn't think you did, Rosie."

The night they'd met she had told him to call her Rosie, though no one who knew her well used that nickname. For that single evening, she had wanted to be someone different, someone more frivolous, someone who didn't weigh out each decision as if it would have an effect on national security.

His lips edged into a smile that reminded her of his kisses, which had felt like conversation, as if he'd been speaking to her with each press of lips.

He had held her in the dark of early morning, and after his breath had steadied in her ear, she'd lain awake, bewildered by the fact that the most passion she'd ever experienced had happened in the arms of a stranger.

Frightened by the burgeoning desire to turn their single night into something more meaningful, she'd eased out from beneath his heavy arm and the leg he'd slid over hers. Then she'd gotten dressed and left, attempting to put the evening in perspective: she'd made a mistake. She had slept with a man she did not know, who had picked her up in a bar. Better to chalk it up to experience than to turn it into something it wasn't. So, she had decided to go home, shower and take a vow of chastity.

And that was before she'd seen him with another woman.

Remembering that she was a train wreck when it came to judging a man's character, Rosemary nodded to the EPT in Dean's hand and said, "If you'll give me that, I'll let you know what happens."

"You can take the test here."

Incredulous, she shook her head. "In a public restroom?" Her gaze darting furtively, she lowered her voice. "Are you nuts? I would think that you, even more than I, would want to be as discreet as possible. You're a pharmacist. People have to trust your judgment."

Tall, square-shouldered in his white lab coat and looking impossibly composed under the circumstances, Dean raised a brow. "That's never been a problem. And, no, not in a public restroom. There's a private bathroom upstairs."

"I have a private bathroom at home. I'll call you."

The friendly humor in Dean's eyes dimmed. "We took the risk together—we can find out the result together."

Before she could protest again, he added, "Humor me. If the result is negative, we never have to see each other again. Unless you need a prescription filled."

And if the result is positive?

What was he going to say and how was he going to react if the thin pink line appeared? Rosemary, if she'd had the option, would have preferred to find out over the phone. Or by email.

"It might help to have time to process the information on our own."

He shoved a hand through his hair, ruffling the brown waves. "Look, I'm as out of my element here as you are. Let's get this part done right now. We'll have the rest of the day to 'process.'"

The bells at the front of the store jingled again and happy voices filled the pharmacy. Rosemary didn't want to discover whether they were going to be heading in her and Dean's direction. "All right, all right. Let's go."

She was rewarded with one of the calming smiles that doubtless made every spoonful of medicine he parceled out to his customers go down more easily.

"This way," he said and headed to a staircase that led to the building's second story.

Trepidation made Rosemary's legs feel like lead weights. Her anxiety mounting with each step she took, she followed Dean to a single door at the top of the stairs and stood beside him on the landing as he unlocked the door and pushed it open.

"What is this?" she asked as the open door revealed an attractive living room.

"My apartment."

"You live here?" Being in the pharmacy with him was

bad enough. She did not want to be alone with Dean in his home.

Pocketing the keys again, he winked at her. "I can walk to work. Plus, it's only me, Buff and Calamity up here, and we don't take up a lot of space."

"Buff and Calamity. Buffalo Bill and Calamity Jane?"

Stepping back so she could enter, he smiled more broadly. "Exactly. My fish. I don't have enough space for a dog, and I kill plants, but the fish and I have been together so long they're almost fossils."

Rosemary crossed the threshold of the apartment with all the momentum of sap trying to move *up* a maple tree. The room was attractive, with an exposed brick wall and handsome furniture, but her anxiety turned everything sort of fuzzy.

Three steps in, she turned to him. "Look, I do not belong here. It isn't right." *And why was he so damned composed, anyway?* Seeing no point in quibbling, she hit him with her best shot. "Engaged men should be with their fiancées, not with other women. I can't imagine that your fiancée would be okay with the fact that I'm here, much less—" she lowered her voice and hissed again "—with the reason for it."

Dean plowed fingers through his hair then dragged his hand down his face. He also winced.

Crossing her arms, Rosemary waited. Caught red-handed. She'd give him a minute to try to wriggle out of it then take her test kit and go.

"I'm not engaged, Rosie. I was," he hastened to add before she could respond. "We called it quits two days ago."

She was surprised, but hardly placated. "That's two and a half months too late," she pointed out. "You should have called it quits *before you slept with someone else.* And for the record, it is not fair to 'the other woman' not to *tell* her she's the other woman. Some people believe women should stand together, not destroy each other's lives."

Dean shut his front door. "Wait a minute. You think I was engaged the night I met you?"

"Oh, please." Rosemary shook her head firmly. "Don't put a spin on it. Whether you were engaged then or still dating, you belonged with her, not me. I've heard every rationalization there could possibly be for cheating, and they're all bull. There is no justification for that kind of dishonesty."

"You've been cheated on?"

Rosemary stiffened. Concern turned Dean's features into his the-doctor-is-in expression that had hooked her in December.

"We're talking about *you,*" she said.

"Come sit down." He gestured toward a chocolate-colored leather sofa. "I'll try to explain."

"I don't need an explanation. I only wanted you to know how I feel about being drawn into this kind of situation."

"There was no situation when I met you, Rosie." Dean's gaze bore into her as he made sure she understood. "Amanda and I were engaged two years ago. Six months into it, we broke up when her job transferred her to Minnesota. I didn't see her again until a few weeks ago."

Rosemary blinked dumbly as she processed the information. Dean hadn't been engaged to or even dating Good English Cheddar on the night she and he had had their fling? That was excellent news. She wasn't a home wrecker.

And yet…

"You hadn't seen each other for a year and a half, yet you got engaged again in only a few weeks?" She wanted to bite her tongue the moment the words were out, because she understood exactly why she'd asked: she didn't like the idea that he had that passion with someone else. "Never mind. It doesn't matter."

"I wasn't in touch with Amanda in any way when you and I were together." Dean had a disconcertingly direct gaze when he needed to make a point. "Trust is something I take seriously."

Captured by his words and his gaze, she wished he hadn't said that. Without the specter of infidelity, he was once again the strong, attentive stranger who gave more than he took when they made love and who managed to make her feel more comfortable in her own skin than she'd felt in ages.

They stared at each other, lost for words and unsure of their next actions. Then Dean pulled the EPT box from the pocket of his lab coat. Looking down, he turned it over in his hands, and Rosemary knew that one way or another, they had to have an answer. She asked him where his bathroom was.

He extended an arm. "This way."

He seemed to think she was going to precede him to his restroom, but that was where Rosemary drew the line.

Holding out her hand, she gestured to the box. "I'll take that now."

Expecting an argument, she was relieved when all he said was, "Right," and handed the test kit to her.

She progressed slowly down the indicated hallway, feeling more surreal with each step. The only comfort she could dredge up was the knowledge that if she hadn't gotten pregnant in ten years of marriage, it was unlikely Dean had gotten the job done in a single night.

"Rosie."

Nearly jumping when she heard her name, she turned.

He stood with his hands in his pockets, his brows drawn together, even features awash in concern. "Good luck."

For a moment they were comrades, and even though they were bonded by what both now surely viewed as a colossal mistake, Rosemary felt less alone.

She managed a brief smile. "You, too."

Entering the bathroom, she closed the door, sending up a prayer that in just a few minutes all this would be over.

* * *

As Rosemary disappeared from the hallway, the ghost of her frightened smile gave Dean a physical ache.

Immediately after the words *good luck* had left his lips, he'd realized he wasn't sure what kind of luck he was hoping for.

March in eastern Oregon was a cold state of affairs, but Dean began to perspire as if it were August in the Everglades. He wanted to phone someone right now—his sister-in-law, perhaps, or maybe his brother—someone to whom he could confess, *I may have a pregnant woman in my apartment, and I think...that would be okay.*

For weeks he had looked for Rosie, returning to Tavern on the Highway on the off chance he would see her there again. He'd realized the night he met her that she didn't frequent the place, but hoped he might run into one of her friends. He'd grilled every bartender and all the servers about the women, appearing, he was certain, like a stalker, but he hadn't cared. Looking for her—and, when he wasn't looking for her, thinking about her—became his primary occupation. And then Amanda had shown up.

Glancing at his watch, Dean wondered if he ought to offer to time the test for Rosie.

Yeah, she's in there hoping you'll hover.

With restless fingers, he rubbed his temples. Love had never been easy for him—a congenital defect, apparently, which both he and his younger brother had inherited. Fletcher, however, was married now and, as unlikely as it seemed, he had become a devoted father to the three children from his lovely wife's first marriage. Claire Dobbs Kingsley had turned Dean's bad-tempered half brother into the proverbial pussycat. It hadn't been easy, and it had come about only because Fletcher had been forced to wed.

Inexplicably, Fletcher was in a marriage of convenience that had turned into a union of souls.

Consciously exhaling, Dean knew he hadn't breathed properly since the day he'd read his father's will and discovered that Victor Kingsley required each of his two sons to marry or lose what they loved most—in Fletcher's case, the ranch that had been in his mother's family for generations; in Dean's case, the building in which he now stood.

Ironically, Fletcher had been the one who had seethed over the will, refusing at first to abide by its dictates. Dean, on the other hand, had quickly reconciled himself to a marriage of convenience. Why not? He'd never been impetuous, was not prone to infatuation and seriously doubted his capacity to fall head-over-heels in love. He'd been involved in a few longer relationships; no one had ever broken his heart.

He had an excellent career, a good life. He was only deficient when it came to love, but at least he knew it. Therefore, a marriage of minds and shared values, a relationship entered into because both parties considered it mutually beneficial, would be less a hardship than attempting to fulfill some woman's dream of true love. He disliked hurting people.

Mentally, at least, he'd accepted his late father's mandate, relieved to know he would secure title to the building in which he both lived and made his living. He had plans for the block-long set of storefronts, plans that would benefit both the immediate community and beyond.

So when Amanda, his former fiancée, had shown up with several clearheaded reasons why they should rekindle their engagement, he'd told her about the will. The unromantic marriage directive hadn't fazed her a bit. And he had told himself he had no right to be disappointed by that fact.

A slow creak announced the opening of the bathroom door, and Dean's pulse zoomed. He cast around for something to do so he wouldn't look as if he'd been standing idle, waiting for Rosie, then recognized the absurdity of the thought and remained where he was.

He'd rebroken his engagement to Amanda shortly after seeing Rosie in the market. Without divulging the details, he'd told Amanda that the woman from the market was someone he'd "dated" and was not yet over. She'd questioned him, argued, pointed out that he had to be married in just a couple of months or default on the will, but not once had she tried to hang on to their relationship by saying she loved him. Ending their engagement—again—hadn't been nearly as difficult as it should have been.

It seemed to take an aeon for Rosie to emerge from the bathroom, an aeon during which Dean once again wondered what he was hoping for tonight.

Rosie's desire for a negative result on the test was clear and fervent; how could he hope for anything different?

She entered the hallway, adjusting the strap of her purse securely on her shoulder as she headed toward the living room. Dean's heart pounded like the hooves of a thousand horses.

In her left hand, she carried the test stick like a spoon with an egg on it, moving so cautiously it appeared she was afraid the slightest jostle might tamper with the results.

As she approached, Dean offered a supportive nod.

Rosie looked exhausted, as if she needed a stiff drink or a long vacation. Dark shadows rimmed her eyes, marring the silky skin he remembered so well. He wished he had the right to take her in his arms as he had that night.

Whatever had happened to change her mind about him, his attraction to her had not lessened. He didn't expect it to now. Silently, he vowed to see her smile genuinely at least once before she left tonight. In the meantime, he read the stick she handed him. His breath caught and held.

Instantly, his world calmed as he read the results. The thundering hooves slowed and then grew still in his chest. Every tense muscle released. For the first time in a damned long while, he knew exactly what he wanted, and it was exactly what he was getting.

One thin pink line.

Congratulations, Dean Kingsley. You're going to be a father.

Chapter Four

"You have got to be kidding me." Fletcher Kingsley gaped at his older brother. "You knocked someone up? In a one-night stand? *You?*"

Disbelief and—undeniably—enjoyment mingled in Fletcher's expression.

Dean began seriously to regret coming to his brother for "support." For too long Fletcher had played the badass while Dean had enjoyed a golden-boy image around town. Expecting Fletcher not to gloat now had obviously been unrealistic.

"I'll be damned." Fletch shook his head. "I'd guess this is about the will, but that would *really* be out of character." He narrowed his eyes, scrutinizing his brother closely. "It's over with Amanda, I take it?"

"It was over *before* I knew about the pregnancy."

Fixing one of his sons' lariats, Fletcher worked deftly with the rope while muttering, "Thank God for small favors. That would have been a marriage made in hell."

"Fletcher!" Claire Kingsley emerged from the house, shouldering open the screen door, a tray of refreshments in her hands and a look of gentle admonishment on her pretty face.

As the screen door creaked then slapped shut behind her, Fletcher hopped to his feet, taking the tray while Claire repositioned a small table next to Dean's chair.

Dean smiled. His brother had struck gold when he'd met the woman who was now his bride of three months. Fletcher was a new man, happy down to his bones.

"I like Amanda," Claire stated as she set out a pitcher of lemonade, glasses and a plate of homemade molasses snaps. "I know she seems chilly at times—"

"Iceland is chilly," her husband interjected, "Amanda could freeze lava."

"Fletcher!" Shaking her head, Claire poured lemonade. "I know for a fact that beneath her defenses, Amanda is a romantic."

Fletcher coughed loudly as he resumed his seat. Dean didn't want to disrespect his sister-in-law, whom he had come to care for deeply, but even he had a hard time reconciling Amanda with *romantic.*

"How do you know?" he asked, accepting a glass of lemonade.

Fletcher winced. "Please don't go there."

Pinching her husband's earlobe while she smiled at her brother-in-law, Claire replied, "Amanda comes to the bakery every couple of days. No matter what else she buys, she always, always gets two strawberry thumbprint cookies. I'm sure those are for her."

Dean looked at Fletcher for clarification. His brother rolled his eyes. "Wait for it."

"We use a heart-shaped cookie cutter and add jam to the dough so the cookies turn pink," Claire explained. "She's feeding the little girl inside her. The one who still dreams of pink hearts and true love."

Dean stared.

Fletcher ate half a molasses snap in one bite. "Claire believes every baked good tells a story."

"It does. Which is why you like bear claws." She put a hand on Fletcher's shoulder. "They sound scary, but inside they're sweet as sugar."

Fletcher, who had indeed sounded scary before being transformed by his wife, grinned. "Can't argue with logic like that." He pulled her close against his side.

"It still doesn't mean I thought Amanda was exactly right for *you,*" Claire told Dean. "I can't imagine you spending your life with anyone other than your soul mate, will or no will."

"My current situation doesn't have anything to do with the will." Dean confirmed Fletcher's earlier assessment.

"So who's the mother of our future niece or nephew?" Fletcher's tone was amused, but his gaze turned piercing.

Eight years younger than Dean and raised by a different mother, Fletcher had never exhibited any protective instincts where his older brother was concerned. Yet protectiveness was precisely what Dean saw in the concerned gazes of his family.

"Her name is Rosie," he said. "She works at the library."

"Rosie…Rosemary Jeffers, the new librarian? The boys love her!" Claire exclaimed.

"You had a one-nighter with the new librarian?" Fletcher's frown melted, and he gave a hoot of appreciative laughter. "It figures. Even your indiscretions turn respectable."

"This one hasn't." Irritated and guilt-ridden, Dean downed half the glass of lemonade, wondering whether Rosie had told anyone yet and, if so, what kind of response she'd received.

"Are the two of you getting to know each other better now?" Claire offered him the plate of cookies.

"Not really." He accepted one of the molasses snaps, but had no appetite. His guilt swelled. "I don't even know how she feels about the pregnancy, except that she's scared. We agreed to meet in a couple of days to discuss what we're going to do."

"What are the options?" Fletcher squinted at him.

Dean rubbed his head, mussing the hair that was typically neatly combed. "I'm not certain. I don't know yet how she feels about marriage and kids."

"Meaning she could decide to terminate the pregnancy?"

"No!" Dean glared at his brother, outraged that Fletcher had asked. Then he saw Claire's expression—concerned and compassionate, as if she were a step ahead of him in her understanding of the situation—and realized he had no idea what Rosie was thinking. Could abortion be one of the responses she was considering?

"That's not what you want, then," Fletcher stated.

"No. Hell, no!" Dean realized he was firm on that. "If she doesn't want children…I'll raise the baby."

Fletcher and Claire shared a glance, and Dean could see the bubble above their heads. *Famous last words from the perennial bachelor.*

"Mom! Mom! We need cookies for our fort!"

Dean's nephew Will raced up to the porch, followed swiftly by his younger brother, Orlando.

"I want lemonade!" Orlando clambered up the heavy railing Fletcher had installed after Claire and her children had moved in. "We're invitin' Bigfoot to be in our secret club, so we need a *biiig* glass! Hi, Dad!" Orlando's exuberant rush of words ended in a smacking kiss he planted on Fletcher's lips.

Claire reached for the glasses. "Wow, Mom, that looks delicious. May we have lemonade and cookies, *please?*"

Fletcher raised a brow at his sons, and, smiling sheepishly

at their mother, they rephrased their requests. Claire happily complied, preparing a plate of cookies and three glasses of lemonade—one for Bigfoot.

"We'll see you tomorrow for Free Friday, right, Uncle Dean?" Will asked in his more customary well-mannered way.

"Absolutely, Will. It's a Kingsley tradition." A tradition Fletcher had made up the day he'd met Claire and her children. Realizing she couldn't afford to buy her kids an ice cream, and feeling guilty for the way he'd initially treated the small family, Fletcher had invented Free Fridays at the pharmacy soda fountain—one scoop of ice cream and one topping on the house, every Friday. Though it ate into his profits a bit, Dean had soon made it a regular promotion, open to the public. The benefits—the giddy smiles of kids and their parents lured by ice cream—outweighed his losses.

Fletcher rose to help Claire carry everything to the boys' tree house, and Dean watched the young family progress across the lawn, Will sticking close to his new father's side and Orlando instructing his mother to count as he performed an impressive succession of cartwheels en route to their destination. The fifth member of the family, an enchanting fifteen-month-old named Rosalind, was currently napping inside.

Lucky. That was the word that popped to mind when Dean thought of the family that had been created here on this ranch. Three children who had lost their father now had a man to love and protect them again; a woman who had been shouldering numerous responsibilities on her own had a devoted partner who would lay his life down on her behalf; and a man who formerly had had no life at all now lived as fully as anyone Dean had ever known. Love had made them all whole. Exactly as life should be.

Unlike Fletcher, who had once been the king of cynicism, Dean had always believed that a pure and endless love existed.

His doubts around the topic centered on the disbelief that such a feeling would ever happen to *him*. In thirty-five years he had never lost control of his heart.

Still, as he listened to Claire count cartwheels and Fletcher laugh at his son's antics, Dean acknowledged the firm conviction that a child should be raised in a family. And while "family" could be defined in a variety of ways, his desires were crystal clear: he and Rosie had created a baby, and that baby should turn cartwheels someday with two parents to watch him. Or her.

He stood. He'd intended to give Rosie a couple of days to process their "situation" before he spoke with her again. Bad plan, he realized now. Giving her more time to put a wedge between them would not yield the results he wanted.

And he did know what he wanted. He knew exactly.

Downing the rest of his lemonade as if it were a double shot of courage, he set the glass on the table and walked down the porch steps to say goodbye to his brother, sister-in-law and the boys. He had some business to attend to, and there was no time like the present.

Chapter Five

Rosemary had been back at work for a couple of days when Dean walked into the library. As far as she knew it was the first time he'd been here since she'd started the job in January.

Seated at the reference desk, she watched him stride through the double doors, greeting three people by name before he spotted her. Her heart began to beat too fast and too hard.

He wore his white lab coat and carried a bag from Honey Bea's Bakery. When he stopped in front of the reference desk and plopped the white bag in front of her, she strongly doubted he'd come in to ask whether the library had the latest edition of *Physician's Desk Reference.* She glanced at Circulation, where Abby was replacing a bar code, then back at Dean. *Please do not say the word* pregnant. *Do not say anything about us,* she pleaded silently, *or indicate in any way that there is or ever was an "us," or that I know you as anything other than the friendly neighborhood pharmacist.*

Her too-damn-friendly neighborhood pharmacist.

"Rosie," he greeted.

She grit her teeth. *I have got to tell him not to call me that.*

"Nice to see you again." He spoke as calmly and pleasantly as if the only place they'd ever met was a church coffee hour. Raising his voice slightly, he asked, "I wonder if you could help me find something."

She blinked. He was here as a library patron?

"Quite possibly," she murmured. "What are you looking for?" Her trembling fingers poised over the computer keyboard.

Dean leaned forward—way forward—his classic features appearing more handsome the closer he got. He dropped his voice to a whisper. "You." More audibly, he asked, "Do you have the latest Laurence Gonzales novel?" And, softly again, "When do you take lunch?"

"I believe our copy is circulating," she responded loudly to his first question. "Let me check the rest of the system." Her fingers flew across the keyboard. In a low hiss, she told him, "I am not spending my lunch hour with you. This entire library would buzz with gossip." Clicking the mouse three times in rapid succession, she returned to a voice that carried. "Yes, I'm afraid all copies are circulating. Would you like to place a hold?"

"Sounds great," he boomed for anyone nearby to hear. And then quietly, "What kind of hold do you have in mind?"

Rosemary's gaze flew to his.

He winked. "Because I was rather fond of the hold you used when—"

"Shh! Shhhhhh!" She shushed like the classic librarian. Unable to stop herself, Rosemary glanced wildly around, noting that her library was beginning to fill with the noontime regulars. When a couple of people looked over, she peeled her puckered lips back in a toothy smile.

Dean turned and smiled, as well. "Hello, Mrs. Covington," he called out, nodding to an older woman who owned more hats than anyone else in Honeyford. Today she had on a short-brimmed blue straw with morning glory and a purple butterfly springing from the wide band. "You look particularly charming today."

The octogenarian beamed, leaving her place in front of the large-print section to join them at the reference desk.

"Good afternoon, Mr. Kingsley. Miss Jeffers."

Some of the older folks in Honeyford preferred a more formal style of address, Rosemary had discovered. Ordinarily she enjoyed conversing with EthelAnne Covington and being swept into the woman's more gracious era, but today she'd give anything to clear the library of all humans. How much simpler life would be if she were left alone with her books! The most complex tome seemed like kid stuff compared to the tangled web of her current circumstances: pregnant and single only two and a half months into her job in a conservative small town.

"Is there anything I can do for you, Mrs. Covington?" she asked, hoping that if she became involved with her customers Dean would disappear.

"Why no, thank you, dear, not at the moment. I came over to speak with Mr. Kingsley, if I may." *Drat.* "I hope I'm not crossing too many boundaries by accosting my pharmacist in the library," she said to Dean with a near-girlish laugh, "but you were my next stop today."

Sensing an opportunity after all, Rosemary stood. On the verge of excusing herself, she felt her wrist caught in a masculine hold. Surprised, she gazed down stupidly at Dean's fingers as they curled around her.

"If you'll wait just a moment, *Ms. Jeffers,*" he said. "I'm not quite finished with my…questions."

To EthelAnne, he inquired graciously, "What can I do for you, dear?"

The elderly woman obviously adored the endearment.

Rosemary's wrist—no, her entire arm—began to feel hot. She needed an avenue of escape *right now.* Dean was practically sitting on her reference desk, holding her arm as if such a gesture were nothing out of the ordinary. Even if EthelAnne didn't think that was odd, someone else was bound to walk by and take notice. Then questions would begin. Questions Rosemary was nowhere near ready to answer.

When she attempted to extricate herself, Dean's casual hold tightened briefly, as if in warning. She considered picking up her stapler and wrapping him on the knuckles. Before she could make her move, his fingers began to lightly stroke the underside of her wrist, away from Mrs. Covington's view. Goose bumps shivered up Rosemary's arm.

Darn him!

"I've just been speaking to Gabrielle Coombs," Mrs. Covington said, blithely unaware of the drama in front of her. "She's on the July Fourth entertainment committee. Lovely young woman, so civic-minded."

"Yes," Dean murmured. His fingertips began to trace tiny circles while Rosemary considered the various ways she could either break free or murder him in full view of her patrons. Unfortunately her brain grew fuzzier with each slow, tantalizing circle.

"I know you're aware that your brother is Grand Marshall of our Honeyford Days Spring Festival," EthelAnne said to Dean. "We're so appreciative that he agreed. What you don't know is that a few of us 'old-timers'—" she laughed as if they really weren't old-timers at all "—in The Betterment of Honeyford Society have written a play depicting Honeyford's history. Since he's the only professional actor we know, we're wondering whether he might agree to perform a role in our theatrical sortie."

Dean's fingers ceased their circles on Rosemary's wrist. "A play," he murmured, frowning. "Uh…my brother isn't a theatrical actor, Mrs. Covington, he was a bull rider and—"

"Oh, but he's very high-profile. The cities of Bend and Sisters draw tourists throughout the year. If Honeyford can accomplish that, every business in town will benefit. And what better way to draw tourists than to offer them special events they can't find anywhere else? I'm quite certain that with the right cast we can pack the community center to the rafters." Her thin fingers fluttered like angel wings toward the ceiling. "And it's no sin to want to win." Her hands came back to rest in pretty-please position. "Will you ask him?"

Rosemary could see Dean struggling with the desire to be of service and the reluctance to approach his brother. She wondered what kind of relationship he had with his family. Who, for that matter, were his family members? She knew nothing important about him.

You know he's a generous lover.

Heat suffused her face seconds after the thought struck. Still, it was true. By the time they'd arrived at the motel, they'd both been almost comically ready to shuck their clothes. She'd been surprised by her own eagerness, though not by Dean's. Weren't most men in a hurry once they'd determined they were going to have sex?

And yet he'd been considerate, unselfish and…romantic. Rosemary wondered whether it was reasonable to call the actions of someone who didn't even know you romantic. Vi had once dated a man who, she said, could look at any woman as if she were the only woman in the world. It wasn't personal. With Dean, everything had felt personal.

Rosemary knew that her mother and sisters would, if consulted, tell her to get her head out of the clouds. The Jeffers women were historically unlucky in love. Rosemary's mother had jettisoned her own husband when her daughters were still wearing footed pajamas. She'd raised her girls to be independent, strong and, above all, realistic. Rosemary's two sisters had never, as far as she knew, believed in Santa Claus, the Tooth Fairy or any story ending in "...and they lived happily ever after." Which was why Rosemary had always felt like a disappointment to her family. She'd once set out cookies for Santa on a little dish she'd set behind a chair so her mother wouldn't see it. It had taken hours to cut out the tiny arrows she'd taped on the floor after everyone else had gone to bed, in the hope that Santa would find his snack. He hadn't. The Tooth Fairy had never taken any of the teeth Rosemary had slipped under her pillow, either, and as for "happily ever after"... These days Rosemary knew where all the fairy tales were shelved in the library, but never again would she count on real life being so accommodating.

"I share your interest in bringing more tourism to Honeyford, Mrs. Covington." Dean smiled gently at the older woman as he prepared to disappoint her. "And I'll help in any way I'm able, but I can't imagine my brother agreeing to—"

"Bridgett Kramer has agreed to sew his costume from scratch! She's an award-winning seamstress, you know," EthelAnne "It's No Sin to Win" Covington interrupted, trying to cut a refusal off at the pass. "Bridgett found a wonderful pattern for an Uncle Sam costume. It even has spats."

"You want Fletcher to play Uncle Sam?"

"Yes, and Ed Fremont will loan us a top hat that Bridgett can decorate"

"A top hat." Rosemary saw the muscles around Dean's mouth twitch. "White beard, too?"

"Of course." EthelAnne looked at Dean with exquisite hope. "You'll ask him, then?"

Dean's smile spread handsomely across his face. Rosemary

knew instantly that he was laughing at himself and his brother, rather than at EthelAnne. She wondered again what kind of family relationships he had. Fun? Casual? She couldn't recall the last time she had simply laughed with her mother or sisters. When they had dinner or got together for holidays, suits and cell phones were the order of the day. She felt herself frowning then saw Dean turn to her. He winked.

That was all—just a quick, sharing-the-joke wink—but Rosemary felt the connection all the way down to her toes. She felt connected, she realized with a jolt, connected to *him*. She didn't even have time to tell herself how absurd that was, or to get her head out of the clouds. Immediately the warm, knee-wobbling feeling spread through her.

She began to feel queasy. It might have been her pregnancy, it might have been fear, but either way Dean was responsible.

"I'll speak to him at my first opportunity," Dean promised, eliciting a clap of delight from EthelAnne, whose nails, Rosemary noted dimly, were painted a hopeful peony-pink. "May I ask you for a favor now, Mrs. Covington?"

"Why, certainly!" EthelAnne's eyes sparkled with eagerness.

"Do you think you could help convince this lovely lady to have lunch with me?" Rosemary's eyes widened as he gestured to her, his eyes flashing with bald interest. "I haven't had a chance yet to welcome our new librarian to town, and as president of the Chamber of Commerce, I consider it my responsibility."

There might have been a couple of decades between EthelAnne Covington and her last date, but she didn't miss Dean's true intent. She looked between the two of them, clearly delighted, and Rosemary felt her anxiety spike to out-and-out panic.

"That's not necessary." She held up a hand, shaking her

head at the same time. "We're a library—we don't deal in any kind of commerce, so it's not your responsibility—"

EthelAnne laughed. "Oh, dear, you're very literal. Dean is one of Honeyford's most conscientious citizens. I'm sure he won't sleep a wink until he's performed his civic duty."

The laugh lines around Dean's mouth deepened, but he raised his brows innocently. Rosemary's brain scrambled for a way out and latched on to "too much work" as an excuse, but she never got to utter it.

Irene Gould, who led the book club that met in the conference room every Tuesday evening, approached the reference desk and exclaimed, "How lovely! Three of my favorite people in one location!"

Rosemary winced. Why did everyone sound as if they were speaking through megaphones today? "May I help you, Irene?" she said quickly. "Do you have a question?" *Because this is the reference desk, after all, not a singles' bar.*

"We were just convincing Miss Jeffers to—"

Oh, for the love of heaven…

"—allow Mr. Kingsley to accompany her to lunch. As a gesture of welcome." EthelAnne filled Irene in on the topic du jour.

Behind purple-framed glasses, Irene's blue eyes rapidly assessed the situation. "Wonderful idea! The diner has a sublime mulligatawny soup today."

Dean reached for the white bag he'd brought with him. "Actually I picked up sandwiches at Honey Bea's." This time when he made eye contact with Rosie his expression was more sympathetic than humor-filled or victorious.

Less than ten minutes later, Rosemary and Dean were walking side by side down C Street.

"I know I should apologize," he admitted, his voice deep and smooth, "but I can't claim true repentance."

The late-winter day was crisp, but sunny. Rosemary shoved

her hands in the pockets of the thick periwinkle cardigan she'd grabbed on her way out of the library.

"I was under the impression that Honeyford is a conservative town," she complained. "Doesn't anyone care that you were *engaged* just a few days ago?"

"Very few people knew about my engagement, Rosie. We hadn't officially announced it yet, and Amanda lives and works in Salem. She doesn't particularly care for small-town life, so generally we got together in the city. The night you saw us in the market was one of the rare exceptions when she came here."

Their shoes crunched along the gravel that substituted for a sidewalk on a portion of the street.

"Were you planning to move to Salem?" Rosemary asked. If he had, she might never have met him again, even after she'd discovered she was pregnant with his baby. Would that have been better?

They crunched a few more steps, and Dean responded, "We were going to commute to be together on weekends."

He was staring straight ahead, frowning. His former marriage plans were none of her business. Zero. Not a bit. But she'd been married to a man who had worked so much that they'd had a weekend marriage even though they'd lived in the same house seven days a week. They had lost their connection to each other years before the marriage had ended. She wished she'd seen it sooner.

"Marriage has to take place seven days a week," she said, "wherever you are. But it would be a lot harder if you weren't even in the same town. Everyone takes for granted that love will get them through the hard times." She shook her head. "It won't. Love comes and goes—that's natural. If the commitment to an ideal isn't there—" Hearing the fervor in her voice, Rosemary stopped. She felt Dean's gaze on her.

"How long were you married?" he asked quietly.

Panic gurgled through her. Her marriage was too private, too confusing and too much a failure to discuss. "Who said I was?"

Dean's hand grasped her elbow, firmly stopping her when she would have kept walking. He faced her, and she stared at his chest, but he wasn't having any of that, either. Tucking a finger under her chin, he raised her face.

His expression was serious, direct. "One thing we can be with each other is honest," he said. "That's one thing we *should* to be. Our child ought to have parents who talk to each other, at the very least."

The mention of *their* child reminded Rosie that something much larger than her feelings or his was at stake. For better or worse, she had to find a way to get along with this person that one aberrant, passionate night had permanently affixed in her orbit. Still, there had to be boundaries.

"I honestly don't want to discuss my marriage," she said, meaning what she said without saying it meanly. "Not right now."

He wasn't happy with her answer, but he accepted it. "All right. I'm a willing listener if you change your mind." He let go of her chin, glancing at the sky and looking, she thought, like the leader of a lion pride, testing the air to see what the pride's next move should be. When he glanced back to her, she had to give herself a mental shake.

"I took a long lunch break today," he told her. "Half an hour to convince you to join me, and an hour for us to eat and talk." The appealing, self-mocking smile curved his lips again. "I figure we both have about fifty-five minutes left. My place is close by, or it might be warm enough to sit in the park."

"Park," she chose immediately, thinking that it had taken her a decade of marriage to accept that men didn't like to sit and talk. Just her luck that she'd had a one-night stand with a man who wanted to get chatty. At least if they went to the park, where there might be other people enjoying the spring day, she'd feel safer. After days—and nights—deliberating, she had decided how she wanted to handle her pregnancy and his involvement with the baby, assuming he insisted on any. In a public place his reaction would necessarily be tempered, and that was a good thing. Because she was darn sure he wasn't going to like her plan one bit.

Chapter Six

Dean had never in his life wanted anything as much as he wanted to break down the wall Rosemary Jeffers had erected around herself…and his baby.

The child growing inside her was his, and whatever else might be right or wrong about their relationship took a backseat to that singular fact. A month ago, engaged to Amanda for reasons more practical than idealistic, he'd considered a future without children and had thought he might be fine focusing on his business, his plans to open a community health cooperative and spending time with his new niece and nephews. His life would be full enough.

Now fatherhood was an imminent reality. That changed everything, including his approach toward Rosie. Getting past her defenses wasn't an option: it was a necessity.

"The park is up Fifth Street," he said, pointing as they approached Main. Deliberately, he tempered his ground-eating strides to more closely match the steps she took—short and reluctant, as if she were shuffling to her own guillotine. "It's got covered picnic tables and a gazebo."

"I know. I walk by it when I go to work."

"Speaking of work, is that what brought you to Honeyford?"

"Yes."

When she declined to elaborate, Dean persisted. "I'm sure library jobs are hard to come by in this economy, but even so there are people who would resist living in a town of under two thousand. Particularly young, beautiful, single women."

He saw her thin, dark brows arch in surprise, watched a pink blush stain her ivory cheeks, and felt both pleased and annoyed that someone as lovely as she would be surprised to hear a man refer to her as beautiful.

He put a hand beneath her elbow as they traversed Main, but released her once they were safely across.

"Were you coming from another small town?" he asked, determined to discover, one way or another, how she had lived—and with whom—prior to moving to Central Oregon. And prior to showing up at Tavern on the Highway.

"I grew up in Portland," Rosie revealed hesitantly. "I've never lived anywhere but a city."

Dean whistled. "From Portland to Honeyford. Kind of like switching from triple-shot espresso to decaf."

Rosie laughed, and he liked the sound of it. "So you stayed in Portland after school," he prompted. "Where did you meet the women who were at the Tavern with you?"

"We went to high school together."

"It says a lot that you've remained friends through the years. Are you pretty loyal in general?"

Rosie seemed to relax a bit as they moved away from Main Street. She considered his question. "Yes. I'm loyal." She slanted a glance at him. "And, no, I am not going to discuss my marriage with you, and, yes, I know that's where you're going with this."

He laughed. "Still, the least you can do is tell me whether you were a free agent the night we met. Because I'm concerned that *you* might have compromised *me*."

"*You're* concerned?"

"I already told you that you have nothing to worry about. Care to put my mind at ease? I'd hate to go to my grave thinking I was 'the other man.'"

She shook her head, appearing partly amused, and partly *be*mused. "Reassuring my one-night stand," she murmured. "You boy toys are a lot more high maintenance than I knew."

"It's hard not knowing where you stand. We're sensitive that way." Call him old-fashioned, he liked being reminded that he was her first and, so far, only fling. "So?" He waggled his brows, inviting her answer.

"You can sleep like a baby tonight. I was a completely free agent."

A knot of tension in Dean's chest began to loosen at the news. "On the rebound from anyone?"

"Dean…" she warned, still prickly about getting personal despite the fact that they'd already been about as personal as a couple could get. He decided not to back down.

"It's that darn sensitivity issue again. How about you humor me this one time?"

"I have a feeling that humoring you 'one time' is like handing a six-year-old one M&M and expecting him not to ask for another."

Laughter dissolved the rest of the knot. "You're right."

"I wasn't on the rebound. I hadn't been in a relationship at all for a couple of years. And that's all I'm saying," she hastened to add. "So move on now."

"Okay. We'll talk about neutral things until we get to the park."

"The park is only a block away."

"Yeah." He clucked his tongue regretfully. "That's the problem with small towns. The geography makes a lengthy neutral discussion almost impossible."

She cocked her head, looking adorable, he decided. Finally she merely shook her head at him, but he noticed her lips twitching.

When they reached the park, they had a choice between having their lunch at the picnic tables or in the gazebo. Rosie chose the gazebo, a fact he filed away for future use. Gazebos were, after all, pure small-town romance.

Dean couldn't claim a wealth of experience in the realm of romancing a woman. Amanda had been decidedly "anti-artifice," as she referred to the trappings of courtship. His sister-in-law's appraisal that Amanda was a romantic at heart because she had a penchant for pink cookies didn't jive a bit with what he'd experienced of his former fiancée, but now he wondered whether he hadn't tried hard enough to turn their engagement into more of a courtship. The motivation hadn't been there, on either side.

With Rosie, the motivation was a continuous hum.

He couldn't look at her without remembering the sight of her in bed, the feel of her beneath him and the half surprised, half uncontrollable sounds of her pleasure.

That's what he wanted again. He'd wanted it about every fifteen minutes since that night. He wanted it right now, before lunch, in the gazebo if necessary and with as little foreplay as possible.

And then he'd romance her. He'd give her all the hearts, flowers, candlelight and whatever else a woman wanted until the thought of him, of *them,* filled her mind the way it had been filling his. And then—

God willing, sex again.

Sitting demurely on the gazebo's curved bench, Rosie folded her hands on her lap.

Dean loosened the tie he'd worn to work. *You are lusting after the mother of your child.*

Seemed like a good sign.

He sat beside her, leaving enough space between them for her to feel comfortable. He had always, after all, been a polite man. Self-control had never been a chore for him; it came naturally.

He wanted to push her cardigan aside and dip his hand into the loose neckline of her dress, remembering exactly what he'd find inside. And how she had felt, cupped in his palm. And how damn perfect she'd looked to him.

Quickly, he unrolled the white bakery bag. "Turkey?" His voice sounded as if he'd dragged his vocal chords across sandpaper. Sweat popped out along his upper lip. He wiped it away, clearing his throat. "It's warm today."

Rosie dragged the edges of her sweater closer together. "I'm a little chilly." Taking the sandwich he offered her, she gave him a weak smile. "This looks good. Thank you."

"My pleasure. My sister-in-law works at Honey Bea's." He passed her a napkin and a bottle of sweetened iced tea. "She's hoping to become a full partner this year."

"I've been in the bakery once or twice." Delicately his lunch mate peeled the plastic wrap from a thick, soft roll Dean's brother had dubbed The Rozzy Roll in honor of his toddler daughter, who loved to gnaw them until they were paste. Rosie smiled ruefully. "Generally I try to stay out of bakeries. Also ice-cream parlors and candy stores. I have a runaway sweet tooth."

"Your figure hasn't suffered." He squelched an urge to leer. "Take my word for it."

She ducked her head briefly, making it impossible to gauge

her reaction then said, "I'm going to have to be more careful than ever now that I'm—"

Abruptly she cut herself off, as if refusing to discuss the situation with him would make it less real, or would make him less a part of it.

"Pregnant," he finished for her. Polite or no, he by-God wasn't going to let her skirt the issue. If he did, she'd avoid him until it was time for her to push his baby out.

"I'll remember that you're pregnant, Rosie, whether you mention it or not." Though there was no one nearby to overhear, he spoke quietly, intently, declaring the intimacy that linked them more loudly than if he'd shouted. "And I do recall…in detail…how you got that way. I remember every time I look at you." Seeing her eyes grow big and round, he hammered home one final point. "Eat. We Kingsleys love a good meal."

He could tell by her expression that she got the drift: this baby was going to be a Kingsley, and he was going to be a very present father. He hadn't considered the day-to-day reality of that nor had he considered any alternatives, but now that he'd spoken he knew exactly where he stood. The only question worth contemplating was whether they were going to parent together or apart.

And, what he was going to do about the damned will.

Looking away, though he wanted nothing more than to crush her to him and see if she tasted as good as she had that night, he concentrated on unwrapping the sandwich instead of the woman. The hunger in his stomach was weak and puny compared to another, more pressing appetite.

All his adult life, Dean had prided himself on being a gentleman. Animals reacted from instinct; human beings used reason to control their behavior. Fletcher had taken the opposite tack for his first twenty-eight years, generally acting rashly and claiming he left the thinking to Dean. For the first time, Dean envied his younger brother's lack of caution.

The muscles throughout his midsection clenched. Controlling himself with effort, he took a bite of turkey with avocado and Havarti, but his favorite sandwich was tasteless today.

"I have been giving a great deal of thought to our…situation." The voice that came from his right was soft and hesitant, almost as if Rosie were speaking to herself.

At least she said "our" situation, he told himself, swallowing the bite of sandwich and turning toward her fully. "And?"

Her fingers gripped the sandwich. "What you said before—about this town being too small to have a neutral conversation—I know you were being facetious, but it's true in a way. Honeyford's not tiny, but two people with jobs as public as ours are bound to the object of gossip if someone finds out about…"

"Our situation," he supplied wryly.

"Yes."

"Mmm-hmm. I'd say it's more a matter of *when* they find out, not *if.*" He watched her closely, his breath held, feeling clear as a bell that he'd never asked a more important question or waited for a more seminal answer. "Wouldn't you?"

She pressed her lips together, taking time before she answered, and he felt as if he were hanging from the edge of a cliff, waiting for someone either to pull him to safety or pry his fingers loose, one by one.

"If I can find another job," she said, "we might not have to discuss it with anyone for the time being. It could be between the two of us while we figure out the details."

"Another job where?" he asked, hearing the tension in his voice.

"The Tacoma Public Library is looking for someone."

"Tacoma." Dean frowned. "Washington."

She picked at her sandwich, pulling out the tiniest piece of turkey, chewing carefully and swallowing before she explained, "Tacoma is a much larger city. No one there will care if a librarian is single and pregnant."

"Ah." He nodded, setting aside his sandwich. "Right. Because we're pretty provincial here. Burned a witch just last week."

She didn't smile. Just as well. He wasn't feeling particularly good-humored, either.

"I mean that I don't know anyone there, so I won't have to explain anything," she said, her voice stronger now. "And the baby won't have to worry about being the object of curiosity, or worse. When I interviewed for my job, I was told I'd be working with the community a great deal, and it was made abundantly clear that a large sector of that community is conservative." Dean opened his mouth, but she overrode him. "I don't mean 'conservative' as in 'I'd better hide all my copies of *Catcher in the Rye.*' But I was asked how I felt about stocking an abundance of G-rated books. In large print."

He frowned, but Rosie only shrugged. "A return to old-fashioned values was one of the things that appealed to me about moving to this town." She slid him a glance that was both wry and regretful. "I didn't get off to a great start. With regard to the old-fashioned values, I mean."

Dean felt a tiny, figurative knife stick him in the gut. He was the indiscretion she regretted.

"I have friends and family in Portland," Rosie continued.

"Isn't Portland several hours from Tacoma?"

"Only three."

"And Portland is three hours from Honeyford, so I'd have a six-hour drive one way to see my child," Dean pointed out, not even mentioning seeing her at this point. "There's no easy way to fly in, either." She started to respond, but this time he overrode her. "But putting the issue of visitation aside for the time being, you're proposing to move to a city where you don't know anyone, when you're on the brink of one of the biggest changes in your life."

"I told you, I have family—"

"Three hours from Tacoma. Right." Controlling his mounting frustration, Dean, too, set his sandwich aside, abandoning the notion of a friendly picnic. "Listen, Rosie—"

"No one calls me, Rosie. I meant to tell you in the library."

He had a clear memory of her introducing herself as "Rosie." *Rosie Jo,* to be exact. Noting the spreading blush on cheeks the color of vanilla ice cream, he had to smile. "That night really was an anomaly for you, wasn't it?"

"I've been cautious my entire life." She wagged her head, raising a hand to swipe at the tears that were spilling over her lashes. "And obviously I was right to be careful. One misstep and now both of our lives are in complete turmoil. I don't even understand how it happened." He quirked a brow, and her blush deepened. "I know *how.* But I've been wracking my brain—" she sniffled loudly "—and I can't remember *not* using a condom." She looked at him in question, biting her lower lip.

Immediately, his groin tightened. He wanted to soothe that worried lower lip with his own mouth. He couldn't help it: he chuckled, drawing a surprised and resentful look from her. "Sorry, but when I think about that night—which I find myself doing frequently, by the way—condoms are hardly ever the first things that come to mind." Reaching into the bakery bag, Dean pulled out a napkin, but rather than handing it to her, he brought the makeshift tissue to her nose and dabbed lightly.

When she grabbed the napkin to do the job herself, it didn't surprise him. Somehow, in some way, she had been hurt, and he was willing to bet that a man had done the deed. *You nearly messed her up for anyone else, buddy. Nearly.*

Bending over her dark, curly head while she delicately blew her nose, he murmured, "So are condoms really all you think about when you remember that night? When you remember us?"

She gasped so hard, he was afraid she might inhale the napkin. He chose not to relent.

"There is an us, you know. Like it or not, what we started that night is something that owns us both now. Two people, one cause. And, like it or not, passion made that baby you're refusing to feed. So, like it or not, I do care whether you eat. I care where my baby is going to live and how easy or difficult it's going to be to get to him. And, I care that that single night in the motel was the best sex I've ever had. In my life. Bar none. You may be over it, *Rosie,* but I'm not. Not by a long shot."

He sat up straight, reached for his sandwich again and winked at her as he took a bite.

Her eyes were wide and troubled; her soft, plump mouth formed a huge O. A pulse throbbed visibly in her neck, the rhythm reminding him more of a marimba band than a heartbeat.

Yep. He'd made his point.

"Your one-night stand lives in the same town you do, and you were together when you found out you were pregnant even though you hadn't seen each other since that night?" Daphne recapped what Rosemary had just told her, her sweet voice rising in disbelief.

"Yes," Rosemary said, trapping the cordless phone between her shoulder and ear while she rummaged through her kitchen pantry, looking for dinner.

Confused, nervous and tense as piano wire since seeing Dean earlier in the day, she had finally decided to break her silence about the pregnancy. After giving brief—very brief—consideration to phoning her mother or one of her sisters, she had decided to lean on Daphne, the only one of her friends so baby crazy that news of a pregnancy, no matter how it had come about, would be received with joyous anticipation.

"Do you feel any different?" Daphne asked with keen interest. "Do you feel pregnant?"

"I'm hungry all the time." She shoved three baked BBQ potato chips into her mouth, grabbed another handful before she made herself roll up the bag then reached for peanut-butter-stuffed pretzels.

"Are you having cravings?"

"Yeah." The potato chips did a quick disappearing act. "I'm craving food." Biting the tip off the pretzel, Rosemary sucked out the candylike nut butter. "When I'm not throwing up. I hate throwing up. But I'm dizzy and nauseous every morning the second I open my eyes. It doesn't go away until late afternoon, and then I'm ravenous the rest of the night."

"Poor baby." Daphne murmured. "What does your doctor say?"

"I haven't seen one yet. I'm going this Friday for the first time. I found an ob-gyn in Bend. That's over an hour from here, which should minimize the likelihood of anyone seeing me and realizing what's going on. Then if I get the job in Tacoma, I can move before I'm showing, and nobody has to know."

After a brief pause, Daphne commented, "I can't believe anyone would really care in this day and age. And you said Honeyford has almost two thousand people, right?"

"That's what *he* said," Rosemary grumbled darkly.

"You could probably keep it private until you're showing, if you really want to," Daphne soothed then emitted her adorable laugh, confessing, "If it were me, I'd get a Baby On Board maternity shirt and start wearing it while I was still a size six. I'd want everyone to know."

Trying to decide between mac and cheese or sardines with mayonnaise and pickle relish on rye, Rosemary made a face into the phone. "I've never been a size six. Do macaroni and cheese and sardines go together?" She was met with silence. "Daphne?"

"I'm sorry. I just threw up a little. Hey, maybe you're superhungry because you're having twins! Are there any twins in your family?"

Rosemary froze with the box of pasta in her hand. "Not on my mother's side. I have no idea about my father's."

"You should ask your mother."

"Great. Now I think *I* just threw up a little." The suggestion that she should consult with Maeve Jeffries about any aspect of this pregnancy temporarily killed Rosemary's runaway appetite. "I doubt my mother knows anything about my father's family. She used to refer to him as The Donor, and she didn't even say it in a derogatory way. She simply didn't see him as essential to our daily lives in any way. When I'd ask her about him, she'd look totally mystified and answer, 'I don't recall, Rosemary.'" Her best friends had met her mother and sisters and understood that she had not grown up conventionally. Still, she hadn't discussed her family in a while. Frowning, she replaced the box of pasta, exhausted suddenly. "My parents must be the only two people on the planet capable of bringing three children into the world without having a single memorable conversation."

Daphne, who had the kind of relationship with her dad that every fatherless little girl dreamed of, responded with her customary quiet compassion. "I'm sorry, sweetie." Then in a tone equally caring, she nudged, "I bet you want something very different for your daughter."

Whomp. As if they were playing verbal dodge ball, Daphne's comment socked Rosemary right in the gut. It was the one hit she couldn't outrun.

"Maybe I'm having a boy," she mumbled, but she knew the sex of the baby didn't matter. She'd been tagged.

It seemed to take great effort to reach the banquette in her kitchen. Sinking heavily into the cushioned seat, she gazed through fluttering white eyelit café curtains. The street was so peaceful this time of evening. This town was everything she'd dreamed of as a girl when she was growing up in the city.

"I'm scared," she whispered.

"I know." Daphne, who was a legal secretary, but should have been a therapist, asked with no judgment in her tone, "How did you get pregnant? It's a little confusing, given that he's a pharmacist and you're an educated woman. I mean, did the pill fail and the condom broke?"

"I haven't been on birth control in two years. And…" Rosemary hesitated, knowing how utterly irresponsible, immature and downright reckless she was going to sound. "I think we forgot to use the condom at one point."

"At one point? How many times that night did you, um, need a condom, if you don't mind my asking?

Rosemary closed her eyes. "Four. But I think time number three was the problem."

Daphne hooted. "Rosemary Josephine Jeffers!"

"I know, I know!" Her forehead lowering all the way to the wood table, Rosemary groaned. "It was a crazy night. It seemed to exist in its own cosmos." She shook her head against the cool wood. "I sound like I'm seventeen on prom night. Except that I was a lot smarter on prom night. I stayed with the group."

Sitting up, she gazed at two deer picking their way across her front lawn. The does' skinny legs raised and lowered with a kind of slow-motion military precision. Having their evening feed before they moved to the beds they made deeper in the pines around Honeyford, the deer would sleep for only a couple of hours at a time, their instinct for survival dictating that they never get too comfortable. Smart deer.

"The worst part is I wasn't paying close enough attention," Rosemary said, "because I felt this…trust when I was with him."

"Why is trusting him the worst part?"

"Because I didn't know him. Because he picked me up in a bar. Because he's a man, and I could have been any woman. Take your pick."

"Hmm. He didn't look at you like you could be any woman. He looked at you like he was…smitten."

Rosemary's emotions responded instantly, before her mind could overrule the reaction. A coil of pleasure sprang up from low in her belly, sending out frissons of electric longing. So much for her survival instinct.

No matter how she'd been raised, no matter how much she'd learned from her own experience or from her mother and sisters' fretful we-told-you-so's after her marriage imploded, she returned over and over to dreams of white picket fences and forever. Her sisters might be slightly rigid in their approach to life, but at least they stayed away from the kind of pain Rosemary apparently courted.

"I should have phoned Vi," she said. "She'd have been cynical. She'd have reminded me what happened the last time I trusted a man." Pain choked her voice to a whisper.

"Yes, she'd have said that. And she'd have told you that deep down men will never want the same things as women, so we should cut the poor sods some slack and use them like the toys they were intended to be. But you didn't phone Vi," Daphne pointed out. "What does your pharmacist/boy toy want to do about the baby?"

"He wants to be involved."

"How involved?"

Rosemary stood and paced to the living room, where she had no idea what to do with herself. She was so tired, she wanted to crawl into bed and so restless she thought perhaps she should go for a run. "When I told him I was considering moving to Tacoma, he said to let him know as soon as I'd made up my mind so he could start looking for employment there."

Daphne's soft intake of breath spoke volumes. "Wow. All right, don't take this the wrong way, but that's more than your family would do. It's more than your friends *could* do, Rosemary. Is he a genuinely nice guy? Because that night he seemed like a genuinely nice guy."

Rosemary halted her pacing in front of her fireplace, fingering the smooth river rock as she tried to steady her thoughts, which flashed immediately to Dean's eyes—so attentive and penetrating—and to his voice, the timbre rich with humor or deep and strong and sober as he set the ground rules for dealing with each other.

"He insists on open lines of communication," she told Daphne. "He said that if nothing else we should be honest with each other."

"Oh, my. How did that feel?" Daphne knew that Neil's dishonesty had left Rosemary with a wound that no amount of emotional suturing seemed to close all the way. "On your birthday you said you wouldn't have a relationship again until you met a completely honest man."

A dull throb filled Rosemary's temples. "Yeah, and Ginger said I'd never date again if that was my criteria."

They fell silent. Daphne had been hurt plenty by men who took one look at her perfect face and Pussycat Doll figure and were willing to tell her anything in order to start a relationship they had little intention of finishing. Daphne was a diehard romantic who had fallen hard more than once, dreaming of "forever." She'd been hurt plenty, and this past New Year's had resolved to be celibate until she heard the words "You may kiss your bride." Rosemary figured that not even Daphne would suggest she should trust a man simply because he *claimed* to value honesty and communication.

But if he values communication, what was up with that engagement of his?

"Remember when we were in high school and had to carry dolls and diaper bags everywhere for Health Ed?" Daphne's voice was soft and reminiscent.

"And we had to set a timer that woke us up every two hours for an entire weekend." Rosemary nodded at the river rock.

"Half the class didn't even complete the assignment. Vi left the baby in her backpack."

Rosemary smiled. "I remember. She said it needed a quiet place to nap."

"Right." Daphne's sweet giggle reached across the miles. "You and I were the only ones who never got tired of it." More seriously she pointed out, "You used to want a family more than anything. We've talked about the guy. The one thing I haven't heard you mention yet is whether you're happy about the baby."

Tears sprang to Rosemary's eyes. Guilt and regret swelled inside her. "I try not to think about the baby," she confessed in a miserable whisper. "I don't want to let myself. Oh, Daphne, I never, ever imagined I'd be a single mother. It makes me so sad to think about it."

"I know." Daphne's understanding made it feel as if she were in the same room. "It doesn't have to feel the way it did when you were growing up, though. You're completely different from Maeve."

Emotion made it difficult for Rosemary to speak, so she nodded into the phone.

"Right now you're frightened because you see yourself

repeating your parents' choices," Daphne said, still with the utmost kindness. "But if Dean wants to be involved, and if he's a reasonable man, maybe you could find a way to work him into your and the baby's life—peacefully. Couldn't you, Rosemary?"

Turning from the fireplace, Rosemary plodded to the downstairs bathroom, wiping the mascara from beneath her eyes. "I have no idea how to make that work, Daph. In my world, there's no precedent for peaceful shared parenting." She plucked a tissue from a box on the counter. "The Jeffers women take the praying-mantis approach."

Daphne laughed. "Well, then your choice is clear—either you set a new precedent or you bite his head off."

Rosemary produced a watery laugh. "Can I think that over and get back to you?"

Chapter Seven

Rosemary had allowed Dean Kingsley to call the shots at their last meeting. In the two days since, she had arrived at a couple of critical decisions, and she was determined that their next meeting be on her terms. She intended to be reasonable, clear and calmly unmovable in her stance.

The best-laid plans…

"Oh, my God, what do you think you're doing?" she whispered fiercely when she came upon him in one of the library's nonfiction aisles—Women's Health, to be exact—holding a copy of *What to Expect When You're Expecting.*

"Browsing," he answered, a slow smile spreading over his face as he turned toward her. "You look great in pink."

Nonplussed, she stared mutely for several seconds then came to and stabbed her finger at the book. "What are you doing with *that?*"

"I'm going to check it out." He tapped the cover. "I hear it's essential reading for pregnancy."

Darting her gaze around the immediate area, she grabbed Dean's arm and tugged him around the back end of the aisle. "Are you crazy? You cannot check that book out!"

"Is it on hold?"

"Very funny." She held out her hand. "Give it to me."

"Sorry, you'll have to get your own copy." One chestnut brow rose. "Unless you want to read it together. I might be open to that."

She thought at first that he was being glib, but the oceanic gaze that settled into hers was alarming in its authenticity, and a lightening bolt seemed to explode in her chest.

"You used to want a family like Vi wants to be CEO of Neiman Marcus," Daphne had reminded her before they'd hung up last night.

Her heart hammered unevenly. She didn't expect to have a *family* anymore, not in the traditional sense, and she was okay with that, or would be. That was one of the conclusions she'd come to last night.

Holding out her hand, she said, "Give me the book so I can check it out *privately,* and I'll bring it to you."

"When?"

"Tonight."

"Where?"

What were the chances he'd agree to meeting in Bend, an hour away?

"Try not to overthink this one, Rosie."

She glanced around. "Would you please call me Rose*mary,* like everyone else?"

He narrowed his eyes, considering. "We can talk about it later. You *may* be able to persuade me. Time and place?"

"Seven o'clock. At…Tavern on the Highway," she decided quickly.

"Sentimental."

"We're less likely to be spotted there."

"Practical *and* sentimental."

"May I have your library card, please?"

He reached for his wallet. "Okay, but just so you know, I usually share this only with women who are serious about me. I'll make an exception in your case. This time." He handed over the card. "Before I give it to you again, I'll need a definite commitment."

He arrived at the tavern early since it was Saturday, and he wanted to scope out a table as far as possible from the music and the beer. Dean found her choice of meeting locations telling.

As he pushed toward the bar, wading through the noise and memories, his mood plunged to something dull and dark around the edges. For days, ever since he'd seen Rosie…Rosemary…again—and certainly since the discovery that she was pregnant—he'd expected to rediscover the woman he'd met here in December. He'd felt sure that somewhere beneath the distance and the denial, she still existed.

Now, before she even arrived, he felt hope waning. Being here afforded him a visceral reminder of the feelings he'd had that night. He remembered Rosie Jo in vivid detail.

Rosemary Jeffers appeared to be someone else altogether.

Wedging between the patrons at the bar, he placed his order. "Obsidian Stout and—" Damn, what would she want now that she couldn't have alcohol? "Scratch the stout. Orange juice on the rocks. Two."

Waiting for the drinks, he let his gaze wander out to the dance floor. About fifteen people were line dancing, but in his mind he saw a slow dance, with two bodies moving in perfect unison, getting to know the feel of each other and the smell and the sweetness. He saw a woman with no reserve looking up at him, her lovely eyes deep and hazel and promising.

His body tightened with longing. He'd fallen for a one-night fantasy. He felt like a girl.

"Two OJs." The bartender placed the drinks in front of him. "Sip slowly."

Dean set off to locate a table, but hadn't taken more than a couple of steps when he heard an familiar, accent-laced, "Hey, *compadre*."

"Alberto." Balancing the tumblers of juice on one palm, Dean clasped his friend's hand. "I haven't seen you in a couple of months. Where've you been?"

"I was in Medford, working with *un hombre muy rico*—" he laughed "—to renovate a building." Alberto's black eyes glowed with the quiet humor that was characteristic of him. "Old brick and exposed pipes, like your building. I learned a lot that will help us." Holding a drink Dean knew was non-alcoholic, he elbowed his old friend. "I hear you're engaged now. In the nick of time. *Sí?*" he asked, his interest keen. "So the building is guaranteed."

Discomfort engulfed Dean. Alberto knew about the will Dean's father had left and about the marriage codicil that gave Dean ownership of half a block of storefronts on Honeyford's Main Street, as long as he married within the specified period of time and remained so for two years.

Alberto wanted Dean to acquire ownership of the property as much as Dean wanted it.

"When do we get started?"

Alberto's skin was the color of fine leather, lined with more care than a forty-year-old man should have confronted.

Dean met the Flores family eight years ago, when Alberto came to the pharmacy, inquiring about medicine for his daughter, Adelina. The girl had been ill for several days, treated only with home remedies due to the family's financial circumstances and a lack of education regarding health care and the state health-care system.

After listening to Alberto's nervous recitation of the young girl's symptoms, Dean insisted that his father visit the Flores family at their home. Victor Kingsley hospitalized Adelina for pneumonia immediately, but the medical intervention occurred too late.

Accompanying his father to the Flores home, Dean watched the beautiful cinnamon-skinned girl, her ribbons of ebony hair dampened with perspiration, full lips parted with the effort to breathe while her mother whispered to her in Spanish. The walls of the Flores house were cracked, patched, he had later learned, again and again by Alberto himself when he could afford the materials. The girl lay in the family's only bed; Alberto had been sleeping on the floor. Dean had felt a sharp, furious frustration as he realized the Flores family and their neighbors availed themselves of medical care only at the last possible moment—and even then, generally only for their children.

At Dr. Victor Kingsley's stoic insistence, Adelina was transported to the pediatric unit of a medical center in Bend, where she died before her tenth birthday. The Flores family was destroyed.

Alberto began drinking. Eventually his wife sought her solace with family in Mexico, and Dean found the gentle man living on the street.

"Let's have lunch this week, and I'll tell you what's going on," Dean prevaricated, hoping that by the end of the week he might have some ideas about how to salvage his plans to put a low-cost, bilingual health-care clinic in the building his father had owned.

Dean had driven Alberto to his first AA meeting. In the following months, they had spoken frequently. The idea for Clinica Adelina Community Health Care was born in these conversations and out of Alberto's desperate need to deal with what he perceived as his terrible failure.

"It looks as if another grant is going to come through." Dean watched pleasure spark in Alberto's eyes and felt some guilt about not disclosing the demise of his engagement, a crucial component in making the dream of a clinic come true. Perhaps they could find some other venue, someone willing to donate the space….

The music changed, and Alberto grinned. "Time for line dancing." He gestured to the glasses in Dean's hand. "You here with your *novia?*"

After some hesitation, Dean answered, "No. I'm expecting a friend."

They agreed to be in touch the following week, and Alberto moved on. Dean found a table far from the dance floor and waited. Precisely at 7:00 p.m., Rosie walked in.

She wore a camel-hair coat over the same skirt and sweater outfit she'd had on earlier. Curls the color of coffee beans framed her face and bounced thickly on her shoulders. She took several steps into the tavern then stopped and looked around, searching for him.

Dean's hand came halfway up then stopped. Every time he saw her, a smile rose from his chest, but she appeared as tight-laced and miserable as she had since December, and his optimism fell another notch.

One night and a baby did not turn two strangers into a couple. As much as he wanted to rediscover the woman who had smiled like the sun and whose starry eyes had sparkled with humor, it was time to admit that he may have been mistaken about her. It wouldn't be the first time that a man in his family had fallen for the wrong woman.

Was he like his father? Victor had been three-times unlucky in love. By most accounts, he had loved Dean's mother, but she had passed on when her marriage was still young and her son a mere child. There was no telling whether that marriage would have lasted. Dean barely remembered his mother, but he knew that emotional availability had not been his father's greatest gift.

Victor's second marriage, to Fletcher's mother, could only be termed a tragedy, though it had begun with the anticipation of rebuilding a family. Jule Kingsley had been more mercurial than the Oregon weather. A delight one moment, incomprehensibly distraught the next, she had harbored pain and secrets that had nearly destroyed them.

Dean studied Rosie in the subdued tavern light. Had he, like his father, fallen for a woman inherently incapable of—or chronically unwilling to—conduct a relationship in a positive, open, constructive manner?

His mood threatened to tumble further, but he pulled it up with firm resolve, setting aside his own interests. Rosie didn't want him; that was clear. Badgering her would not help matters. No matter what, his child would be raised amid respect and courtesy, with two parents who worked together to create a stable environment. A loving environment…even if they didn't love each other.

Maybe if he backed off, she'd open up. Smile more. Knock a hole or two in the wall she'd erected around herself.

Rising, Dean started toward her, promising himself that his only agenda from now on was to establish a calm cordiality between them and to formulate a sane plan for cooperatively raising the child they'd created.

Rosemary looked around Tavern on the Highway, trying to ascertain whether Dean was already there. She turned her head in choppy motions, like a bird feeling vulnerable in an open field.

After spending the rest of her workday utterly distracted by thoughts that had nothing to do with work, she had come to a firm conclusion.

Well, pretty firm….

Sort of firm….

Not really firm at all. But she believed she was making the least crummy decision she could in a really difficult situation. The thought of sharing that decision with Dean was making her a nervous wreck, however, and she wanted to get it over with quickly.

"Rosemary."

The deep voice cut smoothly through the music and talking.

Dean wore a handsome sweater in cowboy tan, an attractive complement to his blue eyes and nut-brown hair. His shoulders appeared broader out of the white lab coat, and he looked relaxed and very, very…hot.

Rosie felt a dizzying sense of déjà vu, almost as if they were about to reenact the night they'd met. Except that he'd just called her Rosemary—instead of *Rosie*—for the first time.

"I've got a table away from the noise," he said, reaching automatically to put a guiding hand beneath her elbow. Before he connected with her, however, he stopped himself, letting his hand drop back to his side.

Nodding, she followed him, aware of the feminine smiles and lingering glances of appreciation he drew along the way.

When they reached the table, she plopped her large shoulder bag onto one of the four available chairs. As she sat, she noted the drinks waiting for them.

"I ordered for us," he acknowledged. "If you'd like something else, I'll head back to the bar."

Recalling the drinks he'd sent to the table the night they'd met, she frowned. "Is it a mixed drink? I'm not having any alcohol."

"It's orange juice."

She looked at the two tall tumblers. "Which one?"

"Both."

She looked up, remembering that he was a connoisseur of Pacific Northwest microbrews. “Orange juice over beer?”

He shrugged. “You can’t drink. I’m fine with orange juice.”

“That’s nice of you.” Her ex wouldn’t have put himself out that way. Dean sat down, and Rosemary cleared her throat, wondering how to begin.

“Are you hungry?” Dean asked, drawing her attention to the Tavern’s minibuffet.

“I’m ravenous at night, but…I’m a little nervous right now. I’d like to talk first.”

His brows rose, but quickly fell again, his expression a handsome mask that hid his thoughts. He was different tonight, more subdued and…neutral. No hunger in his eyes, no humor lurking at the edges of his mouth. Rosemary told herself that a dispassionate Dean would be far easier to approach regarding the topic at hand.

She coughed lightly to clear her throat.

Then sighed.

Then she reached for her orange juice, took a shaky sip and replaced the glass on its cocktail napkin.

She folded her hands in her lap.

One of her feet began to tap madly, so she crossed her legs to quell the anxious motion.

Spit it out, Rosemary!

“I’ve been thinking about our situation all afternoon. It’s hard to think of anything else, isn’t it? I told one of my friends—she was here the night I met you—Daphne. I don’t know whether you remember?”

“The blonde.” Dean nodded. “My friend Len was smitten.”

“Oh. Well, I told Daphne what was going on. I hope you don’t mind—”

He waved the concern away. “I’d expect you to discuss a

major life event with your friends. I'd be more worried if you didn't. I assume you've told your family, too?"

She shifted uncomfortably. "No. I'd rather not tell my family until we have certain decisions ironed out."

Crossing his arms, Dean settled himself against the ladder-back chair, observing her soberly. He wasn't a husky man, but he was tall and broad-shouldered. He looked too big for the stingy piece of furniture. "Maybe," he said, "your family can help you reach those decisions."

She nearly groaned. If only he could appreciate the irony.

Her mother, after lamenting Rosemary's apparent inability to navigate birth control at the age of thirty-two, would remind her that the decision to forfeit one's independence this way lasted at least eighteen years.

One thing Rosemary had to say about Dean: at no time had he chosen the easy way out of this situation. He could have walked; she'd certainly given him the opportunity to turn a blind eye to her pregnancy.

Frowning, she folded the edges of her cocktail napkin. "We've both had a few days to let this sink in," she began, needing to know more about him before she said what she'd come here to say. "Have you—at any time—considered asking me to end the pregnancy?"

It took her a few seconds to lift her gaze from the napkin and let it focus on his face. She saw an expression she had not witnessed on him before. Blue lasers, his eyes pinned her with a steely intensity. His shoulders grew rigid, and he looked as if only a mighty effort allowed him to control his voice when he responded. "If you don't want this baby, I do. Your body is the one that has to go through nine months of pregnancy, I realize that, but you're carrying something that belongs to me, too. If you need help—with money, time, anything—I'll give it to you, but don't do anything—"

Rosemary held up a hand. "I'm not, I'm not." She shook

her head. "I asked because I wondered how committed you are to the idea of being a father." She smiled wryly. "I guess we're clear on that now."

He watched her closely a moment longer. Slowly, his shoulders began to relax.

What an interesting man he was. Never married although he was thirty-five, not above a one-night stand, yet willing to become a single father if necessary.

"Have you always wanted children?" she asked. "Or is this a philosophical conviction?"

He gave the question the consideration it was due. "I used to want children. In my twenties, I figured I'd be a father by the time I was thirty. Somewhere along the line I became less convinced, and more recently…" he hesitated "…I thought I'd marry, but wasn't sure kids were in the picture."

"That would have been all right with you?"

Again Dean gazed at her a long time before answering. "No. For a while I thought it would be, but…no." Uncrossing his arms, he leaned forward, moving his untouched orange juice to the side and resting his elbows on the table. "What about you? How eager are you to be a mother?"

That's what Daphne had asked her, and after getting off the phone with her longtime friend she'd spent the rest of last night letting the reality sink in. For as long as she could remember, she'd wanted the trappings of family life—dinners around a big table with everyone talking too much; holidays filled with chaos; summers that were lazy and laughter-filled. Neil, her ex, had convinced her that wanting to do family activities and needing to expand the family in order to do them were two entirely different things. They were already a family, just the two of them, he'd insisted, and someday they could seriously discuss the addition of children, when they were *both* ready.

Neil had decided he was ready to add a mistress before he became ready to add children, and even now, two years beyond the discovery, his betrayal still felt like a bayonet slashing at Rosemary's soul. That seemed so melodramatic, but it was true. She wished she could get over it, forget him, forget how good they had once felt. But she had pictured herself at eighty, with children and grandchildren and great-grandchildren… and with Neil, happily counting the wrinkles and the years. She had defied her family's warnings, braved their wagging heads and ignored how often the word *naive* came up in conversation so she could continue to believe in her dream.

Neil had taken much more than himself out of her life. Never before had she believed hope was something that could die; now she knew it was possible. To lose her dream, something so intrinsic to her spirit, was a feeling she never wanted to experience again.

She looked at Dean, waiting patiently for her answer. Was she eager to be a mother?

Last night, she had pictured her future with—and without—a child. She'd imagined being a single mother, in a small town and in a city…perhaps Portland, but perhaps someplace entirely new, where she would be a stranger among strangers. She'd bathed herself in the details and the feelings that had come up, trying not to judge or censor her reactions, and finally she'd found her way to what was, for her, the truth.

Being a single parent, like her mother before her, was not her dream come true. But having a child to hold, to love unconditionally, to introduce to butterflies and rainbows and monster slides and swimming pools, to wipe sticky hands and dry salty tears, and to know that until the end of her own life, she would love someone with every breath she took—

"Yes," she said aloud and without any doubt. "I'm eager to be a mother. I'm excited about the baby." It felt *soooo* good to be able to say it out loud! Hopefully when the time came, she would be able to say the same thing to her family—without stuttering or apologizing for being the sole Jeffers woman who wanted the whole package—mother, father, backseat full of kids. "I don't think it's too soon to start addressing the baby's needs."

Dean shifted, sitting up straighter. He had begun to smile when she said she was thrilled. Once she mentioned the baby's needs, however, he came to full attention, serious as a judge. "I plan to be financially responsible throughout my child's life. If there's anything you need right now—"

"Oh, no, no! I wasn't talking about finances. I don't need money. And neither does the baby right now."

"There are things you'll need. And days you might not feel up to working. I'll see my lawyer and set something up."

"That is not necessary, really." He started to rebut, but she held firm. "If there are things you want to buy for the baby, that's up to you, but *I* do not want financial help, especially not before she's born. Thank you, anyway." She smiled to sweeten the edict, but was careful not to appear to waver, because Dean Kingsley could be stubborn.

He took her words in, not liking them much, though he nodded his acceptance. He raised a brow. "'She,' huh?"

"Or he."

"When it's time to pick out names, do you mind if I help? At least with the middle name."

Baby names. Rosemary blinked in surprise. He wanted to pick out baby names? She nearly laughed aloud at the irony.

Years ago, when she and Neil had still been in college, they'd gone to Canon Beach for the weekend. Two darling chubby toddler girls in tiny bikinis had played in the sand next to them, and Rosemary had asked Neil what he might like to name a little girl if they ever had one. He'd leaped from their blanket as if the sand had caught fire, ran into the ocean and returned twenty minutes later, dripping wet and silent.

Back in Portland, Rosemary had relayed the story to Vi, who told her that playing "What Do We Name the Baby?"

with a man was like "handing him a knife and inviting him to cut off his own testicles." Rosemary had not broached the topic again until they'd been married three years.

Now she managed a wry smile. "As long as your favorite names are pronounceable and have nothing to do with states, cars or local tributaries, I think we can work it out."

For the first time this evening, she got a glimpse of the more relaxed Dean, the one who laughed easily. "Aww. I was hoping for Montana if it's a girl and Nissan if it's a boy. I guess I can bend."

"Montana is kind of pretty, actually."

They shared their first un-tense moment since the night they'd met. Rosemary hated to ruin it by introducing another issue, but she'd come here with an agenda that had to be addressed.

"What?" he said when she hesitated. "You're frowning again. Whatever it is, why not get it over with fast, like pulling off a Band-Aid?"

"I usually use a wet towel and soak a Band-Aid off."

"Sounds time-consuming."

She nodded.

"Gotcha." He reached for his orange juice and settled back. "Okay, take your time."

She took a deep breath. No matter how much time she took, this was still going to be awkward in the extreme. Her heart thumped heavily. If only she knew more about him….

"All right," she breathed, gripping the table's edge as if she were hanging from a cliff. "You asked me once if I was married before. I was. My plan was never to be married again. When I moved to Honeyford, I wanted to focus on my career and the community. I like it here. A lot."

From her first word, Dean gave her his full attention, as usual. His face was a mask of polite interest, using neutrality to invite her to keep speaking.

"Being a single mother will change how I feel about the town," she continued, "and how the town feels about me. I've had half a dozen people describe the scandal of the interim librarian." At his puzzled expression, Rosemary explained, "She had a pierced lip and tried to introduce the book club to erotica."

Dean's mouth twitched.

"I've given a lot of thought to moving away." She saw Dean tense perceptibly, so she stated quickly, "I've decided that I want to stay." Like magic, his shoulders relaxed again. "At least for now," she added cautiously. "But being the single pregnant librarian doesn't sound like a good idea, especially when people discover that you're the father."

Placing his glass on the table, Dean shrugged. "Why? I don't like to brag, but most people in town find me pretty likeable."

Rosemary looked at the thick, earth-brown hair he kept neatly trimmed, at the features that were classically handsome and aging like fine wine, at the blue eyes that smiled even when his lips hadn't moved a bit, and she knew that although he was being facetious, he had told the truth. Women probably faked all manner of ailments merely to visit the pharmacist for advice.

"It's going to seem ridiculous that a librarian and a pharmacist didn't have the sense to use birth control, don't you think?" she said.

Dean's eyes darkened. "Obviously 'sense' is not my forte when you're in my arms." He paused. "Past tense, I mean."

The temperature in the tavern—or simply inside Rosemary—shot up ten degrees. *Concentrate on the topic.* A gentle, ironic smile curved his lips, and suddenly she remembered exactly how they felt pressed to hers…and to other parts of her body. *Concentrate.*

"Anyway, I think there would be a lot of gossip. And even

if it isn't ill intentioned, it would be difficult to deal with. Difficult for the library and, when the baby grows up enough to understand, difficult for her. Or him."

A silence as pregnant as Rosemary ensued. Dean broke it.

"What's your solution?"

Her heart began to race at a dizzying speed. "I think it's not unreasonable to cater to the conservatives in this case. I mean, I think sometimes discretion is the better part of valor."

He raised a brow. "Yeah?"

As gentlemanly as he was, he didn't intend to rescue her. Rosemary broke a sweat.

"Yes. So here's what I propose." She winced when the last word left her mouth. Couldn't help it. Deep breath. "I think we should…or at least *I* would like to…for the baby's sake more than anything…get…" *Say it, Rosemary, say it.* "Mm… Mmm…" She swallowed, licked her dry lips. "Mmm-a…" Oh, God in heaven.

She was going to have a heart attack before she said the damn word. Maybe there was another solution, after all. Maybe she really should move….

Dean reached into his back pocket and withdrew a leather wallet. He pulled out a few bills, tossed them onto the table and reached for her wrist. "Let's go."

Chapter Eight

They wound up driving their own vehicles to Dean's apartment. He led the way, driving slowly enough for her to follow even though she knew exactly how to get there. Upon arriving on Main Street, Dean directed her around the rear of his building, where they parked and walked up the alley entrance to his place.

Neither of them mentioned her botched proposal again until they were seated at the small dining table, eating omelets he'd made expertly with Gruyère cheese, oil-cured olives and thin crescent-shaped slices of avocado.

"You're good at this," Rosemary commented, awkwardly breaking their tense silence. "I'm not a very inspired cook."

"I took a class when I was in college. My roommate and I thought it would be a good way to meet girls."

"Was it?"

"For him. He married someone he met the first night."

"And she got a husband who could cook."

"No. He dropped the class."

"You stayed and learned how to make omelets?"

"And fish tacos and a dangerous chocolate cake." He pointed the tines of his fork in her direction. "*You're* getting a husband who can cook."

With the point of their meeting on the table, they both set down their forks.

Wiping his mouth, Dean rested his forearms on the table and made his usual straightforward eye contact. "I like the idea of getting married."

Rosemary nodded slowly. With that one decision agreed upon, a host of new issues opened up, and her stomach roiled. "It seems like the best solution…for now."

Dean watched her closely. "Are you putting a time limit on it?"

He'd hit fine-point number one solidly on the head. "Yes. I think it should be time-limited from the outset. Everything should be as clear and businesslike as possible to avoid confusion and resentment down the line." She'd already given this point extensive consideration and was able to present her case without stumbling. "Confusion and resentment on the parents' part is toxic for a child. If we plan in advance exactly when and how we're going to separate, then when the time comes we should be able to do it amicably. And that will be good for everyone."

"What makes you certain there'll be a time when we want to part?"

The question truly shocked her. "We don't know each other. We're getting married for the sake of the baby…and maybe our jobs. But mostly for the baby."

"Marriages have begun on flimsier foundations than wanting to create a family for a child."

"I doubt those marriages last."

"I'm sure they take work." He buttered one of the rolls he'd set out. "Then again, all marriages do. We'd be more aware of that than most, which could give us a leg up."

She frowned, watching the steady, even swipes of the butter knife over the bread. "I've already told you, I don't want to be married again. Ever."

"Which seems to be the real crux of the matter." Calmly, he took a bite of the roll then reached for his fork and tucked into the omelet again.

Suddenly they could have been discussing Honeyford's plan to hold a spring parade rather than a matter that would affect the rest of their lives; he was that nonchalant. The tide of tension inside Rosemary rose dangerously. "How can you still be hungry when we're talking about this?"

"About marriage?" He shrugged as he forked up another bite of egg oozing with melted cheese. "See, that's the difference between us. The thought of marriage doesn't kill my appetite."

I have good reason, she almost said, but wisely remained silent. They didn't have to know everything about each other to make this work. *For the length of time that it had to work.*

"All right." Someone had to be reasonable and realistic here, and obviously it was going to be her. "What I'm thinking is that a year and a half of marriage will give us time to have the baby, establish that you are the legal father and that we tried to make the relationship a go. Unfortunately, because we rushed into things, we will realize that we need to separate before the baby is old enough to be confused and hurt by our continual problems. We'll say we did our best, but the writing was on the wall."

"Why didn't we get counseling?"

"Because—" She shook her head and blinked. "What?"

"Counseling. Professional advice about how to make it work."

Rosemary squinted as if that might help her see his point. “We’re not trying to make it work.”

He washed the food down with decaf then nodded. “Ah, right. What if someone asks that, though? It’s a reasonable question, especially with a child involved.”

“We’ll say we tried, and *it didn’t help*.”

He gazed at her. “Pity. So a year and a half. Is there a contingency plan if we decide we don’t want to separate?”

“We’re not going to decide that.”

“*You* might. I’m incredibly easy to live with.” Polishing off his roll, he spied the one she hadn’t yet touched and plucked it off her plate. She regarded him dubiously as he picked up his knife to split and butter *her* bread.

“Why do you want to talk about staying together?” she asked, snatching the roll back. “If you want a wife that badly, why haven’t you gotten married before now?” She took a big bite of roll. She was the pregnant one, after all, the one who needed the most nourishment. If he could eat during this conversation, then by golly so would she.

He looked at his plate, and she wondered if he was going to respond at all. Finally, instead of answering her, he looked up and asked a question. “Why did you go to the motel with me?”

Oh, Lord in heaven, what a question. “Lust,” she said baldly, shoving every other memory from her mind. “I was using you. Sorry, but that’s all.”

He laughed. “That statement doesn’t carry the same negativity for a man that it does for a woman. We’re generally happy to have you go ahead and use us. From whom were you on the rebound?”

“I didn’t say I was on the rebound.”

Dean narrowed his eyes.

Fine. “My ex, of course.” She took another bite of the roll, this time a big one. “Good bread.”

"It's from Honey Bea's. I'll take you there one morning before work for decaf coffee and the best apple fritters you've ever tasted."

"One apple fritter has enough calories to feed a major city," she informed him, seriously tucking into the omelet now while simultaneously shaking her head. "Do they serve dry toast?"

"I sincerely hope not. Why are you worried about calories? Your body's great."

"I've always been kind of fleshy. By month nine of this pregnancy I'll probably weigh more than you."

"Fleshy." This time he muttered an expletive. "Women and body image. This is why I won't carry weight-loss aids in the pharmacy." He buttered the other half of her roll. "So you were on the rebound from your ex-husband. Somehow I was under the impression you've been divorced awhile."

"Two years." She held out her hand. He put the roll into it.

"And you're still rebounding?"

"Not 'still.'" She put a little bit of the omelet onto the roll. "You were my first rebound. And my last. I'm done with all that. I'm going to be celibate now." She popped the impromptu sandwich into her mouth and rolled her eyes in pleasure. "I can't believe how hungry I get at night."

"Join the club."

Rosemary glanced up from the food to find him gazing at her with an appetite that couldn't be misunderstood. Her body responded like a firecracker set alight.

Exploding low in her body, desire rushed through her, making her limbs go weak as noodles. The food lost its appeal.

Dean leaned forward, almost imperceptibly, but his intention was clear in every angle of his tightly wound body. He looked as if he was waiting for her to give him the okay so he could leap across the table to devour her instead of the food.

Wanting him wasn't the question. Whether Rosemary was willing to give in to the urges trying to overtake her—that was the question.

Never one to be carried away by the needs of her body, she could hardly fathom the strength of her desire to rip off his clothes and to feel him again over, inside and around her.

"A year and a half." His voice, deep and gravelly, interrupted her thoughts. "That won't be nearly enough time to burn out this desire. If we make love again, even once, I'll end up wanting you more, not less. So my answer to 'Do you want to get married?' Yes." His mouth quirked. "Great idea. But unless we're going to keep it open-ended—and very real—I think we should call it a night tonight."

Even though he'd made a statement, a question lingered in his tone and in his eyes.

An open-ended marriage…one that was 'real'…

What made a marriage real? Sex? That wasn't enough to turn a legal union for the baby's sake into the genuine article—or to make a marriage last. Sometimes not even the best intentions or the strongest desire could do that.

Edging out sexual hunger came the fear that was never far from the surface for Rosemary. What if she really did fall for Dean? Or for the dream of a traditional family again? What if she bought it all, hook, line and sinker, and he turned out to be another really good salesman?

Her sister Lucy was a family law attorney in Portland, specializing in divorce for women. Lucy had handled the dissolution of Rosemary's first marriage, and Rosemary planned to have her handle this one, too. Lucy was a pit bull, one of the most sought-after attorneys in Oregon. She didn't have a sentimental or romantic bone in her entire body.

Lucy was thirty-four, but she had never thrown herself into

a relationship with the fervor of an Olympic athlete going for the gold. She had never cried for months because a man no longer loved her.

Channel Lucy.

As it turned out, Rosemary didn't have to say a word. Dean read her answer on her face.

"A shame," he murmured, removing the napkin from his lap and setting it on the table.

The evening was over.

She thought—although she wasn't positive—that they had just come to an agreement: a time-limited marriage, no sex.

That was good. That was…that was smart.

The next time she and Dean were together they would need to discuss an actual prenuptial agreement—printed on paper with a watermark, witnessed signatures, the whole nine yards. Lucy would scream if Rosemary entered another marriage without one.

And, her sister would positively murder her if she knew that right now Rosemary wasn't thinking about practicalities at all, but rather imagining what it would feel like to have one more night of astounding sex with Dean then walk to the bakery in the morning before work, thinking of nothing more important than the calories in an apple fritter…and of how fortunate a woman was when her lover thought she was simply delicious just the way she was.

Three days later, Dean had agreed to allow Lucy Jeffers to draft a prenuptial agreement. It would include the details of the apparently inevitable dissolution of his marriage to Rosemary and specify that he agreed to an uncontested divorce when the time came.

"Give me something to do," he told his brother as they stood before a section of barbed-wire fencing Fletcher was working on. It was Sunday, the day Dean typically spent riding his mountain bike when the weather was good, or working on plans for the clinic he dreamed of opening. More recently, he spent his day off here at Pine Road Ranch, playing uncle to his brother's new family and enjoying one of his sister-in-law's stellar home-cooked meals. Today, though, he was here to get advice—from the brother he'd once thought wasn't fit to advise a toddler not to play in the street.

"What are you doing," he pressed when Fletcher continued to work without responding, "twisting those pieces together? Do you have another pair of pliers?"

Fletcher continued to work steadily and with practiced skill. "This is manual labor, Deano. I don't want you to hurt yourself. Why don't you stand there, look pretty and keep talking. So far, this has been the most interesting conversation we've ever had."

"Hand me the damn pliers." Shrugging, Fletcher complied, and Dean attacked the fence, working without skill, but with a fervor fueled by frustration.

Fletcher stepped back and took a long drink of the lemonade Claire had packed for him. Then he sat on the hard ground and recapped what his brother had told him. "So you're going to get married in time to fulfill that one condition of Victor's will, but you're not going to *stay* married long enough to actually claim your inheritance. And this woman, Rosemary, doesn't know you need to be married two years to inherit the building on Main, because you haven't told her about the will at all, even though this isn't a love match to begin with. Have I got that right?"

"That's the gist of it." Dean gave a vicious twist of the pliers.

"Don't snap that wire. If you leave me with more work to do, it'll piss me off, and I've been working damn hard lately to control my temper."

Dean clenched his jaw as he wrapped one piece of wire

around another. "I thought marriage has mellowed you naturally."

"It has. Toward Claire and the kids. Fools still try my patience."

Looking over his shoulder, Dean glared. "Meaning I'm a fool."

Fletcher removed his sweat-stained Stetson and scratched his scalp. "Ah, let's see, how did Claire tell me to word this crap? Oh, yeah. I don't agree with your *decisions* in this *arena*, Dean. I'm afraid you may get yourself into some trouble." He replaced his hat and spit on the ground. "But as soon as you take your head out of your ass you'll be fine."

Dean tossed the pliers into Fletcher's tool kit. "Just say it."

"All right. From what you've told us, Rosemary wouldn't go on a date with you, much less get married, unless she felt she had no choice. So you've got nothing to lose by telling her about Victor's asinine will. Tell her the Kingsleys put the *fun* in *dysfunction* and that you can't inherit the building you live and work in unless you get married by summer and stay married two years. That's only a half year longer than she already wants. No big deal." He reached into a canvas lunch box and withdrew a thick cookie that looked as if it had been made for a giant. Taking a huge bite of his wife's baking, Fletcher grinned. "She knows what I like." He chewed contentedly, and Dean wanted to kill him.

"The thing is," Fletcher continued once he'd swallowed, "you don't want to tell Rosemary the truth even though you had no problem telling Amanda. Seems to me that's because Amanda was the woman you always thought you'd marry—cool, intellectual, didn't give a rat's ass whether you were marrying for love or not. Very safe for you since you don't like to feel anything below the neck."

"Hey, that's bull—"

Fletcher held up a finger—not the index one. "You asked. I respect you too much to sugarcoat the horrible truth."

Dean clenched his fists to keep from picking up the pliers and hitting his brother in the head with them. "And the horrible truth is?"

"Loving a woman is the most ass-kicking, out-of-control, cannot-get-your-head-around-it, frightening feeling in the world." He leveled Dean with a laser-sharp stare. "I'm talking about real love."

"As opposed to?"

"Everything else. The stuff people fill their time with so they won't be alone or be able to think too much. Being with someone because you want a relationship isn't remotely the same as being with a woman because you can't imagine taking another breath without her in your life."

Dean shook his head. "I feel as if I'm having an out-of-body experience, listening to *you* give a dissertation on love."

It was a fact that before he'd met his wife Fletcher had spent his life disdaining affection. He took no offense.

"Thing is," he said, "people assume love is a soft feeling. It hasn't been for me, and I doubt it will be for you. When you need a woman like you need air and water, you'll be on fire until you know she wants you, too. Then you'll stay on fire, wanting to keep her happy, figuring out how to let her know she's the best thing that ever happened to you. Add kids to the mix, and every muscle in your body will be on alert, ready to kill or die for them. It's damned exhausting."

"But you love it."

"Wouldn't have it any other way. Ever. That's what's so freaking terrifying. Once you meet *the* woman, you know damn well that if anything ever happened to her, you'd want to die, too." His gaze narrowed. "When I met Claire, she made me want things I thought I'd given up half a lifetime ago. So how is it for you? You haven't known Rosemary that long."

Dean pulled a hand down his face and took a deep breath. Everything his brother said whomped him smack in the gut. He'd started to feel that way about Rosemary the first night. "I've known her long enough."

Fletcher nodded slowly. "And you don't want to tell her that you need to get married on account of your crazy father's will, because…"

"It'll louse up any chance to make her believe I'm falling in love with her." Dean's mouth was dry as old hay. He couldn't swallow with guilt choking him. "I'm right not to tell her… right?"

Fletcher tossed his big bro a pitying glance. "No, you're out of your mind. She's going to draw up that prenup, and if the marriage only lasts eighteen months, you're screwed. Six more and at least you'll walk away with your business."

"Well, what the hell?" Uncharacteristically, Dean burst into anger. "Now you're saying the inheritance is more important than love?"

"No. But according to the will, the building on Main goes to the city if you default. Doug Thorpe sits on the city council. He's been yammering to everyone who'll listen that a new upscale restaurant downtown will draw tourist dollars. I think the pharmacy itself is safe, but he'd love to get his hands on a couple of the storefronts next door, so there goes your clinic. And, you'll have to start paying rent on the drugstore. With a child to raise, that's going to be a burden. You don't want to have to start working longer hours when you've got a baby. You gain nothing by losing the building."

Frustration turned Dean's limbs stiff yet quivering like plucked strings. "The worst part of this, the absolute worst part, is lying to her. And being terrified that if I tell her the truth I'll lose her and the baby." He eyed his brother. "There better be a solution on the tip of your tongue. You came out of this will debacle smelling like a rose. Give me some coaching here."

Fletcher's features melted into the grateful serenity that the mention of his family never failed to evoke. "Sometimes, Deano, I think that the fact things worked out with Claire was dumb luck." His voice turned into the kinder rumble Dean was still getting used to. "That or divine pity. But Claire was a widow with one good marriage under her belt already. She was a wife and mother through and through. From what you've told us about Rosemary—and you don't seem to know *that* much about her—marriage was the furthest thing from her mind the night you two hooked up. Seems to me that not telling her about the will is playing with fire."

Pressing fingers to his forehead, Dean scrubbed at his brow. He was caught in a damned tangled web. He didn't know whether to blame his father for adding the marriage codicil to his will…or himself, for falling in love when he'd least expected to.

Chapter Nine

"Make him sign in front of a notary. Don't let him off the hook for any reason. But, if his lawyer quibbles over anything—*anything*—in that prenup, then I don't want you getting within fifty feet of the thing with a pen."

Lucy Jeffers's voice sounded like rubber bands snapping as it came through the cell phone. Tucked beneath Rosemary's arm was the prenuptial agreement Lucy had overnighted, and Rosemary held an umbrella over her head to protect the large envelope from the steady rain as she made her way up Main Street to King's Pharmacy.

"Honest to God, Rosemary—" the strain in Lucy's voice was palpable "—I don't know why in heaven you think you need to marry this dude. Women have babies on their own all the time, not that I think *that's* a brilliant idea. But it'd be a helluva lot easier to be stuck with a kid and a nanny instead of a kid and some jerk—"

"Dean's not a jerk. He's not like that," Rosemary muttered,

acutely aware that a) She and her sister had already had this conversation, b) Lucy was never going to be soothed when it came to a man, marriage and one of her family members, and c) She was walking down a public street and did not want to talk about this. "Dean's actually very reasonable—" she began sotto voce, but Lucy cut her off so loudly Rosemary pulled the phone away from her ear.

"Don't!" The severe admonishment echoed like a tuning fork. "Do not romanticize him. Rosemary, promise me you'll save your…" Lucy searched for the right word. "…fairy-tale fantasies for your journal and *this time* apply your brains to the real world."

Rosemary winced. By the time she pressed End Call, she felt as if she'd run several miles in sand. All she wanted was a nap. And a good cry.

"She's trying to protect you. She doesn't want to see you get hurt again. No one does," their sister Evelyn had said when Rosemary phoned last night to tell her about the baby, the decision she'd made and Lucy's help with the prenuptial agreement. *"This is why she's a top lawyer. I only wish you were better at protecting yourself, honey. Have you told Mom?"*

Rosemary hadn't, not yet. She had a one-person-a-day threshold when it came to disappointing family members.

Morning sickness encroached on her previously nausea-free day. She wasn't certain this time whether it was physical or emotional. Loneliness, bone deep and chilling, assailed her.

Clutching the handle of the umbrella in a death grip, she put her free hand over her stomach. *Don't you worry,* she told it telepathically, comforting the tiny, tiny life inside her as if it, too, were concerned about isolation, *we're going to be fine, just fine, the two of us. And you'll have your…* Her breath caught just a little. *Your daddy. I think he's going to be very hands-on.*

It was true. She wasn't worried about Dean's involvement with their child. He'd been accepting of and excited about the baby from the start.

She frowned and caught the toe of her pump on an uneven piece of sidewalk. Not once in any of their conversations had Lucy or Evelyn mentioned their future niece or nephew, even though Rosemary's child would be the first baby in the family.

Suddenly, her footsteps, which had been dragging, picked up the pace as she advanced on King's Pharmacy. She would get this over with then phone Daphne for a reassuring pick-me-up. Marriage and babies were always positives for her.

Reminding herself of Lucy's admonition to be businesslike and unemotional when dealing with the prenup, Rosemary closed her umbrella, shook out the water and swung open the pharmacy door. Amid the tinkling of the bells, she walked briskly into the store. At this time of morning, the pharmacy would be open, which meant Dean would be in the back, filling prescriptions and doling out advice.

Heels clicking along the linoleum, she looked neither left nor right, hoping as she always did when she entered the pharmacy that she wouldn't run into anyone she knew.

Gonna have to get over that one, she thought, *if you're going to be married to the pharmacist...married for a while, anyway.*

Immediately when she walked in, the inherent friendliness and charm of the place struck her. The store could be divided into three distinct parts: the dry-goods aisles occupying the center of the shop; an old-fashioned soda fountain, which was past the dry goods to her left; and the pharmacy, tucked all the way in the back. Displays of candy and small gift items greeted her on the way in, but Dean spared his customers the usual commercial assault. Here, the candy was locally made and attractively packaged. Ditto on the gifts. Rosemary got the feeling Dean was selling Honeyford as much as anything else. *Welcome locals. Welcome tourists,* this store seemed to say. *I hope you like it here as much as I do.*

Unexpectedly, Rosemary felt as if she were on the verge of tears. "Hormones," she muttered under her breath and decided to get this done quickly so she could head to the library and keep herself busy.

"Rosemary!" Her name, sweetly accented with a Southern drawl, drew Rosemary's attention. "The boys and I were just talking about coming to story hour this afternoon."

After an initial clutch of apprehension, Rosemary glanced left to see a woman who was a frequent patron of the library. The young woman had a daughter still in diapers and two young sons who seemed to love the library as much as their mother did.

"Hello, Claire," she greeted, pleased that she was remembering the first names of most of the people who came to story hour at the library. "I almost didn't recognize you without Rosalind on your hip."

Claire rolled her eyes. "I know. My husband says I need to stop wearing her in the sling all the time. She's fifteen months, and she'd still rather ride than walk." Claire's joyful laugh further relaxed Rosemary. "I love carrying them, though. That time of their lives doesn't last long enough for me."

A strong yearning assailed Rosemary. How wonderful it would be to sit down with a mother and discuss everything baby—strollers and slings, diapers (cloth or disposable?), first smiles and first foods and the best methods for helping them sleep through the night. When should she and Dean announce that they were going to have a baby? When were they going to get married? There were still so many details to iron out.

Eager suddenly to see Dean, she politely excused herself. "It was good to run into you, Claire." She tilted her head in the direction of the pharmacy. "I need to see…the, um, pharmacist, so—"

"Dean's at the soda fountain." Claire reached for Rosemary's arm—somewhat eagerly, Rosemary thought. "Come on."

Young voices rang out as they approached that end of the store.

"How'm I doin', Uncle Dean? How'm I doin'?"

"Outstanding, buddy. Good job eating all the malt balls that fall."

"I don't want to waste 'em."

Claire's younger son, Orlando, stood behind the soda fountain as he ladled candy atop a dish of ice cream. His older brother, Will, very carefully spooned thick hot fudge over a sundae already gilded with toppings. And supervising it all was the man she had come to see, handsome as sin in his white pharmacist's coat, holding Claire's youngest child, the toddler Rosalind, as she experimented with putting chocolate fingerprints on the cheek of the man cuddling her.

It all looked so…right.

I wonder if this is what an out-of-body experience is like? Rosemary wondered, feeling as if she were floating.

"Hey!" Laughing, Dean reached up to capture the sticky fingers painting his cheek. Holding the tiny hand, he pretended to be horrified by the chocolate smears, but then stuck out the tip of his tongue and gave one short finger a swipe.

The boys *eeewwed,* Rosalind squealed, and, beside Rosemary, Claire laughed softly. "He's great with them."

Uncle. Belatedly, Rosemary realized what Orlando had called Dean. Her jaw dropped enough for her open mouth to accommodate a waffle cone. Of course, people used *Uncle* simply as a term of affection all the time, so it could be that—

"I was a widow when I met Fletcher," Claire confided in

a quiet voice. “I thought my boys would grow up without a man around and that having a mama would have to be enough. Now they’ve got two wonderful men—their daddy and their Uncle Dean.” She looked at Rosemary, her eyes aglow if a bit tentative, and her voice soft. “He’s going to be a terrific father someday.”

She knows. The realization hit Claire like lightening on a hay bale.

“You and Dean are…” she pointed toward him, her brain moving like sludge through a sewer “…related by marriage?”

“Yep. Dean is my husband’s brother. I met him, though, before I met Fletcher, which was a good thing, because Fletcher made me wonder whether Kingsley men were fit to be around little ones.” Once again, her gay laughter put Rosemary at ease…almost.

“What’s, um, *wrong* with Fletcher?”

“Oh, he just needed a good woman to smooth his rough edges.” After a brief pause, Claire grinned beautifully. “And I needed him to rough up some of my smooth ones.”

She looked at Rosemary, and suddenly seemed unsure of whether she should speak again. Rosemary both dreaded and couldn’t wait to hear what Claire was going to say next.

“Dean’s the opposite of my husband in so many ways. They’re like dark and white chocolate. Fletcher still keeps his distance with everyone except family. But Dean…” Claire smiled with sincere fondness. “He puts everyone at ease. He’s got a heart for people that’s as big as the sun. Fletcher says Dean’s carrying half the town on his ledgers. If someone doesn’t have insurance, he finds a way to make sure they get their prescriptions filled no matter what. People aren’t afraid to come to him when they need something. He never makes you feel foolish or small for asking.” Appearing slightly apologetic, Claire concluded, “That was probably more than

I should have said, but I think sometimes Honeyford takes Dean for granted because he's always been good."

Rosemary's gaze strayed from Claire—her future temporary sister-in-law if Dean signed the prenup—to the man who, Rosemary knew, had not "*always* been good." In fact, the night they'd first met, he'd been quite, quite bad.

A disturbing thought—the kind of thought that sounded exactly like her mother's voice—made her breath catch. Maybe Dean did that kind of thing—seduced women in out-of-the-way bars and motels—more than anyone knew. *May*be he was like a politician, smooth as butter when people were looking, but with a secret life that could curl a horse's mane. Maybe he—

"Hey, give me that spoon, you little monkey." Rosemary emerged from her blind panic to see Dean laughing as he tried to pry a spoon from the resistant Rosalind's tiny hand. "Soon as you're steady on your feet, Uncle Dean is going to teach you how to play T-ball." He glanced up and grinned as Claire approached the marble-topped counter. "This one's got quite a grip—" For the first time, he noticed Rosemary, still standing several feet away. His words stopped, and his gaze lingered.

"What did you give her?" Claire asked, nodding to the spoon.

"White Chocolate Peppermint Patty," he responded, his attention still on Rosemary. "I needed her expert opinion. Hello."

Rosemary wasn't certain whether he mouthed the greeting to her or murmured it. Either way, the intimacy made her toes curl.

Claire reached across the counter to take the spoon from her daughter and laughed when Rosalind protested. "If that's a new flavor, I'd say it's a winner. Here, let me wipe her mouth."

Returning his attention to his sister-in-law, Dean came around the counter to transfer his wriggling niece to her mother's arms. Then he turned to Rosemary.

Her body began to tingle. An ocean of sensation rose up from her toes until it roared in her ears. *It's nothing, nothing,* she told herself. *You are not your feelings. You are a sane, intelligent, levelheaded person—*

He smiled. Just for her.

Hic.

Her eyes widened as a painful hiccup jerked her body. *You are in charge of how you react to any given situa—*

Hic!

"Ow." She pressed a hand to her sternum.

"Ooh. Are you okay?" Claire looked at her, mild concern tinged with amusement.

"Yes, I—" *Hic.* "'Scuse me."

Dean reached a hand beneath her elbow. She tightened her arm against her side so as not to drop the prenup. His touch was gentle, his expression gorgeously disturbed by her discomfort. *Oh, God, a woman could get lost in that expression—*

Hic!

"Can you take a deep breath?" Dean modeled the breath he had in mind, making his chest rise and fall slowly.

"I'm fine. Really."

"Mom!" Orlando, Claire's younger son, called from behind the counter. "Uncle Deano! Look! I'm finished. Lookit how big it is!" He pointed a spoon dripping with strawberry sauce at a lopsided sundae. He'd covered the ice-cream mountain in candy. A landslide appeared imminent.

"Oh, dear," his mother said.

But Uncle Dean gave him the thumbs-up. "Good job, buddy. Any day you want to work here after school, you let me know."

The older boy, Will, whom Rosemary had always found very sweet, looked up from his more circumspect creation. "Me, too, Uncle Dean?"

"Of course. You'll be in charge of the daily audit. I'll rely on you to keep our food costs down." Will had no idea what his uncle meant, but the job sounded impressive, and he puffed up like a peacock as he smiled at his mother.

Family. Place. Permanence. That was the fourth part of King's Pharmacy, and it was almost as tangible right now as the dry goods, pharmacy or soda fountain.

Glancing back at Rosemary, Dean winked, handsome creases edging his grin. "Training the next generation of Kingsley soda jerks," he quipped. Then his gaze dropped, briefly and privately, to her stomach.

The tides of feeling surged again from Rosemary's toes and by the time they made it to her head, she was dizzy. *Oh, no...*

Hic...hic. Hic! Hic! Hic!

"If you drink apple juice backwards with your fingers in your ears, hiccups go away," Will advised sagely.

Dean glanced at Claire, who shrugged and whispered, "I made that up."

"Come on." He began to pull on Rosemary's elbow to guide her. "Hold down the fort, guys. Claire, if you need to head out before I get back, just leave everything." Guiding Rosemary, he said, "Let's get those taken care of."

With her thoughts buzzing like an active hive, Rosemary let herself be led up the stairs in the back of the store and into Dean's immaculate-as-before apartment. Once inside, she stood in her trench coat, body straight and tense, her stillness punctuated only by the intermittent bounce of the hiccups.

Closing the door, Dean came up behind her and tried to slip her purse off her shoulder. Startled, she grabbed the strap.

"Sorry. Why don't you put down everything you're carrying, and I'll help you get rid of those hiccups."

Embarrassed that she was so jumpy, Rosemary said, "I'm sure they'll go away soon. I almost never get hic—*hic!*—cups." Shifting the large envelope beneath her arm into her hands, she got down to business, hoping that would calm the jittery sensation in her body. "I brought the prenuptial agreement my sister drew up."

He hesitated before accepting the envelope. "You want a cup of coffee?"

"Now? No. I mean, you don't have to read it now…and I have to get to work."

"I wasn't going to read it now. I just thought you might like to relax a minute. And talk."

"Talk?" *Hic.*

"Yes, Rosie. Talk. That's when two people sit, sometimes opposite each other, sometimes side by side, and they converse about any topic that has meaning for them." He looked at the envelope, a frown between his brows. "In this case, our marriage might be a good conversation starter."

He closed his eyes briefly, brought his thumb and forefinger up and rubbed before looking at her again. "Sorry. Sarcasm is not my favorite mode of expression."

She smiled. Who said things like "mode of expression" in normal conversation these days? Every now and again Dean would pop out some comment or action that made him seem as if he came from another era. Like his store downstairs. She liked it. "You're not sarcastic. Usually."

"Really? I feel sarcastic lately."

The tilt to his lips and the wry, almost sad expression in his eyes gave the moment an intimacy that for a moment made Rosemary *feel* married to him.

Hic!

"Oh, for God's sake," he muttered. Tossing the envelope

onto a slim buffet table that stood against the back of the couch, he reached for her purse again without asking and tossed it onto the table, as well. "Give me your coat."

Don't wanna. Rosemary knew she should leave before her thoughts ran away with her, but she did have something—a little point she and Lucy had changed in the prenup—that she needed to mention to him.

"I'll only stay a minute," she assured him, unnecessarily as he didn't seem concerned about getting back to work quickly this morning. Untying the belt of her trench coat, she let him grab it in one hand and toss it, too, over the buffet.

"Come on." Taking her arm, he pulled her casually around the sofa, where he directed her to one of the leather cushions and seated himself beside her. "Turn," he said.

"What?" *Hic.*

Shaking his head—*I'm not doing this dance again, Rosie*—he turned her shoulders, forcing her either to shift the rest of her body or to twist herself into a yoga pose guaranteed to squoosh the teeny tiny baby.

Dean's hands settled onto her shoulders. She felt his palms through the thin material of the wrap dress she'd donned this morning. His touch was warm and heavy and grounding. *Hic. Oh, man. Hic, hic, hic.*

"I, um, I do have something…a little point…I need to discuss with—"

"Shh. We'll talk in a minute. Relax first." Sliding his hands down the outside of her arms, he lifted her shoulders until they were hunched around her ears, held them there a moment and then let them drop. Not at all a sexy move, which was rather reassuring, but definitely relaxing.

Stretching her shoulders back, he used his thumbs to work into the muscles, the massage rhythmic and efficient, and her body began to settle into his capable hands.

"Hiccups can be caused by tension in the diaphragmatic

muscle," he murmured, his mellow voice seeming like yet another aspect of the massage. "Once they begin, the muscle contraction takes on a life of its own." His fingers walked slowly down either side of her spine. Rosemary had been tense for so many weeks, she almost moaned. "Some people try to relax the muscle by distracting themselves."

"Like drinking apple juice upside down with their fingers in their ears." She remembered Will's suggestion.

Dean chuckled softly. "I'd never heard that one before. But yes, like that." He used the entire surface of his hands to knead his way slowly back to her neck. *That feels sooooo good.* "Most people still believe in the scare tactic, catching someone by surprise." He began to work on her nape…into her hairline…behind her ears… "I've never found that to be effective. Have you?"

She responded with something that sounded vaguely like, "Mmm-nnnnrrfflephlumph," and didn't trouble herself to clarify. He palmed the back of her head, his fingers pressing circles into her scalp like a hat with benefits. Nothing, *nothing* had ever felt this good, except…

Except for the last time he'd touched her with this kind of freedom. Well, more than this kind of freedom. Last time, he had touched her naked body, and relaxation wasn't quite the release they'd been after.

Well on her way to cooked-noodle state, Rosemary couldn't summon even a smidge of alarm over that thought. Why had touching never felt this good before? She'd been married, and for the ten years, everything had been hunky-dory—from her perspective. She'd had no complaints about sex, either the frequency or the intensity. Although…

In comparison to the fireworks Dean's lovemaking had set off, her ex-husband was more of a…sparkler.

Desire had crashed upon her like a tsunami when she and Dean were on the dance floor. Her body had needed him, or so it had seemed at the time, the way bread needed flour to exist. *Don't dance with him, not ever again,* she'd commanded herself the morning after.

Dimly she realized that letting him massage her was not in line with her decision *never to lose control again.* But this massage wasn't about tsunami-like sexual heat. No, no, it was…gentle. Relaxing. Platonic, right?

His hands made a return trip down her spine, stopping to work an extra minute on her lower back. As she was wearing a dress rather than pants, Dean did not need to fight a waistband in order for his magic fingers to press and knead, working into her hips. A haze of sensation dulled Rosemary's thoughts until they felt about as fluid as oatmeal.

Never felt sooo good…

Do… Not… Stop, she thought.

"I won't," Dean whispered back.

Oops.

When his palms slipped up her back like smoke, Rosemary leaned into them. She didn't mean to, really… Although she didn't exactly mean *not* to. Regardless of how she tried to care about the future and about not being weak or impulsive, she couldn't seem to access the principles her mother and sisters wore like a second skin.

True to his promise, Dean did not stop massaging. When he tilted her neck, pressing his thumb and fingers along the stiff muscles, cupping her jaw in a palm as warm and soothing as a summer day, Rosemary sighed and leaned into the caress. She turned her head to say, "Thank you," but no words emerged. Instead they locked gazes, and the words she should have spoken became a kiss she should not have given.

Really should not have.

Should not have brought her hand up to reach for his neck and pull him closer…

Should not have moaned into his lips as she tasted him for the first time in months.

This was what had stunned her so the night they'd gotten together, this hunger. It made her feel alive, strong. It made her feel daring and bold and free. And she'd never felt that way, not even as a kid. Life had always been a field filled with land mines to avoid. Caution had to be exercised, and her family's brand of caution generally involved "healthy cynicism," which translated to "Trust no one."

But none of that mattered now, with Dean. As the eddying sensation pulled her deeper and deeper to its center, Rosemary knew the physical spell he cast was not the sole reason she was abandoning her cloak of protection; she couldn't ignore the way he interacted with his family, his Mr. Rogers naturalness with children….

Bet you never wanted to shag Mr. Rogers, though, did you?

It was Dean who brought them face-to-face. And Dean who pulled back long enough to look into her eyes, to make sure she knew that this was no mere indiscriminate lust, not on his part.

He began kissing her again, his mouth hot and ravenous, and soon they were lying on his couch, their legs tangling discourteously, her hands running up his sides and traveling across his back as she noted for the first time that he'd ditched the lab coat.

Rosemary's breasts tightened and tingled even before his hand found the generous mounds. As he touched her, managing to tease her nipples through her thin dress and lacy bra, she thought she might levitate off the couch.

She began to yank his shirt from his trousers, needing to feel his skin…needing, really, to feel his skin on her skin… and recognizing the precise moment when she decided she couldn't stop, wasn't going to stop until the sharp, painful ache inside her had been soothed—

Then, suddenly, it was over.

Rosemary wasn't sure what had happened at first. Her eyes were closed, so all she knew was that one moment her body felt like an inferno with a gasoline drip and the next moment she was cold, floundering, wondering what was wrong.

She opened her eyelids with extreme effort, blinked at the light coming through the windows on the other side of the apartment and saw Dean sitting up, one of his hands on her tummy as if he required the continuity, his chest rising and falling visibly as he panted his way back to normal.

When he was sufficiently recovered, he helped her sit, straightened her dress at the shoulders and with a small smile noted, "This probably isn't a good way to kick off a celibate marriage." Running first one hand then the other through his hair, he expelled a breath filled with pent-up energy. "How are those hiccups?"

Rosemary figured her options at this moment were a) embarrassment, b) relief or c) frustration. Since she'd always been rotten at multiple choice, she aimed merely for coherent. "Fine." Her voice sounded hoarse and thready. "Gone." Attempting an urbane laugh, she said, "I think you found a new cure."

"I doubt it's new." Reaching out, he looped one of her curls around his forefinger. "Effective, though." Hovering on the brink of speaking again, he changed his mind, released her hair and stood. "I'll take a look at that document after work." Again she had the sense he had something more on his mind.

Rosemary couldn't regroup nearly as quickly as he seemed able to and stood more slowly. Lucy had told her to tell Dean something about the prenup, but what was it…? She frowned. Oh, yeah—

"Um, my sister wanted me to mention something that's a bit different from what we discussed. About the marriage. A little detail."

"Oh. Uh-huh." Dean cleared his throat. "Yeah…. Changes—they happen."

"Yes."

His tie had loosened during their…activity…and yet he tugged on it now as if it was choking him. "In fact, I was going to talk to you about… I wanted to mention…" He shook his head. "What's the change?"

Rosemary stared at him. Up to now he'd always seemed enviably sure of himself. "What do you want to ask?"

"What's the change in the prenuptial agreement?"

"Oh, it's not actually written into the prenup. It's part of our verbal agreement…about the length of time we're going to be together. Married."

His brows rose abruptly then swooped lower than before as he awaited elaboration.

Rosemary hadn't thought the change would be a problem since this marriage was destined to have a short shelf life from the get-go, but now anxiety fizzed inside her.

Silly. It's not going to matter. Just tell him. "Well, originally, we agreed to one and a half years of marriage from our wedding day, if you remember? But Lucy said the divorce might be smoother if we stick it out two years. I think she considers two years some kind of magic number for proving you gave the marriage the old college try." Rosemary swooped her fist through the air. *Cute. That made you look like an idiot.* Dropping the smile and her hand, she shrugged at him. "Are you okay with that?"

Dean lowered his head and pressed two fingers to his eyes. Imminent migraine. Probably not a good sign. Although he was the one who'd been pro-marriage from the start, anything could have changed since they'd spoken about it. Maybe it appeared to him that she was trying to manipulate their agreement to her advantage, which…well, she was. Sighing, Rosemary told herself to be prepared if he was perturbed.

Despite that note to self, she was *not* prepared when Dean started laughing. Laughing.

"What?" she asked, watching him warily. *Was that ha-ha-funny laughter or demonic "I'll be damned if I let you screw with my life, sister," laughter?* "Um, look, if it's not going to work for you, just say so, because it was Lucy's idea, anyway. She's probably just being extracautious. She's like that. Personally, I think it's a little silly to assume that a few more months—"

Dean sobered abruptly. "It's Lucy's idea?" Looking away, he nodded to himself, wiping a hand down the face that only seconds before was wreathed in laughter. "You, of course, would have preferred not to add six more months to this marriage." He didn't wait for her to answer. Rising as if he were very tired, he walked around the sofa, grabbed his lab coat and shrugged into it. "Two years suits me fine. Another six months in the same house with my child—can't argue with that, can I?" He smiled, but it failed to reach his eyes. "I'll be happy to sign."

Rosemary didn't know how to respond, which seemed to be a continual state for her lately.

"You want me to bring the papers to you or send them to your sister?" he asked.

"Whatever you're comfortable with."

Without telling her what that would be, he crossed to the door, leaving Rosemary still buzzing with lust and confusion.

With empty eyes, Dean gave her a brief nod. "I've got to get back to work. Come down when you're ready. Just pull the door shut on your way out."

Chapter Ten

Things moved fairly quickly after that. Dean sent the signed prenuptial agreement directly to Lucy, who texted Rosemary, "He signed. 0 changes. Lucky U."

Rosemary applied herself to her work at the library, but her mind never strayed far from the realization that it wouldn't take long for her pregnancy to show, so if she and Dean planned to go public as a couple, it would behoove them to do it sooner rather than later.

Even though there was a family physician right here in Honeyford, Rosemary had begun seeing an ob-gyn in Bend. Perhaps after she and Dean came out of the closet (or bedroom?), so to speak, she would change doctors and save herself the drive.

Listening to the library's grandfather clock chime noon, Rosemary reached for one of the peppermints she kept in her drawer at the reference desk. Thus far on her list of fun ways to spend the day, pregnancy and salmonella were running neck and neck.

Nearing the end of her first trimester, she expected her morning sickness to abate. That was what the books she'd purchased from Amazon suggested (Dean still had the library's best pregnancy guides). Unfortunately, Rosemary's nausea had increased in the past few days, and now it seemed to be a loyal companion. Gone were the ravenous nights that allowed her to fill up on the food she couldn't even squint at during the day. She'd lost a pound this week.

No one stopped by the library on his lunch hour to wave a pastrami sandwich under her nose, either. She hadn't seen or heard from Dean for several days, not since she'd dropped off the prenuptial agreement.

Interestingly, just thinking about their romp on the couch ignited inside her an inferno of sexual heat that temporarily burned off the nausea. And made her hiccup.

"Are you hiccuping *again?*" Her clerk, Abby, joined her at the reference desk. Abby's wardrobe changed along with her choice in reading material. Currently she was devouring *The Catcher in the Rye* at Rosemary's suggestion and had replaced the 1940s shoulder pads with a pearl-buttoned sweater set, full skirt and saddle shoes. "You should get those hiccups checked out," she said. "My boyfriend's brother hiccuped for thirty-five days straight and didn't stop until they took him to the hospital."

"What did the hospital do for him?"

Abby helped herself to a mint. "They ran a CAT scan and found out he'd swallowed a quarter at his cousin's bar mitzvah."

A shiver of alarm pattered up Rosemary's back. *Hic.* "That's what was causing him to hiccup?"

Working the mint around her mouth, Abby shrugged. "Doubtful. He'd gone to the bar mitzvah two years earlier. Good to know there was a quarter in there, though. I think they operated. I'll ask. In the meantime, want me to scare you?"

"You just did." *Hic.* "I'm going to refill my water bottle."

"Okay. Oh!" Reaching into the folds of her pink skirt, Abby withdrew an envelope. "Here. For you."

Rosemary accepted the square linen envelope, noting her name—and nothing more—printed neatly on the front. "Where'd you get this?"

"My friend Polly brought it by when she came to drop off books."

"Polly?" Frowning, Rosemary tried to remember if she'd met a Polly in town.

"She's in high school with my cousin Emily. Polly works at the pharmacy."

The tips of Rosemary's fingers began to itch with the desire to rip open the envelope. Controlling herself, she shrugged her eyebrows and said, "Hmm." *Look at me, all indifferent.*

Forcing herself to toss—not place carefully, but actually toss—the envelope next to the keyboard on her desk, as if she wasn't the least bit curious, Rosemary feigned a businesslike glance at her watch.

"Why don't you take lunch now," she suggested. "I'll hold down the fort until story hour."

"Okay. Cool. I brought leftovers, so I'll be in the back, reading, if you need me."

Rosemary sat calmly until Abby was out of eyesight and then, because no one else was nearby, she fumbled the envelope open with shaky fingers and pulled out a simple ivory card with an embossed *K* at the top. She hiccuped once before she read the message:

Rosemary,
Hoping you will join me for dinner tomorrow evening at the Honeyford Inn, 7 p.m. Regrets only.
Dean

Above the too-rapid beat of her heart, Rosemary reread the inked lines. This was the first time she'd seen Dean's handwriting—clear, bold letters, not too fancy yet with a distinct style. He'd drawn a small happy face after "Regrets only."

This was also the first time he had formally invited her on a date.

Rosemary's hand wandered to her tummy. She patted the baby. "Sorry we've done this backward, sweetie pie. Mama has never had a good sense of direction where men are concerned."

Her breath caught in her throat almost painfully as she realized another first: the first time she referred to herself as Mama. the image of herself holding a baby with hair as soft as kitten fur, teensy fingers with teensy nails and toes that looked like bay shrimp filled her with a flood of emotion that made tears spring to her eyes. Instantly, however, worry chased the love. Her mind began to reel with *What if* and *Oh, no* statements.

What if she had a daughter, and her wonderful, beautiful, tenderhearted girl had the same rotten luck with men that Rosemary, her mother and sisters had? *Oh, no!*

What if she had a son, and he sensed that his mother was weak, confused and cynical about men? *Oh, no!*

What if she and Dean disagreed about parenting techniques, and their child grew up confused, angry and disillusioned? *Oh, no, no, no!*

The nausea returned so strongly Rosemary was sorry she'd told Abby to take her break.

Scrabbling for the peppermints again, she sucked air like

a fish in cloudy water. This settled it: she had to establish a good relationship with Dean. One that was open, mutually respectful and, above all else, sane. The youngest of her sisters, Rosemary didn't remember their father at all, but Lucy had once purchased two Siamese fighting fish, housing them in a small bowl with a clear divider. The fish would puff their fins and glare at each other as if they'd like to bust through the plastic separating them and rip each other's heads off. Lucy had named them Mom and Dad.

"And look what happened to us," Rosemary muttered, wondering what her patrons would think if she put her head between her knees to calm the dizziness.

Slipping Dean's card into the pocket of her cardigan, she knew they would need to talk, to map out exactly how they planned to parent, how to conduct their relationship, and precisely how to end it when the time came. And they needed to arrive at these understandings quickly, before they could harm their child in any way. Nothing should be left to chance or the whims of the day.

It began to occur to Rosemary that life was handing her an opportunity she had given up on completely—the chance to be someone's mother and to do it well.

A sense of wonder began to rush like an un-dammed river through her veins. She had already resigned herself to reading *The Dr. Seuss Sleep Book* during library story hour, but never with a sleepy, pajama-covered bundle of her own tucked beneath her arm. She'd stopped imagining making animal-cracker zoos and Lego Ferris wheels. Out of a sense of self-preservation, she had changed her goals and told herself it was…okay. Now the dreams she had relegated to the discard pile could be pulled out again.

Where nausea had dominated only moments before, Rosemary now felt like a balloon, so filled with joy she might pop. She covered her belly with both hands.

"It's going to be so good, sweet darling baby. You're going to have the best life. And you don't have to worry about your father and me. We'll find a way to do this so everyone gets along." Her promise was a solemn whisper. "We'll never, ever, ever hurt you."

The Honeyford Inn occupied a three-story brick building downtown. Hotel rooms comprised the top floor, with a restaurant serving Eastern European cuisine making up the main and lower levels.

Rosemary had heard the food was excellent and was actually looking forward to her evening with Dean. In fact, she hadn't felt as queasy today and was hungry as a bear.

After work yesterday, she'd driven over an hour to Bend, where she'd hit every major store selling anything related to babies, children, pregnant women or parenting. Onesies and adorable knit hats, a doll-size snowsuit in fire-engine red, a Boppy pillow for breast-feeding, Winnie the Pooh bookends and the most current parenting books filled the shopping bags she had lugged to her car.

She hadn't been able to resist the maternity stores, either, and handed the maître d' her coat to reveal her first maternity-related purchase for herself—a silky, V-necked dress in variegated swirls of hot pink and red. The dress had a stretchy tummy panel (so cute!) and a gorgeous drape. The extra folds of material looked fabulous now and would expand as necessary to accommodate her growing belly. Her budget took a hit when she wrote the check to Angel Kisses Maternity for a garment she didn't strictly *need* yet, but it was worth it. Oh, mama, was it worth it! This dress was a celebration.

"Your party is waiting for you in the cellar," the maître d' informed her formally.

Rosemary followed him down a short staircase to "the cellar," a wonderful room with brick walls, thick wood pillars and five linen-cloaked tables, each a comfortable distance from the next, providing an eminently private and cozy setting. There was even a fire snapping in the wood-burning fireplace.

Dean rose as Rosemary approached.

A twinge of anxiety threatened as she wondered if he was still upset about the prenup, but the look in his eyes calmed her.

"You look…stunning."

His expression reflected every woman's dream response to her dolling-up efforts. His gaze took in her hair, her face, the dress, and his slow-spreading smile made her feel like the only woman in the room even though every table was filled with diners.

"You look nice, too. I like your suit."

He smoothed his tie. Dean looked, she thought, like an ad for Yves St. Laurent for men. Compliments traded, they sat. Rosemary told herself that all she had to do tonight was enjoy the company of the man she had, on one fateful night, found too delicious to resist. Tonight she would be cordial, engaging, interested, but a whole lot calmer. And, of course, she'd keep her clothes on this time, because they were in public, and she didn't want another episode like the one in his apartment.

It was a good plan, and it didn't even sound that difficult. All she had to do was keep a clear head.

Accepting the wine list, Dean lifted a brow at his dinner companion. No alcoholic beverages for her, though they were the only two people present who knew why. Dean hoped she would let him rectify that tonight. He'd done a lot of thinking since their kiss on his couch, and now he had a goal and a plan. It was time to go public with their relationship.

After they ordered drinks and dinner, he kept the conversation light and upbeat, telling her about Honeyford's illustrious history (founded by a family of Italian beekeepers named

Castigliano, many of whom were terrified of bees), the upcoming spring festival—Honeyford Days—and the fact that his limelight-loathing little brother had been roped into being Grand Marshal.

"Fletcher was in the rodeo. Back then he was meaner than some of the bulls he rode, but he's got a movie-star puss the women loved. He wound up doing clothing ads, a few TV commercials. He'd signed on for a role in a movie, a Western, before he had an accident that laid him up for months and finally brought him back home."

"Wait a minute." Rosemary sat back from the bread pudding she'd made a sizable dent in. "Fletcher Kingsley is your brother? Fletcher Kingsley, the Tuff Enuff jeans model?"

Dean winced. "Yeah, let's not refer to him as a 'model' at family gatherings like Thanksgiving or Christmas, though, okay?" He winked. "Best to keep peace in the family."

"Okay, but you have to let me get a signed photo for my friend Vi. She set her TiVo for those jeans commercials."

He laughed then lowered his voice way, way down. "You seem to be feeling better. How's the morning sickness?"

Rosemary didn't seem to mind the topic change. "Better since yesterday."

"Good. According to the book, it gets better after the first trimester, and you're almost there."

"You're still reading the book?"

"I like to follow along, imagine where you're at." Again, he'd spoken softly and was pleased to see that she didn't mind the references to her pregnancy.

"I do feel a hundred percent better," Rosemary offered, spooning up another taste of the custard sauce beneath the bread pudding. "I went shopping in Bend last night as a matter of fact and ate at The Olive Garden. I'm not even going to think about how many breadsticks I had." She leaned over the table and smiled in a way that made Dean's heart skip.

"Maternity clothes have this fabulous expandable panel in the front. All pants should be made that way."

He glanced toward the couple at the table closest to them. The Marsdens had greeted Dean when they'd first arrived twenty minutes earlier. Currently they were occupied with the pierogi appetizer and appeared no more interested in Dean's conversation with Rosemary than Dean and Rosemary were in the pierogis.

Dean knew, however, that he was about to make them much, much more interested. He crossed his fingers that he was doing the right thing.

"More coffee?" The word emerged hoarsely. *Damn.* When was the last time he'd been nervous? Couldn't remember. Clearing his throat, he tried again. "Coffee?"

Setting her spoon on her plate, Rosie leaned back in her chair and held up a hand. "Lord, no, I'm stuffed to the gills. Making up for lost time, I guess. Everything was delicious."

"Here we are." Holding a silver tray, Josef and Annette, owners of the Honeyford Inn, approached the table. "A special dessert, just for you." With great care, Annette set before Rosie a china plate with a thick square of darkest chocolate topped by a marzipan rose. A gold ribbon bow sat on the edge of the plate.

Rosie looked at the creation with something approaching alarm, but recovered well and smiled charmingly at the pair that hovered over the table. "It's beautiful. Did you make it here?"

"Yes!" Annette nodded eagerly. "One of a kind. With a surprise inside."

"Mama, shh." Josef patted Annette on the arm then pointed a gnarled finger at the plate. "Taste." He waggled his thick gray brows.

Dean grimaced. Subtle as a sledgehammer.

Rosie looked slightly sick at the thought of more dessert.

"That dinner was *so* fabulous, and the bread pudding was amazing. I don't think I have room for anything else right now." She lifted the plate to hand it across the table. "Maybe Dean—"

"No!" Josef and Annette both stretched out a hand. Startled, Rosemary clunked the plate back onto the table.

Dean narrowed his eyes at the duo.

"We want *you* to try it." Josef looked at her appealingly. "Dean, he's been coming here since he was young. It will mean more if you tell us how *you* like it."

"Oh. Well…I suppose there's always room for a tiny bite." Picking up the small silver fork sitting on the plate, she sliced a piece of the dense chocolate and chewed obligingly. Her smile was only a little strained. "Delicious."

Josef looked worried. "No, eat the rose."

Dean shook his head. "Maybe you could give us a minute—"

But Rosie was already dutifully forking up a marzipan petal and raising it to her lips. "Mmm." She looked as if she could barely swallow. Once she'd managed the feat, she set down the fork and sat back. "It's a lovely dessert. Are you putting it on the menu?"

Annette and Josef looked at each other in grave concern. Annette began to wring her hands. They both turned to Dean.

It was hardly the way he'd envisioned the moment. Reaching for the plate, he pulled it toward him. Nestled amidst the formed flowers, was the object of the whole dessert. He plucked it out of the marzipan, stood and didn't even bother to try to exile Annette and Joseph.

"Excuse me," he said, shouldering past them. When he reached Rosie, he knelt. Her eyes turned into huge hazel moons as he held the ruby ring out to her.

"It's taken my entire adult life—and no small part of my

adolescence—to find you," he began. "I've imagined what life would be like with a woman who was my best friend, my partner in all that's good and my bulwark against the tough times. I've imagined what it would be like to be that person for someone else, and I've never trusted that I could be, not a hundred percent. Until now."

He reached for one of her hands, resting limply in her lap while she gaped at him. Holding her fingers and the ring, he gazed steadily into her eyes, unmindful of the whispers that circled the room.

"Rosemary Josephine Jeffers," he said, "will you be that woman, that partner and friend, and allow me to be yours? Will you believe in me when the going is rough and trust that I believe in you, too? Because more than anything in my life right now, I would like to be your husband." He took a breath and hit the bull's-eye. "Will you marry me?"

Josef sniffled. The room went utterly silent, save for a watery "Awww" in the background. Dean's heart pounded the seconds as he awaited a response from the woman who appeared, currently, like a photograph taken immediately after someone had jumped out and yelled, "Surprise!"

Well, he thought, swallowing around a knot in his throat that felt as if he'd overtightened his tie, *that went well.*

The first time a man had asked her to marry him, she'd choked on a pepperoni. Choked in joy, of course.

Rosemary had been dating Neil for three-and-a-half years. At the time of the proposal, he'd been preparing for his second year of law school, and she had recently packed all her worldly goods to move to Seattle, where she was going to earn her Master's degree in Library and Information Sciences.

"Maybe we should get married," Neil had said over a large pie—half pepperoni and green pepper for her, half kitchen sink for him (if only she'd realized then that he had trouble discriminating).

"I'm leaving for U of W in two weeks," she had protested (admittedly weakly) once the pepperoni had gone down. Washington had one of the top-ranked Library Sciences programs in the country. She'd been planning since high school to get her degree there. She'd had an apartment, her student loans and a part-time job at a local public library all lined up. Neil had known that. They'd talked about it, talked about how they would navigate a long-distance relationship.

"You can get your Master's in Portland." His goofy smile had massaged the cavalier comment into something romantic, daring almost. *Give up your plans for me, baby. Love will make it worth the while.*

And she had seen it then, if she'd been honest enough to admit it—his fear that the "the long-distance thing" would not work. He had known he would stray.

At the time, however, Rosemary had told herself Neil couldn't wait to marry her, that he was itching to be a family man. She'd insisted to herself and her sisters and mother that true love really did exist and that marriage wouldn't hold them back; it would be the wind beneath their wings.

It hadn't even bothered her that her student loans had not transferred, that she'd wound up working full-time in the Multnomah County Public Library System—first shelving books and then as a clerk—while she went to school, that she had developed migraines, or that she'd slept an average of four hours a night for two years. What difference did any of that make, she'd told herself, in the long run? She and Neil were bound to start a family soon, anyway; she'd be staying home for several years once their first baby arrived since no way was she going to repeat her own childhood. She would get her degree now and use it in the future.

She and Neil had gone ring shopping together and purchased

what they could afford at the time—Black Hills Gold bands with a diamond chip for each of them. He'd lost his on a river-rafting trip (white water, after all) before their second anniversary. She had cherished hers until the day she'd taken it off for good.

Now, a good decade after that first proposal, she stared at what appeared to be a diamond-crusted platinum band with a heart-shaped ruby nestled in the center. *Yowza.* Unless Dean's morning cereal had come with an unusually good piece of costume jewelry, this was the real deal, and it was a ring like nothing she had ever imagined on her finger. The only thing that brought the confection down to earth was the marzipan gumming up one row of tiny prong-set diamonds.

"Will you…" he had just asked on bended knee. With a great preamble.

What he had not said: *Will you marry me, Rosemary Jeffers, mother of the baby we did not plan, even though we've already agreed we're going to divorce before we've picked out a preschool?*

He knew and she knew they were going to get married; he needn't have bothered with the trappings of a proposal.

A muffled whimper cut through Rosemary's thoughts, and she glanced beyond Dean to Annette, who clutched Josef's hand and compressed her lips so as not to sob out loud.

Unlocked, Rosemary's gaze traveled the intimate, candlelit room to see that the customers at all five tables in the Honeyford Inn's cellar were glued to the action as if it were the final rose ceremony on *The Bachelorette.*

Surely the news would travel upstairs to the main dining room before the end of the evening. By tomorrow more and more people would know that the hometown pharmacist had proposed to Honeyford's new librarian as prettily as any man deeply in love.

And suddenly Rosemary realized: he'd done it this way to

get the ball rolling. By the time people discovered she was pregnant, the myth that she and Dean loved each other to distraction would be the stuff of local legend. Their child could grow up in Honeyford and never hear that he or she had been "an accident."

She looked again at the man who knelt before her. In the dim light Dean's blue eyes looked like a calm sea, steady and eternal. *Take your time,* his gaze told her. *I'm not going anywhere.*

Surely she was supposed to speak now. A small dining-roomful of people waited for her to complete this über-romantic moment. But über-romantic dialogue required some emotional investment, and she had no idea what her emotions were at present. Was it normal to feel numb and sort of dazed and that was all when a man said all the right things and then presented you with a ring that would rock the world of any girl who had grown up staging and restaging her engagement with Barbie dolls?

Finally Rosemary had a good proposal with which to entertain her children and grandchildren. Dean's proposal was one she could recite again by heart for their fiftieth anniversary party at the Governor Hotel in downtown Portland. It was a proposal from which tender excerpts could be culled for inclusion on side-by-side tombstones.

Damned shame that none of it was real.

Probably fewer than thirty seconds rolled by, during which Dean remained calm and charitably patient, but a quiet murmur arose in the peanut gallery. "Did she hear him?" someone whispered.

She knew she should respond immediately, but…

This could be my last—and best—proposal. I should at least know what I feel.

Gratitude. She felt grateful that he'd wrapped their child—and her, as well—in a gauzy fairy tale, for the time being anyway. Maybe it wasn't very forthright or very modern, and perhaps Oprah would frown, but she'd rather have people gossip about her whirlwind courtship than her one-night stand.

Besides gratitude, she felt…affection, actually. Dean Kingsley had taken this entire situation better than most men would have. He was kind. And he had integrity.

And besides gratitude and affection, there was that feeling of lust that kept cropping up, especially when she looked at his ears. It was weird, her reaction to those ears, but he had longish earlobes. Longish earlobes that had felt velvety when she'd nibbled on them back in December. There was something about long lobes that said *stability.* You could grow old with them.

For an instant an image slashed across her mind. Two old people, one with curly gray hair and one with long ears, sitting on the porch of a sweet two-story house with dormers, a stone chimney and a birdhouse they'd made themselves hanging from the branch of an oak tree. The old couple laughed as they reminisced….

"Remember when Montana told the neighbor boy she had a magic hat that made people fly, and they climbed onto the roof to test it out?"

"Remember how Nate used to sit under the oak tree with Buster and tell that old dog all his secrets?"

Oh, my gosh, they even had an old dog….

There was a for-sale sign on the front lawn, because now that it was just the two of them, they were moving to something smaller. Their new place still had a formal dining room, though—she'd insisted on that—for big family Thanksgivings and Christmases. And on the wall of their new living room they intended to hang a photo of the house that had held their family so sweetly during the growing-up years….

Swallowed tears put a lump in Rosemary's throat.

She looked at Dean, so calm, so steady, and her foolish heart began to hope.

What if she was getting one more chance at forever? Maybe…just maybe…this time—

Hic.

Oh, no.

Hic-hic. Oh, holy heaven. She slapped a hand to her breast-bone. Her worst case of hiccups yet began the assault on her diaphragm. *Hic-hic-hic.*

"Rosie?" Dean's expression, previously the picture of for-bearance, began to exhibit some tension. "You all right?"

Her eyes bugged at Dean. Poor Dean. This was not a proper response at all. "I'm fine—" *Hic.* "Ow. Maybe a little water—" *Hic-hic.* Ohhh, why did she eat the whole bread pud-ding? Every hiccup felt like a blender churning the contents of her stomach.

"Push under her ribs, once. Hard," Josef instructed as Dean stood.

"That's for choking." Annette slapped her husband's arm. "She should suck on a hard candy while drinking a glass of water with one tablespoon of cider vinegar. I'll get it."

Rosemary groaned. "No—" *Hic-hic.*

Dean put a hand on her shoulder. It was warm and com-forting. "Is another massage in order?" he whispered, a brow hooked.

She hiccuped in his face.

"Have her jump up and down on one leg and—"

"She should sing the national anthem while—"

"Put your fingers in your ears and hold your breath for a full minute."

Pelted by advice, Rosemary's head began to ache as much as her stomach. Only the hand on her shoulder provided re-lief, and she wanted to lean into it, to rest against the body in front of her. She was tired. All the worries and uncertainty and secrecy of the past few weeks had been exhausting. Was Dean exhausted? Her eyes met his. He cocked his head.

Oh, Dean. Poor, poor Dean. He had publicly proposed and earned a spate of hiccups in response. She looked for the ring in his free hand, prepared to give him the public acceptance he deserved. He really was a gentleman, a decent person, a—

Hic!

A glass of water was lifted to her lips. Dean again. Gratefully, she took long, breath-stealing gulps and then waited a moment. Calm. *There. Now please let that be the end of it.* She pushed the glass aside. Where was the ring?

"Dean." She focused on his eyes. Kind and, yes, honest eyes. "Dean, I—"

Abruptly, droplets of sweat popped onto her forehead and above her upper lip and then…pretty much everywhere else very quickly. Rosemary had a sudden mental image of the food in her stomach looking like dozens of crazed beavers building a dam against white water. Her hands went round her middle.

Hold on, Rosemary. Just hold on. The man deserves a proper response.

"Dean." She shoved a smile to her lips. "I…I… Uh-oh."

The restroom was on the main level of the restaurant, ten steps up from the cellar.

Rosemary wasted no time. She made a run for it, leaving behind a roomful of spectators and Dean, who doubtless would remember this moment for the rest of his days.

It looked as if the second proposal she'd received in her life was going to be even harder to put a spin on than the first.

"Rosemary, it's Dean. I'm coming in."

Too busy to argue, Rosemary continued giving up her dinner as Dean entered the women's room. Unoccupied save for the pathetic barfing pregnant woman, the bathroom was not, alas, as soundproof as Rosemary would have wished. She heard the clinking of china and glasses and the hum of the diners. Then, directly behind her, came Dean's softly uttered swear.

"Aw, Rosie..."

He held her hair, stroked her back then brought her a moist paper towel. Any embarrassment Rosemary might have suffered dissipated beneath the quilt of comforting murmurs and Dean's immensely soothing back rub.

Who knew how many minutes passed before he asked, "Is it always this bad?"

Rosemary shook her head, dabbing her brow with the towel as she leaned against the sink. "Days aren't great, but I stick to crackers and toast so I can't get too sick." Folding the damp paper, she tossed it in the trash. "Nights are usually fine."

"Unless you're proposed to?" His voice was rich with irony, but devoid of anger.

"Oh, my. You really are a nice man," she said softly, surprising a wince out of him.

"Rosie—"

"No, truly. I...I can see that, and I'm sorry I've made things so difficult."

"Rosie, I need—"

"I accept your proposal." She made a face. "Obviously I accept it. I mean, we planned it, but...you didn't have to do it this way, with so much thoughtfulness, and I appreciate it."

"Yeah. Ro—"

"Unless, of course, you want to rescind it after all this." She laughed, but became acutely aware that every part of her, every tiny little part of her, hoped he would say, *Hell no, I'm not rescinding anything.*

Good golly crackers, she truly was starting to believe in him. Maybe she'd begun to believe in him a while ago, and that accounted for the nerves—

"Oh, my gosh," she realized suddenly. "I'm not hiccuping." She blinked at the realization, waiting to be sure. "They're gone. I'm accepting a marriage proposal to a genuinely nice man, and I'm not hiccuping!" The hope she'd squashed so ruthlessly began to peek through her season of disillusionment, like the sun finding it's way through a break in the clouds.

Dean arched a brow. "This is progress, I take it?"

She nodded and whispered, "This is progress."

Some expression she couldn't identify lingered until at last his gaze cleared to azure blue. He reached a hand into his coat pocket.

In the modest but homey ladies' room of the Honeyford Inn, Dean proposed to Rosemary again, without the bended knee and tender words this time (they really did need to get out of the bathroom), yet Rosemary felt more content accepting him than she'd ever imagined she could be.

Slipping the ring on her finger, he said, "I guessed at the size. And the gemstone."

She ought to have protested a ring so costly, particularly when theirs was a union with start-stop dates. If the marriage ended—*when* the marriage ended—she would give the ring back to him, but for now, after upchucking at his first attempt to formally propose, Rosemary was determined to be gracious. "I think rubies are lovely. So different."

"We began differently." He held her hand, the low lights making the heart-shaped stone glow warmly. "Maybe we'll end on an up note."

Or, Rosemary thought for the first time, shocked when she didn't freak out at the thought, *maybe we won't end at all.*

They exited the restroom together, and Rosemary was stunned to find a group of people from the cellar waiting for them, plus most of the upstairs diners turned their way to see what the fuss was about.

"Isn't that the new librarian?"

"Really? Was she drinking?"

"So did she say yes or no?" asked one of the women from the cellar. "I didn't hear."

Rosemary felt her left hand clasped and squeezed. She glanced up.

Dean smiled, just for her. His upstage eye closed in a private wink. Then, turning toward the dining room, he raised their hands for everyone to see. The ruby ring drew wide-eyed stares. And a gasp from Annette.

"You're looking at the luckiest man in the world," he said.

Annette's sweet face crumpled as she burst into happy tears. She and Josef embraced. "In our restaurant," he blubbered, patting his wife's back.

Applause erupted from the small crowd gathered outside the bathroom and "Congratulations!" echoed around the dining room.

Rosemary couldn't help it: she started to cry, too…because everyone was so sweet, and because Dean sounded so sincere and because, if only in this moment, she was able to set aside the facts surrounding her engagement and focus on the feelings. And what she felt—even if it would only be for this one moment—was like the world's luckiest woman.

Chapter Eleven

"You're playing with fire."

Fletcher leaned against the outer wall of a horse stall, eating his pecan roll while Dean viciously stabbed clean hay with a pitchfork.

"I know it," Dean growled, spreading the straw around the interior of the stall. "Don't you think I know that?"

Fletcher shrugged. "If you know it then why are you here shoveling hay instead of coming clean about the will with Rosemary? And what is it about my ranch chores that attract you when you're hiding out? Not that I'm complaining." Lifting a red Honey Bea's travel mug, he took a long pull of coffee.

"I need the physical outlet." Dean pushed the words through gritted teeth. "I can't release tension counting pills."

"Understandable." Fletcher swirled the coffee inside the mug. "According to Claire, half the town is babbling about your engagement. Very romantic and all that crap. You might have been better off keeping things private if you're not going to tell Rosemary the truth. Keep things a little more low-key to spare her feelings in the long run."

"Thanks for the tip, Dr. Phil." Dean took another ferocious stab at the hay. "How many people know about the will?"

"Aside from you and me?" Fletcher popped the rest of the pecan roll in his mouth and thought. "Claire, of course. Gwen."

Dean nodded. Their father's mistress was the mayor of Honeyford and the executor of Victor's will. Fortunately, Gwen was also an eminently reasonable woman. She believed the marriage codicil to be a huge mistake. Although she loved Honeyford and had numerous plans to bring more revenue to the often-struggling town, she did not want to feather Honeyford's nest with Fletcher or Dean's inheritance. She'd sold Pine Road Ranch back to Fletcher for a dollar.

Dean stopped working and backhanded sweat off his brow. "I approached Gwen about buying the building on Main if I default on the will. She thinks she'll get resistance from the city council. You were right—Doug Thorpe's been badgering the city to buy up stores and find lessees with upscale businesses. He's not going to go for a low-cost, bilingual medical clinic."

Fletcher nodded. "So why aren't you telling Rosemary the truth? That inheriting the building is going to benefit people who sorely need a medical clinic."

Dean sighed, feeling out of touch with himself for perhaps the first time in his life. "I planned to. The morning after I proposed. After I made it clear to the town how I feel about her, so there won't be any question about why we're marrying." Fletcher would understand that. He had been bound and determined not to allow any demeaning gossip to affect his wife on account of the blasted will. "I was going to tell her about the will and the clinic and then let her know that I'm going to forfeit the building, because I don't want that hanging over our heads for the next two years. I want to make this marriage work. I need this family to work."

"So what happened?" Fletcher asked.

"I got a letter." Dean rubbed the back of his neck. He was working on a forty-eight-hour headache ibuprofen hadn't been able to touch. "From a doctor who wants to help open and then work in the clinic."

"I didn't know you'd started recruiting already."

"I haven't," Dean said. "I've been working on grants. She found out about it from an aunt who knows Alberto."

"She. The doc is a woman?"

"Esmeralda Duran. Her mother is Guatemalan. Father's Spanish. Esmeralda trained as an EMT then went to UC Irvine for her medical degree. She's coming off two years of volunteer work in Guatemala."

"Speaks Spanish then."

"Fluently. Wrote eloquently about how she wants to support the community not only with medical aid, but also education. She heard about Clinica Adelina from an aunt who lives in the area. The aunt heard about it from Alberto."

Fletcher whistled. "Perfect. But if you default on the will..."

"I'll have no building. I've got a real-estate agent combing the area for something suitable."

"But you'll have to buy the building or pay rent."

"Right. It'll be a setback, not one I'm sure we can conquer soon. How do I tell Alberto the plans are on hold, indefinitely? And how do I turn away a doctor who can make it all come together?"

"By keeping your mouth shut, getting married to the mother of your child and hoping she'll understand when the truth comes out?"

Grimacing, Dean nodded slowly. "That might be my plan," he admitted.

Fletcher wagged his head. "Poor dumb, love-struck bastard. I mean that in a good way." He swirled the coffee in his mug, his expression changing from something almost affectionate to a thoughtful frown. "All these years I've never asked you…what was it like for you, growing up with Jule as a stepmother?" His mouth quirked ironically. "And me as a brother? That must have scared you off starting a family. At least a little."

The question caught Dean by surprise. Though they shared the same father, he and Fletcher had been born to vastly different mothers. Victor Kingsley had married twice in his life—first Dean's mother, by all accounts a gentle and gracious woman who had died from cancer when Dean was only five, and then Jule, a far more flamboyant, mercurial and, ultimately, troubled young woman.

"I thought the early years were good," Dean said carefully. "Until Jule's bipolar disorder got really out of hand, there were some happy times for all of us. But I've never blamed her, Fletch—or you—for the problems."

Fletcher nodded. "Well, thanks for that. The problems, though…the fights and the separations…they make you wonder whether you can do it differently, don't they? Victor wasn't the greatest role model when it came to open lines of communication. I've had nights when I've woken up in full panic, wondering if I can give my kids a decent childhood, wondering whether I even know what that looks like."

Perspiration that had zilch to do with physical activity covered Dean's brow. He had an abrupt urge to bolt, leaving the stall—and the conversation—unfinished.

"You seem to be doing a good job," he told his brother. "The boys are happy. And you're already your daughter's hero."

The cowboy who had once seemed impervious to a

vulnerable moment began to look slightly green. "Yeah, that's now. I just thank God for Claire. She straightens me out when I start to stress."

"Well, this is great. Two grown men panicked over relationships."

"You want to email Dr. Phil?"

"Nope."

Dean shook his head. He was so screwed. Smitten by a woman—utterly, thoroughly smitten—for the first time in his life. About to become a husband and, in a few months, a father. Beneath the fear, he was excited about all of it, yet he couldn't get to know Rosemary—or rely on her for support—because of this thing, this lie, hanging over them. In addition to his headache, he'd been nursing serious nausea all day and wondered if he was experiencing sympathetic morning sickness or simple guilt.

"I'm forfeiting the building. I have to. I can't explain this to Rosemary in a way that will make sense."

"You mean you can't explain it in a way that won't make her think she's marrying into a family of lunatics."

On even the worst days of his life, Dean had been able to calm his mind and his body, to keep his reactions sane and focused. Millie, who'd worked at King's since Dean was a kid, had once told him he would never need a blood-pressure pill. It appeared those days were gone; he felt as if the pressure in his body were going to pop his head off like a cork.

Smacking his fist again the stall, he said, "I need the kind of chance we'd have if this were a normal relationship."

"Kingsleys don't do normal."

"I do."

"You gave it the old college try," Fletcher agreed. "But you were alone. Try to do 'normal' now that you're alive below the neck."

Dean longed to take offense. Before Rosemary, he'd have

argued that his emotions were present, simply calm and sane, unlike Fletcher's. Now he knew better. Now he knew what passion was.

"I can't tell Rosemary about the will, not yet. I've started my family with more baggage than we can handle. I've got to get rid of the problem, and that means forfeiting the building."

Once the words were out, Dean felt a weight lift from his shoulders. "I'll talk to Doug and the rest of the city council, try to make them understand how necessary the clinic is for the underinsured. Maybe they'll do the right thing and donate the building for the clinic."

"Will you tell Alberto?"

The weight pressed down again, like a lead yoke. "I'll have to. But not until I speak to Gwen and the others. And look around for another venue if I have to. Alberto has the most riding on this." His stomach began to churn, and he wondered if love made that a continual state of affairs. "He's got to make sense of his daughter's death."

Fletcher's sober gaze skewered his brother. "And Rosemary? What's next?"

"That's easier," Dean said, praying he was right. "We get married. Fall in love and have a baby. In that order."

Dean and Rosemary sittin' in a tree. K-i-s-s-i-n-g. First comes marriage, then comes love, then comes Dean Jr. in a baby carriage….

Rosemary stared at the skinny platinum band that had joined her engagement ring four days ago, the singsongy lyrics of the old children's melody playing in her mind as she wondered what to wear. Dean would be home…home to her house…in half an hour.

She had dinner—chicken, shallot and baby portabello casserole in a sublime Burgundy sauce—bubbling in the oven. She'd set the table with multicolored braided tapers and the blown-glass stemware she'd purchased after regifting Vi with her wedding crystal. Three potential outfits were laid out on the bed, awaiting her decision. A lot had changed in four days.

She had married Dean in Reno on Saturday. They had "honeymooned" for a couple of days then returned to Honeyford last night. This evening he was going to begin the process of moving into her place.

Rosemary stood at the foot of her queen-size bed, trying to decide between jeans and a boat-necked pullover in powder blue or a more formal skirt and sweater combo, when the phone rang.

Checking the caller ID, she smiled. "Hi, Daph. I was going to try you tomorrow."

"That is way too late." Her friend's voice sounded muffled.

"Watcha doin'?" Rosemary asked, holding the blue sweater up and tilting her head at the mirror. "You sound funny."

"I'm eating coconut-milk ice cream," she said around an apparently large mouthful. "It's *sooooo* good. Have you ever tried it?"

"Which flavor?"

"Coffee chip for dinner. I had Almond Joy as a midafternoon snack—that was good, too—piña colada for lunch, and triple-fudge-brownie for breakfast. My commitment to celibacy is going really well."

Rosemary smiled. "Sounds like it."

"So how about you? You've been married four whole days…and nights. Are *you* still celibate?"

"Yes."

"Bummer." Daphne shoved another spoonful of coffee chip into her mouth. "How was the wedding?"

Rosemary returned the sweater to the bed and moved to her dresser to pluck a pair of turquoise drops from an earring tree. "It was nice. I thought we'd get married at city hall or next to a blackjack table, but Dean found a chapel that was actually kind of sweet. Pitched roof, white gingerbread trim, pansies out front…."

"Awwww. Were you married by a minister?"

"I don't know. He had teased hair and offered an Elvis option. Does that say *minister* to you?"

Daphne laughed. "From the church of Elvis, yes. Did Dean kiss you?"

"Um, chastely."

"Darn. What did you do after you got married?"

"Well—" Rosemary poked the earrings into her lobes "—as we left, the minister's wife tossed birdseed and then handed us a pamphlet of their services, which include but are not limited to shuttle service to and from local casinos, infant baptism and marriage-dissolution counseling should the need arise."

"Sounds like every girl's dream wedding."

"Yup. Once we were alone, there was a moment of, shall we say, extreme awkwardness outside the chapel. Then Dean kissed my hand and said, 'Thank you for marrying me. Let's go somewhere else for the infant baptism.'"

Daphne laughed. "I like your husband."

Happy bubbles, reminiscent of the champagne she hadn't been able to drink, floated up from Rosemary's stomach. "I like him, too," she whispered, so softly she wasn't sure her friend heard until Daphne whooped.

"Details, please!"

Rosemary smiled. She and Dean had "honeymooned," otherwise known as Making the Marriage Look Real, by driving to Virginia City, where they had shopped, played slot machines (Rosemary won forty dollars on an old-fashioned nickel machine) and ate excellent chili at a little hole-in-the-wall. They returned to Reno at night, went to their—*separate*—

rooms, changed and attended a performance of Cirque du Soleil. And they talked.

They talked about Dean's college days and hers, about their favorite childhood hobbies (bug collection and tennis for him; cooking in her Easy-Bake Oven and ice skating for her), and about child-rearing philosophies (they had both purchased Patrice Moore's *Back to Basics* and loved the common-sense approach).

Every night, Dean walked Rosemary to her hotel room, held her hand, kissed her cheek and said, "Thank you."

Every night, she imagined how it would feel if he stayed.

When she admitted that out loud, Daphne's voice filled with wonder. "Honestly? You're falling for him?"

Rosemary closed her eyes. "I'm weak. Tell me I'm weak and that I'm conducting my life like a romantic comedy and that carpe diem dating is the only good idea I've had since I bought the Barbie-and-Ken wedding suite."

"Carpe diem dating is a really good idea," Daphne said dutifully, "in theory. In reality, it's kind of like crocheting a zip line. You can try and try, but it's never gonna hold. We're die-hard romantics, Rosemary."

"But you're committed to celibacy. That's a plan to keep from being hurt again. It's okay not to want to be hurt, right?"

On the other end of the line, Daphne sighed. "Well, I'm still planning to date, so I'll probably still get hurt. I'm just trying to weed out the real contenders from the phonies."

"Which makes excellent sense!"

"Yes. For me. But, Rosemary, what if you've already found your real contender? What if Dean Kingsley is your destiny, and you keep resisting until it's time for you to split up and then it's too late?"

Rosemary felt hiccups coming on. "If Dean Kingsley were

my destiny, I would know for certain, wouldn't I? I mean, I would be feeling peace right now."

"I don't know. Destiny could be like coconut ice cream. You'll never know how right it's going to be unless you dive in and take a bite. Then…kismet."

"Kismet," Rosemary murmured.

"One more thing you might want to consider," Daphne said, and Rosemary could tell she was enjoying the ice cream again. "This whole celibacy thing?"

"Yeah?"

"It's really fattening."

Dean arrived bearing a suitcase and a gift for his bride.

"Crystallized ginger," he announced, handing her a package of cellophane-wrapped candy. "My sister-in-law swears there's nothing better for morning sickness. If it works, we'll start carrying it at the drugstore. And these—" he whipped a bouquet of two dozen long-stemmed yellow roses out from beneath his arm and lowered his voice to the intimate caress that sent goose bumps racing down her arms "—are for the beautiful lady of the house."

"Thank you." Rosemary accepted both gifts, leading the way into her cottage-style home. Nerves rattled her bones. Dean always managed to appear utterly sincere when he said things that made him sound as if he'd walked out of a Frank Capra movie. In fact, he *looked* as if he'd walked out of a Frank Capra movie.

His chestnut hair was thick as turf; his jaw looked as if a master sculptor had formed it. Broad shoulders, a flat stomach and a perpetual smile in eyes as blue as a Honeyford summer sky could make any woman feel good about being alive. But with Dean, Rosemary often got the feeling that his sole purpose was to make *her* feel good.

Smiling shyly over her shoulder, she caught sight of his suitcase—evidence that he truly was moving into her home.

They had discussed it, of course, while in Reno, and both agreed that moving into her larger two-bedroom cottage made the most sense over the next couple of years. Still, her heart thumped heavily at the prospect. She had never lived with anyone other than her family and ex-husband. Leading Dean through the living room, she paused in the small square hallway that opened onto the downstairs bedroom, the stairwell leading to the upper floor and the sole bathroom in the house.

"You remember those girls in college who were completely comfortable living in coed dorms and diving into swimming pools in their underwear at parties?" she asked.

Bemused, Dean nodded. "Uh, yeah. I do."

Rosemary broke the sad news. "I wasn't one of them." She opened the glass door that closed the attic bedroom off from the rest of the house. "I'm putting you upstairs. I moved my things down here so I can use the bathroom and kitchen a little more easily once my pregnancy progresses. Since I'm an early riser, I thought I'd take my shower first in the morning. Or, we can talk about it. It's actually a claw-foot tub with a shower attachment… I hope that's okay."

He nodded.

"I usually start a pot of coffee first thing, too. You're welcome to share if you're a coffee drinker in the morning."

Another nod.

"All right." She wished for a little more from him. Making plans was very calming. Why did men not get that? "Well. Then generally I take a walk—I pack my breakfast and bring it along—and I wind up at work."

Dean mulled over what she was telling him, but made no comment other than a noncommittal, "Ah."

"When the baby comes," Rosemary persisted, certain her

tension would subside once all strategies, present and future, were neatly laid out, "I can have the crib in my room. All the floors are hardwood with the exception of the upstairs bedroom, but when the baby starts serious crawling I'll go rug shopping for something soft on the knees. And we might need to replace this glass door." She tapped it. "A solid wood panel would be much safer. Or we could use a baby gate down here and install a door to the bedroom upstairs for privacy. What do you think?"

He smiled gently. "I think you're an intelligent, conscientious woman who is understandably ambivalent about having a roommate she didn't anticipate. Now you've got the next two years planned out down to the minute. You're remarkable. But I find that where you're concerned, Rosemary Josephine, I've got my hands full just taking it one night at a time."

From someone else that could have been a put-down, but Dean wasn't telling her not to plan, just saying he needed to evaluate things in the moment. Rosemary realized he possessed the quality of stillness. Even on that first night, as he'd flirted with her, there had been something steady and unshakable about him. It wasn't that he hadn't cared about the outcome, but rather that he trusted the outcome to be okay, whatever it was.

"Wow," she whispered, "that was *such* a nice way of saying I'm uptight."

He leaned toward her, or maybe she was imagining it, because *she* wanted to be several inches closer. "I like you uptight. Gives me an excuse to try to relax you."

Rosemary licked her dry lips. "Do you have a *plan* to accomplish that?"

The smile in his eyes expanded to a grin. "Why, yes, Rosemary. As a matter of fact, I do." He raised his suitcase. "I'll show myself upstairs and put this away. Meet me back here in fifteen minutes."

She laughed at the notion of specifying a place to "meet." The entire first floor of her cottage occupied eight hundred square feet. "Okay, fifteen minutes."

Rosemary watched him head upstairs, easygoing, relaxed, taking this next step in his life with enviable calm.

I hope the baby has his personality.

Her breath pinched in her chest. It was the first time she'd thought about whom the baby would take after or whom she hoped the baby would take after.

Placing a hand on her stomach, she felt a near-overwhelming urge to follow Dean upstairs and show him the little mound of her belly.

Here, she would say, *feel. That's her, little Montana Jeffers Kingsley.* And Dean would laugh and argue lightly. *You mean little Nate Jeffers Kingsley.* Then he would put his warm, gentle hand on her stomach, and his expression would change, assuming the serious, contemplative air she was coming to know. Their eyes would meet, the pressure of his hand would increase a bit, and she'd see again what she'd noticed several times already but had deliberately glossed over—desire. The hunger he had to touch her bare skin, to possess the woman who carried his child.

As if her feet had brains, they danced with the yearning to race him to the attic. And the queen-size bed. Would the sex be as good now as it had been that first night?

Gritting her teeth, she pivoted from the stairs, marched herself to the kitchen and grabbed a vase for the roses. Before she attended to the flowers, however, she turned on the faucet and stuck her arms beneath the stream of water, giving herself the cold shower she so desperately needed.

"Ohhhh," Rosemary groaned. "Mmm…amazing. I'm so glad I married you."

Dean laughed. "Stick with me, baby. I've got connections."

He forked up another piece of the Double Trouble Chocolate Pie his sister-in-law, Claire, had baked for them.

After he'd come back downstairs, he'd handed Rosemary a DVD then went out to the car he'd parked in the gravel alongside her front yard and returned with the pink bakery box wrapped in string.

They'd watched the first half of *The Music Man*. "Featuring," Dean had said, explaining his movie selection, "Marion the Librarian, in honor of the most beautiful librarian I know." He'd kissed the tip of her nose.

They'd sat a thigh's width apart on her green velour couch while Professor Harold Hill played his con game and wooed the übercautious librarian. When Marion sang "Goodnight, My Someone" to the soul mate she believed she might never find, Rosemary burst into wet blubbers, feeling as mature as a nine-month-old, and causing Dean to scoot over and put his arm around her. That arm had felt perfect, and she'd cried some more until he'd tipped her face up to his, wiped the tears and looked as if he was going to kiss her.

She'd waited, lips parted, hoping the leaky-nose issue was all taken care of, because she was so going to kiss him back. With the snuffling past, her libido went on the rampage *again* (horny pregnant women were obviously no old wives' tale), and she waited for him to make the move.

Which turned out not to be a kiss.

He'd clicked off the movie, called "Intermission" and stood up to cut the pie.

Damn good thing it had two layers of fudge and a rich cookie crust, because extra shots of chocolate were the only way she was going to medicate her sexual frustration tonight.

She honestly couldn't remember feeling sexually frustrated before. Ever. Dissatisfied, yeah, but climb-out-of-my-skin, gotta-jump-your-bones, don't-talk-just-do-it-to-me-now frustrated? Uh-uh.

"This should be made an illegal substance," Rosemary said, licking the back of her fork. "I'll drop by the bakery before work tomorrow and thank Claire in person."

"She'd love to see you, I'm sure."

Tilting her head back against the sofa, Rosemary sighed. "Daphne was right. Celibacy is fattening."

Vaguely surprised she'd said that out loud, she glanced at Dean, who had taken a sip of the decaf they'd made and now struggled not to spit it out. Once he'd swallowed, he said, "Daphne the cute blonde is celibate?"

Rosemary nodded. "Although I'm not sure I should have said anything. It's probably too much information."

Dean wagged his head. "Len is going to be very disappointed. He's been all over me to get her phone number from you."

"Don't tell him," Rosemary insisted, though she didn't think Daphne kept her celibacy a secret. In fact, quite the contrary when it came to men, since she currently viewed the willingness to wait as something of a test. "Why is sex so important to men, anyway?" Rosemary wondered aloud.

"To men?" Dean's mouth twitched. "It's important to women, too, isn't it?"

He was amused, which made Rosemary feel about forty years older than she was and not very sexy. She'd brought it on herself, of course, and considered dropping the subject altogether, but she was slightly drunk on sugar and for much of her sexually active life she had honestly wondered what the big deal was.

"What I mean is, making love can be…fun. But sex changes, like everything else in a relationship. I suppose it's never been that important to me."

"Why not?"

She shrugged.

"Describe sex in one word. An adjective," he challenged.

"I can't—"

"I bet you have a bachelor's degree in English," he guessed. She did. "Give me a word."

"Well, it's…nice."

He set his plate on the coffee table. "'Nice?' Rosie Jo," he said, his voice a velvet lion's purr, "are you saying what we did at the motel was only 'nice'?"

If she were a match, she'd be lit now. "No. That was more… that was…um…"

"Yes?"

"More than nice."

Blue sparks of humor and challenge shot from his eyes. He seemed half amused, half disgusted when he shook his head. "Nope. You're a librarian. Pick an *accurate* adjective to describe you, me and that king-size bed."

Rosemary tried to swallow, but there was nothin' doin'. Her throat had frozen up on her. She croaked out a weak, "Well…" then cleared her throat and started to perspire. "What would you call it?"

His eyes narrowed, his gaze locked on her. "Astonishing. Inimitable. Transforming. Scorching."

Oh. Scorching. Good adjective. Yes, definitely scorching….

Do not confuse sex with love. Do not confuse sex with love. Do not confuse sex with love.

Rosemary recalled the eleventh commandment in her mother's home, imparted with all the gravitas of Moses on the Mount.

"All I meant," she said, speaking slowly and laboriously since she didn't have a drop of spit left in her mouth, "when we started this conversation was that if Len is serious about getting to know Daphne, then he shouldn't care whether she's fully clothed or bottoms-up naked. That's all."

Dean looked at her. A long time. Finally he said, "With all the books in that library of yours, there's got to be one that explains the natural science of man and woman."

Rosemary bristled at the implication that she didn't have a grasp on male-female relationships. Which, okay, she didn't. Even though she'd been married ten years, and that made the situation especially sad. But she did know about lust. She knew that it could start a relationship and that it could end one. What it could not do was make a relationship last.

"I understand physical desire," she insisted. "I know that lust can start a relationship. It can also end one. But it can't make a relationship last, which is why focusing on personality is important."

"Personality is job one," he agreed easily. Putting his elbow on the back of the couch he leaned against one bent knuckle and regarded her at length. "The thing is, if I had you naked, with that dark, curly hair falling around your shoulders—" he was back to the low, velvet voice that gave her shivers "—and those big cat eyes staring up at me, and if you were willing, I would not be concentrating on your character traits, as much as I admire them." He reached out to loop one of the loose curls around his finger. "I'd be taking the opportunity to get to know you intimately…very intimately…and most definitely involving every part of that gorgeous body. More than once. So—" he continued to play idly with her hair, and Rosemary felt the combustion from the desire building inside her "—your friend Daphne is probably right. If she wants Len, or any man, to know her mind and heart first, then celibacy is a good idea."

All the while he talked about celibacy, he caressed Rosemary with his eyes and toyed with her hair, winding the curls around his fingers until he reached her jawline. Then he burrowed his fingers through the thick brown strands behind her ear and at her nape. His palm cupped the back of her head.

Rosemary's vision began to blur. *Hang on, Rosemary, hang on,* she encouraged herself, but deep down she feared she was about to become fodder for The Learning Channel: *Internal Combustion—Real or an Urban Legend?* He looked at her as if she was already naked. *Damn it, kiss me already.* They were going to set the city on fire.

She leaned forward. He did, too.

"Fortunately," he said, "I'm already in touch with your personality. So if you're really, *really* concerned about celibacy being fattening…"

"I am," Rosemary breathed, "I *really* am."

Dean smiled. "Well, then I'm going to help. I refuse to allow my wife to worry unnecessarily."

He tugged her all the way toward him, and Rosemary went. Willingly.

Chapter Twelve

"You did it. You did the naughty bump with the pharmacist."

"Vi, for heaven's sake—"

"You did. I can hear it in the way you say his name. 'Dean,'" she sighed, her voice high and breathy.

"I don't sound like that. I've never in my life—"

"Was it recreational sex or are you hoping this marriage is going to go live?" She didn't let more than a couple of seconds elapse. "Oh, my God, you're hoping. So much for carpe diem dating."

Rosemary considered knocking herself unconscious against a bookshelf in the Travel aisle. The library was going to open in ten minutes. She shouldn't be having a conversation about this now, but Daphne had phoned Vi to give her the details on the wedding, and Vi had called Rosemary to heckle her and to ask whether there was going to be a reception.

There was, at the Honeyford Community Center, in one

week's time. Both she and Dean had tried to talk his…their… sister-in-law, Claire, out of planning the party, but she had a cadre of townspeople working with her, and they wouldn't take no for an answer. Moreover they wanted to stage this shindig soon, because the Honeyford Days spring celebration was coming up in late April, and the community center would be unavailable.

Rosemary's first wedding reception had taken place at the Governor Hotel in downtown Portland. She'd had a wedding planner, a caterer, several other people on cell phones orchestrating the entire thing, plus Vi, Daphne and Ginger running interference between Rosemary and her weddingphobic family.

"Daphne says Dean wants a real marriage, open-ended," Vi said, her voice subdued for her. "Do you think this guy is the real deal?"

It was an unusual question for Vi. As long as Rosemary had known her tough, independent friend, Via Lynn Harris had assumed that no man was the real deal regarding love and fidelity.

Pressing *Fodor's Italy* neatly on the shelf so its spine aligned with the other titles, Rosemary closed her eyes, allowing mental images from the past two days to shimmer tantalizingly behind her closed lids….

She and Dean making love, with tenderness and with abandon, with humor and with utter earnestness. Appropriate adjectives? Stupendous, staggering, indescribable, astonishing.

The non-naked hours had been just as good. Better, because those were the hours that were making her a believer again.

Dean had discussed parenting philosophies with interest and opinions. He was, he told her, going to be front-row-center for all ball games and dance recitals.

"What if we have an introverted child who isn't into sports teams or performing? she had asked.

He'd given that some thought. "We'll start Team Kingsley with his cousins. No pressure. Pure fun and physical fitness."

"What if *she* doesn't want to be in a dance recital?"

"Every kid likes to perform for her family. Fletcher and I will build a stage on the ranch. She and Rozzy can put on plays. I'll hang the out-to-lunch sign and run over for a noon performance."

He would, too.

Rosemary had stared at his gorgeous, smiling, gonna-be-the-proudest-pop-on-the-block expression, and…oh, good golly. *Help, I've fallen and I can't get up.*

They hadn't talked only about children, either. In fact, up to that point he had spoken directly to her tummy only once, a quick, "Hellooo. How's the view in there? Everything is A-OK up here."

Hanging around the house in the evening, they had discovered a shared fondness for Shakespeare and had both seen the Oregon Shakespeare Festival's production of *Much Ado About Nothing,* which they'd happily dissected. Oddly, they had both chosen the actor in the smaller role of The Friar as their favorite performer. "He had a great grasp on the language without seeming stiff or less human," Dean had said.

"Hmm." Rosemary had thought back to what made the actor so appealing to her at the time. Daphne and Ginger had wanted to wait outside after the show to get his autograph. "He seemed to truly care about Hero. And I loved the way he calmed everyone down and told them how to fix the mess they were all in." *Just the way you would.* "He seemed like the kind of guy you'd want around during a natural disaster. And that voice! When he took charge…" She'd shivered conspicuously. "Quite a looker, too, as I recall." She'd peeked at Dean mock shyly as she'd washed a bowl in the kitchen sink. "Daphne and Ginger were crushing."

Dean had narrowed his gaze. Under her guidance, he'd been rolling chocolate-chip cookie dough into balls and setting them on a baking sheet. He'd been quite dutiful about it, too, eating only every other dough ball, but now left his post to advance on her with exaggerated gravity. "And you, Mrs. Kingsley? Were you 'crushing,' too, or is your interest strictly thespian?"

"Oh, my interest is arts-related, for sure." She'd nodded broadly. "And he was some work of art. I wonder if he lives in Oregon? I could invite him over—"

"That does it." Dean had grabbed her round the waist, burying his mouth against her neck and nuzzling the spot that gave her goose bumps from head to toe. "The next play you go to is *The Trojan Women*."

Grinning, Rosemary had turned her head until their lips met. Dean hesitated not a second before kissing her more deeply than he ever had. Soon she had turned against his chest, and they were clinging to each other—arms, lips, legs tangling. Rosemary's bones had melted on the spot as she'd realized she loved everything she knew about the man: the way he spoke to people—so focused and considerate; the myriad collection jars he displayed on his counter at work and the fact that he helped fill them up every night; his kindness toward Honeyford's elderly population; and his humor.

She also liked the way he glanced over to see if she was looking before he popped more cookie dough into his mouth; the lingering looks at her bottom (one of her better features if she did say so herself) and then the grin and raised brows when she caught him.

She loved the way he smelled, too, the pure physical yumminess of the man. Every pore of her body opened to let him in, and she didn't want to—she couldn't—stop it.

Kissing him back with no reservation was like turning a key in the ignition of a race car that had been waiting for the chance to go from zero to a hundred. Dean roared to life. He'd kissed her back with a hunger that sucked her onto the speedway with him. All she could do, all she wanted to do, was hang on for the ride.

She wasn't sure how long they'd stood in the kitchen, wrapped in and around each other, but when he'd picked her up and headed out of the room, she was more than ready. Their lips had connected the entire way with Dean muttering between kisses, "No actor playing a friar is going to make love to you the way I'm going to."

Rosemary had grinned, kissing him hungrily until he practically sprinted up the stairs. Never had a discussion about classical theatre been more gratifying.

"Hey, you there?" Vi prodded.

"I'm here." Rosemary opened her eyes and straightened away from the shelf she'd been leaning against. She checked the clock above periodicals. Two minutes to opening time. Dean had developed a habit of dropping by for lunch. She couldn't wait.

"Vi, I'm going to tell you something, but don't respond with anything sarcastic or even teasing, okay? I'm very sensitive lately." She took a deep breath. "Here's the thing—I think I've been given my second chance at the picket fence. Dean seems like that too-good-to-be-true guy, except that he's also authentic and dependable. He loves kids, and he's so good with them, Vi. And I know it's too early to be sure, but he doesn't seem like the kind of man who would play around. He has integrity."

"How is he in the sack? Wait, scratch that. Insensitive." Vi sighed heavily. "Okay, I'm glad it's happening for you. And I'm not being sarcastic. The whole 'happily ever after' thing… I guess I just stopped buying into it. But if you believe it, I'm on board."

Rosemary could see Mrs. Spinelli-Adamson waiting at

the door with her customary shopping bag full of books to return. She cradled the phone and spoke softly. "Vi, that year you spent studying in Rome…we all knew there was a special guy, but you've never said why you broke up other than that he didn't want to move to America. When are you going to tell us what really happened?"

There was a brief silence then a too-brittle laugh. "When pizzas fly, *cara*." Before Rosemary could say anything else, Vi said briskly, "So what's the 411 on your reception? Daphne, Ginger and I are driving down together."

"Oh, my gosh, no. Don't—I mean, really do not—come all the way out here for this thing. It's just a little get-together at the community center. My sister-in-law had to book it between Friday night bingo and a Sunday meeting of the Honeyford Succulents Garden Club. We'll probably have a cactus on every table. Don't come. I'd rather keep things low-key and very, very brief."

Vi made a rude buzzer sound. "Uh-uh. You're having a wedding reception, and you think your three best friends in the world aren't going to come? Especially when *I* was the one who encouraged you to sleep—I mean, dance—with the man in the first place? Guess again, little mama-to-be. Now, you tell me the when and where of this shindig, and we'll make it a party befitting the potential last husband you're ever going to need."

Claire had promised Dean and Rosemary a "simple," "low-key," "modest" wedding reception.

"Don't even think of it as a reception, then," she had urged when Rosemary begged her to keep it small. "Think of it as a welcome-to-the-neighborhood party, just an opportunity for people to stop in and say hi and acknowledge that you're a couple now. Not a big deal."

So Rosemary envisioned the multipurpose room of the

Honeyford Community Center dotted with a few balloons, a bouquet of spring flowers from Geri Evans's garden, a portable CD player—perhaps with "Because You Loved Me" on repeat mode—a cake from Honey Bea's and some punch. Maybe thirty people with nothing better to do on a Saturday evening would show up at the community center.

Low-key. Where she and Dean and their so-new relationship would not be held up to scrutiny.

"I'm not going in," she said stubbornly, ducking behind a large planter of Cordyline as she peered in horror at the festivities inside. Twinkle lights festooned the room. Irene Gould walked by in a floor-length gold lamé skirt, hauling Henry Berns, the baker, along with her toward a makeshift dance floor. A crystal ball rotated slowly overhead while a live band—not Celine Dion via boom box but a *live* band for pity's sake—played Faith Hill's "This Kiss." A fountain of punch graced the center of a table bearing the weight of chafing dishes and platters of hors d'oeuvres.

"This is no good!" Rosemary hissed at Dean from her spot behind the plant. "I'm getting fatter by the second! We were supposed to let a few people guess the truth and then spread it around town while we look the other way." She gestured angrily toward the door. "Half the town is in there right now!"

Standing with his hands in his pockets, lips compressed and eyebrows raised, Dean obligingly glanced inside the noisy room. "Nah. The community center can't hold half the town. And it's against the fire marshal's rules. There's probably no more than...one third in there." He sniffed the air, redolent with the aroma of food. "I smell Josef's cabbage rolls. The Honeyford Inn must have catered. Let's go." Rosemary groaned, which elicited a sympathetic smile from her husband. "Did you bring your ginger?"

"I'm not worried about that!"

He approached the planter. "Rosie—"

"Go away. I'm not coming out. Tell them I have the flu."

"Again? That's what we told everyone the night I proposed. And didn't you tell everyone at the library you had the flu when you threw up?"

"All right, all right! Then say I caught a terrible cold." She coughed as an example of "terrible." "You go in. It's dark. I'll stay close to the bushes and run on home."

Dean grabbed her as she commenced her great escape and pulled her in for a hug, stroking her hair with the soothing touch that made her feel immensely comforted. "You're only showing a little, Rosie Jo." When she began to protest, he cut her off. "It looks like a lot to us, because we're excited about the baby." In fact they had spent much of last night looking at the bump from all angles in the mirror after a steamy, sexy shower. "But to the people in there, that tiny mound could look like nothing more than too many of Claire's Honey Bunz."

He nuzzled behind her ear, and Claire melted against him. She was so easy. "I just don't want to be asked a lot of questions that have private answers."

"Stick with me kid. I won't let the paparazzi get you down."

Claire smiled against his lapel and socked him lightly in the ribs. "Fine. I'm making too big a deal of it. I plead the hormone defense."

"Plead any defense you want." He kissed her long and deep then murmured, "Let's get this over with so we can go home."

Putty to his sculptor's hands, Rosemary followed without another word. Going home at night had become her favorite part of the day. Sometimes she beat him to the cottage and made dinner; sometimes he arrived home first and had her favorite mac and cheese waiting for her. But almost always before they ate, they satisfied the other, stronger hungers that had built up during the hours apart. Though his baby grew inside her, they were newlyweds experiencing all the excitement and wonder of setting up house.

"There they are!" Someone—Rosemary couldn't identify the voice—shouted above the music to draw the crowd's attention to the door as she and Dean walked in.

"This Kiss" changed to a surprisingly sincere rendition of The Captain & Tenille's "Muskrat Love," with the band, Honeyford's own Crystallized Honey, a group of sixtysomething musicians who had come out of retirement for Dean's brother's wedding, altering the lyrics to "Muskrat Rosemary, Muskrat Dean, do the jitterbug in their muskrat dreams…"

Dozens of people flocked to the door, shaking Dean's hand, hugging Rosemary and telling her how thrilled they were that one of the town's favorite sons had finally found his bride.

"Love couldn't happen to a more deserving man," Dolores Schenk sighed, holding Rosemary's arm in a grip made tight partly from emotion and partly because the nonagenarian refused to use her walker. "He gives me all my medications at cost, bless his heart. I've prayed every day that he would find himself a good woman. And now he has. A librarian." She waxed eloquently about the importance of education for a woman until her great-granddaughter eased her away.

Rosemary didn't see much of Dean for an hour as the confidences and back slapping continued. The party was in full swing when Vi, Daphne and Ginger swept through the community center's double doors. They found Rosemary immediately and spirited her away from her library clerk, Abby, who had dressed in a black lace Victorian ensemble reflecting her current reading material—*Tess of the d'Urbervilles*—and Abby's boyfriend, Colin, who wore black leather jeans and bore a striking resemblance to Johnny Depp in *Edward Scissorhands.*

"Great band," Vi yelled above the noise. "Haven't I seen them on *The Lawrence Welk Show?*"

"Shh." Rosemary shook her head at her friend. "Apparently they came out of retirement for my brother-in-law's wedding and now they're unstoppable."

"Speaking of your hottie brother-in-law." Vi grinned wickedly, her red lips parting to reveal even teeth that had obviously undergone another round of laser whitening. "Where is he? I need a photo so I can lord it over my Pilates class—I stood next to the Tuff Enuff jeans butt."

Rosemary gazed at her three best friends and broke out in a huge, tear-filled smile. "I'm so glad you're here." They shared a group hug. "I've been ridiculously nervous about tonight."

"Aw, why, sweetie?" Daphne, who wore a powder-blue knit dress that made her look like a Victoria's Secret angel but with more clothes, slipped a comforting arm around Rosemary's waist. "You look wonderful. Refreshed and happy."

"Do I?" Rosemary sniffed, accepting a tissue from Ginger as she tried to stem the waterworks.

Ginger nodded. "You do. You were meant for marriage and motherhood, honey. And it appears you and your man are well-loved." She glanced around. "There's a lot of support in this room. Isn't this everything you wanted?"

Those words—*everything you wanted*—felt like ice cubes bobbing in Rosemary's blood. No, this wasn't everything she'd ever wanted. It was more.

She'd dreamt of the man and the children, but now she had an entire community around her, too. Every day the library became more and more her home away from home. She had started a book club and a Read to the Dogs program. When she went to the bank, the tellers greeted her by name, and yesterday Jan Tuma, the owner of Yellow Jacket Gently Used Clothes, had rushed from her store when Rosemary walked past, eager to tell the librarian that her son, Alex, who previously had thought he was a poor reader, just finished the entire *A Wrinkle in Time* trilogy Rosemary had suggested.

She belonged.

And it all felt *sooooo* good that it frightened her. Losing her dreams the first time, with Neil, had been hard. She'd been in a scary depression for months after the divorce. If she fell for Once Upon a Time again and lost it when she was this close, lost Dean and the family she'd dreamed about since she was a child, she didn't know how she'd survive. And she had to, because now her—*their*—child was involved.

"Family-of-origin alert. Mother and sisters heading through the doors." Vi nodded toward the group that entered the Honeyford Community Center.

As Rosemary looked over her shoulder, her friends stepped closer, circling the wagons around her.

Rosemary's heart rate approached panic mode as her mother and sisters hovered on the threshold of the large multipurpose room, collectively looking like three earthling tourists who had been dropped off against their will on Mars.

Dressed in a Carolina Herrara suit that probably cost more than Rosemary's mortgage, and flanked by two of her daughters garbed in their own designer ensembles, Maeve Jeffers gazed at the small-town festivities—the twinkle lights, the Congratulations, Rosemary and Dean banner decorated in poster paints, the shiny ivory and white balloons, and the flowers stuffed in any vase that would have them, and you could tell she was sure she'd died and gone to Purgatory.

"Oh, holy heaven, I begged Lucy not to say anything about tonight." Rosemary's gaze jerked around the room.

"Are you looking for Dean?" Daphne put a hand out to steady her friend.

"No. I'm looking for an escape route."

"Rosemary, you cannot leave your groom alone with new in-laws." Vi wagged a finger whose red-painted nail bore a skull-and-crossbones tattoo. "Especially *his* new in-laws.

Ginger, you help Rosemary find Dean. Daphne and I will handle Medea and the Greek Chorus. Come on, Daph."

Only Daphne could make nausea look sexy. "Nothin' doin'. It's nothing personal, Rosemary, but Maeve scares me."

Vi rolled her eyes, but reassigned the jobs, pulling Ginger along and shooing Daphne and Rosemary away.

They located Dean standing near the refreshments table, speaking to a thirtysomething woman who looked like Holly Hobbie come to life. Rather than the striking bottle-red locks that Vi sported so well, this woman's naturally curly hair was Opie-orange, thick and gorgeously unruly, a perfect complement to the amber freckles that dusted her milk-white skin. Gi-normous blue-gray eyes claimed most of the real estate on her face, leaving room for a small, rounded nose and puffy, cupid's-bow lips. Viewed individually, her features were quirky, but they worked in harmony to create a face one could look at a long time and not tire of.

Dean was nodding and smiling as they spoke.

"Wow, this is the first time I've seen your man since December," Daphne said as she and Rosemary approached, arm in arm. "He's even hunkier than I remembered. Who's the woman?"

"I don't know her name, but I understand she owns the barbershop on Main Street. I've seen her through the window a few times."

"The barbershop?" Daphne's energy picked up. "She's around men all day? Is she married?"

"I don't know." Rosemary frowned at her friend's tone. "Why?"

"If she's around men for hours at a time, she ought to be comfortable with them, but she's nervous as a cat with Dean. Watch her. Keeps pushing her hair behind her ears, nervous smile. Major crush there."

After several days without morning sickness, Rosemary began to feel ill.

"You have nothing to worry about, though," Daphne assured her.

"How can you tell?"

Daphne stopped walking and looked at her friend in fond amazement. "Honestly, Rosemary, you're such a babe in the woods sometimes. Dean has no idea that woman is the slightest bit interested. Look at his eyes and his smile—extremely polite. One-hundred-percent platonic. He's oblivious. Which is very sweet where you're concerned, but übersad for her. I wonder how long she's been carrying a torch?"

Rosemary marveled at her friend's boy-girl acumen. Indeed, as they closed in on the chatting duo and Dean looked up to see his wife's approach, his expression transformed completely. The well-mannered attention he showed the redhead clicked into an expression that was keenly alert and pheromone-soaked. His eyes smiled, physical tension tightened his body and his lips broadened in a grin that was all for his wife. He didn't even glance at Daphne, who, Rosemary figured, was sexier than she could hope to be in this or three more lifetimes.

Her blood sang, the attraction one-hundred-percent mutual.

He's mine. The sense of connectedness that had gone missing for the past few years was back, and now she yearned for more. *I want Dean Kingsley to be my best friend.* The thought stopped her in her tracks. She wanted all the things Dean talked about when he proposed.

Beside her, Daphne squeezed her arm. "Rosemary Jeffers Kingsley," she whispered with a smile in her voice, "get a room."

"Tried that," Rosemary whispered back, her gaze on Dean. "That's why we're here."

When they reached Dean, he introduced Gabriella Coombs, owner/operator of Honey Comb's barbershop, and Rosemary reintroduced him to Daphne, but their eyes never strayed long from each other.

"Congratulations, Rosemary," Gabriella said, sweetly and politely. Rosemary shifted her focus from Dean to his friend long enough to see the pain that clouded her rainy-day eyes. "I hope you're enjoying H-Honeyford."

Oh, sweet baby Jane, she's going to cry. Daphne was right: the barber was in love with Dean.

Compassion, not jealousy or fear, filled Rosemary. She gave the woman a smile. "Thank you. It's a wonderful town. I hope...I hope we'll get to know each other better, Gabby."

With a brave nod and a last, sad glance at Dean, Gabby excused herself.

Daphne began to chat about the party, engaging Dean, who slipped an arm around his wife's waist, while Rosemary collected herself. Gabby Coombs's loneliness was a palpable thing, and Rosemary knew that if it hadn't been for one aberrant night in December, she would be looking at a future far, far different from the one that currently opened before her.

She studied Dean as he spoke animatedly about small business with Daphne.

Two years of marriage will never be enough. Dean's hand made gentle up and down strokes along Rosemary's expanding waist. Last night he'd treated her to a full body massage, placing his palm protectively over her stomach and whispering in Rosemary's ear, "Ours."

She had waited all her life, it seemed, to feel like this, like part of something sweet and strong and timeless as the sea—a family. Because she had stopped expecting it to happen, she'd almost missed it. Dean had sneaked up on her, moving staunchly through her fears like a soldier marching through a sandstorm.

Thank you, she thought. *Oh, my God, thank you for not giving up.*

"What do you think, Rosemary? Yoo-hoo. Rosemary!"

Hearing her name after it had been called a couple of times, Rosemary blinked. "What?"

Daphne gave them her angel's grin. "I said the food smells great, but something tells me that's not what's on *your* mind." She nudged Dean. "Dance with your wife. I think she'll be putty in your arms."

He grinned. "Try the pierogis," he said to Daphne as she strolled away, then leaned down to nuzzle his wife's neck. "And I'll try you."

Crystallized Honey began "My Eyes Adored You" as Dean and Rosemary took to the floor. The silly crystal ball spun slowly above them; the balloons bobbed as children played with their strings; the twinkle lights looked cheap, but charming as heck. Dean looped his hands at the small of his wife's back while she circled her arms around his neck. There was nowhere on earth she would rather be.

"Thank you for going along with this," Dean murmured as they swayed. "In Honeyford, the longtime residents tend to think of each other more as family than neighbors. They figure it's their right to throw us a reception."

"I'm glad they did," she said, meaning it. "I'm sorry I made such a fuss earlier. I can see I'm going to have to get used to a lot of community involvement if I'm going to be married to Honeyford's favorite son."

Dean laughed. "I am not their favorite son."

"You're definitely in the top five."

They grinned at each other. The urge to say more made Rosemary's heart thump with nerves.

Do it. You've been making love with the man, for heaven's sake. His baby is growing inside you. Tell him how you feel.

Like a softly running stream, their gazes flowed in the space between them. It felt so easy, this moment of intimate connection on a crowded dance floor…except for the confession that hovered on Rosemary's tongue.

As he often seemed to, Dean paved her way. "How about for you?" he questioned softly. "Have I made it to your top five yet?"

Chapter Thirteen

The pulse in Rosemary's throat shimmied. She shook her head. "Not the top five, no. I'd say…" Heat filled her face. *Take the plunge, Rosemary. Take the plunge.* "I'd say—"

Hic!

Not again! She hadn't hiccuped once since she'd said, "I do."

Hic!

Oh, for the love of heaven.

Leaning back a few inches, Dean watched his bride with wry acceptance. "You want some water?"

"No!" *Hic.* She pulled her arms from around his neck and slapped her chest in disgust. "This is so ridiculous."

Releasing his dance hold, Dean brought his hands up to cradle her face. "It's all right. I've learned to speak hiccup where you're concerned. You get them every time you're about to take a step toward me, did you know that? I have a theory."

Rosemary fell into his eyes. How could any man be so patient? So calm and so strong at the same time? "What is it?"

"Part of you wants to dive into the rabbit hole with me, but there's another part that wants to stay right where you are. The closer you get to jumping, the more tense you get, and—hiccups."

Rosemary frowned. "Rabbit hole? You're saying our relationship is like the rabbit hole in *Alice in Wonderland?* That's not very comforting. It was chaos down there."

"Yep. Chaos. Scary and unknown, and sometimes nothing seems to make any sense. I figure jumping into the hole together is what brings the comfort. Staying the course together. Although so far, Rosie Jo, that's just a theory."

She understood what he was saying. He needed a partner to turn hypothesis to reality. He'd been ready for a while, waiting for her.

Though her mouth went dry, Rosemary spoke. "Let's test your theory." *Boom, boom, boom.* Her chest cavity felt like a kettledrum being played too hard. She swallowed hard around the pounding. "I'm willing to jump. With you."

Dean stared at her a long time. Then a grin broke like sunshine over his face. He threw back his head and whooped. It was loud, out of character and wonderful. She laughed as he whirled her around then kissed her before her feet hit the ground. After so many gray days, the future sparkled with color.

"Well, I'd like to meet my son-in-law." Maeve Jeffers's ever-determined voice broke into the festivities. "I assume this is he?"

Dean set Rosemary down and together they turned toward four women—Maeve, Rosemary's sisters, Lucy and Evelyn, and Vi—all of whom stared back with a decided mix of reactions. Rosemary's mother, the only attorney Rosemary knew who was scarier than Lucy, looked much the way she did when going after a deadbeat father in court; her sisters appeared faintly appalled, and Vi was amused.

"Hi, Mom," Rosemary greeted, hoping she could hang on to the good feelings despite an immediate flashback to the day two decades ago when her mother found her practicing the wedding march with a pillowcase bobby-pinned to her hair.

"Rosemary," Maeve had told her twelve-year-old romantic, not ungently, *"do you know that some of the world's great feminist writers have compared marriage to slavery?"*

Face-to-face with her daughter's second husband, Maeve extended her hand with a kind of militaristic grace. Like a marine sniper at high tea. "How do you do? I'm Maeve Jeffers, your new mother-in-law…apparently."

"Dean Kingsley." Dean accepted her hand graciously, glancing at Rosemary. "Luckiest man alive."

Despite the pleasure rush that engulfed her, Rosemary knew too well that Dean had just slapped a bull's eye on his own forehead. Her mother and sisters were always extrasuspicious of a man who appeared besotted and had the temerity to talk about it. At their cousin Madeline's wedding to a man who toasted his bride by tearfully quoting Elizabeth Barrett Browning, Lucy had leaned in to Rosemary and cracked, *"I'll be seeing him in court when he uses the child support to pay for his mistress's boob job."*

For the first time, Rosemary wasn't concerned about her relatives' opinions, not on her own behalf. They could think whatever the heck they wanted; she was happy, dang it! She did, however, feel a ferocious surge of protectiveness toward Dean.

Hugging her mother and sisters, Rosemary whispered, "Play nicely," and wondered how to draw Lucy aside to make sure her lawyer sister had kept mum about the prenup and

Rosemary's pregnancy. Lucy's thin body was as tense as piano wire, not an unusual state for her, but she appeared particularly stiff this evening.

Rosemary made bug eyes at Vi, hoping for a little inspiration about how to handle the moment, but Vi mouthed *Lotsa luck* and took an extralong swig of diet soda.

"You look lovely, Rosemary," Maeve admitted, scrutinizing her youngest daughter closely then turning her attention to Dean. "Do you mind if I pull you away from my daughter for a moment? I'd like to get to know you a little better before I head back to Portland."

"I'll come, too, Mom," Rosemary said immediately. "I haven't seen you in months."

"We're hoping you'll stay in Honeyford a few days," Dean added, including Evelyn and Lucy as well, which caused Vi to choke on her soda and Rosemary nearly to gag on her own spit.

"Unfortunately that won't be possible," Maeve declined. "I'm due in court on Monday and need to prepare. I'm going to put the screws to a multimillionaire who had the audacity to suggest his wife of twenty years should be happy with a lump-sum settlement that doesn't even reach seven figures." She smiled brightly at her new son-in-law. "Men can be so naive."

"Mom," Rosemary chastised at the blatant warning. *This* was what she'd had to overcome all her life in order to believe in romance.

Dean squeezed her waist and merely smiled. He'd asked about her family a couple of nights ago, and she hadn't held back. He'd laughed at some of the things she'd told him, winced at others and commiserated. He hadn't grown up in a Beaver Cleaver world, either. Though his parents' brief marriage had been happy, his father had apparently had a far more difficult second union. Dean had also divulged that the current *mayor* of Honeyford, Gwen Gibson, had been his father's mistress for many years.

"In the end, though, my father believed a committed marriage was the most important ingredient to happiness," Dean had surprised her by saying. *"I'm sure he wished he'd married Gwen. My father's problem was that he had no idea how to achieve the kind of marriage he believed in."*

For several moments after that conversation, Dean had seemed distracted, distant for the first time since she'd met him. Glancing at him now, she saw that he was plenty connected and assessing the situation with his new in-laws correctly.

With great politeness, he invited, "I'd love to have some time to know you better before you leave, Maeve. And, I'm sure you have a number of questions I'd be happy to answer." He squeezed Rosemary's waist again, a pointedly reassuring caress, and added, "Sweetheart, why don't you introduce your sisters around. I see Fletcher and Claire over by the fireplace."

"Fletcher?" Vi perked up. "Absolutely let's go see Fletcher. I've got my camera."

"Fletcher...Kinglsey?" Evelyn, the senior director of advertising at a firm that served the west coast from San Francisco to Anchorage, busily put two and two together. "Your brother-in-law is the Tuff Enuff jeans model?" she asked Rosemary.

Vi raised her can of soda. "Ain't life grand?"

"I'll tag along with Mom and Dean," Lucy announced, far more interested in interrogating a new victim than ogling a cowboy—or snagging him for an ad campaign, which Rosemary figured was Evelyn's angle.

Rosemary looked at Dean, undecided. Should she allow her mother and sister, two self-avowed man-distrusting divorce attorneys, to be alone with her new husband when there was no telling what kind of shape they'd leave him in?

She looked Dean square in the eye. He winked.

Team Kingsley vs. Team Jeffers, his expression said. *This one's a slam dunk.*

The silent communication made her feel more than ever like part of a couple, and her nervous heart settled.

All right, then, she winked back. *Good luck.*

All the while she stood beside Vi and Evelyn—and eventually Daphne and Ginger, who made their way over, too—as they pelted Fletcher with requests for photos and his agent's phone number, Rosemary knew she had found her needle in the haystack, the man who made her want to believe again.

Yesterday she had seen her obstetrician, making the two-hour round-trip trek to Bend for what she hoped would be the last time. Now that she and Dean were married she could see a doctor here in town. Maybe Dean would even come with her. There would be gossip, no doubt, when folks did the math, but if they knew that she and Dean loved each other…

Love. A grin spread across her face. After promising herself that never again would she have expectations of any man, here she was, expecting. Expecting like crazy! Expecting Dean's baby, expecting his friendship, expecting a lifetime together.

They had gone into this relationship entirely backward and had a lot of catching up to do. Thankfully they'd gotten a good head start: he was becoming a wonderful friend already.

Her thoughts a million miles away, she didn't notice her sister-in-law trying to catch her attention until Claire tugged her away from the group. "Fletcher says I shouldn't ask, but you look so happy I just have to. How are things? Are you and Dean enjoying marriage?" She put a hand to her mouth, adorably. "Oh, shoot, that sounds way too personal. Scratch that. Are you getting excited about the baby?"

Rosemary grinned. "I am. I really, really am."

"Do you know what you're having?"

Glancing around to be sure no one else could hear their conversation, Rosemary nodded. "I found out yesterday. I've been trying to think of a creative way to tell Dean."

Claire's eyes glowed with sweet remembering. "I loved that part—telling Arlo what we were going to have. I usually strung it out a good long while."

Dean had told Rosemary that Arlo was Claire's first husband. He'd died before their third child, Rosalind, had made her appearance. Rosemary could tell by Claire's expression and by the tone of her lovely Southern voice that her marriage to Arlo had been a good one. Now that the young woman (Rosemary guessed Claire to be several years younger than her own thirty-two) was in a second happy marriage, Rosemary wondered whether she and Fletcher would add a fourth child to their brood. She decided to ask and earned a sigh.

"Well, I have brought that up, and Fletcher has agreed to discuss it in ten years or so."

"Ten years," Rosemary laughed. "Oh, no. I was hoping for lots and lots of cousins for our little one."

Claire glanced lovingly at her husband, surrounded and looking none too thrilled about it, by Rosemary's sister and friends. "Well," Claire mused, "Fletcher is a new daddy still. He's in that deer-caught-in-the-headlights stage where he's afraid he'll make a mistake that will destroy the world as we know it. Poor baby dreamed last night that he dropped Will on his head. And Will's seven."

"No kidding." It was hard to believe they were talking about the six-foot-plus rodeo star. "Wasn't Fletcher a bull rider?"

"Yes. But I haven't met a bull yet that could bring a man to his knees quick as a baby can." Claire inched closer and lowered her voice even though the music and chatter would have made it hard for anyone to overhear their conversation. "Also you've got to remember that Fletcher and Dean's daddy left them fairly confused about what it takes to be a husband and father. It's hard to understand that man's motives, isn't it?"

Clueless, Rosemary didn't bother to mask her bemusement. "Sorry? I'm not sure what you mean by 'motives.' Motives for what?"

The change in Claire's expression was swift and more confusing than her comment. The cheerful openness from a moment before fled, replaced by a shuttered, uncertain look. "Oh, it was nothing. I don't know why I even brought it up." She looked at Fletcher…a little desperately, Rosemary thought. "I'd better rescue my husband. I wonder if your sister or one of your friends just used the word *model,* 'cause he's wincing like he's in a lot of pain."

Rosemary smiled, but watched curiously as Claire pulled her husband away. The girls began to animatedly discuss Fletcher's assets, but Rosemary's attention was halfhearted at best. When she found an appropriate moment to excuse herself, she took it.

Wandering the room in search of Dean proved to be futile. Every few steps, someone stopped her to chat, but no one knew where Dean had gone. Finally she came upon Irene Gould and Henry Berns, the owner of Honey Bea's Bakery.

Henry, a couple of inches shorter than Irene and obviously no more than a hundred and twenty pounds soaking wet, carried a full plate of food and was about to bite into a sauce-covered cabbage roll. Irene, who had known the little baker most of their lives, hovered over him. "Henry Berns, you're closer to eighty than eighteen. What are you thinking, eating like that?"

"Eighty? Speak for yourself. I may be no spring chicken, but I can still crow like a rooster." He winked at Rosemary, popped the cabbage roll in his mouth and scooped up kasha *varnishkas.*

Irene compressed her lips and turned to Rosemary.

"Congratulations, darling. So exciting. Marriage is a wonderful thing."

"How do you know?" Henry asked good-naturedly enough, scraping the plate with his fork.

Irene's eyes widened, shocked and, if Rosemary was correct, deeply hurt. "Why you old—" she began then clamped her lips shut. Her chest rose and fell heavily.

Rosemary's heart went out to her, but she had no idea how to help. *Major history there.* "Um, have either of you seen Dean recently?" she asked in the uncomfortable silence.

"He walked Gwen Gibson to her car," Irene informed stiffly, shooting a dagger-sharp glance at Henry. "*He's* a gentleman."

Ouch. "Thanks. I think I'll get a breath of fresh air myself."

The little baker looked up. "What do you mean, 'He's a gentleman'? Are you saying I'm not a gentleman?"

Yikes. With a wave, Rosemary left the two to whatever they had to work out and threaded through the crowd, escaping finally to the brisk spring night.

Embedded in the clear sky, stars winked more brightly than the twinkle lights in the community hall. Stretching her arms, Rosemary breathed deeply, thinking about the scene that had just transpired. Relationships were so complex. Did anyone find her way through the maze unscathed?

A powerful need to see her husband, to feel the comfort of his solid arms and his eminently reassuring calmness, arose in Rosemary. She squinted in the darkness. Cars had been parked along the curbless street, beside old hitching posts that remained from horse-and-buggy days. A black iron streetlamp flickered, shedding just enough light to see by, but there was no sign of Dean.

Realizing she should have grabbed a coat, Rosemary hugged her arms and made her way around the corner to the small parking lot behind the community center. It was nice of Dean to walk Gwen Gibson to her car. Rosemary had met the mayor twice—once shortly after she'd been hired to run the library, and once when Ms. Gibson had checked out a book on civic government. Nice lady. Widowed. Probably around sixty, she came across as very poised, with a comfortable elegance and a truckload of natural charm. She'd been in a long, somewhat tumultuous relationship with Dean's father, and though she'd married someone else and had a college-age son from that relationship, she and Victor Kingsley had become, at the very least, good friends again at the end of his life. Dean seemed to like and respect the woman, which was enough to make Rosemary more than happy to get to know Gwen better.

Before she'd completely rounded the brick building, Rosemary heard a female voice.

"It's incredible the way everything's worked out, isn't it? First for Fletcher and now for you."

The masculine response seemed to rumble through her own chest. "I couldn't have asked for it to turn out better."

Rosemary smiled. *Found you.* She felt her body relax even as anticipation fizzed along her nerves. *I'm like a teenager,* she thought with sappy surrender, *happy just to be getting closer to my guy.* She picked up her pace, but before she reached the parking lot, Gwen spoke again. This time, the words made Rosemary stumble on the gravel.

"I was so afraid your father's will was going to cause a disaster. I don't have to tell you how much I loved Victor, but requiring you to marry to gain an inheritance was incredibly risky. I knew you'd be more tolerant of the situation than Fletcher, but honestly, I thought the will might deter you both from ever marrying."

Rosemary's brain began to spin inside her skull. She reached reflexively for the brick wall, but her hand only scraped its rough surface. For several moments she couldn't see, couldn't hear, couldn't think. Then the words just spoken collided with the puzzling comment Claire had made, and her mind filled so horribly with dark thoughts she almost screamed.

She had the presence of mind to do one thing—back away. Stumbling a little, feeling her way along the wall as her legs turned to jelly, she reached the front of the community center. Go back inside? Not possible. Whirling left, adrenaline kicking in, propelling her like a hunted deer, she headed for the cover of the building on the other side of the driveway. *Good choice, Rosemary. Keep moving, keep moving.* Grateful for the Western-style building's deep porch, she headed for its farthest reaches, leaned against the rough wooden facade and hyperventilated.

God in heaven, she couldn't have made a mistake of such magnificent proportions. She couldn't be so wrong, so blind about a man, about their relationship…. Could she? Not this time, not…

With a baby on the way.

Her thoughts progressed to near hysteria.

Dean had married her because of a will. Gwen knew. Claire knew! And how many others?

Rosemary buried her head in her hands. "No, no, no." Things like this didn't happen to people in the real world; they happened on soap operas and *Jerry Springer* episodes and in nightmares.

Sobs built inside her, but she refused to let them gain power. She needed every wit she possessed. Lifting her head, she felt her heart buck as Dean walked around the community center, his shadowed form as tall and straight as ever.

Liar. Fake. Criminal.

If what she'd heard held even a kernel of truth then there were no words bad enough for what he'd done, for the way he'd misled and encouraged her to trust in him. For the way he'd made her love again.

I have to talk to Lucy. I have to dissolve this marriage!

A car rolled out of the parking lot and down the block. Gwen Gibson, the mayor of their fair town. *"I don't have to tell you how much I loved your father."* The Kingsleys wove a large and tangled web.

The town that had seemed like such a haven mere minutes ago now felt about as wholesome as Wisteria Lane.

"I've got to get out of here." Rosemary struggled for breath as Dean disappeared inside the community center. *Run. Run as fast and as far as you can.*

Two years ago Rosemary was supposed to have worked on the evening of her tenth wedding anniversary, which had been her birthday, too, because Neil, bless him, had insisted, "I want to get married on the day God made the perfect woman for me."

When her boss had let her go home early, she'd made reservations at their favorite restaurant and rushed home to surprise him. He'd looked surprised, all right. Naked, having sex on their couch with his paralegal, and surprised.

Rosemary had been too stunned to say a word. She'd simply run out the door while Neil yelled after her, "I didn't use our bed, Rosemary!"

That was true: he hadn't used their bed—that time. During their divorce, however, there had been a steady stream of informants, more than willing to assure her that divorce was the right decision, that her husband had been cheating on her for years.

Slowly Rosemary walked to the edge of the porch, hot now despite the chill night air. She had loved Neil once, would never have suspected him capable of such treachery, yet even during their marriage she had known there was something missing, an elusive, soul-deep sense of…rightness…of completion, a click for which she had reached and reached before finally telling herself it would come with age.

Then she met Dean. What had scared—and thrilled—her most that first night was that she had felt the click the first time his eyes had crinkled at her.

Tears gathered, then began to squirt like projectiles.

Blast. She pressed a hand over her mouth and prayed for calm, for composure, for a shot of Novocain straight to the heart. What lesson, damn it, was she supposed to be learning?

Don't run.

As if the voice were outside her, loud and clear, she heard the message: *Stop running. Stand and face up to your life. Face your dreams, even the ones that are broken, and for pity's sake, face the sonofabitch who's breaking them.*

Stock-still, but panting as if she'd broken the tape in a marathon, Rosemary waited for her mind to catch up with that voice.

She'd fallen in love. Again. More wildly than before. And unfortunately, being duped didn't change that fact.

Now she was going to have a daughter to raise. That was the news she'd planned to give Dean tonight. They were having a baby girl. And no matter what her mama told her, that baby girl that would someday be a young woman who yearned to love and be loved. What could Rosemary teach her? What kind of role model would she be?

Just don't run.

Maybe she couldn't keep her daughter's heart safe or pain-free. Of course she couldn't. If Maeve and all her preaching against the myth of the romantic fairy tale hadn't worked, what would?

Not a damn thing, probably.

Like Rosemary, her daughter would choose her own path to tread. God willing, she'd be lucky. As for Rosemary…

"I'm done."

There was only one thing left to do, as far as she could tell. Wiping her eyes, she sniffed hard. Time to be a big girl, broken or not.

Rosemary headed resolutely toward the building where her wedding reception was still going strong despite the fact the marriage had tanked. Her family and friends were in there. They'd driven three hours to celebrate with her; she wasn't going to abandon them. No. She was going to go back in there and finish this reception. In style.

Allowing a moment's grief for the loss of the beautiful future she had planned, Rosemary sucked it up and kept walking. She couldn't stay in Honeyford after this. The details of where she would move and when could be settled in the light of day. Right now, she had a surprise for the man who had turned her dream to dust. It was time to toast the groom…or turn the groom to toast.

Chapter Fourteen

Something was wrong. Damn wrong.

For the past hour, Dean had watched his bride work the room—her smile wide and ready, her gaze sharp, her laughter bold. But to him, she looked like a piece of crystal—solid and beautiful, yet teetering on the edge of a table over a hardwood floor, about to shatter at any minute. Worse, she wouldn't let him get anywhere near her.

Five minutes ago he'd spotted her dancing with his nephew Will. As he began to make his way through the crowd, which hadn't thinned a hair since the start of the evening, Rosemary glanced up, ignored his smile and twirled Will over to her friend Vi. Then she whispered something in the redhead's ear and took off without another glance in Dean's direction.

Enough was definitely enough, so he'd pressed after her, but Len had stopped him, having a *man*ic (man in panic) attack, because Daphne had just revealed that she planned to be celibate until she met her future husband, no matter how long it took. "She thinks a man's going to go for that? Partner, that's like saddling a racehorse then putting it in the barn."

It had taken a few minutes to calm Len down. Now Dean was looking for Rosemary again.

A loud, amplified whistle rent the air. "Ladies and gentleman, may I have your attention, please? Up here."

Dean turned toward the far end of the hall, where the band played on a raised stage. Eugene Brock, former sheriff and current lead guitarist of Crystallized Honey, was speaking into the mike. Rosemary stood next to him, looking nervous, but brave.

"Folks, we're here to celebrate another couple God put together right here in Honeyford. Now it happens that the very last time we were here in this room 'cause of a wedding, Dean's brother, Fletcher, had just tied the knot. Seems like the Kingsleys are having more than their fair share of luck this year."

Laughter and ribbing erupted from the crowd. "Yeah!" Reginald Jacobson, who owned a small sheep ranch outside of town, hollered, "Two pretty women move to town, and the Kingsleys get 'em both. What's up with that? The next one's mine!"

"Well, soon as you take care of that comb-over, Reg, I believe you'll have better luck." More hooting followed Eugene's comment. He patted the air to calm everyone down. "We've got to give our attention to the guest of honor here. The brand-spankin'-new Mrs. Kingsley would like to make a toast." Detaching the microphone from its stand, he handed it to Rosemary. "Mrs. Kingsley, the floor is yours."

Dean tensed as his wife accepted the mike with a nod and a deep breath. Shouldn't he be up there with her? One of Claire's more elaborate cakes had been carried out and placed on the end of the buffet table. He'd assumed they would make their toasts while cutting the tiered creation. Perhaps Rosemary wanted to surprise him, and that's what her avoidance had been about. He began to move toward the stage, this time propelled by shoulder slaps.

As he reached the steps leading to where his wife stood, their gazes locked. Instead of the melting sugar look he expected…wanted…to see, Rosemary's brow puckered. Her lids lowered, narrowing her expression to a cloud-covered puzzle. He stopped walking, remained at the foot of the steps and knew instantly she wanted it that way.

Instead of inviting her husband onto the stage, Rosemary raised the microphone, turned toward the crowd and gave them a smile they may have believed was genuine, but which he realized went no further than the stretch of her lips.

"Thank you." She acknowledged the former sheriff then expelled a breath that reverberated in the mike. "Thank you all for coming." Taking a moment, she centered herself, looking poised and self-possessed as the toast began. "It's no secret that I arrived in Honeyford a single woman. Yet now here I am, very unexpectedly married." Happy applause punctuated the comment. She nodded to recognize it. "Some might say I let Dean sweep me off my feet—" increased cheerful hollers "—or that we rushed things. And maybe that's true."

Her eyes skittered toward his again. Dean felt his heart drop heavily toward his gut. What the hell… Her glance was brief. Brittle.

He considered this one of the most important nights in his life. Earlier today he had contacted his father's lawyer, instructing him to sell the building on Main Street to the city of Honeyford for the bargain-basement price of one dollar. The only stipulation was that he be allowed to lease the space occupied by the pharmacy for the next ten years and that Clinica Adelina be allowed to lease the two neighboring storefronts at current market value for the same period of time. He'd told Gwen as much this evening when he'd walked her to her car.

She was the executor of the will and believed, as he did, that the city would go for the terms. Because he had married in time to meet the will's demands, he held the cards. What they didn't have to know was that he would relinquish the building no matter what. He couldn't conduct this marriage under the shadow of his father's will.

All his life Dean had tried to do the right thing. Now the "right thing" was whatever it took to make his relationship with Rosemary work.

So that glance of hers, sharp as glass, raised an alarm in his head. He met her eyes with a question in his own.

"The thing is," she said, again addressing the room, managing to look poised yet vulnerable, "all my life I wanted to marry a man I knew would never let me down. A man I could trust, because his word would be as good as gold, and his love…" for a breath of space, her voice hovered before she completed the thought "…his love would be immovable. I wanted to look into his eyes and know that the man I loved when I was thirty would be standing beside me fifty years later. And nothing would have changed except the lines on our faces." She looked at the crowd of neighbors, friends and family, her smile inviting their comradeship and offering her own. "When you get down to it, that's what most of us are looking for, isn't it? To know that the person we go to sleep beside each night will be in our corner the next day?"

Dean heard a feminine sniffle. In his mind, a bull's eye began to take shape on his back.

His own brother, formerly the devil incarnate, had pointed out that Dean had been lying by omission for the duration of his relationship with Rosemary. Now he stared at his wife, at the hazel eyes that looked like a lake on fire, and though he had no idea what had transpired between their dance and this moment, he knew she delivered no ordinary toast.

Rosemary held the microphone with both hands. "Some

people—people in my own family, even—" she grinned to minimize any implied judgment "—say true love is a fairy tale. That to keep from falling down, a strong woman has to stand up alone. Well, to tell you the truth, after surviving a broken heart once, I was all set to agree with them. I even told my friends I wasn't going to date again. *Ever.*" More laughter from their guests. Rosemary nodded. "I know, I know. You speak, the universe laughs. And, of course, then I met Dean." As the chuckles died down, she lowered her voice, sounding almost wistful. "I never expected to meet someone so caring. So willing to put other people first. So deeply, deeply moral. I don't mind telling you that at first I thought he was too good to be true. And I decided to keep my distance. But that Dean, he's a persistent—" she paused, slightly but significantly "—devil. When I married him, I knew that with a man like him, I could put my fears to rest." Her eyes cut to her husband, who felt her gaze like the point of a saber aimed at his heart. "Because Dean Kingsley—the honest, up-front man you all know, the Prince Charming I had started to believe didn't exist—that man would never, ever, *willingly* let me fall."

There was more sniffling. Rosemary raised her glass of punch, and while their guests drank, she and Dean looked at each other with one thing crystal clear between them: the honeymoon was over. In spades.

Rosemary pressed her shoulder against the Prius's passenger-side door, gazing out the window at the clear, sharp night. They'd left the party five minutes ago; it was almost 11:00 p.m.

In the driver's seat—literally, but most definitely not figuratively—Dean had been mostly silent. He hadn't said much at all, in fact, since her toast, and she wasn't sure whether she was glad or angrier than ever.

Now as they neared her cottage, he asked, "Do you want to talk now or wait until we get home?"

If she were a porcupine, he'd be covered in quills right now. When she'd discovered the extent of Neil's cheating, Rosemary had left her house and hadn't returned. She'd let Neil live there until they'd sold the lovely Lake Oswego three-bedroom in the divorce settlement. Not this time. The cottage belonged to her, and she was no pushover. Not anymore.

"My home is on 4th Street," she said quietly but firmly. "Yours is above the pharmacy." They would have to talk, yes, but she wanted the ground rules established: the marriage, as they had so briefly known it, was over.

Still a couple of blocks from the house, Dean pulled over and cut the engine. He turned toward her. "Who told you?"

"Who told me what, Dean? What is there to tell? Honeyford's favorite son is an open book, right?"

"Rosie—"

She held her hand up between them. "Refrain from using nicknames or endearments, please. These days they tend to make me gag."

Dean kept a hand on the steering wheel. His knuckles tightened around it, whitening. He shook his head. "I'm an ass. Whether you believe it or not, Rosie—" She glared at him. "Rosemary—I was going to tell you about my father's will tonight."

"You were going to tell me *tonight*. After our wedding reception." She blinked, affecting a broad smile. "Gosh, that makes all the difference. Thanks. Oh, wait." She began counting off points on her fingers. "Four months after we slept together, two months after you found out I was pregnant and almost three weeks after we got married, you were just going to tell me that according to your father's will you *had* to get married. Ooh, you know what? I'm not that grateful, after all." She shrugged broadly. "Sorry." Dropping the sarcasm, she went for the jugular. "What is the matter with you? What kind of person does something like this? Who gets married because of a will? And *deceives* people about it?" The interior of the small car filled with her wrath. She had plenty more to say, but then remembered something. "Oh, my god. Amanda found out about the will, didn't she? That's why she broke up with you."

"Amanda did not break up with me." Twisting as fully as he could toward Rosemary, Dean said, carefully and clearly, "I broke up with her, because when I saw you again I knew I couldn't marry anyone else. Amanda was aware of the will from the start. She wasn't in love with me."

Rage, hot and furious, exploded within her, and Rosemary kept her arms rigidly by her side so she wouldn't attack him. Never in her life, not even with Neil, had she felt so outraged, so dangerously furious.

"I don't know Amanda, I didn't know your father, and I obviously *don't know you,* but it's clear that not one of you understands or cares that marriage is something sacred, not a game. You don't play with it, and you don't mess with other people's lives."

Dean's face knotted with regret and contrition. He looked so aggrieved, in fact, that she might have comforted him if she hadn't wanted, at that moment, to turn his male parts into pudding.

"Rosie—" he began. Once more channeling one of the witches in *Macbeth,* she raised a brow. "Rosemary," he corrected, "only a handful of people know about my father's will. I'm not sure who told you—"

"Nobody told me," she said, omitting what she now recognized as a slip on Claire's part, earlier. She didn't want to involve anyone else in this mess. "I was coming to look for you and overheard Gwen Gibson say how beautifully everything had worked out for you and Fletcher. Imagine my surprise when I heard the mayor congratulate my husband on his *forced* marriage."

Dean closed his eyes briefly, swearing beneath his breath. "I'm sorry. That isn't what I intended—" He stopped as a new realization dawned. "Wait. If you overheard Gwen and me then you—" He shook his head. "You didn't stay for the whole conversation, did you?"

"No. Although, golly, that would have been fun. What'd you two talk about next? Insurance scams? Pyramid schemes?"

Dean did not answer. He merely started the car again, and Rosemary was glad. Sarcasm was not her usual modus operandi. She felt as if an alien force had taken over her tongue, and she was already sick of it, sick of the hatred she felt. She wanted to be done.

Exhaustion, as swift and global as her fury, drained her. When Dean passed her cottage without stopping, it took her a moment to react.

"What are you doing? Go back, please. I want to go home."

Dean didn't look at her. "We're going to see Gwen." He set his jaw as if steeling himself to press forward no matter what.

"I don't want to see anyone, and it's eleven p.m. I doubt Gwen will be happy to see us."

Dean turned right on Oak Street then made a left on Second, heading for an area of lovely old Victorians. "You heard a fraction of our conversation," he said. "You're not going to believe anything I tell you right now, and I don't blame you. So you're going to hear the rest of it from Gwen." He stared forward, through the windshield again, his face illuminated by the occasional streetlamp. "From the second I saw you, I felt differently about you than I've felt about any other woman in my life. I didn't tell you the truth right away, because—" Now he glanced her way. "How the hell do you tell someone your father's will requires you to marry? I was afraid I'd lose you before we ever got started."

Through the darkness, Rosemary saw the turbulence in his usually pacific blue eyes. Emotion roughened his voice like sandpaper. "I didn't want to lose you, Rosie. So I tried to control everything, and you're right—I screwed up. But you're mistaken about one thing. Kingsley men do value marriage. Fletcher and I valued it to the point that we were too scared to make a move toward it. Our father valued it so much, he tried to force us into it. The problem isn't that we don't want love—it's that we haven't got the faintest idea how to make it work."

They pulled up in front of a grand home with only one small light glowing from an upstairs room. Dean cut the engine and opened his door.

"It really is too late to disturb someone," Rosemary protested mildly, trying vainly to digest everything that had happened tonight and all Dean had just told her.

He came around to her side, opened the door and bent down to look at her. "It *is* too late to disturb someone. And maybe what Gwen is going to tell you won't matter in the end. But I'm not giving you—or our family—up without a fight, Rosemary Kingsley. The only ammunition I've got left is the truth."

He stepped back, letting Rosemary decide what it was going to be: end things here or listen to what Gwen Gibson had to say.

Life seemed so ridiculously complex, so unbearably painful that Rosemary wanted to run from all of it. Even as she tried to steel herself against Dean, her heart thumped against her chest as if it were trying to move closer to him. She wanted to listen, wanted him to reassure and convince her that this issue of the will and a forced marriage was all some big misunderstanding.

Magical thinking.

She tried to remember that she had just left three friends, two sisters and a mother, all of whom were single and in a lot less pain than she was in right now.

Dean waited at the curb, his expression as intent as she had ever seen it. Anxious finger-combing had mussed his usually neat hair.

Not two hours ago, you were my knight in shining armor, and I was lucky in love, Rosemary thought with a sadness that penetrated her bones.

When she got out of the car, it was not with hope, precisely, but rather with the weary conviction that if nothing else, perhaps Gwen Gibson would weave the loose threads of this insane tapestry together.

As she stepped onto the curb, Rosemary looked into Dean's troubled eyes.

The only ammunition I've got is the truth, he'd said.

Truth was good. Maybe truth was all she needed. Because she certainly sensed she was finished with fairy tales, forevermore.

Lucy Jeffers sat on the floor of her sister's living room, picking food from a plate on the coffee table, which currently was set like a Thanksgiving buffet.

"Thanks for coming over and bringing…a snack." Rosemary pushed a halfhearted smile her sister's way. Because Lucy never ate junk food, she had arrived at Rosemary's door with a whole roasted chicken from the market, a quart of wild-rice pilaf, salad, rolls, a Dutch apple pie, a pesto-crusted cheese ball and water crackers.

Eschewing the real food, Rosemary had curled into a corner of the couch with an open bag of cheese puffs—the natural kind, because she refused to feed the baby anything fluorescent, but still something that resembled food therapy. She was depressed, miserable, wretched; roasted chicken and a green vegetable were not going to cut it.

"I still can't believe you stayed in town after Mom and Evelyn left," Rosemary said, watching her sister carefully remove all visible fat from a bite of poultry. "How was the Honeyford Inn?"

"Good. They put me in the honeymoon suite, though." She snorted. "What a crock." Jamming a fork into the meat with unnecessary aggression, Lucy put the chicken in her mouth and chewed as if the bird still needed to be killed.

"Um, why did you stay exactly?"

Lucy looked up. "My sister having a nervous breakdown onstage at her wedding reception isn't a good enough reason?"

"I wasn't having a nervous breakdown," Rosemary protested, hugging her cheese puffs. Apparently the veiled irony in her little toast hadn't been so veiled, after all. Daphne had phoned her three times on the trip back to Portland and once since. Vi had videotaped most of the toast with her cell phone and threatened to post it on YouTube unless Rosemary called to tell her exactly what was going on. "You, Mom and Evelyn should be proud of me," Rosemary protested in a wobbly voice that sounded dangerously like whining. "I was refusing to be a patsy."

"We are proud. It was just hard to figure out what was going on last night. 'Oh, wow, my sister must have found out her husband had to marry her to inherit a building' is not the first thing that crosses your mind before the wedding cake is cut, you know?" Picking walnuts out of the wild-rice pilaf, Lucy raised a skinny brow, dark as soot against her pale skin. "Unbe*effing*lievable that he thought he'd get away with it. *Putz.*"

Squirming painfully on the sofa she had purchased originally for its uncommon comfort, Rosemary reminded Lucy dejectedly, "Except that he wasn't trying to 'get away with it.' Remember? I told you, Gwen confirmed that he's selling his building to the city. He just wanted to keep the will quiet as long as possible, because he knew there was no way to explain it to me so that it would make any kind of sense." *Gee, put that way—*

"Don't romanticize him, Rosemary," Lucy snapped, and Rosemary jumped guiltily.

"I'm not romanticizing him. He still lied to me…by omission…for months, and…that's a deal breaker."

"Damn straight. Because if a man lies once, he'll do it again. Men are such shmucks." Abandoning the wild rice, Lucy plunged her fork into the Dutch apple pie.

Rosemary stared. "Luce, is there something *you* need to talk about? I mean, other than my being duped into a marriage of convenience, did something else happen to make you take this…vacation?"

Filling her mouth with apples and streusel topping, Lucy affected an amazed expression. "What? No. I am here for you."

"Luce—"

"I said, no! Look, it's no big deal." She shoveled in more pie, expanding her normally gaunt cheeks. "One of the partners at my firm got engaged, and his fiancée—" shifting from apple pie, she aimed her fork-weapon at the cheese ball "—joined the firm. Like being around each other 24/7 is going to contribute to marital bliss. Whatever. Anyway, no time like the present to claim some unused vacation time now that Lindsay the Perfect is there to pick up the slack. Not that there was any slack, because, of course, I have busted my butt for that ma—that firm practically my entire adult working life. But that's okay, because now there's plenty of lawyers on board to cover any emergency, so I can have a—" she looked as if she was going to cry or spit "—vacation."

Stunned, Rosemary poked as gently as she could at her sister's huge, gaping, utterly unexpected wound. "Was Dustin Phillips the lawyer who got engaged?"

Lucy had worked for Dustin's father's firm since her college internship. Dustin was very into civic action, and Lucy had hammered nails alongside him for Habitat for Humanity. Five years ago, Rosemary noted that her sister hadn't been able to take her eyes off Dustin at the annual Phillips, Phillips, Arnold & Locke company softball game. She'd hovered around him, fetched bats and lemonade, laughed too loudly, nodded too hard. Rosemary had wondered then if her sister was finally smitten, but Evelyn had insisted Lucy was merely trying to score points with the boss.

Now tears filled Lucy's eyes, an occurrence about as frequent as a Sasquatch sighting. She tried heroically to sniff them back.

"Aw, gee, Luce." Rosemary made to rise, but her sister shook her head, using the side of her fork to massacre the cheese ball.

"Don't romanticize it, Rosemary."

Right.

Sinking back into the corner of her couch, Rosemary tugged the collar of her sweatshirt up over her chin and sighed. Lord knew that in the Jeffers family romanticizing anything—men, women, snow geese that were faithful for life—was a sin punishable by a lifetime of regrets. Hadn't Rosemary proved that point? Twice?

Releasing the sweatshirt, she plunged her hand into the cheese puffs, stuffing a handful of their all-natural selves into her mouth.

After descending on Gwen, she and Dean had returned to the cottage. Midnight had come and gone with Dean explaining how conflicted he had been about relinquishing the building, how responsible he felt for the success of Clinica

Adelina and how that had informed his original decision to comply with his father's nutty will.

"I'd never been in love. Not really." He had looked sad and gorgeous, like Hubbell Gardner telling Katie Morosky he couldn't be what she needed in *The Way We Were*. "I honestly thought there was something broken inside me. So I resigned myself to a marriage that was sensible and figured everyone would be happy, myself included…or happy enough."

Too agitated to sit despite the late hour, Dean had logged multiple laps across the living-room floor while Rosemary huddled on the sofa in her reception dress, her brain hurting from confusion, her hands ice-cold though the gas fireplace hissed and blazed. "Then I went to Tavern on the Highway and saw you, licking salt off the pretzels and trying to be cheerful for your friends…. You were the most beautiful thing I'd ever seen."

He had stopped dead center of the couch, gazing at her with sorrow and longing, making her wish they were upstairs, spooned with one of his big, warm hands on her breast and the other on her belly, the way they had been for a small collection of the most delicious nights of her life.

"I wish I knew how to love you better." His voice cracked. "The way you deserve to be loved. I'm not even sure what that means, that's the damn truth of it."

It was the most vulnerable statement she'd heard a man utter. Though her body felt stiff and as fragile, she had wanted to hurl herself off the couch and into his arms. To kiss and reassure him that she had enough trust and courage for the both of them.

He said he loves you, the romantic in her encouraged. *You'll be all better now. You'll be fine.* They would make love every night, spend weekends at the coast, go on a hundred second honeymoons—

Stop. No one present said, "I love you." The practical,

Jeffers side of her gave the romantic one upside the head, knocking her off her fluffy cloud. *That's beside the point, anyway, isn't it? Do you want the pain that comes with the kind of love you're mooning about? You think your heart's going to keep beating when it's that swollen and sore? When Dean lets you down or lies or decides he doesn't l-o-v-e you anymore? Will you be glad then that you tried again? Right, didn't think so.*

Instead of diving for Dean's chest, Rosemary had stared at her husband of three weeks, her heart shuddering like an engine struggling to keep working just before it ran out of gas. Her throat had ached and suddenly she'd wished she had spent her thirty-second birthday at a Buddhist monastery or a verbal-fast retreat on Whidbey Island or just about anywhere but Tavern on the Highway.

Instead of reliving last night's final moments with Dean, Rosemary now demanded of her sister, "Tell me about Frank." *Frank.* They never referred to the man who had sired them as Father. Or Dad, Daddy, Pop or any other name that might identify him as family. "Tell me about the day he left."

Lucy coughed, spitting a little cheese onto the table. She swore beneath her breath. "God, Rosemary, what is it with you? Ever since we were kids, you've wanted to hear about it like it's a freaking bedtime story or something."

"I want to remember."

"What for? It's not one of your fairy tales."

"I know that." Not that there was anything wrong with the fairy tales that, yes, okay, had given her hope and comfort during the dark childhood fears. Fairy tales were kind… ultimately. The bad stuff happened mostly before the declaration of true love. Once the hero and heroine found each other, you knew nothing would tear them asunder. Ever. Sure, Cinderella had to return to the cellar and wait for the townies to try on her shoe, but that was a small price to pay for lifelong devotion, a castle full of adorable singing mice and, eventually, babies.

On the other hand, Lucy had a point. Rosemary did like to hear the story—in excruciating, full-color detail—of the day her father had left their family for good. For decades now, she had examined the fine points like a CSI picking over evidence, sure she'd find something that could have prevented the crime.

Had she been in charge of the situation, she might have found a word, a touch, a promise to alter the outcome. She'd clung to that idea, using it to convince herself that she could dodge the land mines of pain that had detonated in the wake of her parents' divorce.

I romanticize everything, because reality scares the crap out of me.

Clutching the bag of cheese puffs like a teddy bear, she stared, wide-eyed, at her sister. "Luce, do you think you, Evelyn and I might be in good relationships today if we'd grown up in a healthy family? Or do you think everyone gets driven through the wringer when they love someone? I mean, I used to think people who were compatible and madly in love had easier relationships. But lately I wonder if it's this hard for everyone, and some people just have a higher pain tolerance."

With a look that begged the universe to stop the torture, Lucy, previously her nutritionist's star client, ripped a white roll in half, shoved the entire piece into her mouth and chased it with pie. "Thith ith the motht deprething aftuhnoon evuh," she mumbled through the mouthful.

Rosemary sighed. With Dean standing before her, openly confused and vulnerable—not at all the absolutely certain, fear-slaying, unequivocal man she'd always imagined—she had panicked.

Wait. Rewind that. She'd been panicking all her life, and with Dean in front of her, as perplexed by relationships as she was, she hadn't known what to do with her fear. Neil had always told her not to worry. About anything. Prince Charming was supposed to kill the nasty dragons, right?

That is so yesterday, the Jeffers voice taunted. *Remember—*

"I know, I know. Don't romanticize."

She had believed the right man would provide a lifetime guarantee. But that kind of thinking was as magical as believing she could protect herself from pain by remaining alone.

She shook her head. Real life was about as clean as an oil spill. Last night, when faced with the possibility of accepting Dean and their marriage as the works in progress they were, she had cowered on the sofa and whispered, "I can't. I'm sorry. I just…can't."

Dean had stayed at his apartment above the pharmacy last night, and Rosemary, confused and conflicted, had slept not a wink.

Okay, big girl, it's time to face facts: if you want a guarantee, go shopping. Relationships do not come with the Good Housekeeping Seal. More's the pity, but there ya go.

Wow. That wasn't the Jeffers or the romantic voice. It was just…her.

Perhaps a person could hedge her bets by falling for someone who was as willing as she to keep the fires burning during the tough times or when love temporarily went MIA. Someone who believed in relationships and fidelity and trust. And by learning to forgive when one—or both—of them messed up.

Someone like Dean.

"I've got to go," she breathed.

"Wha?" Lucy lifted her head from the container of salad. "Where?" Understanding dawned. "No! Don't you dare. I…I…forbid it!"

Rosemary cocked her head. "Seriously?"

Lucy's customary certainty faltered. "Yes. I'm your sister and...your lawyer."

Smiling gratefully, Rosemary tucked the bag of cheese puffs between the chicken and the apple pie then rose, slipped her feet into purple flip-flops and headed for the door.

"Oh, God. Oh, God." Lucy, who made feral cats look relaxed by comparison, half rose, sat back down and rose again. "Change your clothes, at least," she called after her baby sister. "And brush your hair!"

"No time! But thanks."

Grabbing a set of keys off a hook and her Oregon Ducks cap from the coat tree near the door, Rosemary smashed the hat onto her head, unfortunately making her curls stick out like clown hair, and raced into the spring afternoon with Lucy's conflicted "Good luck" following her out the door.

Chapter Fifteen

Because the pharmacy was closed on Sundays, Rosemary took the alley staircase to Dean's apartment, hoping he was there. If not, her plan was to let herself in with the key he'd given her and wait. Regarding what she would say… Uh, yeah, not a clue.

Her heart, which had done more emotional aerobics these past few months than ever before in its life, thumped with nerves and excitement. She was nearly five months along in her pregnancy and had thrown on leggings with an oversize Oregon Shakespeare Festival T-shirt that masked her growing tummy, but did nothing for her fashion sense. Oh, well. If Dean wasn't there, then she'd take the time to freshen up a bit, maybe scrunch some gel, if he had any, into her curls while she waited.

Reaching the landing, glad there was no one else in the alley this afternoon, Rosemary raised her hand to knock on the glass-paned door. Noticing a movement inside, she hesitated, pressing her nose closer to the glass. Her busy heart skidded to a momentary halt.

Dean was inside the apartment, tall and handsome and tempting as always. But he wasn't alone.

"What?" Rosemary breathed, blinking as if she could make the scene inside disappear.

Seated on the leather couch that faced the alley windows, Dean gazed at an exotically beautiful woman as she leaned toward him, speaking animatedly.

Instantly, Rosemary reverted to the little girl who'd wondered endlessly why her father hadn't stayed. And to the wife who felt betrayed and foolish when her "perfect" life had turned out to be nothing more than an empty shell.

The urge to bolt came on strong. In the past twenty-four hours, she had gathered enough circumstantial evidence against Dean to write him off for good. If Lucy were here with her fork, she'd stab first and ask questions later. But the evidence was only circumstantial.

Fortunately for Dean, she was not one of her sisters. Or her mother. Or her friends. She was, finally, just Rosemary, and she knew exactly what she needed to do.

Her entire girlhood had been steeped in the quiet and desperate fear that she might end up alone. Her adulthood until two years ago—an exhausting exercise in trying to keep that from happening. More recently she'd attempted to tame the anxiety by convincing herself she embraced being alone.

Now she dived straight into the heart of the terror and discovered something amazing: the longer she stood inside it without flinching, the more it dissolved, like clouds. Behind the fear was the far more substantial soul she had never learned to trust.

Rosemary raised the hand holding the apartment key. Her other hand drifted to her abdomen, eyes narrowing speculatively as she patted the baby. "I can't fix the past, but I can do things differently now. Watch this, kiddo. Mama's going to show you how it's done."

Slipping the key into the lock, she moved swiftly, claiming the element of surprise as she burst into Dean's living room.

The gorgeous Latina woman with the sexy, straight black hair jumped, as did Dean, although when he saw who the intruder was, his surprise turned to, at first, concern and then bemusement. And finally, hope.

He stood, his attention all on Rosemary. The last thing he'd said to her the night before was, *"I'll be waiting. For as long as it takes you to forgive me, I'll wait."*

This afternoon all he managed was a surprised and questioning, "Rosie?"

She almost felt sorry for him. If he expected a quick and easy reunion this afternoon, he was in for a bit of a shock. *I've got a much better plan than that.*

Stomping forward, she halted only when her knees hit the coffee table then stabbed her index finger at Dean's admirable chest.

"Don't you 'Rosemary' me, bub. I come over here to bring you home, and what do I find?"

The woman, who really was lovely, jumped to her feet. "Oh, no! No, this is not what you're thinking—"

"Save it, sister." Adopting a growl that had never before emerged from her mouth, Rosemary realized that the poor woman was ready to whip out her iPhone and key in 9-1-1. *Sorry,* she tried to communicate telepathically. *But I have to make a point here.*

Gesturing toward her husband, she said, "That is *my* man. *Mine.* And I don't share."

"Oh, but, really, I'm not—"

Rosemary gave her a talk-to-the-hand. "Please," she said. "Believe me, I understand *why* you want him." Dean deserved some grandstanding after all he'd been through the past couple of days, and, by golly, he was going to get it. "He's gentle, he's kind, he's incredibly patient. Except for a little trust issue regarding his father's will and my ability to love him in spite of it—and I do love him in spite of it—the man is near perfect."

She turned to Dean, and their gazes locked. "Perfect enough for me, anyway. It took a while for me to figure out that I can't put my faith in anyone else until I've put it in myself, but I think I get that now. And just for the record, I like that you haven't fallen in love easily in your life." She smiled, her heart in her words and in her eyes. "Because I know this one's for real."

She paused, wanting to soak in Dean's expression in that moment, the awe and the pleasure, the hope that looked so boyish and dear on his handsome face, and—oh, yeah… lookee there—the lust. They would have to take advantage of that soon. Very, very soon. She had only one more point to make….

"I don't want a fairy tale, anymore, Dean. Really. Well…I wouldn't mind the singing mice…but trying to live in a fairy tale is exhausting. What I need is a man I love and respect, who loves and respects me. I expect our marriage to be the shelter and strength for our family. So I'm not going to run away anymore. This is my life, and I intend to stand and fight for it."

She put both fists on her hips. "Now. You're coming home with me, Dean Kingsley. And don't get lippy about it. You give me any guff, and you'll see what angry does to a librarian."

His eyes glowed a deep spring-blue she wouldn't mind looking at every day for the rest of her life. Stepping around the table, Dean stood close enough to swap pheromones and sent his gaze appreciatively up and down his very adamant wife. "I love it when you go gangsta."

Taking her face in his hands, he kissed her, that honey-pouring, knee-melting, I-know-you-and-love-you kiss that she'd like to bottle for use every day when they were apart for more than, say, ten minutes. This was what she had almost given up.

When he lifted his head, he remembered they had an audience of one. Keeping a hand on Rosemary's back (and making sensuously slow circles that could drive a girl crazy), Dean addressed the woman who, at the moment, looked as if she'd been in a bad episode of *Punked.* "Esmeralda, this is my wife, Rosemary. Rosie, this is Dr. Esmeralda Duran. She'll be working with Dr. Gill until Clinica Adelina is up and running. Then she'll head the health center."

"Oh, hello! A pleasure to meet you." Rosemary leaned forward to offer her hand, which Dr. Duran took warily.

"Uh-huh. Why don't I leave you two alone…." Esmeralda edged to the alley-entrance door. "Sounds as if you need some time. Dean, thanks so much for showing me the apartment. I'd like to move in a couple of days from now if that's all right." Her coal-black eyes shifted to Rosemary, who understood her hesitation immediately.

"Here's the extra key." She offered it to the other woman. "And no copies have been made. Promise." She was definitely going to have to make a second first impression on Dr. Duran.

Esmeralda plucked the key gingerly from Rosemary's fingers. "Okay, thanks. Well." She nodded again, halfway out the door. "Have a really…interesting evening."

"We will." Rosemary waved. "'Bye." When the door shut behind the beautiful physician, Rosemary cocked her head. "Is she an ob-gyn, by any chance? I could use someone local."

"Hmm," Dean studied his bride. "We may have to shop around."

"Okay." She smiled up at him. "So you're renting your apartment."

"I thought I would, yes. I had hoped to live with my wife till death we did part and all that. But then she realized what a lame-brained jackass I'd been—"

"You weren't that big a jackass—"

"Yes, I was."

He looked sincere and contrite, and she realized this was another apology for the will and that he had to get it off his chest, even though she was ready to move on. "Okay, have it your way."

"Thank you. So I was going to stay away for a couple of days while I figured out how to make a very dramatic statement about how much I love you."

"Really." She smiled brightly. *He said it!* "And what did you come up with?"

Dean raised a brow, wry with regret. "Nothing like what you came up with. I'm going to have to go back to the drawing board."

"Please don't."

Dean shoved his hands in his pockets, a huge disappointment when Rosemary wanted them around her. "You can't get to know someone who's deceiving you. So obviously I have a lot of work ahead, introducing myself to my wife. Becoming the best friend she wants and deserves."

A thrill shot through Rosemary, from her skin all the way down to her soul.

"That sounds time-consuming," she said.

"Bound to be." He nodded solemnly. "Labor-intensive, too. Is your schedule clear?"

"You bet." She nodded back, just as solemnly, picturing weekends at the coast…staying up all night to make love…a hundred second honeymoons…. Heaven. "Of course, five months from now your daughter will have something to say about our free time."

"Daughter." Dean's solemn expression softened to the boyish, wonder-filled sweetness she knew reflected the best of his heart. "A girl?"

Rosemary feared her face might not be big enough to host the smile that stretched across it. But her throat tightened when she saw the telltale sparkle fill her husband's eyes.

"With her mother's curls," he said, reaching out—finally!—to gather Rosemary into his arms.

"And your eyes, I hope." She snuggled against him. "I think I'll teach her to talk gangsta."

Dean's chest bounced beneath her ear. "Librarian gangsta."

Rosemary socked him lightly. They kissed until it was time to come up for air then she leaned back and said, "Want to begin getting to know each other *really* well?"

Brushing the curls off her forehead, Dean nodded, a man who knew exactly what he wanted and understood that he already had it. "We've got at least fifty years of intense work ahead of us. May as well get started."

"May as well."

Rosemary grinned. Once upon a time, she'd chased a fairy tale. Now she stood squarely in the middle of reality and it was everything she'd ever dreamed. Plus a whole lot more.

* * * * *